VA

Val McDermid
community ther
a journalist for sixteen years, spending the last three years as Northern Bureau Chief of a national Sunday tabloid. Now a full-time writer, she divides her time between Cheshire and Northumberland.

The Torment of Others is Val McDermid's fourth book featuring criminal profiler, Tony Hill. The first, *The Mermaids Singing*, won the 1995 Gold Dagger Award for Best Crime Novel of the Year. The series has now been adapted for television under the generic title Wire in the Blood, starring Robson Green as Tony Hill and Hermione Norris as DCI Carol Jordan.

Visit www.authortracker.co.uk for exclusive information on Val McDermid.

www.valmcdermid.co.uk

Praise for *The Torment of Others*:

'A long awaited return to the scene of the crime for Dr Tony Hill. No one compares to McDermid when it comes to the deviant side of human nature'

Maxim Jakubowski, *Guardian*

'This is a disturbing high-tension book, unstinting in its portrayals of psychological distress. One of McDermid's finest, which is saying a lot' Marcel Berlins, *The Times*

'Val McDermid is an intelligent, supremely talented novelist and with this latest tale she is writing at the height of her power. It may not be comfortable, it may be neither pretty nor pleasant, but it is utterly compelling'

Allan Laing, *Glasgow Herald*

'Even as Hill and Jordan are unravelling the truth, McDermid intersperses their efforts with the hideous insights into the deviant megalomania of the voices. Serial killers, though meat and drink to crime writers, are thankfully rare. It is a tribute to the power of Val McDermid's imagination that she made this one seem so believable' *Daily Telegraph*

'This is McDermid on top form – pass the Valium' *Daily Mail*

'It's hard to know what to praise first here: the impeccable plotting or the sharp social relevance of the narrative. Most of all, though, it's the relationship between her two central characters that makes [it] work so well. This is a real, adult relationship; complex, combative and nuanced' Barry Forshaw, *Express*

'Val McDermid, as ever, is adept at engendering irresistible suspense, as the fearsome attractiveness of the ever more benighted and bloody predicament works its effect on readers'
Patricia Craig, *Times Literary Supplement*

'Convincing and intelligent'
Cath Staincliffe, *Manchester Evening News*

'Some excellent writing from an author who is building a formidable reputation. There are some terrific twists: just as the reader feels something has been securely settled, McDermid gives a new jerk to the storyline and the chase is on again'
Jane Jakeman, *Scotland on Sunday*

'This story is a cracker, complicated – with two enquiries run in harness – genuinely surprising, often upsetting, ultimately credible and intellectually satisfying'
John Bowen, *The Oldie*

By the same author

The Grave Tattoo
The Distant Echo
Killing the Shadows
A Place of Execution

TONY HILL NOVELS
The Last Temptation
The Wire in the Blood
The Mermaids Singing

KATE BRANNIGAN NOVELS
Star Struck
Blue Genes
Clean Break
Crack Down
Kick Back
Dead Beat

LINDSAY GORDON NOVELS
Hostage to Murder
Booked for Murder
Union Jack
Final Edition
Common Murder
Report for Murder

NON-FICTION
A Suitable Job for a Woman

VAL McDERMID

The Torment of Others

HarperCollins*Publishers*

This novel is entirely a work of fiction. The names, characters and incidents portrayed in it are the work of the author's imagination. Any resemblance to actual persons, living or dead, events or localities is entirely coincidental.

HarperCollins*Publishers*
77–85 Fulham Palace Road, London W6 8JB

The HarperCollins website address is:
www.harpercollins.co.uk

This paperback reissue edition published 2005

1

First published in Great Britain by
HarperCollins*Publishers* 2000

A catalogue record for this book
is available from the British Library

ISBN 978-0-00-787941-0

Typeset in Meridien by Palimpsest Book Production Limited,
Polmont, Stirlingshire

Printed and bound in Great Britain by
Clays Ltd, St Ives plc

Extract from The Four Quartets by TS Eliot
(published by Faber and Faber Ltd) reproduced by
kind permission of Faber and Faber Ltd

Acknowledgements

As usual, I owe a debt of thanks to those who generously give of their time and expertise in a bid to keep me within the bounds of accuracy. I am grateful to the Greenfield Girls for letting loose the dogs of narrative; Angus Marshall for advice on the forensic aspects of computing; Dr Ray Murray for geological assistance; Dr Sue Black for matters pathological; Brigid Baillie for legal procedure; and the late Kathy Wilkes for first introducing me to the mind/body problem.

For their perennial support, Julia Wisdom and Anne O'Brien at HarperCollins; Jane, Broo, Anna, Claire and Terry at Gregory & Company; Trina Furre at Riverdale; and Sandra, Ken and Robson at Coastal.

For Leslie, Sandra, Julia, Jane, Maria, Mel, Margaret, Nicky, Jenni, Mary, Julie, Paula, Jai, Diana, Stella, Shelley, Daphne and Bunty Al – my personal monstrous regiment of women who brought back the wounded from the battlefield and tended me till I was better. With love and thanks.

But the torment of others remains an experience
Unqualified, unworn by subsequent attrition.
People change, and smile: but the agony abides.

TS Eliot
'The Dry Salvages', *Four Quartets*

All torment, trouble, wonder, and amazement
Inhabits here. Some heavenly power guide us
Out of this fearful country!

William Shakespeare
The Tempest

PART ONE

Just because you hear voices, it doesn't mean you're mad. You don't have to be well smart to know that. And even though you did all that stuff that made the jury look sick to their stomachs, at least you're clever enough to know that doesn't make you a nutter. All sorts of people have other voices in their heads, everybody knows that. Like on the telly. Even though you can believe it when you're watching it, everybody knows it's not real. And somebody's got to have dreamed it up in the first place without them ending up where you have. Stands to reason.

So you're not worried. Well, not very worried. OK, they said you were insane. The judge said your name, Derek Tyler, and he tagged you with the mad label. But even though he's supposed to be a smart bastard, that judge didn't know he was following the plan. The way to avoid the life sentence that they always hand down when somebody does what you did. If you make them believe you were off your head when you did it, then it isn't you that did the crime, it's the madness in you. And if you're mad, not bad, it stands to reason you can be cured. Which is why they lock you up in the nuthouse instead of the nick. That way the doctors can poke around in your head and have a crack at fixing what's broke.

Of course, if nothing's broke in the first place, the best thing you can do is keep your mouth zipped. Not let on you're as sane as them. Then, when the time is right, you can start talking. Make it look like they've somehow worked their magic and turned you into somebody they can let out on the street again.

It sounded really easy when the Voice explained it. You're pretty sure you got it right, because the Voice went over it so many times you can replay the whole spiel just by closing your eyes and mouthing the words: 'I am the Voice. I am your Voice. Whatever I tell you to do is for the best. I am your Voice. This is the plan. Listen very carefully.' That's the trigger. That's all it takes. The intro that makes the whole tape play in your head. The message is still there, implanted deep inside your brain. And it still makes sense. Or at least, you think it does.

Only, it's been a long time now. It's not easy, staying on the wrong side of silence day after day, week after week, month after month. But you're pretty proud of the way you've hung on to it. Because there's all the other stuff interfering with the Voice. Therapy sessions where you have to blank what the real nutters are going on about. Counselling sessions where the doctors try and trick you into words. Not to mention the screaming and shouting when somebody goes off on one. Then there's all the background noise of the day room, the TV and the music rumbling round your head like interference.

All you have to fight back with is the Voice and the promise that the word will come when the time is right. And then you'll be back out there, doing what you've discovered you do best.

Killing women.

Find them in the first six hours or you're looking for a corpse. Find them in the first six hours or you're looking for a corpse. The missing children mantra mocked Detective Inspector Don Merrick. He was looking at sixteen hours and counting. And counting was just what the parents of Tim Golding were doing. Counting every minute that took them further from their last glimpse of their son. He didn't have to think about what they were feeling; he was a father and he knew the visceral fear lying in wait to assail any parent whose child is suddenly, unaccountably not where they should be. Mostly, it was history in a matter of minutes when the child reappeared unscathed, usually grinning merrily at the panic of its parents. Nevertheless it was history that left its mark bone deep.

And sometimes there was no relief. No sudden access of anger masking the ravages of ill-defined terror when the child reappeared. Sometimes it just went on and on and on. And Merrick knew the dread would continue screaming inside Alastair and Shelley Golding until his team found their son. Alive or dead.

He knew because he'd witnessed the same agony in the lives of Gerry and Pam Lefevre, whose son Guy had been missing now for just over fifteen months. They'd dragged the canal, combed the parks and wasteland within a two-mile radius, but not a trace of Guy had ever surfaced.

Merrick had been the bagman on that inquiry, which was the main reason why he'd been assigned to Tim Golding. He had the knowledge to see whether there were obvious links between the cases. But beyond knowledge, his instincts already nagged that whoever had snatched Guy Lefevre had now claimed his second victim.

He leaned against the roof of his car and swept the long curve of the railway embankment with binoculars. Every available body was down there, combing the scrubby grass for any trace of the eight-year-old boy who had been missing since the previous evening. Tim had been playing with two friends, some complicated game of make-believe involving a superhero that Merrick vaguely remembered his own sons briefly idolizing. The friends had been called in by their mother and Tim had said he was going down the embankment to watch the freight trains that used this spur to bring roadstone from the quarry on the outskirts of the city to the railhead.

Two women heading for the bus stop and bingo thought they'd caught a glimpse of his canary yellow Bradfield Victoria shirt between the trees that lined the top of the steep slope leading down to the tracks. That had been around twenty to eight. Nobody else had come forward to say they'd seen the boy.

His face was already etched on Merrick's mind. The school photograph resembled a million others, but Merrick could have picked out Tim's sandy hair, his open grin and the blue eyes crinkled behind Harry Potter glasses from any line-up. Just as he could have done with Guy Lefevre. Wavy dark brown hair, brown eyes, a scatter of freckles across his nose and cheeks. Seven years old, tall for his age, he'd last been seen heading for an overgrown stand of trees on the edge of Downton Park, about three miles from where Merrick was standing now. It had been around seven on a damp spring evening. Guy had asked his mother if he could go out for another half-hour's play. He'd been looking for birds' nests, mapping them obsessively on a grid of the scrubby little copse. They'd found the grid two days later, on the far edge of the trees, crumpled into a ball twenty yards from the bank of the disused canal that had once run from the railhead to the long-silent wool mills. That had been the last anyone had seen of anything connected to Guy Lefevre.

And now another boy seemed also to have vanished into thin air. Merrick sighed and lowered the binoculars. They'd had to wait for daylight to complete their search of the area. They'd all clung to a faint hope that Tim had had an accident, that he was lying somewhere injured and unable to make himself heard. That hope was dead now. The frustration of having no leads bit deep. Time to round up the usual suspects. Merrick knew from past experience how unlikely it was to produce results, but he wasn't prepared to leave any avenue unexplored.

He pulled out his mobile and called his sergeant,

Kevin Matthews. 'Kev? Don here. Start bringing the nonces in.'

'No sign, then?'

'Not a trace. I've even had a team through the tunnel half a mile up the tracks. No joy. It's time to start rattling some cages.'

'How big a radius?'

Merrick sighed again. Bradfield Metropolitan Police area stretched over an area of forty-four square miles, protecting and serving somewhere in the region of 900,000 people. According to the latest official estimates he'd read, that meant there were probably somewhere in the region of 3,000 active paedophiles in the force area. Fewer than ten per cent of that number was on the register of sex offenders. Rather less than the tip of the iceberg. But that was all they had to go on. 'Let's start with a two-mile radius,' he said. 'They like to operate in the comfort zone, don't they?' As he spoke, Merrick was painfully aware that these days, with people commuting longer distances to work, with so many employed in jobs that kept them on the road, with local shopping increasingly a thing of the past, the comfort zone was, for most citizens, exponentially bigger than it had ever been even for their parents' generation. 'We've got to start somewhere,' he added, his pessimism darkening his voice.

He ended the call and stared down the bank, shielding his eyes against the sunshine that lent the grass and trees below a blameless glow. The brightness made the search easier, it was true. But it felt inappropriate, as if the weather was insulting the anguish of the Goldings. This was Merrick's first major case since his promotion, and already he suspected he wasn't going to deliver a result that would make anybody happy. Least of all him.

Dr Tony Hill balanced a bundle of files on the arm carrying his battered briefcase and pushed open the door of the faculty office. He had enough time before his seminar group to collect his mail and deal with whatever couldn't be ignored. The psychology department secretary emerged from the inner office at the sound of the door closing. 'Dr Hill,' she said, sounding unreasonably pleased with herself.

'Morning, Mrs Stirrat,' Tony mumbled, dropping files and briefcase to the floor while he reached for the contents of his pigeonhole. Never, he thought, was a woman more aptly named. He wondered if that was why she'd chosen the husband she had.

'The Dean's not very pleased with you,' Janine Stirrat said, folding her arms across her ample chest.

'Oh? And why might that be?' Tony asked.

'The cocktail party with SJP yesterday evening – you were supposed to be there.'

With his back to her, Tony rolled his eyes. 'I was engrossed in some work. The time just ran away from me.'

'They're a major donor to the behavioural psychology research programme,' Mrs Stirrat scolded. 'They wanted to meet you.'

Tony grabbed his mail in an unruly pile and stuffed it into the front pocket of his briefcase. 'I'm sure they had a wonderful time without me,' he said, scooping up his files and backing towards the door.

'The Dean expects all academic staff to support

fundraising, Dr Hill. It's not much to ask, that you give up a couple of hours of your time –'

'To satisfy the prurient curiosity of the executives of a pharmaceutical company?' Tony snapped. 'To be honest, Mrs Stirrat, I'd rather set my hair on fire and beat the flames out with a hammer.' Using his elbow to manipulate the handle, he escaped into the corridor without waiting to check the affronted look he knew would be plastered across her face.

Temporarily safe in the haven of his own office, Tony slumped in the chair behind his computer. What the hell was he doing here? He'd managed to bury his unease about the academic life for long enough to accept the Reader's job at St Andrews, but ever since his brief and traumatic excursion back into the field in Germany, he'd been unable to settle. The growing realization that the university had hired him principally because his was a sexy name on the prospectus hadn't helped. Students enrolled to be close to the man whose profiles had nailed some of the country's most notorious serial killers. And donors wanted the vicarious, voyeuristic thrill of the war stories they tried to cajole from him. If he'd learned nothing else from his sojourn in the university, he'd come to understand that he wasn't cut out to be a performing seal. Whatever talents he possessed, pointless diplomacy had never been among them.

This morning's encounter with Janine Stirrat felt like the last straw. Tony pulled his keyboard closer and began to compose a letter.

Three hours later, he was struggling to recover his breath. He'd set off far too fast and now he was paying the price. He crouched down and felt the rough grass at his feet. Dry enough to sit on, he decided. He sank to the ground and lay spreadeagled till the thumping in his chest eased off. Then he wriggled into a sitting position and savoured the view. From the top of Largo Law, the Firth of Forth lay before him, glittering in the late spring sunshine. He could see right across to Berwick Law, its volcanic cone the prehistoric twin to his own vantage point, separated now by miles of petrol-blue sea. He checked off the landmarks: the blunt thumb of the Bass Rock, the May Island like a basking humpback whale, the distant blur of Edinburgh. They had a saying in this corner of Fife: 'If you can see the May Island, it's going to rain. If you can't see the May Island, it's already raining.' It didn't look like rain today. Only the odd smudge of cloud broke the blue, like soft streamers of aerated dough pulled from the middle of a morning roll. He was going to miss this when he moved on.

But spectacular views were no justification for turning his back on the true north of his talent. He wasn't an academic. He was a clinician first and foremost, then a profiler. His resignation would take effect at the end of term, which gave him a couple of months to figure out what he was going to do next.

He wasn't short of offers. Although his past exploits hadn't always endeared him to the Home Office establishment, the recent case he'd worked on in Germany and Holland had helped him leapfrog the British bureaucracy. Now the Germans, the Dutch and the Austrians wanted him to work for them as a consultant. Not just on serial murder, but on other criminal activity that treated international frontiers as if they didn't exist. It was a tempting offer, with a guaranteed minimum that would be just about enough to live on. And it would give him the chance to return to clinical practice, even if it was only part-time.

Then, there was Carol Jordan to consider. As always when she came into his thoughts, his mind veered away from direct confrontation. Somehow, he had to find a way to atone for what had happened to her, without her ever knowing that was what he was trying to do.

And so far, he had no idea how he could achieve that.

Day Two. And still no trace of Tim Golding. In his heavy heart, Merrick knew they were no longer searching for a living child. He'd visited Alastair and Shelley Golding that morning, cut to the bone by the momentary flash of optimism that lit their eyes when he walked into their neat Victorian terraced cottage. As soon as they'd comprehended that he had nothing to offer them, their eyes had glazed over. Fear had gnawed at them till there was nothing left inside but barren hope.

Merrick had left the house feeling bleak and empty. He glanced down the street, thinking ironically that Tim Golding had, in a way, been a victim of gentrification. Harriestown, where the Goldings lived, had been a working-class enclave until enterprising young couples in search of affordable housing had begun buying up decaying properties and restoring them, creating a trendy new suburb. What had been lost was a sense of community. The avid followers of *Changing Rooms* and *Home Front* were interested in their own lives, not those of their neighbours. Ten years before, Tim Golding would have known most of the people on his street and they would have known him. On a summer evening, people would have been out and about, walking to allotments or from the pub, standing in their doorways chatting as they soaked up the last rays of the sun. Their very presence would have protected the boy. And they would have noticed a stranger, would have clocked his passage and kept an eye on his destination. But these days, those residents of Harriestown not whipping up some exotic recipe from a TV chef in their exquisitely designed new kitchens would have been in their back yards, cut off from neighbours by high walls, designing their Mediterranean courtyard gardens or arranging the Greek urns that held their fresh herbs. Merrick had scowled at the blank doors and windows of the street and longed for a simpler time. He'd headed back to the incident room, feeling ill at ease and jaded.

His team had worked through the night, interviewing the known paedophiles on their patch. Not a single pointer had emerged to move the inquiry forward. A couple of punters had phoned in, reporting a white Transit van cruising slowly round the narrow streets at about the time Tim had disappeared. By chance, one of them had remembered enough of the index number to make it worth checking out on the Police National Computer. They'd identified half a dozen possibles in the local area, which had given the incident room a fresh surge of energy.

But that lead had died on its knees within a matter of hours. The third van on the list belonged to a company who made home deliveries of organic vegetables. The driver had been going slowly because he was new to the round and wasn't sure of the layout of the local streets. That alone wouldn't have been enough to get him off the hook. But the clincher was that he'd been accompanied by his fifteen-year-old daughter, augmenting her pocket money by helping him out.

Back to square one. Merrick shoved his hands in his trouser pockets and glared at the pinboard in the incident room. It was pitifully bare. Usually by this stage in a missing-child inquiry, information was pouring in. It certainly had in the Guy Lefevre case, although it had all proved fruitless in the long run. But for some reason all they were getting was a pathetic trickle. Of course there were the time-wasters, calling to say they'd seen Tim on the Eurostar train with an Asian woman; in a McDonald's in Taunton with a grey-haired man; or shopping for computer games in Inverness. Merrick knew these so-called sightings were worthless. Whoever had taken Tim certainly wouldn't be parading him round the streets for everyone to see.

Merrick sighed. The images in his head now were not of a small boy playing with his friends. What he saw when he closed his eyes was a shallow woodland grave. A flash of yellow football shirt in the long grass of a field margin. A tangle of limbs in a drainage ditch. Christ, but he felt inadequate to the task.

He racked his brains for some other avenue of approach, summoning up the images of previous bosses, wondering how they would have handled things differently. Popeye Cross would have been convinced their abductor was someone they already had on the books. He'd be sweating the nonces, determined to get a confession out of someone. Merrick was confident he'd covered that already, even though his team knew better than to exert the kind of pressure Popeye had been famous for. These days, you leaned too heavily at your peril. Courts had no patience with police officers who bullied vulnerable suspects.

He thought of Carol Jordan and reached for his cigarettes. She'd have come up with some tangential line of attack, he had no doubt of that. Her mind worked in ways he'd never managed to fathom. His brain was wired differently from hers, and he'd never in a million years arrive at one of her inspired angles. But there was one thing Carol would have done that he could pursue.

Merrick inhaled and reached for the phone. 'Is the boss in?' he asked the woman who answered. 'I'd like to talk to him about Tony Hill.'

John Brandon climbed the steps up from the Barbican station. The dirty yellow bricks seemed to sweat and even the concrete underfoot felt hot and sticky. The air was stuffy with the thick, mingled smells of humanity. It wasn't the best preparation for what he suspected was going to be a difficult conversation.

No matter how much he'd tried to prepare himself for his meeting with Carol Jordan, he knew he didn't really have a clue what he'd find. He was certain of only two things: he had no idea how she felt about what had happened to her; and work would be her salvation.

He'd been appalled when he'd heard about the botched undercover mission that had ended with the violent assault on Carol. His informant had tried to stress the significance of what her operation had achieved, as if that were somehow a counterbalance to what had been done to her. But Brandon had cut impatiently across the rationale. He understood the demands of command. He'd given his adult life to the police service and he'd reached the top of the tree with most of his principles intact. One of those was that no officer should ever be exposed to unnecessary risk. Of course danger was part of the job, particularly these days, with guns as much a fashion accessory in some social groups as iPods were in others. But there was acceptable risk and unacceptable risk. And in Brandon's view, Carol Jordan had been placed in a position of intolerable, improper risk. He simply did not believe there was any end that could have justified such means.

But it was pointless to rage against what had happened. Those responsible were too well insulated for even a Chief Constable to make much of a dent in their lives. The only thing John Brandon could do now for Carol was to offer her a lifeline back into the profession she loved. She'd been probably the best detective he'd ever had under his command, and all his instincts told him she needed to be back in harness.

He'd discussed it with his wife Maggie, laying out his plans before her. 'What do you think?' he asked. 'You know Carol. Do you think she'll go for it?'

Maggie had frowned, stirring her coffee thoughtfully. 'It's not me you should be asking, it's Tony Hill. He's the psychologist.'

Brandon shook his head. 'Tony is the last person I'd ask about Carol. Besides, he's a man, he can't understand the implications of rape the way a woman can.'

Maggie's mouth twisted in acknowledgement. 'The old Carol Jordan would have bitten your hand off. But it's hard to imagine what being raped will have done to her. Some women fall to pieces. For some, it becomes the defining moment of their lives. Others lock it away and pretend it never happened. It sits there like a time bomb waiting to blow a hole in their lives. And some find a way to deal with it and move forward. If I had to guess, I'd say Carol would either bury it or else work through it. If she's burying it, she'll probably be gung ho to get back to serious work, to prove to herself and the rest of the world that she's sorted. But she'll be a loose cannon if that's what she's trying to do, and that's not what you need in this job. However . . .' she paused, 'if she's looking for a way through, you might be able to persuade her.'

'Do you think she'd be up to the job?' Brandon's bloodhound eyes looked troubled.

'It's like what they say about politicians, isn't it? The very people who volunteer for the job are the last ones who should be doing it. I don't know, John. You're going to have to make your mind up when you see her.'

It wasn't a comforting thought. But he'd since had support from a surprising quarter. The previous afternoon, DI Merrick had sat in his office asking Brandon's sanction to bring Tony Hill in to profile the disappearance of Tim Golding. As they'd discussed the case,

Merrick had said almost wistfully, 'I can't help feeling we'd be doing better if we still had DCI Jordan on the team.'

Brandon's eyebrows had shot up. 'I hope you're not having a crisis of confidence, Inspector,' he said.

Merrick shook his head. 'No, sir. I know we're doing everything we can. It's just that DCI Jordan looks at things differently from anybody else I've ever worked with. And with cases like this . . . well, sometimes it feels like it's not enough to cover all the bases.'

Brandon knew Merrick had been right. All the more reason why he should do everything in his power to bring Carol Jordan back into the world again. He squared his shoulders and headed for the concrete labyrinth where Carol Jordan waited at the epicentre.

John Brandon was shaken to see the change in Carol Jordan. The woman who waited in the doorway for him to emerge from the lift bore almost no resemblance to his memory of her. He might well have passed her in the street. Her hair was radically different, cut short at the sides, the heavy fringe swept to one side, changing the shape of her face. But she had altered in more fundamental ways. The flesh seemed to have melted from her face, giving it a new arrangement of planes and hollows. Where there had been an expression of intelligent interest in her eyes, now there was a blank wariness. She radiated tension rather than the familiar confidence. In spite of the warmth of the early summer day, she was dressed in a shapeless polo-neck sweater and baggy trousers instead of the sharply tailored suits Brandon was used to seeing her in.

He paused a couple of feet from her. 'Carol,' he said. 'It's good to see you.'

There was no smile of welcome, just a faint twitch of muscle at the corners of her mouth. 'Come in, sir,' she said, stepping back to allow him to enter.

'No need for formality,' Brandon said, taking care to keep as much physical distance as possible between them as he walked into the flat. 'I've not been your boss for quite a while now.'

Carol said nothing, leading the way to the pair of sofas that sat at right angles to each other with a view through the floor-to-ceiling windows of the old church at the heart of the Barbican complex. She waited till he sat down, then offered him a drink. 'Coffee, tea?'

'Something cold. It's warm out there today,' Brandon said, unfastening the jacket of his charcoal suit. Catching her sudden stillness, he stopped awkwardly at the third button and cleared his throat.

'Mineral water or orange juice?'

'Water's fine.'

When she returned with two glasses of water still hissing their effervescence into the air, Carol set Brandon's in front of him then retreated with her own to the furthest point from him. 'How are you?' Brandon asked.

Carol shrugged. 'Better than I was.'

'I was shocked when I heard what had happened. And upset too. Maggie and I . . . well, I know how I'd feel if her, or my daughters . . . Carol, I can't imagine how you begin to deal with something like that.'

'There isn't anything like that,' Carol said sharply, her eyes on his. 'I was raped, John. No other violation comes close except death, and nobody's reported back on that yet.'

Brandon took the rebuke on the chin. 'It should never have happened.'

Carol let out a deep breath. 'I made mistakes, it's true. But the real damage was caused by people who set up the operation and never levelled with me about what was really going on. Sadly, not everyone is as scrupulous as you.' She turned away and crossed her legs tightly. 'You said there was something you wanted to discuss with me?' she continued, changing the subject irrevocably.

'That's right. I don't know how current you are with recent changes in the service in the north?'

Carol shook her head. 'It's not what I've been paying attention to.'

'No reason why you should,' he said gently. 'But the Home Office in their wisdom have decided East Yorkshire is too small a force and it should be amalgamated. And since my force is the smaller of the two involved in the merger, I'm the one who's had to give up the top job.'

Carol showed the first sign of animation. 'I'm sorry to hear that, John. You were a good Chief Constable.'

'Thank you. And I hope I will be again. I'm back on my old stamping grounds.'

'Bradfield?'

Brandon noticed Carol's body relaxing slightly. He had, he thought, penetrated the hard outer shell.

'That's right. They've offered me Bradfield Metropolitan Police.' His lugubrious face creased in a smile. 'And I've said yes.'

'I'm very pleased for you, John.' Carol sipped her drink. 'You'll do a good job there.'

Brandon shook his head. 'I didn't come here for flattery, Carol. I came here because I need you.'

Carol looked away, her eyes fixed on the marled grey stone of the church. 'I don't think so, John.'

'Hear me out. I'm not asking you to come and fly a desk in CID. I want to do something different in Bradfield. I want to set up an operation like the Met has for dealing with serious crime. A couple of elite major incident squads on permanent standby to catch the tough ones. All they do is the big cases, the really bad lads. And if there's a lull in the action, the squad can pick up cold cases and work them.'

She turned her head towards him and gave him a shrewd, considering look. 'And you think I'm what you need?'

'I want you to be in charge of the unit and to have hands-on leadership of one squad. This is the sort of stuff you do best, Carol. The combination of intelligence and instinct and solid police work.'

She rubbed the back of her neck with a hand chill from her water glass. 'Maybe once,' she said. 'I don't think that's who I am any more.'

Brandon shook his head. 'These things don't go away. You're the best detective I ever had working for me, even if there were times when you came close to overstepping the mark. But you were always right when you pushed it that far. And I need that level of skill and guts on my team.'

Carol stared down at the brightly coloured gabbeh on the floor as if it held the answer. 'I don't think so, John. I come with rather too much baggage these days.'

'You'd be reporting directly to me. No petty bureaucrats between us. You'd be working with some of your old colleagues, Carol. People who know who you are and what you've achieved. Not people who are going to make snap judgements about you based on rumour and half-truth. The likes of Don Merrick and Kevin Matthews. Men who respect you.' The unspoken hung in the air. There was nowhere else she could expect that sort of reception and they both knew it.

'It's a very generous offer, John.' Carol met his gaze, a world of weariness in her eyes. 'But I think you deserve an easier ride than hiring me will get you.'

'Let me be the judge of that,' Brandon said, his natural air of authority suddenly emerging from the mildness he'd shown so far. 'Carol, your work was always a large part of who you were. I understand why you don't want to go back into intelligence and, in your shoes, I wouldn't touch those bastards with a ten-foot pole. But policing is in your blood. Forgive me if this sounds presumptuous, but I don't think you're going to get over this until you get back on the horse.'

Carol's eyes widened. Brandon wondered if he'd gone too far and waited for the whip of irony that he'd once have earned, regardless of rank.

'Have you been talking to Tony Hill?' she demanded.

Brandon couldn't hide his surprise. 'Tony? No, I

haven't spoken to him in . . . oh, it must be more than a year. Why do you say that?'

'He says the same thing,' she said flatly. 'I wondered if I was being ganged up on.'

'No, this was all my own idea. But you know, Tony's not a bad judge.'

'Maybe so. But neither of you can know much about what it's like to be me these days. I'm not sure the old rules apply any more. John, I can't make a decision about this now. I need time to think.'

Brandon drained his glass. 'Take all the time you need.' He got to his feet. 'Call me if you want to talk in more detail.' He took a business card from his pocket and placed it on the table. She looked at it as if it might suddenly burst into flames. 'Let me know what you decide.'

Carol nodded wearily. 'I will. But don't build your plans around me, John.'

It's never silent inside Bradfield Moor Secure Hospital. Well, not anywhere they've ever let you go. All the films and TV shows you've seen make you think there are probably padded cells somewhere no sound can reach, but you'd probably have to go completely tonto to end up there. Scream, foam at the mouth, deck one of the staff – that sort of thing. And while the idea of being somewhere quiet is appealing, you reckon it won't do your chances of release much good if you fake a full-on madhead attack just to get enough peace to hear the Voice properly.

When you first arrived at Bradfield Moor, you tried to get to sleep as soon as the lock's click signalled you were shut in for the night. But all you could hear were muffled conversations, occasional screams and sobs, feet slapping down corridors. You pulled the thin pillow over your head and tried to blank it. It didn't often work. The anonymous noises scared you, left you wondering if your door would suddenly burst open and front you up with who the fuck knew what. Instead of sleep, you'd get edgy and wired. Morning would come and you'd be exhausted, your eyes gritty and sore, your hands shaking like some fucked-up alkie. Worst of all, in that state, you couldn't tune in to the Voice. You were too wound up to find the technique to beat the background.

It took a few weeks, a few hellish, terrifying weeks, but eventually your slow brain worked out that it might be worth trying to go with the flow. Now, when the lights go out, you lie on your back, breathing deeply, telling yourself the noises outside are meaningless background chatter that you don't have to pay attention to. And sooner or later they fade like radio static, leaving you alone with the Voice. Your lips move silently as you relive the message, and you're gone somewhere else. Somewhere good.

It's a beautiful thing. You can replay the slow build-up to your greatest achievements. It's all there, spread before you. The choosing of a sacrifice. The negotiation. Following her to the place that you're going to transform with blood. The stupid trust they had that Dozy Derek wasn't going to hurt them. And the look in their eyes when you turned to face them with their worst nightmare in your hand.

The rerun never quite makes it to the finale. It's the eyes that do it, every time. You relive the moment when it dawns on them, the terror that turns them the colour of milk and your hand tightens on your cock. Your back arches, your hips thrust upwards, your lips stretch back over your teeth as you come. And then you hear the Voice, triumphant and rich, praising you for your role in the cleansing.

It's the best moment in your cramped little world. Other

people might think differently, but you know how lucky you are. All you want now is to get out of here, to get back to the Voice. Nothing else will do.

PART TWO

Ten weeks later

He can't remember the first time he heard the Voice. It makes him ashamed these days that he didn't recognize it instantly. Thinking about it now, he finds it hard to believe it took him so long to get it. Because it was different from all the other voices he heard every day. It didn't take the piss. It didn't get impatient with him for being slow. It didn't treat him like a stupid kid. The Voice gave him respect. He'd never had that before, which was probably why he didn't get the message for so long. It took a while before it dawned on him what was on offer.

Now, he can't imagine being without it. It's like chocolate or alcohol or spliff. The world would go on without them, but why would anybody want it to? There are times and places where he knows he'll hear it: the message service on his mobile, the minidisks that turn up without warning in the pocket of his parka, alone in bed late at night. But, sometimes, it comes out of the blue. A soft breath on his neck and there it is, the Voice. The first time that happened, he nearly crapped himself. Talk about blowing it! But he's learned since then. Now, in public places, he knows how to react so nobody thinks twice about what's going on.

The Voice gives him presents, too. OK, other people have given him things in the past, but mostly worthless crap they didn't want or second-hand stuff they were finished with. The Voice is different. The Voice gives him things that are just for him. Things that are still in their boxes and bags, bought and paid for, not nicked. The minidisk player. The Diesel jeans. The Zippo lighter with the brass skull and crossbones that feels good when he rubs his thumb over it. The videos that fire him up with thoughts of what he'd like to do to the street girls he sees every day.

When he asked why, the Voice said it was because he was worthy. He didn't understand that. Still doesn't, not really. The Voice said he would earn the gifts, but it didn't say how, not for ages. That was probably his fault. He's not quick on the uptake. It takes him a while to get the hang of things.

But he likes to please. That's one of the first things he can remember learning. Make people smile, give them what they want and there's a better chance of avoiding a beating. So he paid attention when the Voice started to teach him his lessons because he knew that if he kept the Voice happy there was more chance it'd stay around. And he wants it to stay around, because it makes him feel good. Not many things have ever made him feel good.

So he listens and he tries to understand. He knows now about the poison the girls spread on the street. He knows that even the ones who have been kind to him are only after what they can get. This makes sense to him; he remembers how often they've tried to sweet-talk him into doing them a better deal, and how vicious they get when he sticks to what he's supposed to give them in exchange for their crumpled notes. He knows now those bitches have to be cleansed, and that he's going to be part of that cleansing.

It won't be long. Every night when he turns out the light, the Voice whispers through the silence, telling him how it will be. At first, it scared him. He wasn't sure he could handle the way the walls seemed to be talking to him. And he didn't think he could do what was being asked of him. But now when he listens in that half-world between wakefulness and sleep, he thinks maybe he can do this. One step at a time, that's how you get where you want to be. That's what the Voice says. And if he looks at it step by step, there's nothing so hard about it. Not till the very end.

He's never done anything like that before. But he's seen the videos, again and again. He knows how good it feels to watch. And the Voice tells him it'll be a million times better to do it for real. And that makes sense too, because everything the Voice has told him so far has been the truth. And now the time has come. Tonight's the night.

He can hardly wait.

Carol Jordan tossed her briefcase on to the passenger seat and got into the silver mid-range saloon she'd chosen specifically for its anonymity. She put the key in the ignition, but couldn't quite bring herself to start the engine. Christ, what was she doing? Her hands were clammy with sweat, her chest tight with anxiety. How the hell was she going to walk into a squad-room and energize her troops when her mouth was so dry her tongue stuck to her teeth?

She stared up at the small windows high on the walls of the underground car park. Feet hurried past, making their way to work. Polished loafers, scuffed shoes, kitten heels and pumps. Legs clad in suit trousers, jeans, opaque black tights and sheer nylon. City-centre hikers, taking the morning in their stride. Why couldn't she do the same thing?

'Get a grip, Jordan,' she muttered under her breath, turning the key and firing the engine. It wasn't as if she was going to have to confront a room full of strangers. Her squad was small, hand-picked by her and Brandon. Most of them she'd worked with before and she knew they respected her. Or at least they once had. She hoped their respect was still strong enough to withstand the temptation to pity.

Carol eased the car out of the garage into the street. It was all so familiar and yet so different. When she'd lived and worked in Bradfield before, the loft apartment in the converted warehouse that occupied a whole block had been her home, a high eyrie that allowed her to feel both part of and apart from the city she policed. When she'd moved to London, she'd sold it to her brother and his girlfriend. Now she was back living inside the same four walls, but this time as the reluctant cuckoo in a nest created by Michael and Lucy. They'd changed almost every aspect of the flat, making Carol feel even more out of place. Once, she'd have shrugged off that feeling, secure in the knowledge that she had a workplace where she was at home. What she feared today was that she'd feel as much of an outsider inside the police station as outside.

Even Bradfield itself felt like a too-familiar stranger. When she'd lived and worked here before, she'd made a point of learning the city. She'd visited the local museum in a bid to understand the forces that had shaped Bradfield over the centuries, turning it from a hamlet of shepherds and weavers into a vigorous commercial centre that had vied with Manchester to be the northern capital of the Victorian empire. She'd learned of its decline in the post-war era, then the reinvigoration that had been kick-started by successive waves of immigration at the tail end of the last century. She'd studied the architecture, learning to appreciate the Italianate influences on the older buildings, trying to see how the city had grown organically, attempting to imagine what the hideous 1960s concrete office blocks and shopping centre had vanquished. She'd mapped the city in her mind, using her days off to walk the streets, drive the neighbourhoods until she could grasp immediately the kind of environment she was about to enter just from the address of the crime scene.

But this morning, Carol's old knowledge seemed to have fled. New road markings and one-way systems had mushroomed in her absence, forcing her to concentrate on her bearings in a way she hadn't expected. Driving to the central police station should have been automatic. But it took her twice as long as she'd estimated and relief washed through her as she eventually turned into the car park. Carol nosed forward towards the dedicated parking spaces, pleased to see that at least one of John Brandon's promises had already been kept. One of the few empty slots bore the freshly painted designation, 'DCI Jordan'.

Walking into the station itself provided a brief moment of déjà vu. Here at least nothing seemed to have altered. The back entrance hall still smelled faintly of cigarette smoke and stale fat from the canteen on the floor below. Whatever cosmetic changes might have been imposed on the public areas, no decorators had been charged with making this entrance more appealing. The walls were still the same industrial grey, the noticeboard covered with what were possibly the same yellowing memos she'd last seen years ago. Carol walked up to the counter and nodded a greeting at the PC behind the desk. 'DCI Jordan reporting to the Major Incident Team.'

The middle-aged man rubbed a hand across his grizzled crew cut and smiled. 'Welcome aboard,' he said. 'End of the corridor, take the lift up to the third floor. You're in Room 316.'

'Thanks.' Carol managed a thin smile and turned to push open the door as the lock buzzed. Unconsciously squaring her shoulders and tilting her chin up, she walked briskly down the corridor, ignoring the occasional curious glance from uniformed officers she passed on the way.

The third floor had undergone a facelift since she'd left. The walls were painted lavender to waist height, then off-white. The old wooden doors had been replaced with plate glass and steel, the central sections frosted so the casual passer-by could see little of what was going on inside the offices. It looked more like an advertising agency than a police station, she thought as she reached the door of 316.

Carol took a deep breath and pushed the door open. A handful of curious faces glanced up at her then broke into smiles of welcome. First on his feet was Don Merrick, newly promoted to inspector. He'd been her bagman on her first serial killer inquiry, the case that had proved to those who cared about that sort of thing that she had what it took to go all the way. Solid, reliable Don, she thought gratefully as he crossed the room and extended his hand.

'Great to see you back, ma'am,' he said, reaching out to cup her elbow with his free hand as they shook. Although he towered over her, Carol was pleasantly surprised to find nothing unsettling in his bulk. 'I'm really looking forward to working with you again.'

Detective Sergeant Kevin Matthews was right behind Merrick. Kevin, who had redeemed himself after an act of monumental stupidity had nearly cost him his career. Even though she'd been the person responsible for uncovering his treachery, Carol was nevertheless glad to see he'd apparently rehabilitated himself. He had been too good a detective to waste on the mindless routine of uniformed work. She hoped he wouldn't mind too much that they'd once been equals in rank. 'Kevin,' she acknowledged him. 'Good to see you.'

His pale, freckled skin flushed pink. 'Welcome back to Bradfield,' he said.

The others were crowding round now. 'Good to see you, chief,' a woman's voice said from behind her. Carol half-turned to see the slight figure of Detective Constable Paula McIntyre grinning up at her. Paula had worked on the periphery of the murder squad that had tracked down the psychopath who had butchered four young men in the city. She'd only been a CID aide on secondment then, but Carol had remembered her attention to detail and her empathetic way with witnesses. According to Brandon, she'd since established herself as one of the best interviewers in the city's CID. Carol knew exactly how important that could be in a murder inquiry, where everything happened against the clock. Someone skilled at persuading people to remember all they knew could save time at a stage when time could mean lives.

Paula pushed forward a mixed-race man standing

beside her. 'This is DC Evans,' she said. 'Sam, this is DCI Jordan.'

Carol extended a hand. Evans seemed almost reluctant to take it, not meeting her eye as they shook. Carol gave him a quick look of appraisal. He wasn't much taller than she was; he must barely have made the height requirement, she thought. His tightly curled hair was cut close to his head, his features more Caucasian than African. His skin was the colour of caramelized sugar and a fuzzy goatee gave him an air of maturity at odds with the unlined youthfulness of his face. She summoned up Brandon's notes on the young detective: 'A quiet lad. But he's not afraid to speak up when he's got something to say. He's smart and he's got that killer knack for pulling information together and making sense of it. He wants to go all the way, though he hides it well. But that means he'll pull out all the stops for you.' It looked like she'd have to take Brandon's word for it.

One person hung back on the fringes of the group. DC Stacey Chen had a small, fixed smile on her face. She was the unknown quantity. These days, any major inquiry needed an officer who understood how the systems worked and who could manage the volume of information generated. Carol had asked Brandon to recommend someone, and he'd come back within twenty-four hours with Stacey. 'She's got a Masters in computing, she knows the systems inside out and she's a grafter. She keeps herself to herself, but she understands the importance of being part of the team,' he'd said. 'And she's ambitious.'

Carol remembered what that felt like. Ambition had deserted her along with her dignity in Berlin, but she could still recall the sharp burn of desire to be on the next rung of the ladder. Carol sidestepped Evans and offered her hand to Stacey. 'Hi. You must be Stacey. I'm glad to have you on the team.'

Stacey's brown eyes never left Carol's. 'I appreciate the chance,' she said in a strong London accent.

Carol's eyes swept the room. 'We're one short,' she said.

'Oh yeah,' Merrick said. 'DS Chris Devine. We had a message yesterday: her mother's been diagnosed with terminal cancer. She's requested permission to stay with the Met for the time being. The Chief agreed.'

Carol shook her head, faintly exasperated. 'Great. We're under strength before we even get started.' She looked around, assessing the room for the first time. There were half a dozen desks, each with a computer terminal. Whiteboards and cork boards lined one wall, next to an overhead projector. A large-scale laminated map of Bradfield filled most of the space by the door. The windows that ran the length of the opposite wall were obscured by vertical blinds, cutting out the distractions of the cityscape. It was a decent size: not too cramped, not so big they'd feel marooned. It would do, she decided. 'Don, where's my office?'

Merrick pointed to the far end of the room where two doors closed off a pair of offices. 'Take your pick. They're both empty.'

And neither offered much in the way of privacy, she thought. She chose the one that had windows on the outside world and turned to Merrick, who had followed her down the room. 'Call whoever's responsible for housekeeping round here. I want some blinds for the internal window.'

Merrick grinned. 'Don't want us to know when you're playing Solitaire, eh?'

'I prefer FreeCell, actually. Give me half an hour to get settled in here, then we'll have a briefing.'

'Fine by me.' He ducked out of the room, leaving her alone. It was, she thought, a relief. She switched on the computer. Seconds later, she saw Evans approaching, his arms laden with a bundle of files. She jumped up to open the door.

'What's all this?' she asked.

'Open cases – the most recent ones. They were delivered yesterday teatime. What we're supposed to be working on while we wait for the next big thing.'

Carol felt her blood stirring. At last, something she could focus on. Something that might just lay her demons to rest. Or at least shut them up for a while.

Aidan Hart studied the man sitting opposite him with a degree of wariness. He knew many of his colleagues thought he was too young at thirty-seven to be clinical director of Bradfield Moor Secure Hospital, but he was confident enough of his skills to write off their disapproval as the product of disappointment and envy. He knew that none of them presented any professional challenge to him.

But his latest appointment was in a different league. Dr Tony Hill came with a reputation for both brilliance and awkwardness. The only rules he observed were the ones that mattered to him. He wasn't a team player, unless the team in question was one he'd chosen. He'd won loyal respect and engendered fury in equal measures among those he'd worked with. When Tony Hill had applied for a part-time post at his hospital, Aidan Hart's first reaction had been to refuse. There was room for only one star at Bradfield Moor, and that was him.

Then he'd had second thoughts. If Hill was only there as a part-timer, his work could be carefully channelled. His successes could be parlayed into more credit for Hart himself, the visionary clinical director who had tamed the maverick. It was a tempting prospect. He could portray himself as the man who persuaded high-flyer Tony Hill back into clinical practice. He had convinced himself that while the patients might benefit from Hill's famous empathetic skills, the ultimate beneficiary would be Aidan Hart himself. His second thoughts had been reinforced when he'd met Hill in the flesh. Aidan Hart knew all about dressing to impress, but within seconds he realized Hill had obviously missed that particular tutorial. The little guy in the chair opposite with the bad haircut, brown shoes with black trousers and greenish tweed jacket with frayed cuffs wasn't going to make ripples in the sort of pond Hart intended to swim in. Hill had seemed embarrassed by the high profile his work with the police had earned him and had stressed that he didn't want to find himself in the public eye ever again. Whatever profiling he did in future would be behind closed doors and beyond distant borders. Hill's eagerness to get back into harness at the sharp end of clinical practice was almost pathetic.

At the time, Hart had been smugly satisfied that taking a chance on Tony Hill would be the best possible decision. Somehow he'd missed the penetrating intelligence of the eyes, the unmistakable charisma the man wore like a well-cut suit. Hart wasn't quite sure how that had happened. Unless, of course, Hill had deliberately disguised it in order to make a quite different kind of impression. And that was a very unsettling thought. He liked to think of himself as the analyst. He was uncomfortable with the idea that this time, he might have been played by a higher master in the art of reading human behaviour. He couldn't help wondering whether he was the latest object of scrutiny for those startlingly blue eyes that seemed to absorb every nuance of his body language. He didn't like the thought that he'd have to monitor his every word and movement in his newest employee's presence. Aidan Hart had his secrets, and he didn't want Tony Hill probing too closely into them.

He didn't think he was being paranoid. Hill had only been in the building for an hour, but already he'd played a blinder. He'd found out about the latest admission and now he was sitting opposite Hart, one ankle casually propped on the opposite knee, making an irresistible rationale for first crack at the new patient. It was the sort of case that led to published papers in well-respected peer-reviewed publications, and already Hill was staking a claim to territory Hart wanted for himself. 'After all,' Hill said, 'since we've got a new admission, it makes sense for me to take the case on. That way I won't have to go over old ground. And nobody's nose gets put out of joint because I'm taking over their patient.'

'It's a pretty extreme place to start,' Hart said, affecting concern. 'And you have been out of the field for a while.'

Tony's mouth twitched in a half-smile. 'Extreme is my comfort zone, Aidan. And I do have very direct experience of dealing with people who kill for reasons that most people dismiss as madness.'

Hart shifted in his chair and spread his hands, as if discarding responsibility. 'So be it. I look forward to seeing your initial report.'

Carol leaned against the whiteboard and waited for her new team to settle down. Then she moved closer to them and perched on the edge of a desk. 'Before we get down to business, there's something I have to say to you,' she said, trying to sound more relaxed than she felt. 'I know how rumours spread in this job and I expect you've all heard some version of my recent history.' She could tell by the way the men all found something more interesting to study that she'd hit the target.

Don Merrick gazed at the floor. 'Nobody here's interested in gossip,' he muttered. 'Just results. And your record speaks for itself on that.'

The shadow of a smile crossed Carol's face. 'Thank you, Don. Nevertheless, if we're going to make this unit work, we need to have an open, honest atmosphere. What happened to me happened because of secrets and lies. I'm not prepared to work in an environment like that again.' She looked around, saw she had their attention and continued.

'I was selected for an undercover operation that left me in a very exposed position. Because I wasn't thoroughly briefed by my bosses, I couldn't cover my back properly. And as a result, I was raped.' She heard a sharp intake of breath but couldn't identify its source. 'I don't expect to be handled with kid gloves. What happened to me won't affect the way I do my job. Except that it has made me very sensitive to issues of loyalty. This squad can only function if we all put teamwork first. I don't want any glory hunters here. So if any of you has a problem with that, this is the time to ask for reassignment.' She looked around at her group. Stacey and Evans looked surprised, but the others were nodding their acquiescence.

Carol stood up straight and picked up the top file. 'Good. Now, until we land our first job, we're supposed to be looking at unsolved open cases. They've given us two murders, a rape, two armed robberies, a serial arson and a pair of child abductions. Over the next few days, I want you each to go through three separate files. Don, work out a rota so all the cases get looked at. Include me in it – since we're one light, I'll make up the numbers. On each file, I want you to list suggested actions for moving the case forward. Then, when you've all made your lists, we'll sit down together, look at what you've come up with and see which cases offer the most promising prospects for further investigation. Any questions?'

Kevin raised a hand. 'Is this a non-smoking office?'

Paula groaned. 'It's a non-smoking building, Kevin.'

'Yeah, but that doesn't mean we can't have smoking areas, does it? I mean, what is the point of air conditioning if you don't make it earn its keep?'

'It's bad for the computers,' Stacey pointed out.

'We could have one corner,' Evans said. 'Under the air-conditioning vent.'

As the discussion rolled over her, Carol felt the first twinges of homecoming. Never mind the adrenaline of working a case, this was the kind of argument that told her she was back where she belonged. Pointless wrangling about the small issues that made life bearable, that was the hallmark of the police service. 'Sort it out among yourselves,' she said with an air of finality. 'I don't care. I've got a door I can close. Oh, and I've got a job for you, Sam . . .'

He looked up, surprise on his face. 'Guv?' He shifted in his seat, turning slightly to one side. It was the movement of a man unconsciously reducing his target area, assessing the situation before committing himself to fight or flight.

'Pop out to the shops and buy us a kettle, a cafetière and a dozen mugs.' His eyes hardened as Carol's words sank in. 'Tea and some decent coffee, milk and sugar. Oh, and some biscuits. We're not going to win any popularity contests in the canteen, digging over what other officers will see as their failures. We might as well entrench ourselves here.'

'Can we get some Earl Grey tea?' Stacey Chen's contribution sounded more like an order than a request.

'Don't see why not,' Carol said, turning away and heading for her office. She'd learned something already. Evans didn't like what he saw as menial work.

Either he considered it to be women's work or he thought it was beneath his capabilities. Carol stored the information away for future reference. She had almost reached the door when Merrick's voice reached her in a protest.

'Ma'am, do you know why the files on Tim Golding and Guy Lefevre are in here?' he demanded indignantly.

Carol swung round. 'Who . . .?' She was aware of a sudden stillness in the room. Paula's stare was wary, while the others' expressions varied from surprised to incredulous.

Merrick's genial face had tightened. 'Tim Golding's the eight-year-old who went missing nearly three months ago. Guy Lefevre vanished into thin air fifteen months before. We turned the city upside down looking for them. We even got Tony Hill to draw up a profile, for all the good it did.'

It was Carol's turn to feel surprise. Tony had said nothing to her about profiling, never mind profiling in Bradfield. But then, he had been uncharacteristically quiet since they'd discussed whether she should take up John Brandon's offer. He'd encouraged her to accept the job, but since she'd told him of her decision to go ahead, his emails had been curiously bland and noncommittal, as if he was deliberately making her stand on her own two feet. 'What's your point, Don?' she asked.

'Tim Golding was my case,' he said angrily. 'And I was the bagman on Guy Lefevre. There's nothing we left undone.'

'Now you understand why we're going to be the station pariahs,' Carol said gently. 'There are another half-dozen SIOs out there smarting because cases they couldn't close have been passed on to us. I wouldn't be surprised if Tim Golding's case had been put in deliberately to keep us on our toes. So even though I have every confidence that you did all you could, we're still going to treat this case just like the others.'

Merrick scowled. 'All the same, ma'am . . .'

'There are people in this organization who would probably be very happy to see us fail. If you let this wind you up, Don, you're playing into their hands.' Carol gave him her warmest smile. 'I trust you, otherwise you wouldn't be in this room. But we're all capable of missing something, no matter how much we think we've covered all the ground. So I don't want the officers reviewing this case to keep their thoughts to themselves for fear of offending you. Like I said earlier: no secrets or lies.'

Carol didn't wait for a reaction. She walked into her office, leaving the door open. Was this the first sign that someone was out to undermine her squad and, by extension, their new Chief Constable? She knew she fell too easily into mistrust these days, but she'd rather be too cautious than blithely oblivious to someone putting the shaft in. After all, it wasn't paranoia if they really were out to get you.

She'd barely settled behind her desk when Don Merrick appeared in the doorway carrying a file. 'A word, ma'am?'

Carol gestured towards the visitor's chair with her head. Don sat down, holding the file to his chest. 'Tim Golding,' he said.

'I hear you, Don. Hand it over.'

He pulled it even closer to him. 'It's just that . . .'

‘I know. If anybody’s going to poke their nose into your case, you’d rather it was me than one of the new faces.’ Carol reached a hand out.

Reluctantly, Don shifted forward in his seat and extended the file towards her. ‘We couldn’t have done more,’ he said. ‘We just kept hitting brick walls. We couldn’t even give Tony Hill enough to go on to make a profile worthwhile. He said himself it was a waste of resources. But I couldn’t think of anything else to try. That’s why it’s ended up as a cold case this early on.’

‘I wondered about that. It seems very soon to consign it to the back burner.’

Don sighed. ‘There just wasn’t anywhere else for us to go with it. We’ve still got a couple of DCs keeping an eye on it, feeding the press whenever they decide to take another crack at it. But nothing active’s happened for at least a month.’ Don’s misery was written all over him, from the hangdog eyes to the slump of his shoulders.

It provoked a sympathetic echo in Carol. ‘Leave it with me, Don. I don’t expect I’ll see anything you’ve missed.’

He got to his feet, a rueful look on his face. ‘Thing is, ma’am, I remember when I was working the case that I wished you were around. Just so I could run it past you. You always had the knack of seeing things from a different angle.’

‘What is it they say, Don? Don’t wish too hard for what you want because you might get it.’

Tony Hill leaned forward and gazed intently through the observation window. A neat, balding man sat folded in the chair bolted to the floor. He looked somewhere in the region of fifty, though his placid expression went some way towards erasing the lines etched into his face. For a fleeting, incomprehensible moment, Tony thought of a child's lollipop, tightly wrapped in cellophane, Sellotape wrapped around the stick.

His stillness was preternatural. Most of the patients Tony encountered had difficulty with immobility, never mind tranquillity. They twitched, they fidgeted, they chain-smoked, they fiddled with their clothes. But this man – he checked the notes – this Tom Storey had an almost Zen-like quality. Tony glanced through the notes again, refreshing his memory from the previous evening's reading. He shook his head, fighting his anger at the stupidity of some of his medical colleagues. Then he closed the folder and headed for the interview room.

He felt the spring in his step, even in that short journey. Bradfield Moor Secure Hospital wasn't generally associated in people's minds with the notion of contentment, but that was precisely what it had given Tony for the first time in months. He was back in the field, back in the world of messy heads, back where he belonged. In spite of his constant efforts to assume a series of masks that would help him blend in, Tony knew he was an outsider in the world beyond the grim institutional walls of Bradfield Moor. It was a feeling he did not care to examine too closely; it said things about him that he wasn't entirely comfortable with. But it was impossible to deny that the exercise of empathy was what gave meaning to his days. There was nothing quite like that moment when the tumblers of someone else's brain clicked into place for him and allowed him to penetrate the knotted logic of another mind. Really, truly, nothing.

He pushed open the door to the interview room and sat down opposite his latest challenge. Tom Storey remained immobile, only his eyes shifting to connect with Tony. In his right hand, he cradled a heavily bandaged stump where his left hand had been until a few days previously. Tony leaned forward and arranged his face into an expression of sympathy. 'I'm Tony Hill. I'm sorry for your loss.'

Storey's eyes widened in surprise. Then he gave a small snort. 'My hand or my kids?' he said sourly.

'Your son and your daughter,' Tony said. 'I imagine the hand feels like a blessing.'

Storey said nothing.

'Alien Hand Syndrome,' Tony said. 'First recorded in 1908. A gift for horror-film scriptwriters: 1924, *The Hands of Orlac* – Conrad Veidt played a classical pianist who had the hands of a killer grafted on after his were destroyed in a train accident; 1946, *The Beast with Five Fingers*, another pianist; 1987, *Evil Dead II* – the hero takes a chainsaw to his possessed hand to stop it attacking him. Cheap thrills all round. But it's not so thrilling when you're the one with the hand, is it? Because when you try to explain what it feels like, nobody really takes you seriously. Nobody took you seriously, did they, Tom?'

Storey shifted in his seat but remained silent and apparently composed.

'The GP gave you some tranquillizers. Stress, that's what he said, right?'

Storey inclined his head slightly.

Tony smiled, encouraging. 'They didn't work, did they? Just made you feel sleepy and out of it. And with a hand like yours, you couldn't afford to relax your vigilance, could you? Because there was no telling what might happen then. How was it for you, Tom? Did you wake up in the night struggling for breath because the hand was round your throat? Did it smash plates over your head? Stop you from putting food in your mouth?' Tony's questioning was gentle, his voice sympathetic.

Storey cleared his throat. 'It threw things. We'd all be sitting eating breakfast, and I'd pick up the teapot and throw it at my wife. Or we'd be out in the garden and the next thing I'd know, I'd be picking up stones from the rockery and throwing them at the kids.' He leaned back in his chair, apparently exhausted from the effort of speech.

'I can imagine how frightening that must have been. How did your wife react?'

Storey closed his eyes. 'She was going to leave me. Take the kids with her and never come back.'

'And you love your kids. That's a hell of a dilemma for you. You've nothing to fight back with. Life without your kids, it's not worth living. But life with your kids places them in constant danger because you can't stop the hand doing what it wants. There's no easy answer.' Tony paused and Storey opened his eyes again. 'You must have been in complete turmoil.'

'Why are you making excuses for me? I'm a monster. I killed my children, that's the worst thing anybody can do. They should have let me bleed to death, not saved me. I deserve to be dead.' Storey's words tumbled over each other.

'You're not a monster,' Tony said. 'I don't think your kids are the only victims here. We're going to run some physical tests. Tom, I think you may be suffering from a brain tumour. You see, your brain comes in two halves. Messages from one part reach the other across a sort of bridge called the corpus callosum. When that's damaged, your right hand literally doesn't know what your left hand is doing. And that's a terrible thing to live with. I can't blame you for being driven to the point where you thought killing your children was the only way to keep them safe from whatever you might do to them.'

'You *should* blame me,' Storey insisted. 'I was their father. It was my job to protect them. Not kill them.'

'But you couldn't trust yourself. So you chose to end their lives in the most humane way you could. Smothering them while they slept.'

Storey's eyes filled with tears and he bowed his head. 'It was wrong,' he said, his voice choking. 'But nobody would listen to me. Nobody would help me.'

Tony reached across the table and laid his hand on the bandaged stump. 'We'll help you now, Tom. I promise you. We'll help you.'

Carol arched her back and rotated her shoulders, swivelling round in her chair to stare out of the window. Across the street stood a white Portland stone building with a fine neoclassical portico. When she'd last been in Bradfield, it had been a bingo hall. Now it was a nightclub, its cold neon tubes spelling out 'Afrodite' in fake Greek script. Buses rumbled past, advertising the latest movies and console games. A traffic warden stalked the metered parking, his computerized ticket machine held like a truncheon. A world going about its business, insulated from the unpleasantness that was her stock in trade. She'd read the material on Guy Lefevre and now she was close to the end of Tim Golding's file. The words were starting to blur. Apart from a half-hour break for lunch, she'd been reading solidly all day. She knew she wasn't the only one. Every time she'd raised her head, the rest of the squad had been equally engrossed. Interesting how their body language seemed to reveal so much more of their personalities than the slightly awkward and guarded conversation over the lunchtime sandwiches Stacey had fetched from the canteen.

Don sat hunched over his desk, one arm round the file like a kid who doesn't want anybody copying his work. He wasn't the quickest wit Carol had ever worked with, but he made up for it with his stolid persistence and total commitment to the team. And if there was one person whose loyalty she could depend on without question, it was Don. He'd proved himself in the past, but she hadn't realized until this morning how important that knowledge was to her.

Kevin's wiry body sat erect in his chair, papers neatly aligned. Every now and again he would pause and stare into the middle distance for as long as it took to smoke a cigarette. Then he would scribble something on the pad next to him and return to his reading. Carol remembered how he'd always seemed so buttoned up. It had made it all the harder to believe when he'd gone off the rails. But like most repressed individuals, when he had finally broken the rules he'd been more reckless than the wildest risk taker. And it had led him into betrayal. Carol told herself that he'd never make that mistake again, but she was still reluctant to trust. She hoped he couldn't see that in her eyes.

Sam Evans was hunched in the chair opposite Kevin, his jacket carefully arranged on a hanger hooked over a filing-cabinet drawer handle. His shirt was crisp and white, the careful creases of the iron still clean cut on his sleeves. He and Kevin had staked out smokers' corner on the opposite side of the room to Stacey and her computers. Evans' reading style seemed almost nonchalant, as if he were drifting through the Sunday papers. His expression gave nothing away. But occasionally his hand would snake into his trouser pocket and emerge with a minidisk recorder. He'd mumble a few words into it then slip it back out of sight. Carol didn't think much was getting past him.

Paula, conversely, was a spreader. Within half an hour of starting, the whole of her desktop was covered in stacks of papers as she sorted through the file in front of her. But in spite of the appearance of untidiness, it was clear she knew where everything was. Her hand moved, apparently independent of her eyes, confidently picking up the next piece of paper she needed. It was as if she had a mental map of her arrangement, a neat grid stamped firmly on her brain. Carol wondered if that was how she worked interviews; slotting every piece of information into its own socket till the connections linked together and lit up like a completed circuit.

Stacey couldn't have been more different. Even her dress style was at odds with Paula's casual T-shirt and jeans. Stacey's suit fitted as if it had been made to measure, and the fine polo-neck sweater beneath it looked like cashmere to Carol's eye. A surprisingly expensive outfit for a detective constable, she thought. When it came to work, it was almost as if Stacey resented the presence of paper. She'd balanced the file she was studying on a pulled-out desk drawer to leave her work surface clear for interaction with the machine. The twin screens of her computer system held most of her attention. She would swiftly scrutinize the file material, then her fingers would fly over the keys before she cocked her head to one side, ran her left hand through her glossy black hair and clicked a mouse button. Manipulable virtuality was seemingly what she craved over reality.

It was, Carol thought, a group with enough variety in their skills and attributes to cover most of the bases. The key question was whether she could get them to bond into a unit. Until they felt part of a team, they would be less than the sum of their parts. She sighed. Somewhere in her near future, she could see a night out with her officers. On balance, she'd rather have spent a day in the dentist's chair without benefit of anaesthetic. She hadn't been out on the town since she'd come back from Germany. Even going to familiar restaurants with friends had been beyond her. The idea of raucous, crowded pubs and clubs curdled her stomach. 'Get over it,' she muttered angrily to herself as she turned back to the Tim Golding file.

She reread the statement given by the organic vegetable deliveryman. My, how Harriestown had changed in the few years she'd been gone. The previous occupants of the area would have been interested in organic vegetables only as potential missiles. So engrossed was she that the sharp rap of knuckles on her door jamb made her start. The pages she was holding fluttered to the desk unheeded as Carol pushed back in her chair, heart thudding, eyes wide. This was new, she thought. The old Carol Jordan was a lot harder to startle.

'Sorry, I didn't mean to creep up on you.' The woman in the doorway looked more amused than apologetic.

It was Carol's habit to form descriptions of new encounters as if she were registering their details for the National Criminal Intelligence database. Medium height; wiry as Carol herself. Straight shoulders, full breasts, narrow hips. Wavy brown hair cut in a tousle that had been fashionable a few years before, but which she'd probably hung on to because it suited her incongruously cherubic face. The cast of her features made her look as if she was perpetually on the verge of a smile. Only the eyes gave her away; she had the long flat stare of the cop who'd grown weary of the variety of human viciousness and misery. She wore black jeans, a black silk T-shirt and a leather jacket the colour of crème caramel. Whoever she was, Carol was certain she'd never met her before. 'I was miles away,' she said, getting to her feet.

'And who wouldn't be, given half a chance.' The woman's eyes crinkled in an easy smile as she moved forward, extending a hand. 'Detective Sergeant Jan Shields. I work Temple Fields.'

'DCI Jordan,' Carol said, accepting the warm, dry handshake. She gave a wry smile. 'You're the Vice, then?'

Jan groaned. 'Oh please. One bloody TV series and we're back with a label from the bad old, sad old days. Yeah, I'm the Vice. That'd be why we get the scuzzy office and you get the management suite. How are you settling in?'

Carol shrugged, slightly uncomfortable with the assumption of camaraderie from an officer junior in rank though probably roughly equal in years. 'We're feeling our way. So, Sergeant Shields, is this a social call? Or is there something I can help you with?'

'I think it might be me that can help you.' Jan waved a slim manila folder, this smile a tease.

Carol raised her eyebrows, moving back behind her desk. 'Really?'

'Your team's working cold cases till you hit a fresh jackpot, right?'

'We're taking a look, yes.'

'And one of those cases would be Tim Golding?'

'You're well informed, Sergeant.'

Jan shrugged. 'You know how it is. Gossip travels faster than a speeding bullet.'

'And we're today's hot news.' Carol sat down. She wanted to give the impression of confidence. 'So what is it you have for me?'

'It's a bit of a long story.' Jan gestured to the chair opposite Carol. 'May I?' She sat down and crossed her legs with easy confidence.

Carol leaned forward. 'Let's have it, then.'

'When you were here before, I was on secondment to a Home Office team working with the FBI on a long-term investigation into paedophiles using the internet. You've probably heard of Operation Ore?'

Carol nodded. The news media had leapt on

Operation Ore with the avidity of a starving coyote in a meat-processing factory. The investigation had netted thousands of potential arrestees on both sides of the Atlantic: men who surfed the net and used their credit cards to buy access to sites where they could download child pornography. But the sheer scale of the results had made Operation Ore a victim of its own success. Overstretched law enforcement agencies looked at the mountain of evidence and threw their hands up in despair. Carol had heard one colleague estimate that with the officers at his disposal it would take nine and a half years simply to interview all the names from his patch, never mind to seize and analyse their hard drives. 'You were involved in that?'

'In the early stages, yes. I've been back here two years now, and most of what I've been doing since then has been prioritizing our hit list, in between the usual shit on the streets. In the last six months, we've started pulling in our prime candidates. What we do is kick their doors down and seize their computer equipment. After a preliminary interview we usually release them on police bail till the analysis is done.'

'Which can take weeks, I imagine?'

Jan's mouth twisted in a half-smile. 'If we're lucky. Anyway, I got a stack of stuff through yesterday from the techies. They'd stripped out a pretty rich seam from a guy we pulled in a couple of months ago.' She shook her head. 'You'd think I'd be used to this by now. The guy's a senior NHS manager. You need a hip replacement or a new knee at Bradfield Cross? He's the one you blame for the length of the waiting list. Respectable house in the suburbs, wife's a teacher, two teenage kids. And his computer's like a fucking sewer. So, I'm wading through his shit and I find this –' She flipped open her file dramatically and pulled out a print of a digital photograph, blown up to cover most of an A4 sheet. She passed it across to Carol. 'I recognized the kid from the media blitz.'

Carol studied the photograph. The background showed a dramatic rock formation. Slender birch branches crisscrossed one corner. A skinny child stood naked and hunched in the middle of the frame. Sandy hair, Harry Potter glasses. Features she'd memorized in the course of her long day's reading. There was no room for doubt: this was Tim Golding. She felt the familiar rush that came with a fresh lead and hated herself for it. This wasn't something to rejoice over. Carol understood that now better than she ever had before. 'Are there any more?' she asked.

Jan shook her head. 'I've been right through the archive. Nothing.'

'What about the other missing kid – Guy Lefevre?'

'Sorry. That's the only one. And it doesn't mean my guy is the one you're looking for. These sick bastards swap shots all the time. The fact that there's only the one pic of the Golding boy would suggest to me that my target wasn't the photographer.'

'I'm inclined to agree with you. But I want to talk to him nevertheless.' Carol met Jan's eyes in a long, measured stare. 'I'd like his file now and I'd like him in an interview room first thing in the morning. Do you want me to clear that with your senior officer?'

'Sorted already. My guvnor agrees you get first crack. Full house beats a flush.'

'Thanks, Sergeant. I appreciate it.' Carol slid the

print back towards Jan. 'This background – any idea where it might be?' She pointed to the unusual rock formation.

Jan shook her head. 'Not a clue. I'm a city girl, me. I get the shakes if I'm more than five miles from Starbucks.'

'It looks pretty distinctive to me. But for all I know, there could be rocks like this from Land's End to John o'Groats.'

'Yeah. But there's only one Tim Golding.'

Carol sighed. 'Wrong tense, I think.'

'Sorry?'

'Looking at this, I think we should be saying there *was* only one Tim Golding.'

His hands are sweating. They slither and slip in spite of the thin layer of talc inside the latex gloves. It makes the preparation difficult. He's not really used to anything that requires finer control than rolling a joint. When his fingers fumble and a blade nicks him through the glove, he swears out loud at the beads of blood that ooze from the wound.

He's glad the Voice isn't here to see him fucking up. And that reminds him that he has instructions about what to do if his blood gets on the stuff. 'Put anything stained with even the smallest drop of blood to one side. Replace it and start again. Only one blood, that's what we want. Only one blood.' The words echo in his head and he does what he's told. He pulls a page out of that evening's paper and places the bloody blade on it. Then he strips off the gloves and adds them to the pile. He doesn't have an Elastoplast, so he tears off a corner of the newsprint and sticks it clumsily over the place where the blood is seeping. Then he takes another pair of gloves from the box. And starts again.

He really wants to get it right. He knows that if he gets it right, this will be the best thing he's ever done. He knows because that's what the Voice told him. And everything else the Voice has said has been right.

All day, he's been thinking about what's to come. All day, his mind's been in a spin. Though he tried to keep it hidden, people noticed. But they don't expect much of him at the best of times, so they didn't notice in a way that they'll remember afterwards. Mostly, they just made a joke of it, although one or two used his slowness or stupidity as an excuse for giving him a bad time. But he's used to that too. Until the Voice came along and said he deserved better, that was how it was for him. The tree every dog pissed up. The one who was so crap everybody else looked good next to him.

Tonight, he's going to prove them wrong. Tonight he's going to do something none of them would dare. And he's going to do it right.

Isn't he?

The car park was a place of shadows, hemmed in by high brick walls topped with razor wire. When it had been built, nobody could have anticipated the explosion in car ownership, so it was always over-full, double-parked and a source of irritation to those who had to use it.

It was also supposed to be secure. A sturdy metal barrier had to be raised to permit entry or egress, and the officer in charge of it was supposed to monitor each entrant carefully. But the man leaning on one of the cars understood how to circumvent systems. When he'd been here before, he'd made allies of the security team, aware that there would probably be a time when he'd want to come back without the necessary authority.

That time was tonight. He'd been waiting for the best part of an hour, resting against the bonnet of the silver saloon, reading steadily through the papers he'd stuffed into his briefcase, his peripheral vision alert to anyone leaving the tall building in front of the car park. But the light was fading fast and the air held the crisp promise of winter. Waiting was becoming less attractive. He glanced at his watch. Just after six. He'd give it half an hour, then he'd slip away into the night. He didn't want to lurk in the darkness, for a variety of reasons.

A few minutes later, he saw what he'd been waiting for. A gleam of blonde hair caught in the security lights by the back door, and he was on the move. He shoved the file back into his briefcase and stood upright, moving towards the back of the car to cut off his target before she could reach the driver's door.

She looked over her shoulder, calling out a farewell to a colleague. When she turned back, he was only a few feet from her. Shock and astonishment shot across her face and she stopped dead. Her mouth formed an exclamation, but no sound emerged.

'Hi, Carol,' Tony said. 'Fancy a curry?'

'Jesus,' she exhaled, her shoulders dropping. 'You nearly gave me a heart attack. What the hell are you doing here?'

He spread his arms wide, a parody of innocence. 'Like I said, inviting you out for a curry.'

'Freaking me out, more like. What are you doing in Bradfield? You're supposed to be in St Andrews.'

He raised one finger in admonishment. 'Later. Now, are you going to unlock the car? I'm freezing.'

With an air of bemusement, Carol obediently popped the locks and watched him walk round to the passenger seat. She couldn't help smiling. There was, she thought, nobody quite like Tony Hill.

Twenty minutes later, they'd found a relatively quiet corner table in a cheap and cheerful Bangladeshi café on the fringes of Temple Fields, the area of the city centre where the gay village sat uneasily alongside the red-light district. Their fellow customers were a mixture of students and individuals poised to go looking for love in all the wrong places. Carol and Tony had discovered the café when they'd first worked together on a case centred on Temple Fields, and it seemed the obvious place for this reunion.

'I can't believe you're here,' Carol said as the waiter departed to bring them a couple of bottles of Kingfisher.

He held out his arm. 'Go on, pinch me. I'm real.'

She leaned forward and gave his shoulder a gentle punch. 'OK, you're real. But why are you here?'

'I jacked the job in. I was a fish out of water there, Carol. I needed to get back to the work I know I'm good at. I'd already got an offer of consultancy work over in Europe. And when John Brandon told me you were coming back to Bradfield, I got on to Bradfield Moor and asked for part-time clinical work.' He grinned. 'So here I am.'

'You came back to Bradfield because of me?' Carol's expression was guarded. 'I don't want your pity, Tony.'

'It's nothing to do with pity. You're the best friend

I've got. I have some idea of how hard this is for you, Carol. And I want to be around if you need me.'

Carol waited for the waiter to deposit their beers, then said, 'I can manage, you know. I've been a cop for a long time. I'm capable of catching villains without your help.'

Tony took a long drink from the bottle of Indian lager while he considered how to deal with her wilful misunderstanding. 'I'm not here to help you do your job. I'm here because that's what friends do.' He gave a crooked smile. 'And besides, it suits me to be here. You should see the nutters they've got locked up in Bradfield Moor. It's a dream come true for a weirdo like me.'

Carol snorted, spraying the paper tablecloth with beer. 'Bastard! You waited till I had a mouthful of beer to make me laugh.'

'What do you expect? I'm trained to provoke reactions. So, where are you living?'

'I'm camping in Michael's spare room while I look for somewhere to rent.' Carol studied the menu.

Tony pretended to do the same, though he already knew he'd choose the fish pakora followed by the chicken biryani. The lack of commitment implied by Carol's decision to rent rather than to sell up in London and buy in Bradfield was understandable. She wanted to leave herself an escape route. But it troubled him nevertheless. 'That must feel strange,' he said. 'It having been your flat in the first place.'

'It's not ideal. I don't think Lucy's crazy about having me there. She's a barrister, remember? She does a lot of criminal defence work, so she has a tendency to regard me in the same light as a chicken farmer regards a fox.' The waiter returned and they ordered their meals. As he departed, Carol met Tony's eyes. 'What about you? Where are you living?'

'I was lucky. I sold my cottage in Cellardyke practically overnight. I've just bought a place here. Near where I used to live. A Victorian semi. Three bedrooms, two receptions. Nice big rooms, very light.'

'Sounds good.'

The waiter plonked a plate of poppadums and a tray of relishes in front of them. Tony took the opportunity to busy himself with something other than Carol. 'Thing is, it's got a cellar. Pretty much self-contained. Two big rooms, natural light. Toilet and shower. And a little boxroom you could easily turn into a kitchen.' He looked up, the question in his eyes.

Carol stared at him, clearly unsure if he was saying what she thought. She gave an uncertain laugh. 'What would I do with a kitchen?'

'Good point. But it does give you somewhere to put the washing machine.'

'Are you seriously offering me your cellar?'

'Why not? It'd solve your accommodation problem. And having a copper on the premises would give me a sense of security.' He grinned. 'More importantly, Nelson would keep the mice away.'

Carol fiddled with the lime pickle. 'I don't know. Does it have a separate entrance?'

'Well, of course. I wouldn't want to compromise your reputation. There's a door that leads to a flight of steps up to the back garden. And an internal door down from the house, obviously. But it would be a simple enough thing to fit a lock to that.' He smiled. 'You could have bolts too, if you wanted.'

'You've been thinking about this, haven't you?'

Tony shrugged. 'When I viewed the house, it seemed like a good way of making it work for a living. I didn't know what your plans were. But the builders started work on it yesterday. And I'd rather have you living there than a stranger. Look, don't make a decision now. Think about it. Sleep on it. There's no hurry.' There was an uncomfortable silence while they both tried to figure out where to take the conversation next. 'So how was your first day back in harness? What are you working on?' Tony asked, moving the conversation away from treacherous shoals.

'Until we get a new major case, we're taking a look at a bunch of unsolveds.' Carol looked up as the waiter brought their starters.

'That must be pretty soul-destroying.'

'Normally it would be.' She reached for her aloo chat. 'But amazingly enough, we actually scored a break this afternoon. Purely by chance, a detective from another squad stumbled across a new lead. I can't help seeing it as a positive omen.'

'That's a great start.'

Carol's expression was rueful. 'Yes and no. You remember Don Merrick? He's the DI on my team. And the trouble is that the break came on one of his cold cases. Which makes him feel pretty sick.'

'Not Tim Golding?'

Carol tipped her head in acknowledgement. 'The one he called you in on. Thanks for telling me, Tony,' she added ironically.

He looked embarrassed. 'To tell you the truth, I was afraid of muddying the waters while you were considering coming back to Bradfield. I didn't want to influence your decision one way or the other.'

Carol smiled. 'Oh, you think your presence in Bradfield would have been such a draw?'

He put down the pakora that was halfway to his lips. 'The truth, Carol? I was afraid if you knew I was here, it would be the last place on earth you'd want to be.'

Don Merrick stared glumly into his pint of Newcastle Brown Ale, his Labrador eyes sad and brooding. 'Stop looking on the fucking bright side, Paula,' he grumbled. 'Because there isn't a fucking bright side, all right?'

Paula ran her finger down the condensation on her bottle of Smirnoff Ice. They were the last survivors of the bonding session the team had decided on after DCI Jordan had called it a day. There hadn't been much of a celebratory atmosphere, truth to tell. Stacey and Sam had excused themselves after the first round, and Kevin had been sucked into a drawn-out game of pool in the pub's ratty back room. Neither Paula nor Merrick minded. They'd worked together long enough to slip the bonds of rank once they were on their own time. 'Please yourself, Don.'

'That photo . . . I can't help thinking about what that lad went through before he died. And don't try to contradict me,' he continued, holding up a hand to fend Paula off. 'We both know that the kind of scum who'd do that to a kid wouldn't leave a witness. Tim Golding's dead. But he was alive long enough to be taken off somewhere in the middle of nowhere and subjected to Christ knows what. That picture was taken in daylight, which means he was still alive the next morning. And that's what I'm having trouble with. If I'd done my job, we'd have found him.'

Paula reached across the table and helped herself to one of Merrick's cigarettes. 'If you're getting maudlin, I need a smoke.'

'Thought you'd stopped.'

'I have.' She inhaled deeply. 'That's bullshit, what you were just saying. We worked that case into the ground. You've got to stop beating yourself up like this, Don. Apart from anything else, we need you not to be fucked up. We've already got a fucked-up DCI. The last thing we need is a fucked-up DI as well.'

Merrick looked at her in surprise. 'You think Carol Jordan's fucked up?'

'Of course she is. She was raped, Don. And it happened because a bunch of suits thought so little of her they staked her out like a Judas goat. However you cut it, she's not playing with a full deck right now. Her judgement's compromised.'

Merrick shook his head. 'I don't know, Paula. She seemed pretty much on her game to me.'

'It's easy to talk the talk when there's no pressure. But I'm not sure she'll be able to walk the walk any more.'

Merrick looked doubtful. 'It's far too soon to be talking like that. Carol Jordan's the best guvnor I ever worked for.'

'I thought so once too. But now . . .?' Paula swigged the rest of her drink. 'Let's see if you're saying that in six months' time. So what do you make of the newbies?'

'Early days.' Merrick shrugged. 'That Stacey knows her way round the machines, that's for sure.'

'I keep catching myself wondering if she is a machine,' Paula giggled. 'She's not one of the girls, that's for sure. I keep trying to get her talking, but she's definitely not one for idle chit-chat.'

Merrick grinned. 'Yeah, somehow I can't see her gossiping about men and make-up in the toilets. But she's quick enough to weigh in when somebody needs a bit of help with the computers.'

'What about Sam? What's your take on him?' Paula asked.

'Seems all right. He doesn't have much to say for himself.'

'I'm not sure about him. There's something a bit creepy there,' Paula confided. 'One of my mates used to work with him over at Downton, and she said he was slimy. Never said much, but never missed a chance to put one over on everybody else. And always incredibly well informed about what everybody else was up to. Apparently, he likes to look good to the bosses, does our Sam.'

'Well, we all like to make a good impression,' Merrick said.

'Yeah, but not necessarily at the expense of our colleagues. Oh, and she said he was never at ease with her or the other women on the squad. She thought he was a bit of a secret sexist.'

Merrick laughed. 'Paula, these days we're only allowed to be sexist in secret or else you and the sisters come down on us like a ton of bricks.'

She punched him affectionately on the arm. 'You know what I mean.' She contemplated her empty bottle. 'You ready for another?'

'I should be getting home,' Merrick said reluctantly.

Paula got to her feet, grinning. 'That'll be another brown ale, then?'

He knows these streets like the inside of his pocket. He's walked them, worked them since he was a kid. He knows the faces, he knows the places where certain people can be found at particular times of the day and night. He never thought anything of it before, it was just the way the world turned. But the Voice has made him understand that knowledge is power, that what he knows makes him king of the streets.

He shambles along in his usual fashion, trying his very best to look like he would on any other night. He does a bit of business, just to cover himself, just to make it look like any other night. The Voice said he should do that. So that when the questions come, people will place him in the usual haunts, doing the usual things.

But soon it's time. He knows where to find her. It's where she always is between punters. He clears his throat and walks up to her. He tells her what he wants. She looks amused, as if she can't quite believe it's him asking for it. 'No discounts for mates, mind,' she says. He blushes and squirms. It makes him uncomfortable that she calls him a mate. Because what he's about to do to her is nothing like the things that mates do to each other, no way. But she doesn't see what's in his mind. She sees what she expects to see: a punter who feels awkward because he's a fish out of water.

He tells her he wants to go back to her room. He knew

about the room even before the Voice. He knows much more about what goes on round here than anybody gives him credit for. He follows her round the corner into the ginnel where her room is, giving a quick glance over his shoulder. Nobody is paying any attention. Even if they wanted to, it's too dark round here; the dealers smash the streetlights so often the council's given up replacing them. And even if they had eyes like a cat, they'd assume it was him working, not getting her to work for him.

Up the stairs she goes, her arse tight in her short skirt. It's amazing, but he feels himself getting hard at the sight of it. He's seen these girls a million times before, they're just part of the landscape, they don't normally register any more. But tonight, watching Sandie's gyrating hips, he's turned on. He remembers dimly what he's supposed to do at this point and he pulls out the digital camera and snaps her as she goes. The flash makes her stop in her tracks and whirl round. 'What the fuck are you up to?' she demands.

He waves the camera at her. 'I just wanted something to remember you by,' he says, the rehearsed words tripping out with hardly a stumble.

She frowns for a second, then laughs. 'That'll cost you.'

He snaps another shot. 'I can afford it,' he says. She carries on upstairs and he follows. At the door, she stops. 'Let's see the colour of your money,' she says. 'You want to tie me up, you pay upfront.'

He takes out the money the Voice left with his instructions and peels off some notes. Sandie snatches at it and shoves it into her little handbag. 'Business must be better for you than it is for me,' she says, her voice bitter as the coffee in Stan's Café. She opens the door. 'Come on then, let's get it over with.'

He smiles. She wouldn't be saying that if she knew what

he's got for her. But then, if he does what he's told, she won't be saying anything again. Ever.

Temple Fields hadn't changed much in the past couple of years, Carol thought as they walked back to her car. The same litter tumbling along the gutters, the same mixture of self-conscious seekers after what passed for pleasure rubbing awkward shoulders with those who had already found it and lost all inhibitions along the way. Her police officer's mind clocked them as she passed: the frail-looking rent boys, the bored hookers, the shifty sellers of chemical promises, and the easy marks who moved among them, obvious in their fake confidence. But the woman behind the badge shivered at the traffic in human flesh and folly. She didn't want to think of the acts that would take place in this square mile before morning. Carol felt as though she'd lost a layer of skin somewhere, and wondered how long it would take to grow back.

'Same old same old,' she said wearily. 'Look at them – they think they've made a deal with the world that will keep them safe. They've no bloody idea how fragile they are.'

'They can't afford to think about it,' Tony said, his eyes taking in the parade on streets splashed with garish neon from the bars.

They walked on in silence. 'I'll give you a lift,' Carol said as they neared her car.

'No, you're all right. I feel like walking.'

Carol raised her eyebrows. 'Thinking time?'

Tony nodded. 'I saw someone today and I need to figure out how to keep the promise I made him.'

'Your latest crusade?' Carol smiled.

Tony looked surprised. 'Is that how you see what I do?'

'I think it's how you see what you do. A one-man crusade to mend the damage.'

He shrugged. 'I wish it was that easy. So, you'll come round tomorrow night to see the house?'

'I will. Then maybe I can decide if I want to be the mad woman in the cellar. Shall I bring pizza?'

He considered. 'Chinese,' he said finally.

'OK.' She reached for the driver's door. 'Tony – thanks for tonight. And for being here in Bradfield.'

He looked surprised. *Why would I be anywhere else? Everything I need is here*. Instead of speaking his thoughts aloud, he patted her awkwardly on the shoulder. 'See you tomorrow.'

She climbed into her car and drove off, conscious of him in her mirrors, standing on the pavement, watching her out of sight. She knew it was guilt that had brought him there. Once, that would have made her uncomfortable and angry. But she was a different woman now and that woman had learned to be grateful for good things, however complicated the package they arrived in.

Sam Evans edged the office door open cautiously. No lights inside. He slipped through the narrow gap and closed the door behind him, turning the lock. Then he flicked the light switches on. The fluorescent strips flickered then settled their hard glare over the Major Incident Team's squadroom. Sam surveyed the array of desks and made straight for Paula McIntyre's.

He sat in her chair and noted the position of the piled paper on the desktop. The case she was working on would come to him next. Carefully, he riffled through each stack, trying to figure out the reason for the alignment she'd chosen. He flicked open the notepad and read down the list of points Paula had made. Some of them were pretty perspicacious, he thought, storing them away in his mind for when he came to review that case.

He inched open Paula's desk drawers one by one, stirring the contents with a pencil, leaving no prints to indicate he'd been there. It was always useful to see what people kept out of sight but close at hand. Tucked right at the bottom of the drawer, he found a photograph of Don Merrick with his arm round a woman in what looked like a pub or a club. On closer inspection, he realized with a jolt of surprise that the woman was Carol Jordan. Her hair was longer, her face fuller, but it was undoubtedly her. They were both toasting the photographer with what looked like glasses of champagne. Very interesting, he thought. And almost certainly useful.

He closed Paula's drawer and moved on to Kevin Matthews' desk, where he repeated the same process. People said you should know your enemies. But Sam Evans also believed in making damn sure he knew the people who were supposed to be on the same side. He was, as John Brandon had spotted, ambitious. But he didn't just want to excel; he wanted to make sure nobody outshone him. Ever.

Knowledge was power. And Evans knew that nobody ever handed out power as a gift. You had to grab it whenever and wherever you could. If that meant stealing it from someone else, so be it. If they were too weak to hold on to it, they didn't deserve it.

He did.

He checks the image in front of him against the one planted there by the Voice and the videos. Sandie's spreadeagled on the bed, her wrists handcuffed to the cheap pine frame. Her feet are tied to the legs. He had to use rope for them because the ankle cuffs wouldn't stretch that far. It's not right, but it's the best he can do. He's grateful to the Voice again for reminding him to take rope as well as the cuffs in case the bed wasn't right.

He wishes the room was nicer, but there's nothing he can do about that. At least the lights are dim. It's easy to ignore the needle tracks on her arms and the fact that she's too skinny. She could almost be the dream girl from one of the videos, the trimmed triangle of hair hiding the secrets he's about to possess.

He turns away from her and snaps the latex gloves over his hands. 'Come on,' she says. 'What are you waiting for? I haven't got all night.'

Only he knows how true that is. He reaches into his back-pack and takes out the padded leather gag. He turns back to face her and now she's starting to look worried. He moves towards her and she starts to shout. 'Wait a fucking minute! You never said nothing about that . . .' But her words are lost as he rams the gag home, jerking her head forward to fasten it behind. Her eyes are bulging now as she struggles to scream. But all that can be heard is the faintest of grunts.

He remembers to wipe the handcuffs clear of any finger-prints, then he grabs the video camera and sets it up on its little tripod, checking that he can see the whole bed. Next, the laptop and the webcam. Sandie pushes against her restraints, but there's no point.

He takes out a bundle wrapped in a thick wad of kitchen towel. He steps into shot and slowly unwraps it. When Sandie sees what he's holding, the veins in her neck stand out. The air fills with the smell of piss. He smiles sweetly. He's hard now, harder than the videos ever got him. But he mustn't lose control. He needs to make the Voice proud of him, and that means no evidence.

He takes a deep breath, trying to steady his pounding heart. He's sweating, he can feel it running down his neck and soaking his T-shirt. He grips his weapon tightly. The razor blades glint sharp and savage in the lamplight. 'I hope you're ready for me, Sandie,' he says softly, just like the Voice told him to.

Then he begins.

Carol stared through the two-way mirror at the man in the interview room. Ronald Edmund Alexander looked nothing like the popular image of a paedophile. He wasn't shifty or sweaty. He wasn't dirty or sleazy. He looked exactly like a middle manager who lived in the suburbs with a wife and two children. There was no dirty raincoat, just an off-the-peg suit, an unassuming charcoal grey. Pale blue shirt, burgundy tie with a thin grey stripe. Neat haircut, no vain attempt to hide the way he was thinning on top. He'd been complaining bitterly when the two uniformed officers had brought him in. They had no right, he insisted, no right at all to come marching into his office at Bradfield Cross as if he was some common criminal. He'd co-operated, hadn't he? All they had to do was pick up a phone and he'd have been straight over. There was no need, no need at all to embarrass him at his place of work.

Carol had watched from across the custody suite, trying to work out if she disliked him more because of what she knew he held on his computer or because he exemplified every petty bureaucrat who had ever driven her to thoughts of violence. She'd wanted to get straight into him, but had been frustrated by the tardiness of his solicitor.

So they'd stuck him in a cell while they waited for his brief to arrive. He'd been remarkably calm, she thought, wondering what Tony would have made of Alexander's demeanour. He'd taken a look round then calmly sat on the bunk, legs apart, arms folded across his chest, gazing into the middle distance. Zen and the art of façade maintenance, she thought wryly.

Finally, the door to the observation room opened. Paula stuck her head round the door. 'Showtime, chief. His brief's here.'

'Who is it?' Carol asked, dragging her eyes away from Alexander.

'Bronwen Scott.'

Carol remembered the defence lawyer from her previous spell in Bradfield. Unlike most legal aid lawyers, Scott seemed to have the wherewithal to dress in Dolce & Gabbana, with matching shoes and handbags from Prada. Her perfectly groomed shoulder-length black hair and flawlessly painted nails always made Carol feel like she'd been dragged straight out of bed into their interviews. It would have been almost bearable if the lawyer hadn't been as sharp and combative as she was expensively immaculate. The general view was that if you could afford

Bronwen Scott, you'd probably done it. 'Oh good,' Carol said, heading for the door.

She came face to face with Scott as she emerged into the corridor. 'Inspector Jordan. What a surprise. I thought you'd left us for pastures more glamorous,' Scott said, her voice cool and amused.

'It's Chief Inspector, actually. And you should know better than anyone that there's nothing glamorous about what we deal in. Shall we go?'

Scott shook her head. 'I don't know where you've been hiding, Chief Inspector, but up here in Bradfield we still allow lawyers to talk to their clients in private. And before I do that, I'd like some disclosure.'

Nothing unexpected there, Carol thought. 'When your client was arrested, his computer equipment was confiscated. It has subsequently been analysed. He will be interviewed fully about that at a later date, but there is one image on his machine that links directly to a major inquiry which I am leading. It is that single image I want to talk to him about.'

'That image being . . .?'

'I'll be happy to discuss that in the interview. And to show you and your client a copy.'

Scott shook her head. 'You really have forgotten your manners, haven't you, Chief Inspector? Before I can have a meaningful conversation with my client, I need to know what we're talking about here.'

There was a long silence. Carol could feel Paula's eyes on her back, measuring her. There really wasn't anything to be gained by holding back at this point. It wasn't as if Ron Alexander was a serious suspect in the disappearance of Tim Golding. If she refused to give Scott anything, then she'd end up with a 'no comment' interview, nothing surer. If she tried waiting until the interview to spring the photo on him, Scott would simply demand time out to talk to her client. Carol considered. She wanted co-operation. She didn't care what that might or might not do to any wider case against Ron Alexander. 'We might as well speed things up,' she said. 'Your client's computer held an image of Tim Golding. The eight-year-old –'

'Yes, I know who Tim Golding is,' Scott said impatiently. 'But since you people disseminated images of the child all over the country, it's hardly a big deal that my client has a photo of the boy on his computer.'

'It's a big deal when the picture in question shows a terrified, naked child.' Carol turned on her heel and walked off. 'Let me know when you're ready to talk,' she said over her shoulder as she rounded a corner, Paula hard on her heels. 'I see Bronwen Scott hasn't mellowed with age,' she commented.

'It's a pain you had to give away so much,' Paula said, falling into step beside her boss.

'You know the rules, Paula. They ask for disclosure, we have to give it.'

'Couldn't you have held back on the ID, chief? Then hit him with it in the interview?'

Carol stopped and gave Paula a speculative look. 'You think I was weak back there, don't you?'

Paula looked horrified. 'I never . . .'

'Giving in isn't always a sign of weakness, Paula. There was no point in holding out. I know how Scott works. Alexander would just have gone "no comment" from the off. This way, she might just see it as a bargaining chip.' Carol walked off, feeling the tension in her shoulders. Maybe they didn't trust her quite as much as she'd thought.

He sleeps late. It's nearly noon when he wakes, and even then he has to force his eyes open. He feels like somebody spiked his brain with Valium. His head's muzzy, it takes him a moment to realize where he is. At home, in his own bed, curled into himself like a baby. But it's a different person inside his body this morning.

He's not the fuck-up that everybody laughs at any more. He did it. He did exactly what he was supposed to. Just like the Voice told him to. And he's got his reward. He's got the money, even though he explained that wasn't why he'd done it. He'd done it because he understood. It's not the money that makes him feel like he finally made it. It's hearing the Voice say good things about him. It's knowing that he's done something hardly anybody else could do. Something special.

Thank God he managed to hide the way he really felt when he reached the moment itself. He'd been excited, aroused, on the point of coming inside his pants like a teenager. But when it came to it, when he had to stick that thing inside her again and again, he wilted. It wasn't sexy. It was bloody and terrible and frightening. He knows it was the right thing to do, but at the very end, it wasn't exciting at all. Just messy and sad.

But the Voice didn't see that. The Voice just saw that he'd done what he was supposed to do, and he'd got it right.

As he wakes up properly, he feels a buzz in his veins. It's pride, but it's fear too. They're going to be looking for him. The Voice promised he'd be all right. But maybe the Voice has got it wrong.

Maybe he wasn't as clever as he thought.

* * *

Tom Storey stared out of the window, watching the leaves detaching from the trees and swirling in the brisk breeze that had sprung up towards noon. He sat motionless, his bandaged stump gripped in his other hand. Tony watched him for a good ten minutes, but Storey never budged.

Eventually, he walked across the day room and pulled up a chair next to Storey. He noted the purple bruise along his cheekbone. According to the orderly who had shown Tony in, one of the other patients had punched Storey during a group therapy session. 'Even these mad bastards draw the line at child killers,' the man had said casually.

'We've all got two personalities, you know,' Tony said conversationally. 'One in each hemisphere of the brain. One's the boss, it shouts down the weaker one. But you sever the diplomatic links, and there's no telling what the subservient one will do once it gets the taste for power.'

Storey still didn't move. 'I can still feel it,' he said. 'It's like a malevolent ghost. It won't leave me alone. Supposing you find out I've got a brain tumour. And supposing that doesn't kill me. There's still going to be a war going on in my head, isn't there?'

'I won't lie to you, Tom,' Tony said. 'There's no quick fix here. See, you've got the dominant left side of the brain. That's in charge of the three R's – reading, writing and arithmetic. And you've got the right side. It's illiterate, but it comprehends form, solid geometry, music. I suspect it gets frustrated because it can't express itself readily in the ways that humans generally communicate. That's why it goes off the rails when the left side loosens its grip. But that's not the end of the story.'

'Just the end of Tom Storey.' His voice was bitter.

'Not necessarily. The brain's an amazing structure. When it gets damaged, it retrains other areas to take over the jobs that used to be done by the bit that's redundant. And there are things we can do to retrain the rebellious part of your brain. I can help you, Tom.'

Storey took a breath so deep it raised his shoulders. 'Can't bring my kids back, though. Can you?'

Tony looked out of the window at the flurry of golden and scarlet leaves. 'No, I can't. But what I can do is help you live with that absence.'

Tears spilled out of Storey's eyes and trickled unheeded down his cheeks. 'Why would you want to do that?'

Because it's the only thing I'm good at, Tony thought. What he said was: 'Because you deserve it, Tom. Because you deserve it.'

Carol walked into the interview room with an assumption of confidence she didn't really feel. It had been many months since she'd interviewed anyone, witness or suspect, and she was afraid of her emotions bleeding into the professional sphere. It didn't help that she was conscious of Paula at her side, weighing her up. At least Ron Alexander's composure seemed to have slipped a little. He was refusing to meet her eyes, fiddling continuously with his wedding ring.

'Right,' Carol said, settling into her chair. 'I'm Detective Chief Inspector Jordan and this is Detective Constable McIntyre. As your solicitor will have explained, Mr Alexander, we're looking for your help in respect of another inquiry that's not related to the reasons you were originally arrested. We would appreciate your co-operation.'

'Why should I talk to you?' Alexander blurted out. 'You'll only twist anything I say to make a case against me.'

Bronwen Scott put a hand on his arm. 'You don't have to say anything, Ron.' She looked directly at Carol. 'My client is concerned that any co-operation he offers you will be reflected in any subsequent proceedings.'

Carol shook her head. 'You know it's not up to us, Ms Scott. It's the CPS who make the deals. But I'm perfectly willing to make representations to them at the appropriate time.'

'That's not good enough.'

Carol shrugged. 'It's the best I can do. Your client might like to consider the converse, however. If he fails to help us in such a sensitive case, nobody's going to cut him any slack anywhere down the line.'

'Is that a threat, Chief Inspector?'

'Just a statement of fact, Ms Scott. You know as well as I how emotions run high in the case of a missing child. Sex offenders have a hard enough time in prison without adding to their problems. It's up to you, Mr Alexander.' Carol eyed Alexander, who was shifting uncomfortably in his chair. She opened the folder in front of her and took out the photograph Jan Shields had supplied. She placed it in front of him. 'We found this on your computer. Do you recognize this child, Mr Alexander?'

He glanced at the image then looked away,

desperately scanning the wall as if it would give him the answer. 'Yes,' he said, his voice barely above a whisper.

'Can you tell me who it is?'

'His name's Tim Golding.' He picked up Scott's pen, gripping it in both hands as if trying to snap it in two. 'His picture was in the papers. And on the TV.'

'When did you acquire this photograph?' Carol leaned forward slightly, forcing warmth and intimacy into her voice.

He flashed a look at Scott, who nodded. 'I don't know exactly. A few weeks ago, I think. It came in an email attachment. I was shocked when I opened it.'

'Shocked because you recognized Tim Golding?'

He nodded. 'Yes. And because of . . . because of how he looked.'

'What? You're not used to receiving pictures of naked, frightened children?'

'Don't answer that, Ron,' Scott said quickly. 'Chief Inspector, if we're going to make any progress here, I must insist you stop asking questions whose answers might tend to incriminate my client.'

Yeah, right. Carol took a deep breath. She slid another photograph from her folder. 'Do you recognize this boy?'

Alexander frowned. 'Isn't he the one who went missing last year? Guy something or other?'

'Guy Lefrevre,' Carol said. 'Have you ever been sent photographs of Guy Lefevre?'

'No.' Alexander's eyes flicked from side to side. Carol couldn't decide whether he was panicking or lying. But with Bronwen Scott patrolling her every question, there was nothing to be gained by pressing the point.

'What did you do when you recognized Tim Golding?' she asked.

'I erased the picture right away,' he said. 'I didn't want it on my machine.'

Carol stripped her voice of challenge and tried to sound sympathetic. 'You didn't think about contacting the police? You could have printed it out and sent it to us anonymously. You've got children of your own, haven't you, Ron? How do you think you'd feel if one of them went missing? Wouldn't you want to believe that anyone who had information that might help the inquiry would pass it on to the police?'

A sheen of sweat appeared on his forehead. 'I suppose,' he said.

'It's not too late to put that right,' Carol said. 'Who sent you the photograph, Ron?'

He breathed out noisily. 'I don't know. People don't use their real names on email, you know?'

Carol knew. They used nicknames and mixtures of letters and numbers even when they had nothing to hide. Her own personal email address was a combination of her surname and the last four digits of a previous phone number because, when she'd signed up, 'caroljordan' had already been taken. 'OK. You didn't know the identity of the sender. So what was his email address?'

He spread his hands. 'I don't know. I didn't pay attention. I just wiped the whole thing. The email and the attachment.'

'Presumably it was someone who had sent you things before?'

'I'd advise you not to answer that, Ron.' Scott laid a hand on his arm again.

Carol glared at the lawyer. 'You seem to be losing sight of what's at stake here, Ms Scott. A child is missing. We both know the chances are he's dead. I'm trying to find out what happened to him, and that's all I care about.'

'Very commendable, Chief Inspector. But my concern is my client's best interests. And I will not sit quietly by while you draw him into potentially incriminating statements.'

Carol gathered herself together and turned her attention back to Alexander. 'Ron, can you remember anything that might lead us to the person who sent you this picture?'

He shook his head. 'Honestly, if I knew anything useful, I'd tell you. I want to help, I really do.'

'OK. Let's try a different tack. Why do you think he sent it to you? Why would he have thought this was the kind of thing you might like to see?'

'I don't think . . .' Scott began.

'It's all right,' Alexander said. 'I don't know the answer to that either. Everybody gets unsolicited email. Spam blockers don't get rid of it all.' He sat back in his seat, clearly more relaxed now he'd figured out how to play the game.

Carol felt irritation rising. 'Fine. If that's how you want to play it, Mr Alexander, that's the way we'll go.' She pushed her chair back. 'This interview is over. But I should tell you that we're going to be trawling every byte on your hard disk. We're going to follow your footsteps round the web. You may think you've cleaned up your computer, but our technicians are going to demonstrate just how misguided you are. You've had your chance, Mr Alexander. And you just blew it.'

Carol marched out of the interview room and headed back to her office, not even bothering to check if Paula was following her. 'Stacey? My office, now,' she said as she crossed the squadroom. Paula and Stacey arrived together. 'What did we get from the techies on Ron Alexander's computer?' Carol asked Stacey, waving a hand to indicate they should sit down.

'Not as much as they'd hoped for,' Stacey said. 'People are so dim about this stuff. Alexander thought he'd erased everything from his hard disk. He probably panicked when he saw the earlier newspaper reports about Operation Ore. But like most people, he thought if he just deleted them then emptied the Recycle Bin, they were gone for good. And like most people, he never bothered to reformat or even defrag –'

'Defrag?' Paula asked faintly.

Stacey rolled her eyes. 'It's when you –'

'Never mind,' Carol said. 'So there was still stuff lurking there?'

'Well, yes, of course there was. File fragments, some complete files. Like the photo of Tim Golding.'

'And can we find out where that came from?'

Stacey shook her head. 'Not a trace. It's an orphan.'

Paula opened her mouth but before she could speak, Carol said hastily, 'Never mind, Paula, we get the idea. That's a blow, Stacey.' She rubbed the bridge of her nose between her fingers. The lead that had seemed so promising the day before was turning into another dead end. 'What about his email service provider? Any chance they could help?'

Stacey shrugged. 'Depends when he got the email. They're not really techies, ISPs, just bean counters,' she said disparagingly. 'They're only interested in billing, not in keeping records of traffic. Most only keep detailed records for a week. Some for a month. If he got that attachment more than a month ago, we've got no chance. And we'd need a court order before they'd hand over the information anyway.'

'So we're screwed.' Carol's flat statement hung in the air.

Stacey pushed her hair behind her ear. Her self-satisfied smile and her dark almond-shaped eyes made her resemble a cat. 'Not necessarily. Images like this, there's more to them than meets the eye. Literally. You sometimes get other information encoded in them.'

Carol perked up. 'Like the sender's details?'

Stacey's sigh fell just short of obvious exasperation. 'Nothing that straightforward. You might get the serial number of the camera that took the picture. Or the registration number of the software the photographer used to process the image electronically. Then it's a matter of contacting the manufacturer or the software licence holder and seeing what information they can provide.'

'That's scary,' Paula said.

'It's bloody good news,' Carol corrected her. 'So what are we waiting for?'

Stacey stood up. 'It's going to take time,' she warned.

'Doesn't everything?' Carol leaned back in her

chair. 'Anything you need, Stacey, just let me know. Paula, find out who Ron Alexander's ISP is and see what they can tell us. It's time we brought Tim Golding home.'

The doorbell came as a welcome relief. Tony pushed aside the philosophical text on the mind/body problem that had been stretching his brain and hurried down the hall. He opened the door to find Carol leaning against the porch, a bulging plastic carrier in one hand. 'You ordered a takeaway?' she said.

'You took your time. It's at least twenty-two hours since I placed my order,' he said, stepping back and following her down the hall. 'The kitchen's straight ahead.'

Carol looked around, taking in the pine units and the tiled breakfast bar. 'Very eighties,' she said.

'Is it? You think that's part of the reason I got it so cheap?'

She smiled. 'Could be. It looks in good nick, though.'

'All the drawers work, which is a definite improvement on anywhere I've ever lived before. Now, do you want to eat first or tour the cellar?'

'What I'd really like is a glass of wine. It's been a frustrating day.'

'OK. Wine we can do.' He reached for an opened bottle of Australian Shiraz Cabernet and poured them each a glass. 'Here's to . . . I don't know, what should we drink to?'

'An end to frustrations? For both of us?'

Tony raised his glass and chinked it against hers.

'That's as good as anything. An end to frustrations.' He watched her drink, noting the dark shadows under her eyes and the wariness in her body language. She was, he thought, a long way from herself. 'So, would you like to see the cellar – sorry, basement flat?'

Carol smiled. 'Why not?'

She followed him back into the hall. He opened a door that looked as if it should be the cupboard under the stairs. Instead, it gave on to a narrow, steep flight of steps illuminated by a bare lightbulb. Tony led the way into a surprisingly high-ceilinged space. 'This would be the living room,' he said, ushering her into a large room that had two shallow but wide windows set high in the walls. 'It gets a fair bit of natural light. And we could put glass panels in the outside door and build a little porch at the bottom of the steps for security,' he added eagerly. 'I already suggested that to the builder. I know it's hard to imagine now, with the walls still being bare brick, but all this will be plasterboarded. Wood floors. It'll look really nice.'

It was a good size. Plenty of room for all she would need, Carol thought. The bedroom was almost as big as the living room, with a surprisingly large bay window. Carol looked around, a smile tugging at the corners of her mouth. 'It's not bad, you know. I can imagine waking up here.'

Tony looked at the floor, suddenly embarrassed. 'Good,' he said. 'Think about it.'

On the way back upstairs, he showed her the recently installed toilet and shower room. White tiled walls gleamed bright under their ceiling spotlights. *Clean, fresh, untainted. New,* she thought with a surge of excitement. *A place without ghosts*. 'I don't need to think about it,' Carol said. 'When's it going to be ready?'

Tony grinned like a small boy. 'The builder reckons three weeks. Can you stand it at Michael's till then?'

Carol leaned against his breakfast bar. 'I can stand anything if I know it's going to end. You think you can stand having me as your downstairs neighbour?'

'Only if you promise always to have milk.' He pulled a wry face. 'I'm very good at running out of it.'

Carol smiled. 'I'll stock up on UHT.'

Waiting is never easy. Especially when he knows exactly what he's waiting for. By the time he got out on the street today, he was expecting cops everywhere, police tape cordoning off the ginnel where Sandie worked. He was expecting huddles of people on street corners, muttering about murder and mutilation. He was expecting uniformed officers with clipboards asking people where they were and what they were doing last night.

He remembers what it was like last time. The whole of Temple Fields felt like it had overdosed on whiz. Everybody talking nineteen to the dozen like speed freaks, even the miserable gits who never normally had the time of day for him or anybody else. Until the bizzies walked in. Then silence fell like somebody dropped a blanket over everybody's head.

That's what he expected this time. But when he went into Stan's Café and ordered his usual bacon butty and mug of tea, it was just like any other day. A few of the working girls clustered round greasy tables, taking the weight off their feet for half an hour. A couple of kids from the rent rack cuddling cups of coffee. Various eyes clocking him, wondering if he was carrying any gear. Looking away in disappointment when he gave them a slight shake of the head. He'd get hassle off Big Jimmy when he showed up to collect today's stock. He'd bollock him for being late. He'd hoped the excitement on the street would give him an excuse, but there isn't any.

So he finished his breakfast and moseyed on round to Big Jimmy's flat for some stuff to sell. Luckily, the big man wasn't in and he only had to deal with that fuckwit scaghead Drum who's too far out of the world to care what anybody else is doing. Within the half-hour he was back on the pitch, doing the business, hoping nobody wondered where he'd been all morning. Hell, most of them had probably still been out cold themselves.

But now it's evening, and still nothing's stirring on the streets. It makes him uneasy. Part of him begins to wonder if he dreamed the whole thing. He almost wants to walk round to Sandie's pitch to see if she's standing on her usual corner, acting as if nothing out of the ordinary had happened.

He wishes the Voice was here right now to tell him what's going on. But since he delivered, he's heard nothing. He begins to wonder if he's been abandoned, if all the promises were a dream too.

It wouldn't be the first time.

Tony raised his glass and reached across the debris of the Chinese. 'Here's to one of our rare non-Catholic meals.' They chinked glasses.

'Non-Catholic meals?' Carol frowned.

'Mostly, when we eat together, it's in the middle of a case.' He picked up a piece of pancake. 'Here is my body which I sacrificed for you.' He ate the pancake, then raised his glass again in mock-ceremony. 'Here is my blood which I shed for you.'

Carol nodded, getting it. 'Only, in our case, the confession comes after the communion.'

'Only if we're right.'

She pulled a rueful face. 'Right, and lucky.' She took his glass from him and sipped from the opposite side. She felt a crackle of electricity in the curiously intense moment. Before she could hand back the glass, the intimacy was shattered by the insistent ring of her mobile. 'Damn,' she said, scrabbling for her bag.

'Speaking of lucky . . .' Tony muttered.

'DCI Jordan,' Carol said.

Don Merrick's familiar voice sounded in her ear. 'We've got a body. I think you'll want to see this one.'

Carol stifled a sigh. 'Fine. You'll have to send a car for me, I've had a couple of glasses of wine.' Tony stood up and started shovelling the tinfoil containers into their plastic bag.

'No problem, ma'am. You at your flat?'

'Actually, no, Don. I'm at Dr Hill's house.' She caught Tony's glance and raised her eyes heavenwards as she gave Merrick the address. She was aware of muffled conversation at the other end of the phone. Then Merrick came back on.

'I've asked a car to pick you up there.'

'I'll see you shortly, Don,' Carol said, ending the call. She drained her glass of wine and said, 'Seems we've got a body.' She got to her feet. 'I didn't exactly mean the evening to end like this.'

Tony picked up the dirty plates. 'Well, it's probably best to stick to what we know we're good at.'

* * *

Temple Fields' tawdry glitter was blurred by the slant of autumn rain. The car tyres hissed on the block paving of the pedestrianized zone at the heart of the area. The driver turned into a narrow side street. Redbrick and seedy, it harboured shop fronts with little allure and small entrepreneurial businesses with bedsits on the floors above. Halfway down, access was blocked by a pair of parked police cars. Vague figures hurried beyond the cars, heads down against the weather. As the car pulled up, Carol lowered her head, took a deep breath and climbed out.

Approaching the squad cars, Carol saw that the entrance to a smaller ginnel was closed off by crime-scene tape. Her stomach lurched in anticipation of what she was about to be confronted with. Please God, let it not be sexual. She ducked under the tape, giving her name and rank to the officer logging access to the scene, and spotted Paula standing at a grubby door leading to a stairwell. Seeing Carol, she broke off her conversation with a uniformed officer and turned to her.

'It's upstairs, chief. Not a pretty sight.'

'Thanks, Paula.' Carol paused on the threshold, snapping a pair of latex gloves over her hands. 'Who found the body?'

'One of the street girls. Dee. She and the dead girl used to share the room. Somewhere to take punters.'

'Was Dee with a punter, then?'

Paula gave a grim little smile. 'According to Dee, as soon as he realized there was something wrong, he was out of there like a rat off a sinking ship.'

'Where's Dee now?'

'On her way back to the nick to make a statement. With Sam.'

Carol nodded in satisfaction. 'Thanks, Paula.' She edged past a fingerprint technician lifting prints from the narrow banister and headed up. At the top of the steep, uncarpeted stairs, an open door cast an oblong of pale light on to the landing. The air was thick with the coppery smell of blood and the darker, deeper stink of human excrement. Though she'd been steeling herself against it, Carol felt herself slide into flashback and almost lost her footing. But the sight of the SOCOs coolly going about their business anchored her back in the present, banishing the kaleidoscope of images that threatened to overwhelm her. *Further up and further in.*

As she reached the doorway, Carol was conscious of Merrick and Kevin turning to look at her. At first, she concentrated on the external details, working up gradually to deal with what lay at the heart of the room. It was a spartan space, shoddy and cheaply decorated with old stained woodchip emulsioned in what had once been magnolia. A pine bedstead, a couple of armchairs that looked like they were rescued from the tip, a sink, a card table and not much else. Nothing to distract her from the body on the bed.

The woman was tied down, her legs and arms spread in a hideous parody of ecstasy. Her blue eyes stared blankly at the ceiling. It wasn't hard to read panic and pain there. Her short bleached blonde hair was plastered to her head; the sweat of fear had soaked it and time had dried it into a stiff helmet. She was still dressed, her skirt a blood-soaked ruck around her hips. A sea of gore engulfed her lower body and soaked the thin, sagging mattress. Carol cleared her throat and moved closer. 'That's a hell of a lot of blood,' she said.

'According to the police surgeon, she pretty much bled out,' Merrick said. 'He reckons it took her a while to die.'

Carol struggled with the emotions tormenting her and tried to remember how to do her job. 'He's been and gone already?'

'Yeah, so happened he was at a dinner at the Queensbury. We'd hardly got here ourselves.'

'So, what have we got?' she asked.

Merrick consulted his notebook. 'Sandie Foster, twenty-five, prostitute, convictions for soliciting and possession. But before we get into that . . . ma'am, this is the identical MO to a series of four murders that happened two years ago, not long after you left us.'

'Were all the victims clothed, like this?'

'Like I said, it's identical.'

'Well, maybe this time we can solve them.'

Merrick and Kevin exchanged a glance. Kevin looked faintly apologetic. 'That's the thing, guv. We already did.'

'What?' Carol said.

Merrick shoved his gloved hands into his pockets. 'Kevin and I worked the case. Derek Tyler – he pleaded guilty. He's in a secure hospital.'

'Could we have got the wrong man?'

Merrick shook his head, his lower lip jutting in stubborn denial. 'No room for doubt. The forensics nailed him. DNA, fingerprints, the lot. Derek Tyler. He pleaded guilty. He even made a confession of sorts, claiming the voices in his head told him to do it. And as soon as Tyler was arrested, the killings stopped. Even more proof, as if we needed it. They locked him up in Bradfield Moor and he refused to say another word about the murders.'

'Can we check if Tyler has been released?' Carol asked.

'I already have. I just came off the phone. Tyler is tucked up in bed, sleeping far better than he has any right to, so it's not him.'

'Perhaps we missed something last time.'

'The forensics nailed him,' Merrick insisted.

'Maybe we should talk to Dr Hill,' Kevin said. 'Making sense of things is his line, isn't it?'

'Good idea, Kevin,' Carol said. Tony was always complaining he was never called in early enough on complex murder inquiries. She stepped outside the room and dialled Brandon's mobile. When he answered, she briefly outlined the circumstances. 'On the face of it, it looks impossible,' she said. 'I'd like to bring Dr Hill in for a consultation.'

'Isn't it a little early for that?' Brandon asked.

'Normally I'd agree with you, sir, but if there's any possibility we're looking at a copycat, I think he could give us a quick answer. Like he did the first time we all worked together.' Carol held her breath while Brandon considered.

'All right, go ahead. We'll talk more fully in the morning.'

As the call ended, Carol stepped to one side to allow the mortuary staff access to the crime scene. 'Does Dr Vernon know about this?' she asked.

The one bringing up the rear nodded. 'Yeah, he

wants to cut and shut early tomorrow, he's got some conference or other to go to. He said to tell you he'll be ready to roll at seven.'

Merrick and Kevin joined her on the landing, to allow the technicians room to manoeuvre the dead woman into the body bag. 'Kevin, Sam's interviewing the woman who found the body. I want you to come back to the station with me and sit in with him. You worked the case before, there might be something you pick up on that Sam wouldn't know about. Don, you and Paula start organizing door-to-door inquiries. We need to talk to all the street girls and rent boys we can get our hands on, as well as bar staff, punters and the like. Find out where Sandie Foster worked. Somebody must have seen her with her killer.' She stripped off her gloves and shoved her hands in her pockets, unconsciously hunching her shoulders. 'And let's all keep an open mind for now.'

Kevin found Sam Evans slouched against the wall outside one of the interview rooms. 'How's it going?' he asked.

'Am I glad to see you,' Evans groaned. 'That woman in there most definitely does not like people of colour. How come we say one word out of place and we get hit with a complaint of racism, but she gets to call me a jungle bunny?'

Kevin winced. 'You want me to take a crack at her?'

'Be my guest.' Evans waved a hand at the door. 'I can't get a single word out of her. I'm going for a smoke.'

He handed Kevin a folder and walked off. Kevin

opened it and saw a single sheet of paper that told him nothing more than name, age and address. 'You weren't joking, were you, Sam?' he said softly.

Kevin looked through the spyhole in the door to see a bleached-blonde woman in a short, tight, black dress. The notes said she was twenty-nine but, from this distance, she looked closer to nineteen. She was pulling her skimpy jacket close to her as if the room was chill. She was smoking, and judging by the thickness of the air, it wasn't her first cigarette. So much for Brandon's non-smoking policy. Kevin remembered the first day he'd tried to enforce it. The suspect he'd been interviewing had threatened him with a complaint under the human rights legislation for cruel and unusual punishment. He wasn't going to be telling Dee Smart to put her fag out. She was the nearest they had to a useful witness so far, and this case was far too important to take chances with.

He walked in and treated her to his best sympathetic smile. 'Thank fuck,' she said. 'A human being.'

'You have a problem with my colleague?' Kevin said, a sympathetic smile on his face.

'He gives me the creeps,' she muttered. 'He's got that Ali G chip on his shoulder. "Is it because I is black?" No, mate, it's because you is an arsehole. Somebody should tell him even whores are higher up the food chain than the shit on his shoe. Where does he get off, looking down his nose at me?'

'He's a bit lacking in the social skills department.'

'You can say that again.' She blew out a stream of smoke and scowled. 'So are you going to treat me any better?'

Twenty minutes later, the two of them were almost

cosy. The mugs of tea he'd brought as an ice-breaker were empty, and they'd got through the hardest part, the actual discovery of the body. 'Just how long had this arrangement been going on?' Kevin asked conversationally.

Dee lifted one shoulder in a half-shrug. 'About three months, I suppose. Sandie used to share the room with another girl, Mo, but she moved back to Leeds so Sandie asked me to come in with her.'

'How did it work in practice?'

Dee flipped open her cigarette packet and looked in disgust at the three remaining cigarettes. 'You're going to need to find a fag machine if we're going to be at this much longer.'

'Don't worry about that. Tell me about the arrangement.' Kevin gave her his best sympathetic smile.

Dee scowled. It brought the fine lines on her skin into sharp relief, making her look her age. 'Sandie has the early shift. Most nights she likes to knock off about ten. She's got a kid. A little lad, Sean. Her mum looks after him. Sandie likes to get home in time to get a decent kip before she gets him up in the morning for school. Any time after half past ten, the room was mine.'

Kevin tried not to think how Sean would be feeling when he woke up tomorrow morning to discover his mother had been murdered. Instead, he concentrated on what Dee was saying. 'So how come you didn't find her there last night?' he asked.

'I wasn't working last night.' She clocked the look of surprise on his face. 'If you must know, I had the shits. I must have eaten something dodgy. There was no way I could turn tricks, the state I was in.'

It made sense. Even whores could throw a sickie, Kevin thought. 'So as far as you knew, everything was normal? When you went up with your punter you expected the room to be empty?'

Dee closed her eyes and shuddered at the memory. 'Yeah.'

'Had you seen Sandie at all earlier in the evening?'

Dee shook her head. 'I wouldn't have unless I was working, and I wasn't. I had a couple of drinks in the Nag's Head before I got started, but I never saw Sandie.'

'Where did she normally work?'

'Down the end of Campion Boulevard. Just past the mini-roundabout.'

Kevin pictured it in his mind's eye. Only fifty yards down the side street and Sandie would have been at the entrance to the alley where the shared room was. 'What about regulars?' he asked.

Dee suddenly lost her composure. Her eyes welled up with tears and her voice emerged as a strangled wail. 'I don't know. Look, we shared the room and the rent, we didn't live in each other's pockets, I don't know what she did or who she did it with.'

Kevin reached across the table and took her hand. Astonishment overcame her emotional outburst and her mouth fell open. 'I'm sorry. We just need to explore every possibility if we're going to have any chance of catching him.'

Dee snorted derisively, pulling away from him. 'Listen to you. Anybody would think it was a respectable mother of three who'd been killed, not some throwaway tart.'

Kevin shook his head sorrowfully. 'I don't know

who you've been listening to, Dee, but we don't treat anybody as a throwaway victim here. My guvnor wouldn't stand for it.'

Dee looked momentarily uncertain. 'You mean that?'

'I mean it. Nobody on this investigation is giving any less than a hundred per cent. Now, I want you to come upstairs with me and look at some photographs. Will you do that for me, Dee?'

'All right,' she said. It was hard to say who was the more surprised.

After midnight, the fluorescent lights in Carol's office seemed indecently bright, turning skin tones grey. Carol was reading the scant computer files on Derek Tyler's murders when the door opened and Tony walked in. 'It's rubbish, you know,' he said without preamble.

Carol, accustomed to the vagaries of his conversational style, humoured him. 'Thanks for coming in. What's rubbish?'

'Copycats. They don't happen. Don't exist – not in sexual homicide.' He dropped into the chair opposite her desk and sighed.

'What are you saying, Tony? That Derek Tyler managed to be in two places at once?'

'I don't know anything about Derek Tyler until I read the files. What I do know is that whatever we've got here, it's not a copycat.'

Carol struggled to make sense of what she was hearing. 'But if the MO is the same . . .?'

'Then you've got the same killer.' He gave her an apologetic smile and shrugged.

'That's not possible. From what Don says, and from what I've read here, there was no doubt on the forensics. And Derek Tyler is behind bars.'

Tony yanked the chair forward and leaned on the desk. His face was inches from hers. 'What is sexual homicide about?' he demanded.

Carol knew the answer to this one. 'The perverted gratification of desire.'

'Good, good,' he said, moving even closer. 'How many lovers have you had?'

Flustered, Carol looked away. 'What's that got to do with anything?'

'More than one, right?' he continued insistently.

Carol gave in. It was easier than the alternative. 'More than one,' she agreed.

'And have any of them ever behaved identically in bed?' Tony asked, as if the answer would settle an important argument.

Carol started to see a glimmer of where he was going with this. 'No.' Tony's intense blue eyes were irresistible. In spite of herself, she grew tense at his physical closeness. Whether he recognized that or not, he gave no clue.

His voice dropped, becoming intimate and gentle. 'My particular needs can only be met by one specific ritualistic process. I need you bound to the bed, I need you clothed, I need your voice stilled by a leather gag, I need you in my power and I need to destroy the manifestation of your sexuality.' He took a deep breath and pulled back. 'What are the chances that there are two of us out there who want exactly the same thing?'

Comprehension dawned on Carol. She relaxed now the immediacy of the intimacy had receded. 'Point taken. But we're still left with an identical MO. Which is a problem for me.'

Tony leaned back and his voice changed. Carol recognized the shift. Now he was thinking out loud, unformed conclusions bumping into each other. It had taken him a while to be comfortable enough with her to riff like this, but now it was almost as if he saw her as an extension of himself in these moments of verbal reverie. 'Unless of course someone wanted to get rid of Sandie specifically and thought it would be clever to do it in a way that made us run around like headless chickens looking for an impossible killer.'

'I suppose that's conceivable,' Carol said reluctantly.

'I mean, if it wasn't for the history, tying it into past cases, it wouldn't be that far out of the ordinary. Extreme, but not extraordinary.'

'Jesus, Tony,' Carol protested. 'You think what he did to her wasn't extraordinary?'

'Divorce your personal response from your professional one, Carol,' he said quietly. 'You've seen worse than that. A lot worse. Whoever did this still has a lot to learn about sexual sadism.'

'I'd forgotten how far from normal you are,' she said wearily.

'That's why you need me,' he said simply. 'Probably the only really interesting aspect of it is that she wasn't undressed. I mean, if you go to the trouble and expense of going back to a room with a hooker, I'd have thought you'd want her to take her clothes off. I know I would. Otherwise, you might as well just do it in the back of the car or up against a wall.'

'So what does that say to you?'

'Rape.' The word hung in the air between them. For months it had been unspoken and unspeakable. But now it was out in the open. Tony raised his shoulders in an apologetic shrug.

Carol struggled to stay in the professional zone. 'Why do you say that? There's no sign of a struggle back there. Presumably Sandie agreed to be tied up. Presumably he'd agreed to pay her.'

'Absolutely. But he wants it to feel like it's rape. So he doesn't want his victim undressed. That way he can fool himself that he's a rapist.'

It was Carol's turn to look puzzled. 'He wants to pretend he's a rapist? And then he kills them? Why can't he just pretend to be a murderer?'

Tony sighed. 'I don't know that yet, Carol.'

It's ironic, but he's calmer now the streets are full of cops. It's what he expected, and it's always comforting when what he expects happens, even if it's bad shit. Because at least then he knows it's not something worse.

He was doing a bit of business in the toilets at Stan's Café when he saw the blue strobe of their lights through the high frosted-glass window. One set of lights could have been anything, but three together had to be Sandie. And he didn't panic. He's proud of that. Before the Voice, he probably would have run, just as a matter of principle. But now he carried on selling rocks to the nervy black kid, acting surprised when he tried to hurry the action along because of the bizzies outside.

The kid had barely walked out the door when the conversation started. 'They've found her,' the Voice said, warm and caressing. 'They're going to be all over Temple Fields tonight. They're going to want to talk to everybody. They're going to want to talk to you. And that's fine. Just fine. You know what you're going to say, don't you?'

He gave the door a nervous glance. 'Yeah. I know.'

'Humour me. Let me hear it again,' the Voice coaxed.

'I was round and about, just like usual. Dropped in at Stan's, had a couple of beers in the Queen of Hearts. I never saw Sandie all night. I sometimes used to see her down the end of Campion Boulevard, but I never saw her last night.'

'And if they ask you for alibi names?'

'I just act thick. Like I can't tell one night from another. Everybody knows I'm a bit slow, so they won't think anything of it.'

'That's right. Vague is good. Vague is what they expect from you. You did a great job last night. Wonderful footage. When you get home tonight, there'll be a little reward waiting for you.'

'You don't have to do that,' he protested, meaning it. 'I'm sorted.'

'You deserve it. You're a very special young man.'

He felt a warm glow inside, a warm glow that's still there. Nobody but the Voice has ever thought anything about him was special, except his educational needs.

So now he's out there, mooching around like usual. He checks out the cops, a mixture of uniforms and obvious CID. They're working their way down both sides of the street. He could go back to Stan's and wait for them to come to him, or he could amble towards them like a fool with nothing to hide.

He recognizes one of the CID from before, when they were all over Temple Fields a couple of years ago. A big Geordie. Geordie didn't treat you like shit. He changes his angle of approach to come close to Geordie and the woman he's working with. They're talking to a punter, but he's got nothing to say, he can't wait to be away. He's probably given them a moody name and address and he wants to skip before they catch him out.

They step back and the punter scuttles off sideways like a crab. The cop looks up and sees him. He's got that 'I know you but I can't put a name to you' look. He gives Geordie a stupid grin and says hi. Geordie says he's Detective Inspector Merrick.

He repeats the name a couple of times to fix it good and proper because he knows the Voice will want to know everything. He tells Geordie his name and address almost before he asks and the woman cop writes it down. She's not bad looking. A bit on the skinny side, but he's learning to like them like that. The cop asks if he'd heard about Sandie and he says yes, everybody's talking. And he comes out with the lines that the Voice has carved on his brain. Word perfect.

They ask if he saw anybody acting strangely. He laughs loudly, playing up to the image of the Gay Village idiot. 'Everybody acts strange round here,' he says.

'You're not kidding,' the woman cop mutters under her breath. 'Can anybody vouch for your movements last night?'

He looks puzzled. Mr Merrick says, 'Who saw you around? Who can confirm where you were last night?'

He opens his eyes wide. 'I dunno,' he says. 'Last night, it was just the same as every other night, you know? I don't remember stuff too good, Mr Merrick.'

'You remembered you didn't see Sandie,' the woman chipped in. Smart-arsed cow.

'Only because that's what everybody's talking about,' he says, feeling a tickle of sweat at the base of his spine. 'That's a big thing, not a little thing like who was in the café or the pub.'

Mr Merrick pats him on the shoulder. He takes a card

out of his pocket and tucks it into his hand. 'If you hear anything, you give me a call, right?' And they're off, ready for the next friendly little chat.

Not a flicker of doubt. Not a breath of suspicion. He fooled them. They were talking to an assassin and they had no idea. So who's the thickie now?

Carol eased the door shut, not wanting to disturb Michael and Lucy. She was aware how even slight noises carried in the high-ceilinged loft. She slipped out of her shoes and padded through to the kitchen at one end of the open-plan living space. The concealed fluorescent strips that cast light on the worktop were turned on, revealing her cat Nelson sprawled on his side, soaking up the warmth. He twitched one ear as she approached and let out a low rumble that the charitable might have interpreted as a welcome. Carol scratched his head, then noticed the sheet of paper he was half-obscuring. She slid it out from under him, ignoring his wriggle of protest. *'Hi, Sis. Lucy's doing an armed robbery in Leeds tomorrow and Thursday, we got last-minute tickets for the opera so I'm staying over there with her tonight. See you Thursday night. Love, M.'*

Carol crumpled the paper and tossed it in the bin, allowing herself to be momentarily wistful about the prospect of a night at the opera in good company. Anything was better than thinking about a night alone in the apartment. Opening the fridge to take out the half-eaten tin of cat food, she was drawn irresistibly to the bottle of Pinot Grigio sitting in the door. She took both out, fed the cat and contemplated the wine.

In her battle for restoration, Carol had resisted the

easy comfort of drink, nervous of its easy promise of oblivion. She'd told herself she didn't want to sleep-walk through the aftermath of the rape. She wanted to deal with it, to unpick its effects and put herself back together in something approximating the right order. But tonight she wanted erasure. She couldn't bear the thought of closing her eyes and seeing the images she'd brought home from the mortuary. Without anaesthetic, there was no way she was going to sleep. And without sleep, there was no way she could effectively lead the hunt for Sandie Foster's killer. Carol raked through the cutlery drawer for the corkscrew and hurriedly opened the bottle. Full glass in hand, she leaned against the worktop and buried her fingers in Nelson's fur, grateful for the beat of his heart against her skin.

Before last night, she'd had nothing in common with Sandie other than their gender. But what had happened to the prostitute had given her a sort of kinship with the woman charged with hunting down her killer. They both possessed a victimhood that had been conferred because they'd both been guilty of being female in a world where some men believed they deserved never to feel powerless. Sandie hadn't merited what had happened to her any more than Carol had.

Carol drank steadily, topping up her glass whenever it fell below the halfway mark. She understood the terror Sandie must have known as she realized there was no escape from her attacker. She knew that sense of utter helplessness, knew the absolute fear of the prey that has no defence against the predator. But in one crucial sense, perverse though it sounded,

Sandie had been luckier than Carol. She hadn't had to find a way to live with what had been done to her.

Tony stood by Carol's side, his eyes focused on Sandie Foster's lifeless face. He didn't mind being present at post mortems. If he was honest, it intrigued him to watch the pathologist uncovering the messages contained by the dead. Tony read corpses too, but his was a different text. What they had in common was that they both received communication from the killer via the conduit of his victim.

The body lay in a pool of halogen light, the surrounding room a collage of shadows. Dr Vernon, the pathologist, stooped over the body. It offered a gruesome illustration in contrast. Below the waist, Sandie's body was still caked in blood, a study in scarlet. Above the waist, she was apparently untouched. The plastic bags covering her hands partially obscured the bruising at her wrists, allowing the illusion of wholeness to persist. 'Poorly nourished,' Vernon said. 'Underweight for her height. Signs of intravenous drug use –' He pointed to the needletracks on her arms.

He leaned forward and gently probed her mouth open. 'Slight bruising on the inside of the mouth. Most likely as a result of the gag we removed earlier. Some indications of long-term amphetamine abuse.'

'I know you hate it when we jump the gun,' Carol said. 'But can you give me any indication on cause of death yet?'

Vernon turned and gave her a wintry smile. 'I see you haven't acquired patience in your time away from us, Carol. So far, I see nothing to contradict the obvious. She bled to death as a result of injuries inflicted vaginally. The tissue in the area is macerated almost beyond recognition. Not a pleasant way to go.'

'She didn't die quickly?' Carol asked. Tony could feel anxiety vibrating from her. He could also smell stale alcohol on her breath. He'd only managed four hours' sleep himself; God alone knew how little sleep Carol had managed to squeeze in between the bottle and the morgue. It certainly hadn't been enough, judging by the bruised smudges under her eyes.

Vernon shook his head. 'No. No arterial bleeding. This was slow exsanguination. She would have been alive probably for an hour or more, in terrible pain and shock.'

There was a long silence as they absorbed the information. Tony hoped Carol was not contemplating Sandie's suffering too closely. He gave himself a mental shake. He had to stop concentrating on Carol. He had a job to do, and while that job might be easier if he could help Carol on a personal level, he had to keep enough distance to allow himself to do what he was paid for. Mapping the mind of a murderer was never an easy task, and he couldn't afford to ignore an opportunity as good as this for finding a way in.

A long, slow, painful death. 'He watched her die,' he said softly.

Carol's head jerked round. 'What?'

'That's the whole point of a lingering death. The killer wants to savour what he's created. He'll have recorded it as well. Video, probably. But you might want to check the room for fibre-optic cameras. It's possible he wanted to watch the discovery of the body too.'

'He stayed around till she was dead?'

Tony nodded. 'High risk. He's confident, this one. He knew enough about Sandie's routines to feel safe that they weren't going to be disturbed. He's probably paid her to have sex before so he could check out the lie of the land. He won't have been able to manage intercourse, but he'll have wanted to talk, to find out her regular patterns. You should ask around, see if she mentioned anything to any of her mates.'

Carol filed the information away for future action. Vernon unpeeled the plastic bags from Sandie's hands and began taking scrapings from under her nails. 'Any thoughts on time of death?' Carol asked.

'An imprecise science at the best of times,' Vernon said drily. 'My best guess would be somewhere between midnight and eight yesterday morning.'

'No way to tell if she had sex before she was attacked, I suppose?' Carol asked.

'No chance. The damage to the surrounding tissues is so severe it will be impossible to tell whether there was any ante-mortem bruising. If it's any comfort to you, there's no apparent sign of any gross anal penetration.'

Before Carol could respond, the door behind them opened. Tony glanced over his shoulder. That single look told him the woman who had entered was a police officer. There was something unmistakable about her casual air of authority in this context. She wore a long black leather coat, the collar turned up against the blustery weather outside, making her look as if she was auditioning for a feminist version of *The Matrix.* She barely glanced at the body on the table before crossing to Carol.

'Morning, DCI Jordan,' she said. 'Mr Brandon said I'd find you here.'

Carol hid her surprise, though not from Tony. He knew her well enough to read the faint rise of the brows, the slight widening of the eyes. 'Sergeant Shields,' she said. 'What brings you here?'

'Mr Brandon didn't call you?' Jan's face showed consternation.

'No.'

'Ah. I expect he's left a message on your voice-mail. I tried to call you myself earlier and I couldn't raise you. Anyway, he's seconded me to your team for this investigation. He said you were a sergeant under strength and thought it might be useful to have someone on the team who knows the street scene.'

'That makes sense.' Carol's voice had ice at its heart. Already Brandon seemed to be reneging on his promise to give her a free hand, and she didn't like what that said about her.

'He seemed to think so,' Jan said, turning towards Tony. 'And this must be the man who reads our minds.'

Tony assumed the expression of a man who's heard it all before. 'Only if you're a sexually motivated serial offender.'

Jan laughed. 'My secrets are safe, then.' She held out a hand. 'I'm Jan Shields.'

Tony returned the handshake. Strong, warm hand. Exactly what he'd expect from someone who'd just demonstrated how sure of herself she was.

Jan turned back to Carol. 'Another one bites the dust, eh?'

'In a particularly unpleasant way,' Carol said repressively.

Jan shrugged, stepping forward to see better what Vernon was doing. 'It's a high-risk occupation.'

'So is being a cop,' Carol said. 'But when one of us dies, we get a little respect.'

Jan gave an apologetic smile. 'Sorry, I don't mean to sound callous. But when you've been in Vice as long as I have, they all start to look like meat while they're still on the hoof.'

Tony didn't find Jan's attitude surprising. He'd met too many cops – and clinical psychologists – on the edge of burnout not to have some sympathy with the defensive positions they adopted. He took a step away, moving closer to the table. 'Did you do the post mortems two years ago?' he asked.

Vernon nodded. 'I did.'

'What do you think?' Tony asked.

'If I didn't know better, I would say this woman had been the victim of the same killer. The pattern of the wounds is quite distinctive. Unique, really. The only time I've seen it before was in the murders Derek Tyler was found guilty of.'

'What did he use? A knife of some sort?'

'As I recall, Tyler never gave up the weapon. At the time, I surmised it was something home-made,' Vernon said. 'The wounds certainly don't match any implement I've ever come across. And I did ask one of my colleagues who's an expert in toolmarks for an opinion.'

'So, what kind of home-made?' Carol interjected.

Vernon studied the blade of his scalpel. 'It's hard to be certain. The wounds are consistent with a narrow, flexible blade. A razor blade rather than a craft knife. But there are dozens, hundreds of cuts. The best guess my colleague and I could come up with was something along the lines of a latex dildo with a series of razor blades inserted quite deeply into it.'

Carol's intake of breath was audible. 'Jesus,' she said.

'Danger, nutters at work,' Jan said bitterly. 'That right, Dr Hill?'

Tony frowned. It made no sense. Nothing added up. If the police had captured the wrong man, the real killer should have reacted by taking another victim then and there. Sexually motivated murderers didn't like other people being given credit for their handiwork. To wait two years to strike again was all wrong. He needed to talk this through. 'Carol?' he said softly.

But her attention was elsewhere. She indicated Tony with a movement of her head without looking at him directly. 'Jan, Dr Hill thinks our man had been with Sandie before. Can you find out who she hung around with, see if she mentioned a punter who wanted her to talk about herself? Chances are he couldn't maintain an erection.'

Jan snorted. 'That hardly narrows it down. You'd be amazed how many punters can't get it up when it comes to it. That's often why the girls get smacked around. But yeah, I'll see what I can come up with.' She pulled her coat collar closer. 'I'll hit the bricks, then. Catch you later.'

Tony watched her melt into the shadows, waiting till he heard the door close behind her before returning to Carol's side. The room was quiet save for the clink of metal on metal as Vernon exchanged one instrument of deconstruction for another. 'Carol, I keep coming back to what I said earlier. This is an impossible scenario. If Derek Tyler really did commit the murders he was convicted of, it's beyond the bounds of credibility that somebody else would find satisfaction in such a precise replication of his crimes. It goes against every psychological truth I know. Somebody's setting the scene, creating what they want us to see.'

'But the forensics –'

'I know what you said,' Tony interrupted her. 'But your team needs to look at those files, to see if there was any possibility of a mistake. And if there was, you need to start looking at men who've been recently released from prison or from Bradfield Moor after a two-year stretch. That's the only explanation for the time lag. Because I'd stake my reputation on the fact that whoever killed those women two years ago also killed Sandie Foster.'

Carol stared at him, the glimmering of an idea at the edge of her consciousness. 'Tony? What if that's exactly what our killer is gambling on?'

'Sorry?' he looked puzzled.

Carol's words tumbled over each other in her excitement. 'What if the person who murdered Sandie Foster is gambling on the fact that we'll be forced to draw precisely that conclusion? What if killing Sandie was incidental? What if the killer's real intent is to have Derek Tyler's conviction set aside?'

Tony cocked his head to one side, considering. 'That would work? You could base an appeal on that? In spite of the overwhelming evidence against Tyler?'

'You could have a damn good try. Especially with someone like you in the witness box staking your not inconsiderable reputation on it.'

'Ah,' he said. 'So I take it you don't want me shouting that from the rooftops?'

'Especially not when there are lawyers or journalists present,' Carol said. 'But what do you think? Is it motivation enough?'

'Hard to say. It would have to be somebody who cared passionately about Derek Tyler and who was smart enough to figure out how to pull our strings. It's not a likely scenario, but it's possible.' He smiled. 'This is why we work so well together. You think like a detective, I think like a nutter.'

After the morgue, it was almost a relief to be back inside Bradfield Moor. Front-desk security told him where to find Derek Tyler. Because he'd been classified as a non-violent inmate, he was allowed to eat his meals with others in the same category in the dining room. It was a low-ceilinged barn of a room that smelled of chip fat with undertones of overcooked brassicas. The walls had been painted indigo and yellow in line with what Tony privately considered to be the junk science of colour therapy. Any beneficial effects that the décor might have provoked were probably compromised by the scuffs and stains that marked the paintwork from floor to ceiling. Through the security-glass windows there was a view of a shrubbery that consisted mostly of spotted laurel and rhododendrons. If they weren't depressed when they came in here, Tony thought, they soon would be.

He asked one of the orderlies to point out Tyler, then he helped himself to a tray of macaroni cheese and peas, choosing a table off to one side, where he could observe the man who had been found guilty of the murders of four prostitutes over a period of six months, a man who had blamed his urge to kill on the voice in his head. A few of the other inmates glanced Tony's way, some openly staring. But nobody made any attempt to approach him.

Tyler was a lanky, scrawny individual in his mid-twenties. He hunched over his sausage, egg and chips like a miser with a hoard of gold, head down so Tony could see little of him apart from the top of his shaved head and the tattoos on his skinny forearms.

Tony absently munched his way through his lunch, washing the bland food down with strong tea. Tyler showed none of the physical tics of the obsessive compulsive. He ate with preternatural slowness, as if he were stretching the meal out as long as he could. It seemed a pretty good strategy for passing the time, Tony decided.

Tyler had progressed to his last few mouthfuls when Aidan Hart slipped into the chair next to him. 'I didn't expect to see you in today,' he said.

'It's all right, I won't be claiming overtime,' Tony said.

'There's better grub in the staff restaurant, you know.'

'I know. But I wanted to take a look at a patient.'

Hart nodded. 'Derek Tyler.' Noting Tony's look of

surprise, he said, 'Security told me when I came in. What's your interest?'

'Bradfield police found a murder victim last night. They've asked me to consult on the case.' At the mention of the police, Hart perked up, his eyes gleaming with interest. Tony reckoned he'd been right when his first instinct had placed Aidan Hart firmly in the box marked 'careerist'. Just what he needed. More of the professional politics he was so bad at. He'd have to be very careful how he handled this. 'On the surface, it looks like a copy of Derek Tyler's murders.'

Hart stroked his cleanly shaved chin. 'Interesting.'

'Oh yes, it's that, all right.' Tony finished his tea. 'He looks a bit young for this kind of offence.'

'I guess the profile has to be off the mark sometimes,' Hart said smoothly. 'Given that we're working with the law of averages.'

'Which is why I always warn the cops it's not an exact science. So, what can you tell me about him?'

Hart looked across at Tyler, who had come to the end of his meal and was staring down at his empty plate. 'Very little. He's one of the most unco-operative patients I've ever come across. Don't get me wrong. It's not that he's disruptive – quite the opposite. He's totally passive. In one sense, he's no trouble at all. But in another, he's completely intractable. He won't participate in any aspect of the therapeutic regime. He won't speak. He's not catatonic. He just chooses not to.'

'Ever had any trouble with him?'

'Only once. They've got integral radios in their rooms. They can choose from half a dozen preset stations, and we can use the system to broadcast announcements. Derek never uses his, but somehow something went wrong with it. The radio came on and it couldn't be turned off. And Derek lost it. Smashed the room up, went for the nurses. We had to sedate him, and he wouldn't go back in his room until we had the radio removed.'

Tony gave a small smile. 'Interesting,' he said. If Hart noticed the echo, he didn't react.

'But not very illuminating.'

Tony let the comment lie. He wasn't ready to share his thoughts with anyone, least of all someone he felt an instinctive mistrust towards. 'What do we know about him before the killings?'

Tony watched the eye movements that indicated Hart was accessing memory not lies. 'Not a lot,' Hart said after a short pause. 'Borderline special needs. According to the report from his GP, he was highly suggestible, eager to please, mild obsessive compulsive. But nothing to merit treatment. And nothing to indicate he was heading for a career as a serial killer. Then again, GPs – what do they know?' His smile was complicit, one expert to another, calculated to build an alliance. Tony read it for what it was and instinctively fought against it. Hart pushed his chair back. 'Do you want to meet Derek?'

'I'd appreciate it if you could arrange it. It'd be good if I could talk to him in his room.'

Hart looked surprised. 'That's not normal procedure. We usually talk to patients in one of the interview suites.'

'I know. But I'd like to see him on his turf. I'd like him to feel he has a measure of control. And you've said yourself, he's not violent.'

Tony could see Hart weighing up the arguments and deciding to keep his powder dry. 'All right. I'll page you when we're set up. But you'll be wasting your time, you know. He's not spoken to a member of the medical staff since the day he arrived here.'

Tony didn't take his eyes off Derek Tyler as Hart bustled off. He spoke under his breath: 'You like the voice, don't you, Derek? You like to listen to it. You don't want anything to interfere with it. So what do I have to do to make you want to listen to mine?'

When she'd woken up only three hours after falling into bed, Carol had blamed lack of sleep for the way she felt. But as the morning had worn on, it became clear to her that she was in fact hung over. She felt as if someone was cutting through her brain with cheesewire after cruelly turning the lights several hundred watts higher. Still, it was almost worth it for the dreamless stupor that had kept the nightmare images of Sandie Foster's death at bay. She swigged from a bottle of water and surveyed her team. They all looked fresher than she felt. She walked out of her office and took up station in front of the white-board that was already adorned with photos of Sandie, alive and dead.

'Good morning,' Carol said, trying to imitate an energy she didn't possess. 'Sandie Foster died at some time between midnight and eight a.m. on Tuesday morning. Which means she was probably attacked somewhere between ten on Monday night and four on Tuesday morning. Given that she normally knocked off at ten, we can assume she was in the company of her killer before then. According to Dr

Vernon, she bled to death and it would have taken her at least an hour to die. Dr Tony Hill, who will be working with us on this case, believes that the killer probably stayed with her while she bled out. So we're looking for someone who has two or three hours they can't account for in that time period.' She turned to the whiteboard and wrote up the crucial times.

'Preliminary forensics indicate we're not going to have much to go on here. Plenty of prints, but none on the handcuffs or the bedstead. They've been wiped clean. The top of the table was green baize, so nothing for us there either. Chances are the remaining prints are from punters who had nothing to do with this. Nevertheless, if and when we get any matches, we need to follow up on that. So far, we've not found any traces of sperm. The blood boys are checking to see if they can find any blood that isn't Sandie's, but that's a slim chance.' Carol perched on the edge of a desk, forcing her thoughts into order.

'I know you're all aware of the similarities between this case and a series of murders that took place two years ago. However, there is nothing to suggest that Derek Tyler's conviction was unsafe. I've read the files, and even without his admission of guilt, that case was as open and shut as we're ever likely to get. So while we treat this as an individual case, we should be aware that it's possible Derek Tyler had a fan a couple of years ago. A sick bastard who sees it as his role to replicate Derek's crimes. It might even be the case that someone is trying to get Derek Tyler out of Bradfield Moor and sees this as the way to do it. Make a case for linkage between the murders, and you make a case for a miscarriage of justice.'

'Don't you think that's a bit far-fetched, ma'am?' Don Merrick interjected.

'At this stage, Don, I'm not ruling out anything, however off the wall it might seem.' Carol noticed Paula catch Merrick's eye and give him a small shake of the head. Indicating that she thought her guvnor had lost it? Or was Carol just being paranoid? Was Paula acting out of team solidarity, signalling it wasn't appropriate for Don to question the boss's judgement when there were others present? Carol cleared her throat and continued. 'We all know this is not a straightforward murder because of the resemblances to the previous series. But I want that knowledge to stay in this room. Nobody talks to the press. Leave that to me and Mr Brandon. Now, what have we got?'

Not much, Carol thought miserably as she listened to the team run through the scant high points of their results so far. Nobody admitted to having seen Sandie with a punter after nine o'clock. Sandie's distraught mother knew nothing of the details of her daughter's other life; it had been tacit between them that what Sandie did to earn her keep was something not to be spoken of in the family home. The only lead they had was that Sandie had been seen getting into a black Freelander 4x4 around half past eight. An obliging prostitute had noted the last three digits of the number plate.

'OK,' Carol sighed. 'Kevin, get on to the number plate. Chances are it's not our man, but at least if we can find out when he dropped her off, we narrow down the time frame for our killer. Don, Paula – I want you to collate all the interviews from the street last night. Work with Stacey to draw up a plan of who was where, when. Then we'll have an idea who might be worth reinterviewing. Stacey, I want you to carry on working on Ron Alexander's computer files as well. Let's not lose sight of our other priorities. Jan, you're with me. Sam, you can start backtracking on Derek Tyler's known associates. The rest of you I want out on the streets in Temple Fields – saturation coverage. I want everybody who was out and about on Monday night interviewed.'

The room filled with the hubbub of conversation as officers organized themselves. Jan Shields wove through the bodies and reached Carol as she was about to enter her office. 'What have you got in mind for us?' Jan said conversationally, following Carol inside.

'Kevin did a good job with Dee Smart, but I think she might have more to give us. It's always worth trying a different approach. And I thought you might know some of the levers to pull.'

Jan leaned against the door frame. 'Sure. We're probably wasting our time, but you never know.'

'It's better than spinning our wheels.' Carol was opening and closing her drawers, looking for the paracetamol she was sure she'd stashed there. No trace. She was going to have to manage without.

'You really think somebody's trying to get Derek Tyler off the hook?' Jan asked.

Carol looked up. 'I don't know. But, frankly, it's a more comfortable notion than any of the alternatives.'

Tony knocked on the open door and waited. Silence. Worth a try, he thought, unsurprised that the tactic hadn't worked. He stuck his head round the door.

Derek Tyler was sitting on his bed, knees bent, arms wrapped round his legs. 'Can I come in?' Tony asked.

Tyler didn't move. 'I'll take that as a yes, then.' Tony walked into the small room, keeping his eyes on Tyler. There would be plenty of time to take in the room without making the man feel his environment was under scrutiny. 'I'll sit down, shall I?' Tony continued, making for the single wooden chair that was tucked into a bare table.

He pulled the chair out and turned it so he was sitting at an angle to Tyler. He deliberately chose a relaxed posture, body open and unthreatening. Tyler moved his head so Tony was out of his line of vision. Tony glimpsed a raw-boned face with deep-set pale eyes. He had the sense that Tyler was perfectly capable of connection but that he chose to avoid it. 'My name is Tony Hill,' he said. 'I work here at the hospital. But I also work with the police. And that's why I wanted to talk to you.' He waited, taking in the bareness of the room. It was like a monastic cell. No books, no family photographs tacked to the walls, no Page Three girls. The only personal item in the room was a large framed black-and-white photograph of Temple Fields, looking down the pedestrianized street with the canal off to one side.

After a few long minutes, Tony decided it was time to get to work. His strategy was, he knew, basic. But it was the best he could come up with on short notice with a patient he'd no previous clinical engagement with. 'I understand why you might not want to talk about it. Who could possibly comprehend what it was like to do the things you did?'

Tyler shifted slightly, but his bony face remained

resolutely turned away. Tony lowered his voice, making it warm and sympathetic. 'But that's not the main problem, is it? The trouble is, when you start to talk, everybody just wants to talk back at you. And that way you can't hear the voice, can you, Derek?'

Tyler jerked his head round momentarily, a flash of surprise on his face. It was over so quickly that Tony could almost have believed he'd imagined the response. 'It's still there, isn't it?' he said. Then he waited a good two minutes before speaking again. 'You can hear it when I shut up, can't you?'

Nothing from Tyler. But that single glance had told Tony he was moving in the right direction. 'But the voice can only tell you stuff from before. It can't tell you what's happening now, outside here. You have to rely on me for that. You know why that is? You know why it's all gone quiet? It's because your voice is talking to somebody else now.'

Tyler's whole body swivelled round till he was facing Tony. He was all attention now, his grey-blue eyes shrouded under his heavy brows. Tony spread his hands in a conciliatory gesture. 'I'm sorry, Derek, but that's the way it is. You're shut up in here, you're no use any more. I told you I work with the police. The reason I'm here is that somebody else is doing exactly what you did, Derek. And that has to be because the voice isn't talking to you any more. It's talking to him.'

Anger flared in Tyler's eyes. His hands tightened their grip on each other, the veins on his thin arms standing out like cords. Tony wondered if anyone on Aidan Hart's team had ever provoked this tightly coiled violence in Tyler. He doubted it. If they'd seen what he was looking at now, he didn't think Tyler would be allowed into the general population. 'I'm not making this up, Derek,' Tony said reasonably. 'The voice has left you for somebody else. All you've got is memories.'

Abruptly, Tyler jumped up and walked past Tony to the doorway. He rang the call button on the wall and banged on the door with his fist for good measure.

Tony continued speaking as if nothing had happened. 'I'm right, aren't I? The voice isn't yours any more. So you might as well talk.'

A nurse in white scrubs appeared in the corridor. Tony could see Aidan Hart hovering behind him. Tyler stood meekly by the door.

'What's happened?' the nurse asked.

Tony smiled. 'I think Derek wants to go away and think about what I've been saying to him, don't you, Derek?'

'You're OK, are you, Doc?'

'I'm fine. In good fettle and in good voice.'

The nurse looked from Tony to Tyler and back again, unable to fathom what was going on. 'Come on then, Derek, we'll take you down to the day room.' The nurse reached out for Tyler's arm.

In the doorway, Tyler turned and growled in a voice rusty from disuse, 'You're not the voice. You could never be the voice.'

Aidan Hart's mouth fell open. He watched speechless as Tyler walked down the hall, head high, narrow shoulders thrown back. Tony stood up and replaced the chair. 'Well, that's a start,' he said cheerfully, walking past his new boss at a brisk pace.

* * *

Stan's Café featured in none of the tourist guides to Bradfield. Even the indie internet websites that prided themselves on offering their readers the *echt* experience normally only available to natives shuddered away from a greasy spoon frequented principally by hookers, rent boys, homeless people and drug dealers. Unlike some low-life dives that made it into alternative guides, nobody went to Stan's for the food. The clientele frequented Stan's because it was somewhere to go out of the cold and rain. When Temple Fields glamorized itself into the Gay Village in the nineties, the bar owners had started to become more picky about who they allowed across their thresholds, especially if they were the sort of customers who could make a half of bitter last hours. The only beneficiary of this more stringent approach was Stan's. Fat Bobby, who owned Stan's, didn't care who occupied the split and sticky vinyl seats as long as they bought food and drink and fags from him.

That morning, half a dozen tables were taken. Two young Asian men were hunched over eggs on toast, a velvet jeweller's roll of knock-off watches half-exposed between them. They were clearly brothers, sharing the same tight, sharp features, the same slack-lipped mouths stained with tomato sauce. In between mouthfuls, they argued prices and pitches. A gangling youth lounged against the fruit machine, frowning at the reels as they spun and settled in response to the coins a chunky lad with classic Black Irish looks was feeding into the machine. 'Why d'you keep doing it when you don't win?' the spectator asked.

'If I don't do it, I won't win, will I?' the player grunted. 'Fuck off, you're bringing me bad luck.'

Dee Smart sat at a corner table near the toilets, back to the door, huddled over a cigarette. Her eyelids were puffy and heavy, her mouth downturned and tight. She stared into a grey cup of coffee, looking miserable. A gawky, slack-jawed youth emerged from the toilets and caught sight of her. He slid into the seat opposite. 'You sad about Sandie, Dee?' he said. He had some sort of problem with his speech which turned everything he said into a long drawl.

Dee took a drag on her cigarette and sighed. Jason Duffy was not what she needed right then. 'Yeah, Jason, I'm sad about Sandie.'

He patted her hand awkwardly. 'You need something to take the edge off? I got some nice skunk.'

'Not a good idea just now, Jason. I'm waiting for the dibble,' Dee said wearily. 'Besides, you know I don't buy from you.'

Jason's face twitched with nervous anxiety and he edged quickly out of the seat, almost falling over his feet in his haste. 'Be seeing you, then.' He headed for the door without a backward glance.

The youth by the slot machine abandoned his post and moseyed over to the counter to order a tea. The door to the outside swung open and Jason Duffy nearly ran head first into Carol Jordan in his haste to be gone. Carol sidestepped him and walked in, her stomach rebelling at the steamy, smoke-filled atmosphere. Stale bacon fat and vinegar conspired in a foul miasma that made her regret her excesses of the previous night once more. Jan followed her, eyes dredging the room for Dee Smart. 'Over there,' she said, indicating Dee with her head. 'You want a coffee?'

Carol wrinkled her nose. 'You're kidding, right?'

'They don't do mineral water,' Jan said acidly. 'A Coke might settle your stomach.'

Carol tried to hide her surprise. 'Sorry?'

'You've been looking off colour all morning. The morgue will do that to you.' Jan weaved through the tables to the counter. Carol followed, checking out the room. She might as well have been invisible for the amount of eye contact she could garner. Every time she looked at someone, their eyes slid off her like water off wax. 'Who's who?' she asked.

Jan's eyes swept the room. 'The lad playing the fruit machine is Tyrone Donelan. He nicks cars.' As if he'd heard her, Tyrone Donelan took one glance over his shoulder and made straight for the door to the toilets.

'The two Asians, that's Tariq and Samir Iqbal. Snide watches, pirate DVDs – that kind of thing. Their old man's a serious player in the counterfeit game. I think he got a tug a year or so back, did three months.' The Iqbals suddenly lost interest in their eggs on toast, grabbed their stash of watches and hurriedly left.

'What about the kid who nearly knocked me over when we came in?'

'Jason Duffy. Low-level dealer. Smack and whiz mostly. He's not the full shilling, Jason. His claim to fame is that his mother was the first person in Bradfield to be arrested for dealing crack.' She indicated the gangling youth with a sideways jerk of the head. 'That's another one from the same mould: Carl Mackenzie. He mostly deals to the street girls. More of a range than Jason, but not much smarter. As far as what we're looking for goes, there's not one of them that would be as much use as a chocolate chip pan.'

Carol nodded. 'Thanks.' She moved at a leisurely pace towards Dee and sat down opposite her. Dee raised her head and gave her a calculated stare. Carol took in the lank hennaed hair and the weary, suspicious eyes.

'Who are you?' she demanded.

'Hi, Dee,' she said. 'I'm sorry I didn't get the chance to meet you yesterday. I'm Detective Chief Inspector Jordan. Carol Jordan.' Carol smiled and extended a hand.

Obviously taken aback, Dee shifted her cigarette from one hand to the other and accepted the shake. 'Right,' she said. 'So you obviously know who I am.'

'I'm sorry about Sandie,' Carol said.

'Not half as sorry as I am.'

'Naturally. She wasn't my friend. But I want you to know that I'll pursue whoever killed her just as hard as if she had been.'

The sincerity in Carol's voice seemed to penetrate Dee's carapace of toughness. 'That's what the other bloke said. That you'd take it seriously.' She sounded surprised.

Jan reached the table, a can of Coke in each hand. She dumped the drinks on the table and plonked herself down in a chair at right angles to the other two women. 'Dee, this is . . .' Carol began.

'I know who this is,' Dee said. Her manner had shifted back to her earlier truculence.

'Hi, Dee. How are you doing?' Jan asked.

'How do you think?' She angled herself away from Jan.

Carol popped the top of her Coke and took a mouthful. Sugar and caffeine and bubbles hit her, giving her an instant lift. 'I know this is a hard time for you, but we do need your help.'

Dee sighed. 'Look, like I said when you phoned. I told everything I know to that bloke last night.'

Jan shook her head. 'There's always more, Dee. We all know that. Stuff you think isn't important, stuff you think is too important. Who did she score from?'

Dee looked panicked. Her eyes swivelled towards the counter, where Carl Mackenzie was leaning, mug in hand, talking to the girl behind the counter. 'I dunno,' she mumbled.

'Course you do.' Jan followed Dee's glance in time to see Carl heading for the door, throwing a nervous glance in her direction.

'Was that Carl Mackenzie going out just now?' Jan asked.

'I don't have eyes in the back of my head. And if it was, what of it? It's still a free country, isn't it? People can have a cup of coffee wherever they want, can't they?' Dee was talking too much, Carol thought.

Jan clearly agreed. 'Sandie scored off Carl, didn't she?'

Dee snorted scornfully. 'Sandie wasn't a low-life. I don't know who she used, but it wasn't Carl, OK? You stay off his back, he's harmless.'

'That would be because he's dealing to you, would it?' Jan drawled wearily.

'Fuck off. Look, she might have got some stuff off Jason Duffy now and again, but that's all I know.'

'Did she have a pimp?' Carol asked.

Dee shook her head. 'There's less poncing round Temple Fields than you'd think. Her lot saw to that,' she said, gesturing towards Jan with her thumb.

'We cleared out a lot of the pimps a while back,' Jan said to Carol. 'We made it clear we were going to nail their earnings under the Proceeds of Crime legislation.' She turned to Dee. 'I'd have thought you lot would be grateful to us for getting them off your backs.'

'We'd have been a fuck of a sight more grateful if you hadn't tried to get the punters off the streets at the same time,' Dee said bitterly. 'You're the ones who pushed us off the main drags and into the side streets. And now it's all happening again.'

Carol felt the rapport she'd started to build with Dee slithering away out of her reach. 'We want to stop it happening,' she insisted.

'Yeah, well, I've told you all I can.' Dee pushed her chair back.

Carol tried a last desperate appeal. 'If you remember anything at all, however insignificant it seems, it could be important for our investigation, Dee. We're here to help.'

Dee snorted. 'Yeah, well, it's not helping me earning a living, sitting in Stan's being clocked talking to the dibble. I'm out of here.'

She grabbed her skimpy denim jacket from the back of her chair and stalked off. Carol looked after her, fed up and puzzled. 'She was a lot more co-operative with Kevin last night,' she said.

Jan shrugged. 'Maybe she prefers men.'

'She seemed edgy about Carl Mackenzie.'

Jan looked bored. 'She scores from him. She doesn't want us taking him off the streets. He's harmless. Mental age of about ten. The girls treat him like a pet.'

'You think Dee was telling the truth? About Sandie not using him?'

Jan considered, rolling her drink between her palms. 'Probably. If Sandie bought off Jason, she wouldn't have been using Carl as well. They're both street dealers for the same middleman. Plus, what's Dee got to gain by lying about it?'

'Like you said, it keeps her source on the street, where she needs it,' Carol pointed out.

Jan pulled a dubious face, making her look like a pouting cherub past its sell-by date. 'I can't see it. I'll check the overnights, see if he's been spoken to, if you like.'

'That'd be good. And if he hasn't, maybe you could have a word.' She'd skimmed the reports herself that morning, but she couldn't remember the detail. 'Same goes for Jason Duffy.'

Carol knew she was clutching at straws, always tempting when an investigation didn't throw up solid early leads. She was beginning to have a bad feeling about Sandie Foster's murder. It was showing all the hallmarks of a case that was going nowhere fast. If they didn't get a break soon, Carol's squad would be transformed from great white hopes to scapegoats. And that wasn't something she thought she could handle right now.

He's big news. Front page of the evening paper. He can't read well, but he can manage big headlines. He wasn't expecting it to be like that, not with Sandie being just a whore. The cops must be pissed off, he thinks. Big headlines about murder make them look bad.

He can tell by the way the streets are full of them, talking to anybody they can get their hands on, that they don't know where to look. They're desperate to find what he knows isn't there. He knows it's not there because he did it exactly as he was told.

He's proud of himself. He can't remember ever feeling like this before. There must have been a time when he did something right, something he could hold his head up about. But when he searches his fucked-up memories, nothing surfaces.

The Voice understands that. The Voice is proud of him too. He knows because when he got back to his place last night, there was a reward. A small parcel was sitting on top of his TV/video combo, wrapped in nice shiny holographic paper with a big gold ribbon round it. It was so beautiful that he almost didn't want to open it. He wanted to swagger round with it so people would realize he was the kind of person who got special presents. He didn't, though. He knew that would be stupid. And he's trying very hard not to be stupid these days.

Instead he sat on the bed for ages, turning it over in his hands. Eventually, he decided to unwrap it and see what was inside. He had a pretty good idea, but he wanted to be sure. First, he untied the ribbon, forcing his clumsy fingers to go slow over the knot rather than ripping it apart with his teeth or cutting it with his Swiss Army knife. Then he folded up the paper and ribbon carefully, before putting it away in a drawer.

Inside was the reward he expected. A video cassette. With sweating hands, he slid it into the slot in the video, reaching for the remote to turn on the TV. And there it was, in all its glory. His first mission, his first cleansing.

This time, he didn't lose his erection.

PART THREE

Three weeks later

He used to have nightmares when he was a kid. He hasn't thought about them in years; they stopped once he started spliffing. He can't recall the last time he went to bed without at least one joint humming in his veins, so likewise he can't recollect the last time a bad dream woke him screaming and quivering between the sheets. But he does remember how there was always someone towering over him. mouth opening and closing, spewing violent words. He seemed to shrink under the attack, while the shouting figure swelled like a monster in a manga comic. He could never make out the words, but they seemed to strip the very skin from him till he felt raw and bleeding.

What made it worse was that he had nothing to make it better when he woke. There was no comforting memory of gentleness or kindness to set against the sound and fury of his nightmare.

It's hard to believe how much things have changed. Now he falls asleep lulled by the rockabye rhythms of the Voice. He wouldn't mind betting that if he gave up the weed, he'd sleep like a baby these days. Not that he's about to give it a try. He likes life without nightmares too much to take a chance.

Tonight, he's making plans. The Voice is in his head, telling him it's time to move again. Time for the next chapter of the lesson, according to the Voice. Time for another cleansing.

Tomorrow night, he'll come home to find his supplies neatly laid out on his bed. Tomorrow night, he'll get set, just like the last time. He tries not to think of the target as a human being. That way, his head won't get tangled up like it did with Sandie right at the end, when he started to feel like he maybe shouldn't be taking her life away, when it all went muddled and only the memory of the Voice kept him going.

This time, he won't think of her as someone with a name. He'll just think of her as rubbish that has to be got rid of before it poisons the world he has to live in. Then he'll ride the dragon all the way to glory. He'll be a hero, just like in the movies. Blood and glory. Blood and glory and the Voice.

Once upon a time the only way respectable people could buy sex toys was to send off for what catalogues described with bizarre coyness as a 'cordless neck massager'. But by the first decade of the twenty-first century, almost every fair-sized town in the United Kingdom had at least one emporium dedicated to the fulfilment of most imaginable sexual desires. They'd started as seedy shopfronts with blacked-out windows regularly picketed by protesters ranging from evangelical Christians to women reclaiming the night. But they'd rapidly progressed to well-lit, inviting retail palaces, shelves stacked with everything from whimsical fake-fur handcuffs to implements whose functions mercifully eluded most of the customers who were intent only on having a good night in.

There was about most of these stores a relentless cheerfulness. The Pink Flaming-O was typical of the breed. It occupied a double-fronted shop that had once been, ironically, a toyshop, at the less fashionable end of the main shopping street in Firnham, one of the half-dozen satellite towns that circled Bradfield. The windows were painted opaque shocking pink to avoid offending those citizens of Firnham who steadfastly maintained their lack of interest in its contents. Given that most businesses at that end of Deansgate had a life expectancy of somewhere between six and eighteen months, and given that the Pink Flaming-O had been thriving for four years, the assumption had to be that the town boasted enough people with a lively interest in the wilder shores of sex to outweigh the censorious.

Certainly there was no lack of custom towards the end of a late autumnal Sunday afternoon. A pair of teenage girls were giggling incredulously at a display of outsize dildos, but the other half-dozen customers were giving far more serious attention to items as various as cock rings, anal-sex kits, bondage equipment, inflatable love dolls and penis pumps.

As the teenagers moved on to wonder at the range of clitoral stimulators, their place by the display of dildos was taken by a customer who had been browsing a rack of videos. A hand gloved in black leather reached out for one of the display models, a lurid scarlet latex imitation penis. Strong fingers tested its pliability and, satisfied, replaced it on the shelf. The hand picked up a boxed example of the dildo and carried it across to the counter, picking up a couple of pairs of handcuffs and ankle restraints along the way.

There was nothing sinister in the cash transaction, nothing to rouse a moment's suspicion in the mind of the shop assistant, who was frankly more interested in Bradfield Victoria's prospects in that evening's premiership match than in the putative sex life of his customers. It was probably as well for his peace of mind that he had no idea that within forty-eight hours, his merchandise would have been transformed into the accoutrements of murder.

The customer walked out of the shop and turned down a side street that led to a busy supermarket. Fifteen minutes later, a blank-eyed checkout assistant rang up a basket of purchases without thought. A loaf of sliced wholemeal bread. Half a dozen premier pork sausages. Four toilet rolls. A bottle of vodka. And three packets of razor blades.

The Voice was ready.

Carol surveyed the stack of cardboard cartons, her good spirits evaporating. It had seemed a good idea at the time to order the furniture for her new home online from a chain retailer. But now she was faced with a couple of dozen flatpacks, and she knew that what lay ahead of her was a long evening of splintered fingernails and muttered oaths. Still, she told herself, it would be worth the effort. The builder had made a good job of turning the basement into an attractive flat. The acrid pungency of fresh paint still hung in the air, but that was a small price to pay for having her own space again.

Carol pulled the cork on a bottle of Viognier, sloshed it into a glass and savoured the cold freshness of the wine as it slid down. It had become a familiar ritual at the end of the working day. After Michael and Lucy were in bed, she had taken to sitting by the window, Nelson wrapping himself round her legs. With her bottle and her glass for company, she would process the fruitless activities of the day and try to avoid thinking about what lurked in her personal shadows. She knew she was growing too reliant on the comfort that came from the wine, but the only alternative that suggested itself was the talking cure, and she had little confidence that she could find a therapist she would respect enough to trust. She could talk to Tony, of course. But she needed his friendship too much to want to turn him into a therapist.

She drained the glass and refreshed it, then set to work. Bed first. Then at least she'd have somewhere to collapse when the frustration of always having three screws and a piece of wood left over grew too much.

Carol was wrestling the slats of the bed base into place when the unfamiliar sound of her doorbell pealed out. She grinned. Nothing like setting the ground rules early on. She walked through to the living room and opened her door to the outside world. Tony stood at the foot of the flight of steps, a bottle of champagne dangling from his hand. 'I would have brought flowers,' he said, 'but I didn't know if you had a vase.'

She stepped back and waved him in. 'Two, actually. They're in the kitchen, stuffed with enough lilies to take the edge off the paint.'

He handed over the bottle. 'Welcome to your new home.'

Carol put a hand on his shoulder and kissed his cheek. It was the closest they'd come in months, and the familiar smell of his skin tripped a chain reaction of confused feelings. 'Thank you,' she said softly. 'You've no idea how much this means to me.'

Tony patted her back awkwardly. 'You're doing me

a favour. Having you on the doorstep might just save me from becoming an eccentric recluse.'

Carol laughed, stepping away from him as the closeness grew too much. 'I wouldn't bet on it.'

He looked around at the cartons leaning against the wall. 'Let's make a start, then,' he said, rolling up the sleeves of his sweatshirt. 'I warn you, I am to DIY what George Bush is to the philosophy of language.'

'That good, eh? Tony, I know it runs counter to your instincts, but all you have to do is follow the instructions.'

Two hours later, they'd assembled all the bedroom furniture, two bookcases and three of the dining chairs. They sat slumped in exhausted stupor, each clutching a glass of champagne in stiff and bruised fingers. 'God, I'm aching in muscles I'd forgotten about,' Carol moaned. 'I keep telling myself it'll be worth it to have a place of my own again. Michael's been very sweet, but it's so wearing, coming home from work and having to make small talk.'

Tony winced. 'You had to make small talk? That definitely comes under the heading of cruel and unusual.'

'It was that or listen to Lucy laying down the law about the incompetence, stupidity or bloody-mindedness of the police.'

'Not what you need,' Tony agreed.

'Especially not when it feels like she might be right. My supposed crack squad has two cases to work, and we're going nowhere fast with both of them. We've come to a full stop on Tim Golding.

Stacey managed to extract the serial number of the camera that took the photo, but whoever bought it paid cash in a superstore in Birmingham and never filled in the guarantee registration. There's nothing fresh on Guy Lefevre either. The Operation Ore techies are trawling all they've got to see if they can come up with any more images of either boy, but according to them, that's like looking for a needle in a field full of haystacks. I've got the three-week review of Sandie Foster's murder tomorrow morning, and it's going to be a nightmare. What have we got to show for all that slog and a huge spend? Bugger all. A handful of dead ends and not a single new idea to bless ourselves with. Canvassing Temple Fields took us nowhere. Chasing up Derek Tyler's known associates took us nowhere. Forensics took us nowhere.' Carol crossed her legs and wrapped her arms across her chest. 'We questioned Jason Duffy, the kid she bought her drugs from. He claims he hadn't seen her for a couple of days, and there's nothing to put him with her that night. So that's another dead end. We had a make on a four-wheel drive that Sandie got into earlier in the evening, but the punter is alibied solid from nine onwards.' Carol longed to tell him that the punter in question was his new boss, Aidan Hart, the squeaky clean poster boy for psychiatric care. Given that he was one of the handful of people with full access to the details of Derek Tyler's crimes, there had been a heartstopping moment when Carol had thought she had the killer in her sights. But his alibi had checked out. While Sandie Foster had been enduring the hellish attack that had killed her, Aidan

Hart had been sharing a late dinner in an expensive restaurant with a senior civil servant and an MP. According to Sam Evans, who had interviewed him, Bradfield Moor's clinical director had nearly crapped himself when he'd realized the woman he'd paid for a blow job was the victim whose killer Tony Hill was profiling. But that was one confidence she knew she couldn't share.

'I'm sorry I couldn't provide much of a profile,' Tony said, breaking eerily across her thoughts.

'Not your fault. It's the nature of what you do, I know that. You need data to work with, and one case doesn't provide enough.'

Tony got to his feet and paced the room. 'No, it doesn't. It's one of the worst things about this job. The more times an offender walks out on the high wire and struts his stuff, the easier it becomes to figure out what the important elements of the crimes are. With a single episode, you can't separate the background noise from the message. But the more he does it, the more I can draw out of his actions. Which leaves me in the outcast zone – I'm the only one who benefits when he strikes again. It's no wonder some of your colleagues treat me like a leper.'

'Maybe he won't strike again,' Carol said, her voice lacking all conviction.

'Carol, he already has. Even though I profiled it as a singleton, this is really number five.'

She shook her head. 'I've been through the original case, Tony. There's no question about Derek Tyler's guilt. And there's no indication that he was working with anyone. You've told me yourself: in all the cases where killers work as a pair, there's a high level of codependency and intimacy. They're inseparable. There was nobody like that in Derek Tyler's life. Sam Evans went through it with a fine-tooth comb. Tyler grew up in care. He lived alone. He didn't have a girlfriend. Or a boyfriend, come to that. He didn't even have close friends. Which also means there's nobody out there who cares enough to replicate his crimes in a bid to get him out on appeal.'

Tony leaned against the wall. 'I hear what you're saying, Carol. And I've no comfort to offer. I don't understand what's going on here. There isn't a workable theory that doesn't fly in the face of everything I know about the psychology of sexual homicide.'

'You've not had any fresh thoughts?'

He shook his head. 'My best shot is what I said to you right at the start. Your killer gets off on the idea of rape. But he wants to take rape way beyond the act itself. He's the ultimate rapist, the benchmark everyone who comes after him will have to measure up to. That's how he sees himself. This is about power and anger, not straightforward sexual gratification.'

Carol snorted. 'Like sexual homicide is ever straightforward.'

Tony waved his arms expansively, tipping champagne down his arm. Startled, he rubbed the dribble of liquid away impatiently. 'It is straightforward, Carol. It all comes down to the acting out of fantasy. Unravel the fantasy and you've got the mainspring of the crime. Ninety-nine times out of a hundred, the fantasy is primarily about getting your rocks off. But this is about more than that. This is about the assertion of absolute power. And part of that is about manipulating us. Controlling our reactions and masterminding the whole production.' He stopped, suddenly lost in thought. Carol knew better than to interrupt, sipping her champagne while she waited him out.

'There's something that's been bothering me about this profile,' he said eventually, pushing himself off the wall and returning to his pacing. 'The typology of rape was established way back in the seventies by Nicholas Groth and, although it's been refined, it's still basically the same. Now, if Sandie Foster's attacker hadn't killed her, he'd be a classic Power Assertive type. He's a planner. He uses bondage because it increases the foolproof quality of his attack. He wants his victim submissive from the start. Rather than take a victim off the street, our guy has used a prostitute that he's paying to tie up. With this kind of rapist, there's no fondling, no kissing, no foreplay – which I'm betting was the case here. He cut away enough of her clothing to let him do what he wanted; that's his idea of foreplay. There's no sign of him taking souvenirs, though I suspect he probably videoed his actions. So far, so classic. But then he kills her. And that's totally off the scale for Power Assertive rapists. All we know about this type tells us that they only use enough force to achieve their ends. They're not sadists, by and large. That's the first problem.

'The second problem is much more significant for us.' He paused in his restless movement to top up his glass. 'The Power Assertive rapist has a high ego. He's assured in his masculinity. He operates in his comfort zone and he is confident that he can con his victim into a position where he can assert his power. That's beyond probability. That's a virtual certainty.' He fixed Carol with the full force of his magnetic blue stare. 'Does that sound like Derek Tyler to you?'

Carol pushed her short blonde hair back from her forehead. 'You know it doesn't. But that's not an argument that trumps the forensics. Do you think there's any point in you having another go at Derek Tyler?'

Tony dropped back into his chair. 'I've tried. But apart from what he said the first time, he hasn't uttered a word. It's like he's learned to tune me out. If you want me to try again, I will. But don't expect anything.'

'At this point, Tony, you're all I've got.'

DC Paula McIntyre drove slowly down the unfamiliar street, looking for the Penny Whistle pub. Rows of cramped sixties houses and maisonettes huddled together, showing the unmistakable signs that came with private ownership of former council housing – ugly jerry-built porches, nasty cheap doors, incongruous diamond-paned windows. A couple of years previously, the only reason Paula would have been in Kenton would have been in response to another drive-by shooting in the drugs war that had ravaged the inner city suburb. These days, Kenton had emerged from its no-go status thanks not to proactive policing but to its location, close to Bradfield Cross hospital and to the university, which had led to its being colonized apparently overnight by young health professionals and anxious parents who wanted to make sure their privileged offspring didn't have to do anything as tasking as search for decent rental property.

Even so, it wasn't a district that Paula had had non-professional reasons for visiting. She knew a couple of women who had bought round here, but not well enough to have been to their homes. It wasn't Don Merrick's usual stamping ground either, which was why she'd been even more surprised by his choice of venue than by his phone call asking her to meet him for a drink.

Although a friendship had grown between the two that transcended rank out of working hours, they seldom made special arrangements to meet, nor did they tend towards the sharing of intimacy about their personal lives. They'd often go for a drink after work, but they both had other concerns that ate up most of their off-duty time. When he'd called to invite her for a drink, her first instinct had been to refuse. She'd been planning to join some friends in a country pub. But there had been something in Merrick's voice that had snagged her attention, so she'd agreed. Now, as she pulled up outside an ugly 1960s barn of a pub, she was regretting it.

When she opened the door, a blast of smoky air, stale beer and male sweat hit her. The only other women in the place occupied a booth on their own. They looked ground down by poverty and children in spite of their best efforts at denial. Several of the men at the bar turned to look at her, nudged in the ribs by their friends. 'Over here, darling,' one of them shouted.

'In your dreams, saddo,' Paula muttered. She spotted Merrick in a corner booth, staring gloomily into a half-drunk pint. His shoulders were slumped, his head drooped. The country music playing in the background and the electronic cacophony of the fruit machine might as well not have existed. Paula walked over to the bar, ignoring the pathetic attempts of the drinkers to catch her attention, and bought a couple of drinks.

Merrick didn't even look up when her shadow fell across the table. She placed a fresh bottle of Newcastle Brown Ale beside his glass. 'There you go,' Paula said, sliding into the booth beside him.

'Thanks,' he sighed.

Paula sipped her Smirnoff Ice, wondering what the hell was going on. 'So, here we are. What's up, Don?'

Merrick folded his arms across his chest. He looked like a man who didn't know how to begin. 'Why should something be up? Can't we just meet up for a drink on our night off?'

'Course we can. But this is far from our usual watering hole in every sense. And you're sitting there with a face like a wet weekend in Widnes. And because I'm a detective, those two facts tell me something's up. You can either tell me what it is, or we can sit here in this charming hostelry like a pair of bookends. Your call.' She leaned forward, reaching for his cigarettes. The light caught her bleached blonde hair, making it luminous against the dark wood of the booth.

'Lindy's thrown me out,' he said without preamble.

Paula froze, the cigarette halfway to her mouth. *Oh shit,* she thought. *Here comes trouble.* 'What?'

'I took the kids swimming this afternoon, and when I came back, she'd packed two suitcases. Said she wanted me out.'

'Jesus, Don,' Paula protested. 'That's cold.'

'You're not kidding. I couldn't even argue, not with the kids there. She stood in the hall, telling them Daddy has to go away for a few days because of work. And that look on her face, like she was daring me to contradict her.'

Paula shook her head, trying to imagine what that must have felt like and failing. 'So what did you do?'

'I picked up my bags and walked. Got in the car and drove around for a bit. I just couldn't get my head round it, you know? I tried phoning Lindy, but she wasn't picking up. I parked up and I just wandered round the city centre. Then I called you.' He picked up his glass and drained the remaining half-pint in one.

'I'm so sorry, Don.'

'Me too, Paula.' He picked up the fresh bottle and poured it carefully into his glass, watching intently as the beer cleared and formed a head.

'Do you know what brought it on?'

He made a wordless noise in the back of his throat. 'What always brings it on for cops?'

'The job,' Paula said heavily.

'The job,' Merrick agreed. 'You know what it's been like the past few weeks. We've been working all hours, then having a pint to unwind, because you need a space. You can't go home till you've put a bit of distance between you and the day, otherwise you just trail the shit in behind you. And when you do go home, it's the cold shoulder. Either that or it's, "You're never here, you never see the kids, you've no idea what it's like trying to cope with everything, I might as well be a single parent." Ever since I got the promotion, it's been relentless.'

'Did you try talking about it?'

Merrick's mouth twisted miserably. 'I'm not good at talking about feelings, Paula. I'm a bloke. I tried to explain about how it is, how what I do matters, but she just twists it round so it sounds like I think the job's more important than her and the kids. It's been brewing a while, but this case has just been the last straw. She accuses me of preferring to spend my time talking to hookers than to her.'

Paula put a hand on his arm. 'From what you're saying, I wouldn't blame you if you did. What about relationship counselling? Have you thought about that?'

Merrick tipped his head back and stared up at the ceiling. 'Thing is, Paula, I'm not even sure I want to go back. I'm not the same man who married Lindy. I've gone in one direction and she's gone in another. We've nothing in common any more. Did you know she's gone back to college part-time? She wants to be an educational psychologist. Can you believe it? Feels like the only psychology she's learned is how to put me down.'

'So you've maybe been staying in the pub a bit longer than you would otherwise?' Paula wasn't quite sure where this was going, nor how she wanted to play it.

'Maybe. But whatever's going on between me and Lindy, I don't want to lose my kids. I love my lads, you know that.'

'I know that, Don. But leaving Lindy doesn't mean losing your kids. You can still be their dad even if you don't live with their mum. You can still take them to the footie, go swimming with them, take them on holiday even.'

Merrick snorted. 'And how easy is that in this job? How often do we knock off when we're supposed to?'

'You're an inspector now. You don't work shifts, you don't have to do the overtime like you used to. You can make a space for your boys in your life. If you want it badly enough, you'll do it.'

He gave her a pleading look. 'You think so?'

'I think so.' Paula glanced over to the bar where a bunch of men in their twenties were arguing loudly about the football. She made an instant decision she hoped she wouldn't come to regret. 'This is a dump, Don. Have you got somewhere to stay?'

He looked away. 'I thought I'd check into a hotel.'

'Don't be daft. If you and Lindy are going to split up, you're going to need all your pennies. You can have my spare room,' Paula said gruffly.

'You mean it?' He seemed genuinely surprised.

'If you don't mind sharing it with the world's biggest pile of ironing.'

The ghost of a smile spread across Merrick's face. 'Didn't you know I'm shit hot with the iron?'

'Perfect. Just don't use my razor, OK?'

* * *

Sam Evans cracked open the window of his car to let a trickle of smoke out. One thing about doing stake-outs in red-light districts was that nobody paid much attention to a lone man sitting in a car. Nobody except the working girls, but they'd steered clear after he flashed his warrant card at the first to approach him. He'd stressed he wasn't interested in them, and they'd left him alone.

Aidan Hart's alibi might have been enough for Carol Jordan, but when he had interviewed the psychologist, Sam Evans had sensed a man with something to hide. He wondered what that something was and whether it might be turned to his advantage. If there was a way to put Aidan Hart in the frame for murder, it would be to Evans' advantage in every possible way.

So he'd taken to watching Hart whenever he got the chance. One thing soon became clear: Hart and his wife led virtually separate lives. He didn't know if that was from mutual preference, or if it had evolved because Hart only seemed to go home to sleep. His evenings were usually spent in bars and restaurants, drinking and dining with men who looked like him – prosperous, well-groomed and self-satisfied.

But there was another side to Aidan Hart's life that Evans wouldn't mind betting was unknown to his drinking buddies. On the nights when he wasn't engaged in career-building and male bonding, he picked up women for sex. The shock he'd had when Evans had confronted him obviously hadn't been enough to still his appetite. All it had done was to relocate it.

Instead of trawling in Temple Fields, Hart had gone further afield. Manningham Lane in Bradford, Whalley Range in Manchester and now Chapeltown in Leeds. From what Sam could glean, he went for women who had a place to go rather than settling for a blow job in his gleaming black 4x4. On two occasions, he'd gone back for seconds after adjourning to an Indian restaurant for a meal.

Hart's apparent addiction to hookers didn't trouble Evans on a moral level. He'd shagged a few of them himself over the years. But it did make him wonder about what was going on inside Hart's head. Certainly, it was providing Evans with ammunition that he might be able to make something of. Everybody knew that sexual murderers often used prostitutes, everybody knew that exposure to extreme behaviour desensitized people. Hart was starting to shape up nicely as a suspect, even if Carol Jordan had taken him out of the picture.

Evans was determined that his assignment to the Major Incident Team would be the next step on his upward climb. And if he had to make Carol Jordan look derelict in her duty to achieve it, well, so be it.

He was the one with the knowledge, after all. And knowledge was power.

The knock on his office door was the usual perfunctory rap of the hospital staff. 'Come in,' Tony called.

One of the nurses stuck his head round the door. 'You wanted to see a patient in here, that right? Not in an interview room?'

'That's right.'

The nurse raised his eyebrows in a sceptical expression as if to absolve himself of any responsibility for what might happen. 'I'll go and get him, then.'

While he waited, Tony wondered about the strategy he was about to pursue. Thinking outside the box was his speciality, but he didn't normally impose his wilder ideas on vulnerable people. He barely had to rehearse the arguments against it, so strong were they: it was unprofessional, it potentially put a patient in danger and it was against all the principles of treatment to ask something of a patient that had no direct relevance to his therapeutic regime. On the other side of the balance, he had constructed his own argument. The possibility of saving lives should override all other considerations. The patient wouldn't be in physical danger because this was a controlled environment. The best thing he could do for this particular patient was to raise his self-esteem, and setting him an achievable task was a good way of doing that. Of course, it was arguable whether this was an achievable task, so Tony would have to take care to make it apparent he thought it was close to impossible, that it was a last throw of the dice.

Which it was, of course.

There was no time for further speculation. The nurse pushed the door open and moved back to allow Tom Storey to enter. He took a couple of uncertain steps across the threshold, then paused. His stoop had become more pronounced, Tony noted. Storey looked around, an expression of faint puzzlement on his placid features. His grey eyes swept round shelves already crammed to bursting with books, box files and padded envelopes with torn corners. They came to rest on Tony, who had swivelled round on his chair so he had his back to the paper-strewn desk and faced out into the room. 'Come in, Tom,' Tony said, getting to his feet. 'Take a seat.' He gestured towards one of a pair of low chairs arranged in a corner.

Storey frowned. 'We don't normally meet in here,' he said uncertainly.

'No, we don't,' Tony said.

'Does that mean you've got bad news for me?'

Tony wondered fleetingly whether an operable brain tumour was good or bad news for a man in Tom Storey's position. 'I have got some news for you, it's true. But also we're here because today I need your help. Come on, sit down.' He took the older man's elbow and steered him to one of the chairs then sat opposite.

'How are you doing, Tom?' he asked.

Storey averted his eyes and stared down at the place where his hand used to be. The club of bandages had given way to a lighter dressing, making it look as if he had a particularly uninteresting sock-puppet on the end of his arm. 'You were right. They say I've got a tumour in my brain.' He rotated his head, as if trying to relieve a stiff neck. 'Funny, not so long ago that would have seemed like the worst thing in the world.'

'It's never a good thing. How would you feel if I told you that the tumour is operable?'

A faint sheen of sweat appeared on Storey's bald head. He gazed mournfully at Tony. 'This is a terrible thing to say, but I'd want them to operate. I'd want to live. I know that a lot of the time I feel like I've got nothing left to live for, but if you ask me whether I'd rather take a chance on living, I'd say yes.'

Tony couldn't help the swelling of pity for Tom Storey's ruined life. So unnecessary, so final. So much the worse because Storey was clearly an intelligent man who now had devastating insight into his condition. 'You feel guilty about that, don't you, Tom? On top of all the other stuff you have to feel guilty about, you feel guilty because you want to live.'

Eyes sparkling with tears, Storey nodded. 'I'm a coward,' he stammered. 'I . . . I can't face myself for what I sent them to.'

'You're not a coward, Tom. Dying, that would be the coward's way out. Living with yourself is what takes courage. You can't give back what you took away, but you can live what remains of your life with good intention.'

'So is it operable, then? This tumour, can they get rid of it?'

Tony nodded. 'So they tell me. Like I said before, it won't cure what's wrong inside your mind, but we can help make that easier for you. You'll have noticed a difference already with the meds we've put you on?'

Storey nodded. 'I feel a lot calmer. A lot more in control.'

That was, Tony thought, good news for his plan. 'And that should continue to improve,' he said. 'What the operation will do is to give you a future. And I think you can make use of a future, Tom. I really do.'

Storey rubbed his eyes with the back of his

remaining hand. 'They won't ever let me out of here, will they?'

'It's not impossible, Tom. A lot depends on you, and a lot depends on us.'

'So I suppose you want to write about me? Make yourself a name by treating me? Is that how you want me to help you?' There was a faint but unmistakable note of resentment in his voice.

Genuinely taken aback, Tony cursed himself for assuming he'd won a more secure place in Tom Storey's confidence than he clearly had. 'I'm sorry you think we're here to exploit your pain, Tom,' he said, trying to recover ground he hadn't even known he'd lost.

'It's how you people get on, isn't it? You put the likes of me under the microscope, then you turn us into articles and books.'

Tony shook his head. 'That's not how I operate, Tom. Yes, I do write up cases sometimes, but not out of ambition.' He spread his hands, encompassing the room. 'Does this look like the habitat of an ambitious man to you?'

Storey looked around him again, this time making his assessment more obvious. There were no degrees or diplomas on the walls, no books with his name on the cover prominently displayed, nothing that indicated Tony wanted to impress anyone with his position or achievements. 'I suppose not,' he said. 'So why do you do it if it's not to make yourself look good?'

'I do it because what I've learned from someone like you could mean my colleagues giving better treatment to the people who come to them for help.

That's certainly the only reason I can be bothered reading what other doctors have to say. If I was ever going to write about you – and at this point, that's not on my list of things to do because I don't know what the outcome's going to be for you – I'd be writing to try and raise the awareness of your condition so that the next Tom Storey gets the support he needs sooner than you did.' Tony spoke with passion and sincerity, and Storey visibly relaxed as the words sank in.

'When you say you want my help, what are you getting at?'

'I've been watching the way you interact with the other people who live here. You're very good with them. You seem to have the knack of connecting with people who don't always respond very well with the staff.'

Storey shrugged. 'I was always good with people before . . .'

'Before you got ill?'

'Before I went mad, you mean. Why don't you just say it? Nobody ever says the word in here. Nobody calls us nutters, or loonies or even patients. You all pussyfoot around, as if we don't know why we're here.'

Tony smiled, trying to defuse Storey's irritation. 'Would you prefer it if we did?'

'It would be more honest. You expect us to be honest all the time in therapy, but you dress our world up in euphemism.'

Tony sized up the moment. If he was going to rewrite the rule book, this was his opening. 'OK, I'll try to be more direct. You're good with the nutters. They trust you. They like you. They see you as one of them, so they don't feel threatened by you.'

'That's because I am one of them,' Storey said.

'But most of the time you're still the person you were before your body betrayed you. And I'm gambling that that's how you can help me.' Tony took a deep breath and leaned back in his chair. 'I have another job. When I'm not here, I help the police. I analyse the behaviour of offenders and try to give them pointers that can help them catch criminals before they commit more crimes.'

'You're a profiler, you mean? Like Cracker?'

Tony winced. 'Not much like Cracker. And even less like Jodie Foster. There's nothing very glamorous about what I do. But yes, I am a profiler. Right now, I'm working with Bradfield police. There's a killer they need to catch before he takes any more lives.'

Storey looked confused. 'What's that got to do with me?'

'A patient in here was convicted two years ago of killing four women. There was no doubt about his guilt. The forensic evidence was compelling, and he admitted what he'd done. But now another woman has died in exactly the same way. Whoever is doing it knows everything about the original crimes, including details that were never made public.'

'And you think the man in here is innocent? And you want me to help you prove it?' Storey sounded eager, his face animated.

'I don't know if he's innocent, Tom. All I know is

that he has information locked away in his head that might help us stop any more women dying. And he won't talk to me. He won't talk to anyone. He's scarcely said a word since he arrived here. What I want you to do is to persuade him to talk to me.'

Storey looked uncertain again. 'Me? You think he'll talk to me?'

'I don't know that either. But I've tried everything else I know to get him to open up, and I've failed. So I'm willing to try anything, however crazy it might seem.'

'Crazy's the word.' Storey gave a little snort of amusement. 'The lunatics have taken over the asylum.'

Tony shrugged. 'Only part of it. So, what do you think? Will you give it a try?'

Carol ran her wrists under the cold tap, trying literally to cool down after her case-review meeting with Brandon. She'd always found Brandon a reasonable boss, someone who hadn't forgotten what the job was like at the sharp end. But today she'd felt demoralized and uninspired, and she knew he'd been disappointed in her performance. She couldn't blame him: she was disappointed herself.

At least she'd managed to persuade Brandon not to pull her budget from under her feet and reduce the level of the Sandie Foster inquiry to her own small team. She could still call on other officers as and when she had something for them to do. But it was galling to feel his frustration mirroring her own and to be unable to suggest a course of action that would remedy it. She knew one of the reasons for her success as a detective was her ability to think laterally, to come up with the tangent that nobody else had considered. But on these two cases, she felt trapped in deep ruts of conventional thinking, unable to see over the rims.

And part of that reason was that another of her gifts had turned into a curse. Carol had perfect recall of speech. It made her masterly in the interview room, enabling her to trap her victims in the toils of their own words. But these days, the tape that kept looping through her brain more often than not had nothing to do with what she was working on. She was working so hard not to hear the fragments of dialogue that crept under her guard that she had no space in her mind for those promptings of her subconscious that might just take her further forward.

Carol leaned her forehead against the cool mirror and closed her eyes. What she wouldn't give for a glass of wine right now.

The door to the ladies' toilets banged open and Paula rushed in. Carol jerked erect, taking in the startled reflection of her junior in the mirror. 'Hi, Paula,' she said wearily. Paula had been even more distant than usual at that morning's briefing. Carol tried not to take it personally, working on convincing herself that Paula had been scratchy with everyone. But she hadn't managed it.

'Chief,' Paula said, hesitating on her way to the cubicle. 'How did the review go?'

Carol pulled herself together, assuming the appearance of calm authority she knew she needed with a detective she feared was already on the road to writing her off. 'As you'd expect. Nobody's very happy with such conspicuous lack of progress in two very expensive inquiries. But at least they're not scaling us back just yet.' Carol made to pass Paula and head for the door. But Paula wasn't finished with her.

'I've been looking at the Tim Golding file again,' she said, her body language already on the defensive.

'Something strike you?' Carol tried to keep her voice as neutral as possible.

'That photo, chief. I don't know much about rocks and stuff, but the background looks pretty distinctive to me. I was wondering if there was any mileage in blacking out the image of the boy and asking climbing and rambling magazines to print it, see if anybody recognizes where it was taken?'

Carol nodded. Once that would have occurred to her. Now her thought processes were blurred with too many bad memories. *And too much wine*, a small voice in the back of her head muttered. 'Good idea, Paula. Ask Stacey to work something up and we'll get the press office to send it out asap.' Carol had taken a couple of steps towards the door when something in Paula's words triggered a faint memory. She half-turned just as Paula pushed open the cubicle door. 'Paula? What do you know about forensic geology?'

Paula looked puzzled. 'Forensic geology? Never heard of it, chief.'

'I heard something on the radio a few months ago. I wasn't really paying attention, but they were definitely talking about forensic geology. I wonder if someone like that might be able to help us narrow the location down?' Carol was thinking out loud rather than talking to Paula, but she was suddenly taken aback to see the DC's face light up in appreciation. It was as if this was the moment she'd been anticipating for weeks. It should have pleased Carol that she seemed finally to be dispelling the doubt she'd felt emanating from Paula. Instead, it saddened her to think that she'd been so far removed from her former self.

'That's a brilliant idea, chief,' Paula said, giving the thumbs-up sign.

'Maybe,' Carol said. 'For all I know, these guys just do the Sherlock Holmes thing of looking at the mud on your trousers and revealing which field you got splashed in. But it's worth a try.'

She walked back to the squadroom, telling the small condemnatory voice inside her that the white wine hadn't completely done for her brain cells. 'Sam,' she called as she crossed the floor. 'Get on to the BBC website and see what you can find under forensic geology.'

Sam looked up from his desk, startled by the unfamiliar vigour in Carol's voice. 'Sorry?'

'BBC website, forensic geology. Print out what you can find then get me somebody local to talk to,' Carol said over her shoulder. 'There's probably someone at the university earth sciences department who can point you in the right direction.' She closed her door behind her, shutting out the main room behind the recently installed blinds. She dropped into her chair and put her head in her hands, feeling a slither of sweat under her fingers. Christ, but it had been a long time coming, this small and blessed inspiration. It wasn't enough to solve anything. But at least it was a start. And she had some breathing space to explore it.

He looks at the tools of what has become his trade laid out before him. The handcuffs, the ankle restraints. The leather gag. The pliable rubber dildo. The razor blades. The latex gloves. The cameras. The laptop. The mobile. All he has to do now is slip the blades into the dildo then swaddle it in kitchen roll so it doesn't take his fingers off.

He presses <play> on his minidisk player and the Voice floods over him, taking him through it one more time. He doesn't need this reminder of what has to be done; he knows it by heart. But he likes to listen. Nobody ever made him feel this good, and what he does in return seems like a very small price to pay for something so right.

The Voice tells him who to pick, makes it easy for him. There's nothing left to chance. Tonight he'll find her round the corner from the shitty hotel just off Bellwether Street where they rent rooms by the hour to women like her. She'll be leaning against the big cast-iron litter bin, like as not. She'll be amused when he tells her what he wants from her, like as not. The women don't expect anything from him except always having good gear. He's just there. Part of the landscape. Not worth paying attention to.

But she'll pay attention tonight. It'll be the last bit of attention she pays to anybody. But it will be paid to him, and that means something.

The streetlights hung like luminous boiled sweets in the thin fog of the early evening. Bradfield's rush hour had spread like a middle-aged stomach even in the few years Tony had been away. But that evening, he was oblivious to his surroundings, working his way across town from Bradfield Moor to his new home on automatic pilot. Music spilled out of the tape player; he'd no idea what it was. Something soothing, minimalist and repetitive. One of his students back at St Andrews had given him the tape. He couldn't remember why now – something about brainwave function. He liked it because it covered up the background interference, shutting out road noise, other people's engines, the low subdued roar of the city's life.

He wondered about the task he'd set Tom Storey. Was he asking too much of a profoundly damaged man? Would Storey feel so pressurized that he'd blow up again? Tony didn't think so, but he couldn't know for sure. He'd gone way outside the limits this time, and he knew how bad he'd feel if it had any adverse effect on Storey.

It dawned on him that feeling bad might be the least of his worries. Aidan Hart would go ballistic if he found out what Tony had done. It flew in the face of every therapeutic regime in the book, but in Tony's view, the book had been written by people with at least as many problems as those they professed to treat. He knew this because he was one of them. His own difficulties with personal relationships of any kind, the impotence that had dogged him for most of his adult life, his failure to turn his feelings for Carol into any functional shape; these were all measures of his closeness to the ruined personalities he tended in his clinical role.

At least he knew he could do that with some semblance of competence. His empathy with their dysfunctionality made it possible for him to tease out useful treatment programmes. If it sometimes left him feeling uncomfortably complicit, that was a bearable trade-off.

What he couldn't reconcile himself to was the guilt he felt towards Carol. Right now, the best way to help her heal seemed to be helping her to do her job. And the key to that was Derek Tyler. Which went some way to providing him with self-justification for the process he'd set in motion.

'Oh, Derek, Derek, Derek. You crave the silence because that way you can still hear the voice,' he said out loud, continuing a conversation he'd been having with himself since he'd left the hospital. 'The voice does what?' He paused, thinking and feeling, before he answered himself. 'It reassures you. It tells you that what you did was good. If you couldn't hear the voice, you might have to consider that what you did was bad. So you need to hear the voice. So you don't talk, because that way nobody talks to you. So who's the voice?'

He turned off the main drag into a side street. It was only when he couldn't find a parking space that he realized he had come home to the wrong house. He was in the street where he'd lived the last time he'd worked in Bradfield. His automatic pilot had taken him to quite the wrong part of town.

Jackie Mayall walked into the hotel lobby. It wasn't much of a reception area; it wasn't much more than a large room with an alcove cut off by a chest-high counter. It had the kind of carpet visitors knew their feet would stick to. She leaned behind the counter, stretching to reach for a key. 'It's Jackie,' she shouted over the muffled hectic sound of Sky Sport coming from a room to the left of the grimy Formica counter. 'I've taken twenty-four.'

'Right. That's ten past six,' a voice called back. 'I'm writing it down, so don't you take the piss.'

'As if,' she muttered, heading for the threadbare narrow stairs that led up to the room on the second floor that she knew too miserably well. She let herself in and tried not to notice her surroundings. It was about as unappetizing a place for sex as it was possible to imagine. It could have served as a dictionary definition of scruffy, grimy or down-at-heel. A worn blue candlewick spread covered the sagging bed. The dressing table's cheap veneer was chipped and peeling. One upright chair sat by a dirty sink.

Jackie looked at herself in the mottled mirror. About time she dyed her hair again. She didn't care about the half-inch of black showing at the roots, but she understood the virtue of window dressing. Her skimpy skirt, halter-neck top, knee-length boots were all smarter than most of the girls on the street. She reckoned that was why she could afford to charge enough to bring most of her punters here, instead of shagging in shop doorways and bobbing over blow jobs in the backs of cars. Impatiently, she turned away, tossing her bag on the bed. She sat down on the edge of the bed, wondering if she should take off her boots or whether he'd want to see that for himself. He was paying her good money, after all. He deserved the best she could do for him.

A tentative knock at the door brought her to her

feet again. She yanked the door hard, to overcome the way it always stuck. She eyed him up and down, sardonic amusement in her eyes. 'Come on then, the meter's running,' she said, turning her back on him and heading straight for the bed. 'I've got no time for men who take all night.'

As soon as Tony walked through the door, he dialled Carol's number. 'Who's the voice, Derek?' he said, absently listening to the ring tone.

'Carol Jordan,' she said abruptly.

'Who's the voice, Carol,' he demanded without preamble. 'It doesn't make sense. None of the usual voices make sense.'

'Nice to talk to you too, Tony,' she said, weary humour in her tone.

'The thing about voices, they're a bit like past-life regression.'

'I'm sorry?'

'When people do those past-life regressions, they've never been a stable boy or a mill hand. They've always been Cleopatra or Henry the Eighth or Emma Hamilton. It's the same with people who hear voices. They don't hear the milkman or the woman who sits behind them on the bus every morning. They hear the Virgin Mary or John Lennon or Jack the Ripper.'

'Well, it's hard to imagine your average milkman giving out detailed instructions about carrying out sexual homicide,' Carol said drily.

Tony paused for a moment. He grinned. 'So you think it's more likely the Virgin Mary would be behind that?' Carol giggled. Tony felt a quick flash of pride. He'd done something very human. He'd made her laugh. He'd almost forgotten how much he liked the sound of her laughter, it had been so long since he'd heard it. 'But anyway,' he continued, covering up his momentary lapse from the professional, 'what I'm trying to get at is that these are grandiose voices. They live inside the head of the person hearing them and they are dynamic. What they say changes according to circumstance. You don't have to worry about silence. You don't need silence because the voice doesn't mind noise. It just makes itself heard when it wants to be, whenever it's convenient. Well, convenient for the person hearing the voice, not usually convenient for the rest of us,' he added hastily.

'And you're saying Derek Tyler's voice isn't like that?'

'That's exactly what I'm saying. It's as if he's scared of losing it. Scared that it might get swallowed up in the background noise. I've never come across anything quite like it, not in life, not in the literature. It's as if . . .' He shook his head. 'I need to go and do some more research. There must be something in the literature . . . Unless we're breaking completely new ground.' His voice tailed off.

'Tony?'

'I'll call you. I need to think about this. Thanks for listening to me.' Whatever she said in reply was lost as he hung up the phone. He'd never encountered anything like Derek Tyler's voice. If it broke all the rules, maybe it was time for him to do the same thing. Instead of working with probabilities, maybe he should start considering improbabilities. He headed upstairs to his study, muttering, 'Six impossible things before breakfast.'

DS Kevin Matthews stood behind the Woolpack Hotel reception desk, notebook in hand. There wasn't much room behind the counter, which meant he was uncomfortably close to the seedy individual who had introduced himself as Jimmy de Souza, night manager. In spite of the stench of sweat, cigarettes and stale pizza that ballooned around de Souza, Kevin preferred this view to what was upstairs in room 24. One quick look had been enough to tell him that interviewing the man who had found the body was definitely not the short straw. Much better to be down here where there was nothing more disturbing to see than a cheesy night manager and a stream of SOCOs and cops going in and out.

De Souza was stocky, with a round belly that strained his grubby white T-shirt and the waistband of his shell-suit trousers. His black hair was greased back from a sharp widow's peak, and a rosebud mouth over a plump, rounded chin gave him a look of petulance. 'Look, I told you,' he said, a faint trace of distant parts underpinning his Bradfield accent, 'I only come out if somebody rings the bell. People like their privacy. That's what they're paying for.'

'By the hour,' Kevin said, his voice acidic.

'So? It's not against the law, is it, renting rooms by the hour? People have needs.' De Souza started to pick his nose then thought better of it as he noticed Kevin's lip curl in distaste.

'So you rented out room twenty-four when exactly?'

De Souza pointed to a thick desk diary lying open on the ledge beneath the counter. 'There. Ten past six.'

Kevin glanced at it. The time and a name scrawled next to it in a clumsy hand. 'And who did you rent it out to? I'm assuming – correct me if I'm wrong – it wasn't Margaret Thatcher.'

'Slag calls herself Jackie. Skinny bit of stuff with bleach-blonde hair. She used to come in most nights a few times.'

'You don't know her surname?'

De Souza leered. 'You kidding? Who's interested?'

'Who was she with?'

'I dunno. I was in the back, watching the football. She shouted through that she was taking the key and I just wrote down the time. She'd settle up on her way out. I like to give the regulars a bit of leeway.'

'So you didn't see who was with her?' Kevin asked again.

'I don't even know if he was with her. Often the blokes hang back a few minutes, so nobody sees them. The girls just tell them what room to come to.'

'Very handy,' Kevin said bitterly. 'So what made you go up there?'

'Her time was well up, wasn't it? Normally, she's out of there in half an hour or so. Like I said, she'd settle up and I'd go and change the sheets. When the match finished at the back of eight, the key was sitting there on the hook. I was pissed off, I thought she'd done a runner on me. So I went up to see if she'd left the money in there. I went to twenty-four and let myself in . . .' For the first time, de Souza looked uncomfortable. 'Christ, I'm not going to be able to let that room out again in a hurry.'

Kevin looked at de Souza as if he'd like to hit him. 'My heart bleeds for you.' He reached over with his pen and snagged the key of room 24 off its hook. He slipped it into a paper evidence bag and tucked it away in his pocket. 'We'll need to hang on to that for the time being,' he said. 'But, like you said, you're not going to be needing it any time soon.'

His words roused de Souza's self-interest. 'How long are you lot going to be keeping us out of business?'

Kevin smiled sweetly. 'As long as it takes. This is a crime scene now, pal.'

As he spoke, the street door opened again and Carol Jordan strode in. 'Where am I going, Kevin?' she said.

'Second floor, guv. Room twenty-four. Don's up there with Jan and Paula. And the SOCOs.'

'I'm on my way.'

Tom Storey hadn't been lying when he'd said he had people skills. His work as a housing benefits officer had been fraught with the underlying threat of violence, both verbal and physical. Until his recent erratic behaviour had seen him sent home on sick leave, he'd always been known as the one the bosses could rely on to prevent an awkward client losing it in the worst way. That was why the task Tony Hill had given him seemed less a burden than a genuine challenge he thought he might be able to rise to.

Incarcerated in Bradfield Moor, burdened both with crushing guilt and the fear of the unknown invader eating away his brain, he'd tried to distract himself by watching his fellow inmates. It helped him stay in control of his mind if he had something outside himself to focus on. Of course, the ones who were allowed a certain freedom of movement were the ones who were regarded as safe in the sense that they weren't about to run amok with a sharpened fork: the obsessive compulsives who were mostly a danger to themselves; the schizophrenics meekly medicated; the manic depressives kept on a level by lithium. In a way, they were more interesting to him than the violent. Tom found it easier to understand how they'd slipped the cogs of normalcy. He didn't like to think of the personality-disordered ones; he'd seen enough sociopaths in the course of his previous professional life to last him the rest of his days.

When Tony had described Derek Tyler, Storey had known at once who he meant. He'd been aware of his silent stillness, mostly because there was so little of it around the place. Even those drugged up to their eyeballs tended towards the twitchy. But Tyler seemed to exist in a little oasis of quiet. Not that there was anything tranquil about him. He gave off an air of tension that made others wary.

He didn't join in, either. That was something else that marked him out. He displayed no interest in social activities, and his passive resistance to anything approaching communal treatment was impressive, all the more so because Storey reckoned he wasn't that bright.

All of this made him easily identifiable. But very hard to reach. This was no straightforward undertaking that Tony Hill had laid on his shoulders. Storey had spent most of the day covertly watching Tyler whenever he got the chance, trying to figure out a way to crack the carapace. Nothing suggested itself.

In the early evening, when most of those conscious and out of their rooms were watching the TV soaps, he saw Tyler sitting alone at a table in the corner of the day room. On the spur of the moment, Storey helped himself to one of the jigsaws stacked on the bookshelves and walked across to Tyler's table. He sat down without asking, struggled to open the box with one hand but managed it at last. He tipped out the pieces, finding a moment to wonder how many of the 550 would be present and correct.

No reaction. Tyler seemed to withdraw further into himself. But Storey could see his eyes drawn to the muddle of die-cut cardboard in spite of himself. Storey started sorting through the pieces awkwardly, looking for edges and sky. 'The easiest bit and then the hardest bit,' he said. 'After you get the sky done, the rest feels possible.'

Tyler said nothing. The silence endured while Storey constructed the border of the picture. It was an Alpine view, a funicular railway ascending a mountain that turned from meadow to icecap. He made a couple of deliberate mistakes, but Tyler didn't react. So he corrected himself and carried on.

'I'm feeling quite cheerful tonight,' he said, carefully not looking at anything other than the jigsaw. 'I've got to have an operation, but after that, I think

I'm going to be out of here.' He glanced up at Tyler. 'You know what I did, right?' It was a fair bet. In spite of the best efforts of the clinical staff to prevent patients gossiping about the past transgressions of others, news travelled Bradfield Moor like rats mapping their nocturnal territory. 'I killed my kids.' He couldn't help it; tears welled up in Storey's eyes and he brushed them away impatiently. 'I thought that was it. I'd never see the outside world again. To be honest, I wasn't about to argue with that. I mean, how could I be trusted? How could I trust myself? If I could take the lives of the people I loved most in the whole world, how could anybody be safe?'

Tyler showed no sign that he had heard a word. Storey persevered. It wasn't as if he had anything else to do. 'And the way the staff treat me, I can see that, behind all their professionalism, they think I'm beyond redemption. They're used to dealing with sick people. But they make me feel like I'm special, like what I've done sets me even further apart than everybody else. That's the one thing nobody ever forgives, killing your children. Or so I thought, until I met this new doctor they've got.' He smiled. 'Dr Hill. He's not like the rest of them. He's big on getting people out of here. He made me see that it's not impossible to be made better. To start again on the outside. I tell you, you want to get out of this dump, he's the one you need to see.'

Tyler reached out a tentative finger and pushed a piece towards Storey. It was the next in a sequence of jagged grey that would eventually reveal itself as a glacier, hard up against the left-hand edge. Storey tried not to show his delight. 'Thanks, mate,' he said nonchalantly. He carried on in silence for a few minutes.

'I wish to Christ I'd met Dr Hill months ago,' Storey eventually said, this time speaking from the heart with genuine resentment. 'He knew right away what was wrong with me. If my GP hadn't just fobbed me off with a bottle of pills, if he'd sent me to see somebody who knew what they were doing, I wouldn't even be here now. My kids would still be alive and I wouldn't be here.'

Tyler shifted in his seat, turning away from the table. Storey sensed he had somehow lost momentum with the silent man. 'But the thing about Dr Hill . . . he's making me see that that's not the end of my life. That I can go back into the world and start again. And next time, I can do better. I can get it right, maybe. With help, I can get it right.'

Storey wasn't sure what it was that he'd said, but something had worked. Tyler moved back towards the table. He studied the pieces, then picked one up and slotted it in. His eyes met Storey's and there was a flicker of some unidentifiable emotion. Tyler nodded slowly, then got to his feet. He walked past Storey, pausing to pat his shoulder. Then he was gone, a silent shadow slipping out of the room and into the hallway.

Storey leaned back in his chair, a faintly perplexed smile on his face. He wasn't sure if his tactics had worked, but he had a feeling he might have earned himself some brownie points with the man who could set him free, both from Bradfield Moor and from the prison of his thoughts.

* * *

Carol had taken one look at the crime scene and called Tony. Now he stood by the bed, his head bowed, reverential. Carol could almost believe that he was blind to the tide of scarlet that had swept the dead woman's life away, so focused did he appear to be on her gagged face. She didn't have that luxury. The corpse on the bed felt like a personal affront, a calculated reminder that she and her team had failed the challenge of this killer's last outing. Intellectually, she knew it was nothing of the sort; men who did this sort of thing were far less interested in their audience than in the contents of their own sick heads. But emotionally, it felt like a slap in the face.

'There's no doubt about it, is there?' she said softly to Tony.

He looked up at her, his eyes unreadable in the weak light from the sixty-watt bulb inside its dusty paper shade. 'None whatsoever. Whoever killed Sandie killed this one too.'

Carol turned to Jan and Paula, standing on the threshold waiting for their orders. 'Do we know who she is?'

Jan nodded. 'Jackie Mayall. She's relatively new on the scene. A smackhead, but one of the more or less functioning ones.'

'Did she have a pimp?'

'Not any more. When she started, she was working for Lee Myerson. But he's doing five for dealing smack. When we lifted him, we put the word out that his team was to leave the girls alone unless they wanted a taste of the same medicine. Since we started waving the Proceeds of Crime legislation around, a lot of shitty little ponces have had to trade in their fancy motors.'

'OK. So Jackie worked solo. But she must have had mates. Jan, I want you and Paula to hit the bricks. Get out there and talk to the women. Find out who else uses this flophouse. Who was here tonight. Who saw Jackie earlier on. Whether she had any regulars. You know the drill.'

The two women were already on the move. 'Paula, where's Don?' Carol called after them.

Paula turned, her face startled. Her voice said, 'I don't know, chief,' but her expression was a wary version of *Why are you asking me?*

'He was here earlier,' Jan said. 'He told Kevin to interview the manager. He got me and Paula to check out the other rooms. Of course, nobody heard anything or saw anything, not even when we threatened to tell their wives. Then after the police surgeon did the preliminaries, I think Don went off with Sam to see what they could pick up on the street.'

Carol hid her irritation. If Don Merrick wanted to be taken seriously as a DI, he had to start behaving like one. Canvassing the streets was a job for junior officers. He should have been here co-ordinating the rest of the team, at least until she arrived, not rushing off into the night. 'I want him at the post mortem,' she said. 'Tell him to liaise with Dr Vernon's team.'

Tony had moved away from the bedside to allow the scenes of crime technicians room to practise their arcane mysteries. Carol crossed to his side, close but not quite touching. 'It looks like she's bled every drop of blood from her body,' she said. 'He's out of control.'

'It's not a lack of control. It's overkill, true, but it's

overkill in a very specific way. It's about power. The abuse of power taken to the nth degree.'

'And he's going to do it again,' she said heavily.

'No doubt about it. He enjoys it far too much to stop now. And I think he's getting more confident.'

Carol's face wrinkled in distaste. 'What do you mean?'

'Remember Vernon said Sandie must have taken at least an hour to die? And yet he set this one up in a room that rents by the hour. He was taking the chance that he would run over time. He must have felt assured enough to deal with that if he had to.'

Carol shook her head. 'That would be a hell of a risk. He'd multiply his chances of being seen, surely?'

'There's that,' Tony agreed. 'But he doesn't seem to be prone to risk-taking. Power Assertive, remember? Keep the dangers to a minimum. Maybe it's got more to do with his confidence levels. Maybe he feels assertive enough now to know that he could kill his way out of the problem.'

Carol drew her breath in sharply. 'I don't like the sound of that.'

'No. But it's something you have to consider.'

'Who am I looking for, Tony? What can you give me?'

He frowned. 'He's white, male, mid-twenties to mid-thirties. He's not good with authority – he thinks he's underestimated by the world. If he has a job, his employment record will be spotty. But I think he's more likely to be self-employed, semi-skilled. Hires himself out casually to whoever has a job for him, but he never lasts long with the same employer because he thinks he knows best. Only he doesn't. Socially he gets by. He doesn't have close male friends, but he's got a circle of acquaintances. He's very unlikely to be in a relationship with a woman.' Tony pulled a wry face. 'And he'll be impotent except when he's doing this.' He shrugged. 'Not much to go on, I'm afraid.'

'It's a start,' Carol said, knowing how often unpromising beginnings led somewhere productive with Tony. 'And God knows, right now any kind of start is something I'm not going to sniff at.'

He feels good tonight. He's kept his promise to himself. This time it worked. He was strong and he was a man. Now, sitting in the bar sipping lager, acting like it was any other night and he was having a well-deserved pint, he hugs his secret to himself, knowing the activity on the street is all down to him.

They found this one quicker, just as the Voice planned. OK, the delay in finding Sandie worked to his advantage. Time had passed and any witnesses had scattered to the four winds, leaving only the regulars who wouldn't even notice him. But it had been nerve-racking, waiting and wondering. None of that this time, though. He knew Jimmy de Souza would be up those stairs like a rat up a drain as soon as he realized the key was back on its hook and he hadn't been paid. Greedy little shit. Served him right, coming face to face with something that would put him right off his food for days. He remembers de Souza taking the piss once, years ago. It feels good to get payback. Two birds with one stone.

But it was scary, being in the hotel room with her bleeding to death. It seemed to take forever, and although that really got him excited, he felt exposed there in that room in a way he wasn't with Sandie. There were other people in the building. There was greedy Jimmy to consider. But the Voice had told him what to do if he was spotted. He hadn't relished the thought of unsheathing his knife and plunging it into someone's belly. It felt out of control, not part of their carefully staged cleansing. But the Voice had explained how it might one day be necessary, and he'd told himself he was ready for it, capable of it.

He looks out of the big picture window of the bar into the street. There they are, the plod, notebooks out, taking names and addresses that'd be bullshit half the time. Asking people what they'd seen, where they'd been. Looking for alibis, looking for witnesses, looking for a killer who was under their noses. But they can't smell him. He's out of their reach, safe and sound in the pub with his pint. He smiles and remembers a tag from childhood. 'Run, run as fast as you can, you can't catch me, I'm the gingerbread man.' That's him, all right. The gingerbread man.

Jan and Paula decided to start close to the hotel. There were a couple of bars in Bellwether Street close to the narrow entry that led to the Woolpack Hotel. As they walked down the street, Jan shivered in the foggy night air and pulled on her gloves. 'It's bitter tonight,' she said. 'The girls who work out of doors won't be doing so well.'

'Bloody awful life,' Paula said with feeling, turning up her coat collar against the chill clinging hand of the mist.

'So what's it like, living with Don Merrick?' Jan said conversationally.

Paula flashed her a look of surprise. 'News travels fast,' she said.

'No secrets in a nick,' Jan said.

'Then you'll know I'm not living with him in the biblical sense,' Paula said sharply. 'He's sleeping in my spare room. Just till he gets himself sorted out.'

Jan laughed. 'He'll be there for a while, then. It's all right, Paula, I know you're not shacked up with Don.'

There was something in her tone that made Paula uneasy. 'Good. So you won't mind keeping everybody else straight on that one.'

'Is that what you want? You really want me to tell everybody how I can be so sure you're not sharing your bed as well as your microwave with Don?' There was a playful, teasing edge in her voice now.

Paula stopped in mid-stride. 'And what's that supposed to mean?' she asked, a hollow feeling in her stomach.

Jan wheeled round to face her, a smile turning her cherub's face into a picture of innocence. 'Rainbow Flesh, Leeds. On the dance floor. I think it was the dance mix of Beth Orton's "Central Reservation". Your partner was very cute. Mixed race. Tat of a snake on her shoulder.'

Paula tried not to show the shock that seemed physically to ripple through her muscles. 'Not me,' she said automatically, not even pausing to figure out that even by asking this, Jan was making her own confession. She started walking again. 'You obviously have more time off than I do if you're out clubbing,' she added, trying to make light of this moment when her worst fear had assumed the shape of reality. She felt sick.

'It's all right, Paula, I'm not going to tell,' Jan said, falling into step beside her. 'Think about it. I've got as much to lose as you do. We both know that, no matter what the brass say, the street cops aren't going to be our friends if we're out.'

'There's nothing to tell,' Paula said sharply. She wanted time to think about this, not fall into false comradeship with someone she didn't know well enough to trust. She headed across the street, not bothering to see if Jan was following her. 'There's a woman over there, looks like she's working. Let's go and check her out.'

Jan followed, the cherub smile still on her face.

Next morning, the fog had thickened to a dismal shroud, a pale grey tinged with sulphurous yellow. Traffic crawled through the city streets and the morning DJ on Bradfield Sound was beginning to betray his exasperation at the length of the traffic reports. Normally, it wouldn't have impinged on Tony, who would have used the time to escape inside his head. But this morning he was impatient to get to work.

He'd come home from the ugliness in room 24 of the Woolpack to a message on his answering machine from Aidan Hart. When he'd returned the call, his boss had sounded both bemused and faintly annoyed. 'Derek Tyler wants to see you,' he'd said.

'He asked?' Tony wondered what on earth Tom Storey had done to break the logjam of Tyler's silence.

'He didn't use his voice, if that's what you mean. He wrote a note, gave it to one of the nurses. "I want to see Dr Hill." That's all it said. But the nurse thought it was enough of a breakthrough to call me on my mobile,' he added petulantly.

'I'm sorry your evening's been disturbed,' Tony said, not bothering to thread regret into his voice. 'That's great news. Thanks for letting me know.'

'I've booked you an appointment with him at nine tomorrow morning,' Hart continued.

Sorry, Carol, he thought. 'That's fine. I'll be there.'

'In the interview room with the observation window,' Hart added. 'I want to see this for myself.'

Tony cursed the weather and the traffic and wished he knew the back streets of Bradfield well enough to get off the main drag and cut through the back doubles to his destination. At this rate, he was going to be late, and he had a feeling that would bring altogether too much pleasure to Aidan Hart.

Suddenly, for no apparent reason, the cars in front of him started to move at something approximating the speed limit. Tony surged forward, saying a prayer of thanks to whatever god governed Bradfield's erratic traffic flow. *Must be a malicious bastard,* he thought irreverently.

He arrived at the hospital with seven minutes to spare. Tony didn't bother going to his office; he made straight for the observation booth behind the interview room. As he turned into the corridor, he bumped into one of the orderlies. 'Sorry,' he said, stumbling slightly.

The orderly put a hand on his elbow to steady him. 'It's OK, Doc. You're here to see Tyler, right?'

'That's right. He's not changed his mind, has he?' he asked, seized by a sudden apprehension.

The orderly shrugged. 'Who knows? Tyler's not saying. Your boss had a crack at him last night and got nowhere.'

'Dr Hart spoke to him last night?'

The orderly nodded. 'Soon as he got the message, he was out here, telling Tyler that he might as well save everybody's time by talking to him instead of you.'

Politics, Tony thought bitterly. *He wants the glory of getting Tyler to talk.* He spread his hands in a gesture of innocence and opened the door of the observation room. Hart was already there, lounging in a chair, one ankle balanced on the other knee. 'Glad you could make it,' he said.

'Traffic,' Tony said. 'Fog.'

'Yes, I was glad I set off quarter of an hour earlier than usual,' Hart said smugly. 'Well, this is a bit of a turn-up for the books. I thought Tyler had put you in your place the last time you spoke. But it seems he wants to say more. How did you do it?' He straightened up and leaned forward. He really wanted to know. But now Tony knew about Hart's attempt to muscle in the night before, he was determined not to tell.

'Natural charm, Aidan. Natural charm.' Tony smiled and walked out. He was waiting in the interview room when the door opened and Derek Tyler entered. He walked with a kind of cramped stoop that made him look older than his years. The knobbly skull gleamed in the lights as he sat down opposite Tony, who gave him an encouraging look. 'Hello, Derek,' he said. 'Nice to see you again.'

Nothing. But at least this time Tyler was staring at

him, not acting as if there was nobody in the room other than himself. Tony stuck out his legs, crossed them at the ankle and put his hands behind his head. It was as open and relaxed a position as it was possible to adopt on a hard plastic chair. 'So, what did you want to talk about?'

Nothing. 'OK,' Tony said. 'I'll start. I think you're just about ready to give up. You've kept the faith. You've stayed true to the voice in your head. But now you're wondering if there was any point in that. Like I told you when we spoke before, somebody else has taken over your job. He's out there, doing what you were doing. And he's cleverer than you, because he's not been caught yet.'

Tyler blinked several times, like a matinee idol fluttering his eyelashes. His lips parted and the tip of his tongue flickered from one side to the other. But he said nothing.

'I think the voice has given up on you.'

Tyler's eyes narrowed and his thumbs rubbed against the tips of his index fingers.

'Because you can't give satisfaction any longer, can you, Derek? You can't take these bitches off the street any more.'

Tyler shook his head. He seemed frustrated. Then his mouth opened and the words spilled out, dry and cracked. 'I know what you're trying to do. You don't want to help me, you want me to help you. But you can't take the Voice away from me. It's mine. I only do what it tells me to. And until the Voice tells me I can talk to you, I can't.' He pushed his chair back and abruptly stood up. He walked to the door and knocked, a demand for release.

He didn't look back. If he had, he would have seen a slow grin spreading across Tony's face.

Carol leaned against the wall of the mortuary, watching Dr Vernon make his initial assessments of the remains of Jackie Mayall. The acrid traces of chemicals combined with the ripe aromas coming from the body to make her sinuses ache. At least, that was how she explained her headache to herself. Vernon was taking the scrapings from under the victim's fingernails when Don Merrick burst through the door, looking anxious and faintly dishevelled. 'Sorry, ma'am,' he said, his eyes hangdog. 'The traffic was a nightmare. The fog . . .'

'Same fog for all of us, Don,' Carol said.

'I know, but . . .' His voice tailed off. He couldn't explain that he'd miscalculated because he was unfamiliar with the traffic patterns where Paula lived. Not without explaining everything else.

'And last night,' Carol said, keeping her voice low so the mortuary staff wouldn't hear her giving Merrick a bollocking. 'What was that about? You were the senior officer on the scene and you left it to go and do a job that should be left to DCs and uniforms. When I arrived, Paula and Jan were standing around like a pair of spare parts, not knowing whether they were supposed to be working the streets or waiting for me.'

'I told them to interview everybody else in the hotel,' Merrick said defensively.

'Which didn't take them very long since only two other rooms were occupied, and by people who were more interested in their own activities than in anything else that was going on. Don, you're not a sergeant any more. I need to know you're on top of things when I'm not there. You can't just walk away from the scene of a murder and expect everybody else to do the right thing.'

Merrick hung his head. 'I'm sorry, ma'am. It won't happen again.'

'It better not. I've got enough on my plate without having to worry about covering your back from above and below.'

Merrick flinched at the sharpness in Carol's tone. He hoped the information he could provide might go some small way to redeeming himself in her eyes. 'At least we got an address for the victim,' he said. 'It took a while, but we tracked her down to a bedsit in Comb Moss. We got the landlord out of bed at three this morning and turned the place over.'

Carol's severe expression relaxed a little. 'So what do we know?'

'Jackie Mayall moved to Bradfield about eighteen months ago. Originally she came from Hayfield. I spoke to one of the local lads on my way in. Usual sort of story. One of four kids, parents long-term unemployed. Left school at sixteen, not much work around. She did casual shifts in one of the factories, but never managed to land a full-time job. Time-keeping wasn't her strong point, apparently. She drifted into heroin and then into prostitution to pay for the stuff. Little place like Hayfield, it was hard to avoid getting nicked, so she moved up to the big city. The landlord says he knew she was on heroin, but he wasn't bothered because she was no trouble as a tenant. I tell you, her bedsit was the cleanest, tidiest place I've ever seen a smackhead living in.' Merrick could see it now: a neatly made double bed, a couple of cheap armchairs with brightly printed throws covering their threadbare upholstery; a spotless cooking area with a combi oven scrubbed to a gleam; clothes hanging neatly on a rail; TV and video free from dust, and half a dozen chick-lit paperbacks on the mantelpiece. It had been pitiful, really. A sad simulacrum of normal life lurking behind the chipped door in one of the poorest parts of town. 'Not much of a life,' he said.

Carol sighed. 'Even so, it was still hers. And then some bastard comes along and takes it from her.' She cleared her throat and stepped forward. 'What do you think, Doc? Same killer?'

Vernon glanced up at her. 'She was killed in the same way. If anything, her injuries were more severe. I'd guess that her killer used a longer implement this time. The internal damage goes deeper. Chances are she didn't live as long as Sandie Foster. The pain must have been excruciating. She would have gone into shock fairly soon after the initial attack.'

Carol shuddered. 'What kind of person does this?'

'That's a question for Dr Hill, not for me. All I can tell you is what he does, not why he does it. Except that he's definitely getting some sort of sexual thrill from it.'

'That's hardly news,' Merrick muttered.

Vernon gave him a sharp look. 'I deal in the realms of fact, Inspector, not theory. I know he's getting some sort of sexual thrill because there are traces of semen on Jackie Mayall's stomach.'

* * *

The steam on the inside of the windows of Stan's Café always made it look as if mist was hanging along the canal in Temple Fields. DS Kevin Matthews pushed the door open and went from cold fog to warm fug. He wasn't sure it was an improvement. He took a folded A4 sheet of paper from his pocket and sat down at the first table by the door. The vacant-looking young man in a hooded top who was already seated there looked surprised, as if Kevin had broken some unwritten rule. Kevin unfolded the paper, revealing a computer printout taken from a snapshot of Jackie Mayall that Merrick had found in her flat. It showed Jackie raising a glass to the camera, her blonde hair bleached white by the flash. Merrick had tinkered with the photograph to get rid of the red-eye. Now it just looked as if her pupils were unnaturally dilated. 'Probably not so far off normal,' Sam had grunted as he'd picked up his copy and set off with Kevin to do the rounds. They'd split up, Sam taking the convenience store and the burger bar round the corner.

'All right, mate?' Kevin asked.

The young man nodded eagerly. 'Yeah. I'm all right. I'm Jason.'

And you're a few bricks short of a wall, Kevin thought, adjusting his attitude without condescending. 'Hi, Jason, I'm Kevin. I'm a policeman.'

He held out the picture of Jackie. Jason looked at it, then raised his eyes to Kevin. 'Why have you got a picture of Jackie? Is she your girlfriend? Have you lost her?'

'You knew Jackie?'

'Jackie. I know Jackie. Jackie comes in here for cups of hot chocolate.'

'I'm sorry to have to tell you that Jackie's dead. She was murdered last night.'

Jason's mouth fell open. 'No. Not Jackie, that can't be right. Jackie's a nice woman. You must have made a mistake.'

Kevin shook his head. 'No mistake, I'm afraid. I'm sorry.'

'That doesn't make sense. Jackie was nice,' Jason repeated.

'Did you ever talk to her?'

Jason looked embarrassed. 'Not really. Not talk talk. Just "Hello, how're you doing?"'

Before Kevin could ask more, a couple of youths unpeeled themselves from the fruit machine and dropped into the other two chairs at the table. 'You a cop?' one asked.

Kevin nodded. 'And you are?'

The stockier of the two youths squared his shoulders in a pathetic parody of manliness. 'I'm Tyrone Donelan.'

'And what do you do, Tyrone?' Kevin asked, trying to keep the sarcasm from his voice.

'About thirty-five to the gallon.' He guffawed at his own joke. 'I'm a mechanic,' he said. 'Anything to do with cars, I'm your man.'

Anything to do with nicking cars, Kevin thought cynically. 'And who's your mate?'

Donelan jerked his head towards the other lad. 'This is Carl. Carl Mackenzie. Say hello to the nice policeman, Carl.'

Mackenzie grunted something and looked away, tracing lines in a scatter of spilled sugar on the tabletop. 'And what do you do, Carl?' Kevin asked.

Mackenzie's mouth twitched as if he wasn't sure what was expected of him. 'Nothing much,' he said.

Kevin pushed the photograph of Jackie towards them. 'Either of you know Jackie Mayall?' Before they could answer, the door opened and Dee Smart walked in. She looked around and, seeing Kevin, crossed straight to the table and stood glaring down at him. The lads all seemed to brighten at the sight of her. 'This is Dee. This is Kevin,' Jason recited like a child who's proud of recently acquired social skills.

'I know Kevin,' Dee said sourly, fixing him with a hard stare. 'I thought you said you lot cared about us? That we weren't just throwaways?' Her voice was loud enough to attract attention from the surrounding tables.

Kevin flushed an ugly red, his freckles seeming to darken. 'You're not,' he said quietly.

'So how come there's another one of us lying in the morgue? And how come you've got nothing better to do than harass an innocent kid? Why don't you get off your arse and find out who's killing my mates?' Dee turned on her heel and teetered off to the counter.

Jason gave a pained smile while Carl tittered. 'I don't think Dee likes you, Kevin,' Tyrone jeered.

Kevin looked around at the hostile stares pointed in his direction. 'I don't think she's the only one, Tyrone.' He stood up wearily, knowing there was nothing more to be gained in the café while Dee was in this mood.

It was impossible to miss the police presence in Temple Fields that morning. Tony saw several officers he recognized as he walked through the streets and lanes.

The fog was slowly dissipating, leaving the odd swirling pocket that seemed to swallow people whole as they walked into it. It was hard not to feel the weather was responding to the atmosphere of foreboding in the city's dark heart.

Tony stopped outside his destination. The window was brightly lit, its contents mostly innocuous: sex, it implied, was always and only fun. He pushed open the door and walked in. He'd been in sex shops before, but not for a while. What surprised him was how matter-of-fact it all seemed. Upbeat techno music played in the background. There was nothing hidden or coy about the items on display; everything was laid out for the customers to choose from. The implied message was that whatever consenting adults wanted to do in private was fine and dandy.

He wandered round, taking it all in. There were things here whose purpose he could only guess at, which he found slightly disturbing, given his area of expertise. Tony stopped by a section of shelves dedicated to bondage restraints. Chains, cuffs, gags. nipple clamps and various arcane objects clustered together like varieties of baked beans in a supermarket. Tony picked up a set of leather ankle restraints that looked similar to those they'd found on Jackie. He looked at the price and raised his eyebrows. 'Whatever you are, you're not cheap. Power has its price and you're willing to pay.' He spoke softly, but not so softly that it didn't catch the attention of the man behind the counter. He emerged from his station and walked over to Tony.

'Can I help you, sir?' he asked.

Tony looked up, seeing a tall, lean figure wearing

a leather waistcoat over tanned and tattooed skin. The salesman had a line of twinkling diamond studs down the ridge of each ear. 'Sell a lot of these, do you?' he said.

'More than you might think. People like to spice up their love lives.' The look he gave Tony seemed to suggest he could well imagine his love life needed spicing up.

Tony fondled the cuffs absentmindedly. 'Maybe that's where I've been going wrong. What sort of people buy them?'

'All sorts.' The assistant looked wary.

Tony tried for the harmless look. 'My interest is purely professional. I'm a clinical psychologist,' he said apologetically.

The assistant rolled his eyes as if he'd heard it all before. 'Like I said, all sorts. You get your obvious S&M types, all piercings and black leather, but you get your suburban housewives too.'

'Sex. The great melting pot. Thanks. I'll take these.' He handed over the ankle cuffs and added a pair of metal handcuffs. 'All in the interests of research.' He headed towards the till, glancing back at the assistant, who was eyeing him as if he wasn't fit to be out on his own. It wasn't the first time Tony had caught such a look directed at himself. He didn't find it insulting; rather, he was impressed by their perspicacity. *Passing for human,* he thought. *Except I don't always succeed.*

He emerged a few minutes later, wondering idly if he could claim the cost back as a legitimate expense from Bradfield Police. On balance, he thought he'd prefer not to try. Carol might understand why he needed them, but he suspected some clerk in accounts would take a dimmer view. Especially once they found out, as they surely would, where Carol was living now.

He headed back towards his car. As he rounded a corner, he spotted DS Jan Shields talking to a woman in the skimpy uniform of a prostitute. The woman's body language said this wasn't a conversation she relished. Seeing him approach, Jan cut the interview short and watched the woman hurry away. As he grew closer, Jan pointed to his bag. 'Who's the lucky lady, then?'

Tony looked bemused. He looked down at the bag and saw the logo of the sex shop plastered along the side. He shrugged. 'Head games. I need to understand the killer's rules. It sometimes helps to play with the same toys.'

'You think this is a game? Women are being slaughtered like stuck pigs and you think it's a game?' Her tone was amused rather than outraged.

'He does. You have to remember that some people take their games very seriously. Life and death stuff, like Bill Shankly said.'

Jan nodded, getting it. 'And your job is to beat him at his own game?'

Tony considered her words. 'No. It's my job to figure out the rules. You're the ones who get to play out the endgame. How's it going?'

She shook her head. 'Slowly. Truth is, we need a lucky break. Someone has to have seen something. It's just a question of finding them before he does.'

Tony looked at her with surprise. It was an insight he hadn't expected. 'I think you're right,' he said slowly. 'I think he's ready for more.'

* * *

Oscar's, Paula thought, was one of those bars that had never been anything other than a dump. She could read the signs. Even on the day it had opened after its last makeover, it still would have looked exactly what it was – a cut-price version of anything approximating style. Everything reeked of cheapness. The lightbulbs were too low a wattage, but it was still possible to see where poorly applied varnish streaked the pine in a vain attempt to make it look like expensive hardwood. The signboards scattered round the walls screamed special offers on beer, shots and happy-hour doubles.

Paula looked around for her target. Her canvass of the streets had turned up a single nugget so far. One of the girls who worked in a sauna on the fringes of Temple Fields had told her that Jackie Mayall sometimes turned double tricks with a young hooker who worked under the street name of Honey. 'This time of day, you'll likely catch her in Oscar's. You can't miss her. She'll be the one in the red rubber dress with the Bacardi Breezer,' the girl had said, looking apprehensively over her shoulder to make sure nobody overheard her passing information to a copper.

It was a description that fitted perfectly the kid sitting at the corner table, swigging her drink straight from the bottle. Her dark hair was streaked with magenta; a shade one of Paula's friends had once characterized as 'prostitute purple' when her home dye job had gone wrong. Paula's heart contracted at Honey's obvious youth. She didn't look old enough to be served legally with what she was drinking, that was for sure. Paula went up to the bar where half a dozen early lunchtime drinkers nursed their pints morosely. She bought a mineral water and another Bacardi Breezer and walked across to the table. She placed the drinks on the table and sat down. Honey's look of surprise shifted to one of hostile suspicion. 'Cop,' she said derisively.

'Cop with a drink for you,' Paula said.

'You think I'm that fucking cheap?' Honey sneered.

Paula sighed. 'I didn't come here to pick a fight, Honey. I came here because one of your friends is dead.'

Honey gave her a look of pure hatred. 'You lot don't give a fuck about us. We're just shit on legs to you. Jackie wouldn't be dead if you useless fuckers did what you're paid for and protected us like you protect the nice people in their nice houses.'

'That's what we're trying to do. But it's not easy when all we get is silence and lies. I'm not after you, Honey. I'm trying to protect you and your colleagues. That's why I need your help.'

Honey snorted. 'Colleagues? Fuck, that's a new word for whores.'

Paula leaned forward, her face passionate, her eyes boring into Honey's. 'Can't have it both ways, Honey. Can't slag us off for dissing you then slag us off some more when we try to show a bit of respect. I don't think you're shit on legs, actually. I save that for the scumbags who use you and abuse you. And I don't think you deserve what you mostly get. The bastard who killed Jackie? I want to put him away for the rest of his natural life. So talk to me.'

Paula's intensity struck something inside Honey. She looked away and muttered, 'What do you want to know, copper?'

'The name's Paula. When did you start working with Jackie?'

'Who said I did?' It was the last defiance. Paula could see her heart wasn't in it.

'It's not exactly a state secret.'

Honey picked at the label on her drink. 'When I first went on the streets, about six months ago. She sort of took me under her wing, know what I mean? Like, I knew nothing. I just put myself out there, I was easy meat. And she kept me away from the bad shit.'

'So you hung out together on the street? What about after hours, Honey? Did she take care of you then too?'

'What are you getting at? She wasn't a fucking lezzie.'

Paula shook her head. 'That's not what I meant.'

Honey eyed her up. 'And neither am I.'

'I couldn't care less,' Paula sighed. 'Did Jackie help you get yourself sorted out?'

Honey wrapped her arms round her narrow frame, hugging herself. 'She got me a bedsit in the same house as her. She was like a big sister, that's all. We used to have a laugh, you know?'

'And when you worked together? How did that go?'

Honey gave her a sideways look, as if calculating how much she could hold back. 'You remind me of her, you know?'

As a diversionary tactic, it worked. Startled, Paula nearly knocked her drink over. 'What? I look like her?'

'A bit. But it's more – I don't know, it's like you listen, don't just treat me like a fucking kid.'

Paula wasn't quite sure if Honey was being truthful, but if she were, it might prove useful in getting the young hooker to open up. 'So tell me about working together.'

Honey pulled her packet of cigarettes towards her and lit up. 'Now and again, like, if some punter wanted to pay for a threesome, we'd take him to the hotel. You know – the Woolpack, where she . . . died.'

Paula tried to hide the excitement she felt at finally getting somewhere. 'Were any of them regulars?'

Honey grinned. It stripped her of her streetwise cynicism and made her look like the teenager she must once have been before the streets put years on her. 'Some of them came back for more, yeah. We were fucking excellent, you know?'

'Any rough stuff?'

'You can't avoid it,' said Honey, her face clouding over. 'Goes with the territory.'

'Anyone in particular?'

Honey shrugged. 'Jackie wouldn't have them back if they'd cut up rough.'

'We think the man who killed Jackie had been with her before.'

'You reckon that narrows it down?' Honey snorted. 'She was good, you know. The men who went with her, they often came back for more.'

'And one of them might have killed her. We need to try to identify them. See if any of them have a record of violence against women. Will you come back to the station and look at some photographs for me?'

'Me? Come to the nick? Are you kidding? You want me to walk out of here with you and come to the nick? You trying to fuck my life up completely? It's bad enough I'm talking to you. I walk down the street with you and I'm screwed.'

Drugs, Paula thought. *She's worried her dealer will see her with a cop and shut her off.* Thinking on her feet, she said, 'OK. You know the car park at the Campion Centre?'

Honey nodded suspiciously.

'Meet me on the top floor there in half an hour. I'll drive you to the station and take you back afterwards. Nobody will see you arrive or leave. How does that sound?'

Honey considered. 'OK,' she said reluctantly. 'But you better keep your word, Paula.' She used the name like an insult.

Paula smiled sweetly. 'I always keep my word, Honey. I'm famous for it.'

Honey gave her a look that stripped her bare. 'I bet that's not all you're famous for. Like I said, you remind me of Jackie.'

Paula blinked. It was an innuendo too far. She got to her feet and said gruffly, 'Top floor of the Campion Centre car park. Half an hour.'

She could feel Honey's eyes on her all the way to the door. It wasn't a comfortable sensation.

The only person in the squadroom when Carol got back was Stacey Chen. She glanced up from her computer screens. 'The Chief was in a while back looking for you. He said if you came in to call his office.'

'Thanks. Let him know I'm in,' Carol said. Just what she needed to take away the taste of Jackie Mayall's post mortem. 'Has Dr Hill shown up today?'

'I haven't seen him. And I've been here all morning.'

'See if you can track him down when you get a minute,' Carol said.

'I'll get right on to it. Oh, and Sam left you a note about the forensic geologist,' Stacey added.

As if she didn't have enough to do, Carol thought wearily. She closed the door behind her and settled behind her desk, raking through her top drawer till she found a bottle of Paco Rabane. She sprayed her throat and wrists, trying to rid herself of the smell she felt clinging to her. If Brandon was about to walk in, she didn't want to reek of the mortuary slab and the wine bar.

Carol reached for the note lying on her desk. In Sam's tight compact handwriting, it read:

I spoke to the Earth Sciences department at the university. They've got a guy who's done some work with the police before, but he specializes in soil samples, so he's not much good to us. But he gave me the number of Dr Jonathan France who apparently is The Man when it comes to limestone. Which is what we've got here. He's based in Sheffield, but he's going to be in Bradfield this afternoon, so I asked him to swing by around three. Do you want me to see him, or will you?

Carol thought about it for a moment. It never hurt to flatter experts with a sense of their own importance. Besides, she could use the sense of forward movement with at least one of her cases. She logged on to her computer and sent Stacey a message. 'Tell Sam I'll deal with Dr France when he comes in.'

She had barely sent the message when the door

opened and Brandon strode in without waiting for an invitation. Carol looked up in astonishment. In all the years she had worked with John Brandon, she had never seen him lose contact with good manners. His entrance told her more clearly than any words that he was under pressure from places she could only guess at. He tossed an early copy of the evening paper on her desk. SECOND CITY PROSTITUTE SLAUGHTERED, the headline blared. In smaller type it read, 'Did Police Catch Real Killer Two Years Ago?'

'He's laughing at us, Carol. Two killings in three weeks, and we're getting nowhere.'

'I wouldn't say that, exactly, sir.'

'No? You have a suspect? You have any notion of where to start looking for a suspect?' His long face was taut with frustration.

'Dr Vernon found sperm on the body of the second victim. It's heavily contaminated with her blood, but he's reasonably confident the lab can extract some DNA from it.' Carol tried to stay calm, but her heart was racing and she could feel a prickle of sweat at her neck.

Brandon made an impatient noise. 'Unless he's already in the database, that's little use until we have a serious suspect. What progress are you making on that front?'

Carol got to her feet, trying to minimize the distance between them. 'We're trying to trace as many contacts of the murdered women as we can, but it's not easy. Men don't like admitting they go to prostitutes.'

Brandon picked up the paper and waved it at her. 'We're taking a caning in the press. They're asking openly if we fitted up Derek Tyler two years ago. I've already had the TV on wanting a statement from me on the evening news. We need to make solid progress, Carol.'

'I've got Dr Hill working on a profile,' she said, desperately trying to find something to say that would give Brandon a life raft.

He shook his head. 'Not enough. We need to be proactive. I think we should smoke him out. I think we should set up a sting.'

Carol couldn't believe what she was hearing. After what John Brandon knew she'd been through, she couldn't believe he was suggesting that she would seriously consider exposing one of her officers to a risky undercover operation. She wanted to scream at him, to tell him he was no better than the men he'd claimed he wanted to rescue her from. She wanted to slap sense into him, to remind him how close she'd come to losing everything because of just such an operation. Somehow, she controlled herself and simply said, 'Surely it's too early to think along those lines?'

'Too early? He's already claimed two victims, Carol. And that's if we don't accept any connection to the four murders that Derek Tyler is inside for. We can't sit idly by and wait for him to strike again in the hope that he'll get careless and give us some hard evidence to work with.'

'We can increase security in Temple Fields, sir. More foot patrols. More CCTV.'

Brandon shook his head, exasperated. 'Carol, you know as well as I do that all that sort of policing achieves is to move the problem elsewhere. If we make Temple Fields too hot for him, he'll take his next victim from another part of town. That's why the Yorkshire Ripper started preying on so-called "innocent" victims – the police made it too hard for him to operate in the red-light districts. I'm not having that on my conscience.' He flipped open a folder he was carrying and spread out the contents. Six women looked up at Carol from enlarged snapshots that showed them looking far happier than their lifestyles had ever merited.

'There they are,' Brandon said. 'Look at the photographs. There's a definite type he goes for. The same type as Derek Tyler took.'

Carol dragged her eyes from the photographs, disturbed at the thought of lives cut short, lives she and her colleagues had failed to save. And, for a moment, transported back to a point where she wasn't sure how long she would hold on to her own life. 'I'm not disputing that. But –'

Brandon cut straight across her. 'And we have an officer who matches his type.'

Paula, Carol thought instantly. *Slim, short bleached-blonde hair, blue eyes.* 'DC McIntyre.'

'That's right. She'd be perfect.'

Carol felt her stomach turn over. The sense of déjà vu was overwhelming. 'I've experience of this sort of thing, sir,' she said as formally and as forcefully as she could manage. 'We'd be putting her at tremendous risk.'

Brandon seemed to collect himself, as if suddenly remembering who he was talking to. 'It's your very experience that makes me feel all the more confident that this will be handled properly. I think you're capable of containing that risk. And I think if we put this to DC McIntyre, she'd jump at the chance to help put this bastard behind bars.'

Just like I did. 'I'm sure she would. She's committed to the job. But I'm not sure we should be putting her on the spot like that. It's precisely because she's committed to the job that her judgement would be clouded.'

Brandon gathered the photographs together impatiently. 'What else do you suggest?'

She had nothing to suggest, and they both knew it. She stalled as best she knew how. 'We need to be sure it's a strategy that will work. I think we need to involve Dr Hill.'

'In the planning stage. Of course,' Brandon conceded.

'I think we need to talk to him before we get that far, sir. I think before we put an officer's life at risk, we need to be damn sure we're going to get the result we want.'

Empathy was always the answer, Tony believed. Every killer operated to his own interior logic. Find the logic and you could find the killer. The only problem was untangling the external symbols and translating their meanings. Everything connected back to the fantasies of the murderer, and every fantasy had its roots in a contorted vision of reality. Sometimes Tony could find his way through the maze with words; sometimes it needed something more concrete.

He had taken his purchases home, and he was working through his own version of the killer's game. He had fastened his ankles to a kitchen chair with the leather restraints, and now he had the handcuffs in his lap. He fastened one manacle round his wrist and tested its strength. 'Tie me up, tie me down. This way, you have to do what I want. Control without consent. That's what I need from you.'

He fiddled with the other manacle, putting it round his wrist without actually snapping it shut. But the ringing phone made him jump, and before he could stop himself, his fingers spasmed on the cuff, the ratchet gripping tight and locking in place. 'Shit,' he shouted as his answering machine cut in.

He heard his own voice say, 'I can't talk to you right now, leave a message after the tone.'

A long beep, then Carol's voice. 'Tony, call me as soon as you get this. I really need to speak to you. If I'm tied up, get them to interrupt me.'

He looked at the machine in wonder, then burst out laughing. 'If *you're* tied up?' He stared bleakly at the key, sitting on the table a few feet away from him. His toes barely touched the floor. He rocked the chair back and forth, trying to get some purchase on the tiled floor. After a few minutes, sweating and furious, he managed to get close enough to the table to pick up the handcuff key in his right hand. It took half a dozen attempts, but he eventually slid it into the lock. He twisted the key and felt the mechanism shift. He pulled against the cuff and miraculously, his left hand came free.

Unfortunately, so did the key. It shot across the room and clattered into the sink. A series of metallic clinks, then a hollow clank. 'Oh no,' he groaned. 'Let it not be the waste-disposal unit.'

He hastily undid the leather straps on the ankle

restraints and rushed to the sink. The key was not in sight. But the open maw of the waste-disposal unit mocked him with its greed. 'I couldn't have done that if I tried,' he muttered.

He glared at the phone. 'Women,' he said. He picked up the handset and dialled Carol's number. 'You wanted to talk?' he said when they were connected.

'Yeah. But not here.'

'Suits me. What about the gardens in Temple Fields?'

'Why there?'

'I need to go to the sex shop,' he said. 'I'll explain when I see you. Half an hour?'

After he left Carol's office, Brandon decided to pay a visit to the incident room. It never hurt to show the troops he was aware of their work. As he walked round from desk to desk, he had a word of encouragement for everyone, showing an interest in what they were pursuing. He was entirely unaware of Sam Evans' eyes on him.

When he turned to Evans' desk, the DC was making notes on his computer screen. 'How's it going, Sam?' he asked.

'Slowly, sir,' Evans said.

'What are you working on?'

Evans shifted in his seat, his expression embarrassed. 'I . . . uh . . .'

Brandon moved so he could see the screen. 'You've been mounting surveillance on Dr Aidan Hart?' He sounded startled.

Evans cleared his throat. 'Not officially, sir.'

'Explain yourself,' Brandon said, a note of severity in his tone.

'Well, we placed Dr Hart with Sandie Foster on the night she died. But he's alibied after nine o'clock, and Dr Vernon estimated the time of the attack later than that. So DCI Jordan decided he was off the hook.'

'And you disagreed?'

'It's all been on my own time, sir,' Evans said defensively. 'I just got a feel off him, like he wasn't totally kosher.'

Brandon frowned. 'And?'

'He visits prostitutes, sir. At least a couple of times a week. But not in Bradfield any more. He's hitting the other big cities.'

Part of Brandon wanted to congratulate Evans on his persistence. But he was too concerned about the implications of him having done the surveillance in contradiction of Carol's orders. What was she thinking, to let a potential suspect off the hook so easily? 'Report this to DCI Jordan at the first opportunity,' he said grimly. 'Well done, Evans. It never hurts to follow your gut instincts.' Even if it did leave Brandon with a problem.

By the time Carol arrived in the scrubby green space that passed for a city park, Tony was feeding chocolate to the pigeons and rubbing his wrist. She watched him for a moment, then walked up behind him and touched his shoulder. He jumped and swung round, startled.

'I know I'm not going to like the answer, but why did you have to go to the sex shop?' she asked, moving round to sit next to him on the bench.

He had honed his experience into an anecdote for her, and by the time he got to his return to the sex shop, she was giggling helplessly.

'So I walked in, and the bloke behind the counter gave me a funny look. Like, *I hoped I was never going to see you again*. And I could tell he really didn't believe my story. Anyway, he finally agreed to open another pack of handcuffs and set me free.' He pulled out the offending cuffs and dangled them in front of her.

'I think that's taking method profiling a little far.'

'You're not kidding. So, you wanted to talk to me.'

Suddenly sober, Carol got to her feet. 'Let's walk.'

Tony followed her down the path that led back to the street. When Carol said nothing, he filled the silence. 'Radio waves all around us. The air's full of voices we don't hear. Why does the killer hear one and not the others? What wiring in the brain makes him hear the world differently from you and me? It's like sexual predators – we see this as a place to walk, they see it as a place to steal sex. What makes the choices?'

Carol shivered. 'Right this minute, I make the choices. I choose a café – I'm freezing out here. But not in Temple Fields. The place is crawling with my officers. Come on, let's go to Starbucks in the Woolmarket.'

Ten minutes later, they were ensconced in a quiet corner of the café, exotic coffees in front of them. 'Remember when a coffee was just a coffee?' Tony said wistfully. 'I tell you, if I brought some of my patients in here, it would give them a breakdown just trying to decide what to drink.'

'Brandon wants us to smoke him out with a decoy,' Carol said abruptly.

Tony's mouth hung open. He'd known John Brandon a long time but would never have thought him capable of such insensitivity. 'He wants you to send someone undercover?' he said incredulously.

Carol took a deep breath and exhaled. 'Yes. He thinks Paula's the killer's type.'

'God spare us from the brainwaves of the bosses.'

'So you don't think it's a good idea either.' Carol's eyes held a plea for help.

'Psychologically, it might work. But we both know what a high-risk strategy it is. And we know the price of failure – you remember the fiasco of the Wimbledon Common case? That set the cause of profiling in Britain back ten years. Rachel Nickell's killer's still walking the streets. Leaving aside any personal considerations, that makes me very wary about anything that smells of entrapment.'

Carol shook her head. 'A judge wouldn't throw this out. We're not talking a systematic campaign targeted at a particular suspect.'

'So this sort of operation wouldn't count as entrapment?'

'You've been watching too many American courtroom dramas. Legally, there's no problem. It's the morality of it that bothers me. Knowing what I know, do I have the right to expose Paula like that?'

Tony's heart went out to her. He couldn't argue against her position. But he also understood the realities. 'Carol, if Brandon really wants this, he's not going to be swayed by your experience or your views. It's going to happen.'

'What if you tell him it wouldn't work?' She toyed with her mug, not meeting his eyes.

'He won't believe me,' Tony said starkly. 'You know as well as I do how dispensable the views of profilers are when it comes to disagreement on operational matters.'

Carol ran a hand through her hair. 'Shit!' she exploded. 'You'd think they'd have learned from what happened to me that you can't control the war once you take it to the enemy's territory.'

'They always think it won't happen to their operation,' Tony said. 'I don't suppose there's any chance that Paula will say no?'

'What do you think?' Carol's expression was sad, her voice resigned.

Tony reached out and took Carol's hands in his. 'Then we better make sure we don't screw up.'

Before she could respond, Carol's phone interrupted her. 'Carol Jordan,' she said impatiently.

'It's DC Chen,' Stacey said. 'Dr France is here. The geologist?'

Carol rolled her eyes. 'I'll be there in ten minutes, Stacey. Apologize for me, would you?' She jumped to her feet, coffee almost untouched. 'I've got to get back. There's a geologist from Sheffield waiting to see me.'

Tony looked bemused. 'I'll take that as part of your female mystique,' he said, following her. 'Can you take me back with you? I want to talk to Brandon about this undercover idea.'

She flashed a quick look of gratitude over her shoulder. 'Thanks. But no pity, remember?'

'No pity,' he agreed.

Whatever Carol had been expecting, it wasn't Dr Jonathan France. Tall, lean and thirty-something, he was dressed in dark blue bike leathers, the top unzipped to reveal a white T-shirt that showed off an admirable set of pecs. He lounged in the visitor's chair in Carol's office as relaxed as if he was in his own living room. He had thick, straight dark hair cut short enough to stand erect as a shoe-brush on top of his head, and his dark blue eyes were nested with laughter lines. For the first time in months, Carol reacted to an attractive man with interest rather than wariness. She was so shocked at her response she immediately retreated behind formality. 'I'm Detective Chief Inspector Jordan,' she said, extending a hand in greeting.

The hand that engulfed hers was warm and large, long blunt fingers ending in square-cut nails. 'Pleased to meet you. I'm Jonathan France,' he said. *Nice voice too,* she thought, hearing what sounded like a faint trace of West Country in his accent. He glanced around, letting her see him taking in his surroundings. 'Not quite what I expected,' he said.

'Me or the room?' Carol said. *God help me, I'm flirting,* she thought, appalled.

'Both,' he said. 'I didn't realize you would be . . .'

'A woman?' she interrupted, forcing herself to sound cold.

He smiled. 'I was going to say, so young. Isn't that a terrible cliché?'.

Outflanked and disarmed, Carol took refuge behind her desk. 'I don't know how much you've been told?' she said.

'Almost nothing,' he said. 'Only that you had a photograph you wanted me to look at to see whether

I could help identify where it might have been taken.'

Carol opened the Tim Golding file and pulled out the blown-up photograph. Before she handed it over, she said, 'Have you ever worked with the police before?'

He shook his head. 'Never.'

'No problem. But I have to stress that everything we discuss is confidential. Even the fact that you are working with us. This investigation is live and we don't want to give the slightest hint to the perpetrator regarding our lines of inquiry. Whatever insight you can offer stays with us. Are you comfortable with that?'

He frowned. 'It's possible I might have to consult one of my colleagues. But I can do that without going into any detail as to why I'm asking.'

'That would be helpful. Of course, if we make an arrest and we get to court, you might well have to appear as a witness, with the attendant publicity that might bring. Are you comfortable with that?'

'Sure.' He gestured at his leathers. 'I clean up well. And I'm happy to have the chance to show the world that geology isn't boring.'

Fat chance of them thinking you're boring. 'Just for the record, can you run through your qualifications?'

'I took a first in Earth Sciences at Manchester, then spent a year doing postgrad work in the Carlsbad Caverns. I did my doctorate in Munich, then came back to teach at Sheffield, where I am a lecturer in geology. My area of specialization is calcite formations in limestone. That do you?'

Carol looked up from the notes she was taking.

'Sounds impressive.' She picked up the photo again. 'The boy in this picture is called Tim Golding. He was kidnapped nearly four months ago. Every possible lead we had is exhausted with the exception of this. If you can help narrow down where it might have been taken, it's possible we could make some progress in finding out what happened to him.'

He held out a hand and took the sheet of paper. He held it up at an angle to the light and studied it. 'This is a digital image, right?'

'It was sent as an email attachment.'

'And you've got the original electronic version?' He spoke absently, moving the photograph closer to his face then drawing it away.

'Yes, we do.'

He looked up and smiled. 'Good. Can you have someone send it to my mailbox? I've got some great software specially designed to enhance geological specimen photos. It should be able to give me something better to work with.'

'You think you can help us?' Carol had almost forgotten what hope felt like.

He cocked his head to one side, considering. 'It's possible,' he said at last. He straightened up in his chair. 'Yes, it's possible. Can I meet you for dinner this evening?'

Carol was surprised. 'You'll have something for us that soon?'

He laughed, a deep, warm laugh. 'Afraid not. But even Detective Chief Inspectors have to eat sometime. What do you say? Pizza, curry, Chinese? You choose.'

'Are you asking me out to dinner?' Carol couldn't keep the disbelief from her voice.

He spread his hands. 'Why not? I'm young, free and single, and if you're not, just say no.'

She couldn't have explained why, but there was something utterly unthreatening about Jonathan France. The idea of sitting opposite him in a restaurant didn't freak her out. For the first time since the rape, she could almost believe it might be possible to have something approaching a normal life. 'I don't know what time I'll be through here,' she hedged, still not quite trusting herself enough.

He fished a card from an inside pocket of his leathers. 'No problem. I've got a couple of meetings later this afternoon, then I'll just plug in my laptop and do some work till you're ready.' He placed the card on her desk. 'Text me when you're free.' He stood up, loose-limbed and unperturbed.

Carol followed him out into the squadroom. 'Thanks for your help,' she said.

'It's a pleasure.'

Stacey looked up from her computer screen. 'The Chief wants to see you in his office. Dr Hill's with him.'

Carol crashed back to earth. Paula. They had to figure out what to do about Paula. And how the hell was she going to explain Jonathan France to Tony?

Tony had marched straight into John Brandon's office, ignoring his secretary's attempts to stop him. The Chief Constable was sitting at his desk, dictating a memo into a hand-held digital recorder. He stopped, astonished, in mid-sentence. 'Tony,' he exclaimed. 'I wasn't expecting . . .'

'I know you weren't,' Tony snapped. He'd grown increasingly angry as Carol had driven him back to headquarters, though he'd made sure she didn't notice. In his professional life, he'd worked hard to keep his own responses battened down. But the more he thought about John Brandon's suggestion, the more outraged he felt. He stalked across the room and leaned on the edge of Brandon's desk, his hands fisted tightly. 'John, what the hell were you thinking, asking Carol to commit one of her officers to an undercover operation?'

Brandon stood up. 'You're well outside your remit, Tony. My operational decisions are nothing to do with you.'

'Don't hide behind protocol, John. You pay me to give you the benefit of my psychological insight. And that's what I'm doing right now. Carol Jordan was thrown to the wolves by people who have the same masters as you do. I understand you're under political pressure to solve these cases, but it was political pressure to get results that motivated the bastards who hung Carol out to dry in Berlin. Can't you see that, in her eyes, that makes you just like them? You held this job out to her as a lifeline, yet here you are, asking her to put a junior officer in the very same position that nearly destroyed her.' The words poured out of Tony in an angry torrent.

A dark blush spread up from the pristine white collar of Brandon's shirt, creeping up his neck and face. 'You're out of line, Tony.'

'I'm not. I'm telling you that you are going to do serious psychological damage to one of your best officers if you force her to run this operation.'

Brandon pounced. 'So it's not the operation you object to? Simply that I'm asking Carol to oversee it?'

Tony flung up his hands in exasperation. 'The operation's questionable. It'll only work if you sow the proper seeds in the media. But yes, my primary objection is the potential danger for DCI Jordan.'

'You think I haven't considered that?' Brandon said, his voice rising. 'Frankly, I'm already having some doubts about her self-confidence. I think it's affecting her judgement.'

Tony was shocked. 'What do you mean?'

Brandon shrugged off his question. 'Nothing I'm prepared to discuss with you. But just how good do you think it would be for her self-esteem if I put another officer in charge of it? This is her case, Tony, and she's desperate to prove she can still cut the mustard. She's the SIO on these murders. If I give the undercover to someone else, she'll think I don't trust her to do her job. And what's worse, her team will think the same. If we try this avenue of approach, Carol has to be in the driving seat. I'm not happy with that, but I don't see any alternative.'

Tony slammed his palms down on the desk. 'So hold off on it. Give them the chance to see if they can get anywhere with conventional methods. Let me try and get some more out of Derek Tyler. He's close to giving me something, I know he is.'

Brandon shook his head. 'Tyler's been silent for two years. Why should he suddenly start to talk now?'

'He spoke to me this morning,' Tony said.

Brandon's head jerked back. 'He what?'

'He spoke to me.'

'What did he say?'

Tony felt cornered. He knew Brandon would dismiss the prospect of getting information out of Tyler if he told the truth. But a lie would only cause more problems in the long run. 'He said he couldn't talk to me until the voice said he could,' he sighed.

'Well then,' Brandon said triumphantly. 'It's hardly progress, is it?'

'Of course it's progress,' Tony said, knowing from Brandon's expression and body language that he'd already lost. 'It'll take time, though.'

'We don't have that luxury. Time means more women dying. You more than anyone should know that,' Brandon said. 'So, what bait do I have to lay in the media?'

Tony rubbed his hands over his face, as if trying to erase his anger and fear and replace it with professional competence. He stared down at the floor. When he spoke, his voice was cold and distant. 'He's a Power Assertive rapist. He prides himself on his control of the scenario. He thinks he's covered all the bases. So you have to tell the press that this second murder has provided some valuable lines of inquiry. That the killer is not as careful as he thinks he is. That you believe you will be able to apprehend him before he can claim another victim. That way you prick his vanity, challenge him to prove you wrong. And then your decoy scenario might just work in the short term.' He straightened up and looked Brandon in the eye. 'And that's what you want, isn't it, John? A nice, quick, clean result.'

Brandon turned away and reached for his intercom button. 'Have DCI Jordan come up, would you?' With his back to Tony, he said, 'Yes, Tony. That's what I want. A nice, quick, clean result. And I think Carol can deliver that with an undercover operation.'

'For her sake, I hope you're right.'

Merrick walked into the squadroom, balancing a sandwich on top of his polystyrene cup of tea. Late afternoon and nothing much doing. Apart from Stacey, the room was empty. He called out a greeting, earned a grunt in reply and crossed to his desk. He was glad of the peace; he'd stuck his head round the door of the murder incident room, seen it was crowded and decided to write up his interview notes at his own desk. He sipped his tea, rubbed his eyes. He wasn't sleeping well. Nothing to do with Paula's spare bed and everything to do with the core of misery eating away at his heart. He missed his sons like a physical ache. Even though he'd often gone a few days without seeing much of them, knowing he wasn't allowed to be with them was a completely different experience.

He missed nothing about Lindy, and that was almost as disturbing. How could he not have noticed how the love between them had shrivelled and shrunk? It wasn't as if there was anyone else. He hadn't even been tempted to read between the lines of Paula's offer of somewhere to stay. Besides, there had been nothing in her behaviour to indicate that she was interested in him as anything other than a friend, even if he had been ready to consider the possibilities of solace. For now, recognizing the death of love between him and his wife had left him feeling curiously desolate.

Merrick sighed and roused his computer from its snooze mode. He'd just started typing in the mostly fruitless results of his interviews when Paula walked in. 'Hi, Stacey. Hi, Don,' she said brightly, walking over to his desk and perching on the corner of it. 'How's it going?' she asked.

He pulled a face. 'Pretty crap, really. I spent a bit of time out on the streets this morning after I'd sent the teams out. But I might as well have stayed here and read the paper for all the progress I've made. I'm just writing up what I've got, then I'm going to plough through the rest of the reports in the incident room.' He flipped through his notebook. 'Oh, I did get one laugh, though. I was talking to this young lad. Rent, you know? And he goes, "I hear the girls are refusing to play bondage games with their customers. You think maybe I should do the same?" I could hardly keep my face straight. "I don't think you're his type, son," I said.'

'At least you got a laugh,' Paula said. 'I've just spent the last hour going through the mug shots with a kid who calls herself Honey. She used to turn twosomes with Jackie sometimes. I thought she might be able to pick out some of their punters, but no joy. It's such a hidden world, Don, that's the trouble. These are lives that feed on secrecy. Jan says they're so used to turning a blind eye that in the end they just stop noticing.'

'She should know, the queen of the Vice,' Don said slightly sourly.

'You don't like her, do you?' Paula said.

'She's a smart-arse,' he said. 'And you know what they say?'

'Nobody loves a smart-arse,' they chorused.

Paula stood up. 'Better crack on,' she said. But

before she could make a move towards her own desk, the door opened and Carol walked in with Tony. When she saw Paula, she turned to share a quick look with Tony.

'Paula,' Carol said. 'Can you come through to the office? I'd like a word.'

Paula raised her eyebrows at Merrick behind Carol's retreating back then followed her and Tony into the office. Tony leaned against the wall, arms folded. Carol sat down and indicated that Paula should do the same. Paula could feel the tension in the room and wondered what was coming. She wasn't nervous; she'd done nothing to be worried about, after all. The only secret thing in her life wasn't something Carol Jordan would summon her to the office to discuss. Especially not in front of Tony Hill.

Carol fiddled with a pen, avoiding Paula's eyes. 'Paula, the Chief Constable has had an idea he wants me to put to you.'

Suddenly the tumblers clicked into place. Honey's words. Carol's unease. Tony's presence. 'You want me to go undercover on the streets. Be a decoy,' Paula blurted out.

Carol's head came up, her expression stunned. Out of the corner of her eye, Paula registered a look of faint amusement on Tony's face.

'How did you know that? Who told you?' Carol demanded.

Paula shrugged. 'Nobody told me. I worked it out for myself. One of the girls I was interviewing said I reminded her of Jackie, and I suddenly realized that, if I was on the game, I'd be his exact type. And we're not getting anywhere with the usual routines, so when you said Mr Brandon had had an idea . . . it just seemed to make sense, that's all.'

'And how do you feel about the idea?' Carol said. 'It's up to you, Paula. It's a dangerous, risky operation. You don't have to agree if you're not comfortable with it.'

Paula couldn't help herself. She was grinning broadly. 'I think it's brilliant, chief.' Her chance to shine, to show what she could do. Not even the look of concern she caught on Tony Hill's face was enough to dent her enthusiasm. 'So when do we start?'

He's watching the streets tonight. He's had a hard day; it's not easy to do what he does for a living when the place is crawling with coppers. But his customers need what he has to offer, so somehow it happens. He shifts the gear, relying on a sixth sense for avoiding trouble that's always kept him clear so far.

There's something soothing about prowling his familiar pitch, now transformed by his own actions. He'd never have believed he could change the world around him, but he has. People are moving differently. He catches the nervous glances every pedestrian throws at those they pass. They don't know if there's a killer among them, and they're scared.

He almost wishes he could stand in the middle of the street and shout, 'It's me. I'm the one you're all scared of.' Just to see the looks of disbelief. Because he knows he's not what they expect. He's not a monster. He's not even scary. He just looks ordinary.

It's what's inside that counts. And they've got no idea what's inside him. They've never heard the Voice. They're the ones that are ordinary. But him, he's become extraordinary. And this is only the beginning.

* * *

The low rumble of the motorbike engine cut through the quiet of the suburban street. Jonathan kept the big machine steady even at low speed. As they drew level with Tony's house, Carol unpeeled one arm from round his ribs and tapped him on the shoulder. The bike slowed to a halt and the engine died, leaving a shivering echo of itself inside her head. Carol dismounted, heart still racing, and took off the spare helmet Jonathan had given her outside the Italian restaurant where they'd eaten dinner.

Jonathan was next to her, placing his own helmet on the padded leather saddle. 'Not too terrifying, I hope,' he said.

'It's years since I've been on a bike,' she said, handing over her helmet. 'I'd forgotten how exhilarating it feels.'

Jonathan opened the topbox on the rear of the bike and stowed the spare. 'There's nothing like it,' he said. He moved closer to her. Instinctively, she put a hand against his chest, feeling the rough tweed of his jacket under her fingers. It was as if all her senses were heightened, on full alert. She could smell the tang of winter in the air, the warm masculine scent that rose from Jonathan's skin. He put his hands on her hips and she could feel a burn on her skin even through her clothes.

'Thanks for a lovely evening,' she said briskly. 'I enjoyed it.'

'Me too,' he said, leaning down for the kiss.

Carol shifted her head to one side so his lips brushed her cheek. Her pulse was hammering in her throat, her tongue dry against the roof of her mouth. The images flashing in her head were not of Jonathan

France, and no matter how hard she tried to tell herself this was not a threatening situation, she couldn't free herself from her history. She knew she wasn't being fair; their conversation had been flirtatious and fun, but that had been in the safe environment of a well-lit, busy restaurant. Here, now, she couldn't maintain the charade that she was like any other woman.

He sensed her tension and drew away, a puzzled look in his eyes. 'Was it something I said?' he asked, his tone light and teasing.

Carol released the breath she hadn't been conscious of holding. 'It's not you,' she mumbled, fixing her eyes on the sleeve of his jacket. She'd been surprised that he hadn't turned up in his leathers, but he'd explained that he always travelled with a change of clothes when he was working. The boy biker look had been replaced by a faintly fogeyish tweed jacket, faded jeans and a crew-neck cotton sweater.

'What's wrong, Carol?' he asked, his voice mild, entirely lacking in accusation.

'I'm sorry, I . . .' She didn't know what to say except the truth and she didn't know how to say that. His hands were still on her body and it was taking all her strength not to wriggle away from what felt like an invasion.

As if sensing her discomfort, he let her go. Her hand was still on his chest, and he gently covered her fingers with his own. 'It's all right,' he said. 'I'll go.' He stepped back, still holding her hand.

Carol closed her eyes. 'I was raped,' she said. The words hung in the air between them. His grip didn't alter. She opened her eyes, expecting to see shock, anger, pity, avidity.

But all she could read on his face was concern. Their eyes met in the silence. Then, tentatively, he said, 'Then it was pretty brave of you to come out with me tonight. Thank you for trusting me.'

She was taken aback. His reaction was unlike anything else she'd experienced. 'I don't know about brave,' she said. 'But I don't think it was very fair.'

He shook his head, the streetlights catching his hair and making it seem to sparkle. 'Don't be hard on yourself. Is this the first time you've been out with someone since it happened?'

Carol nodded. 'With someone I didn't know before? Yes.' She took a deep, shuddering breath. 'Seven months ago, and it still feels more vivid than anything I did today.'

'Then you should be proud of yourself. I'd never have guessed that there was anything preying on your mind other than work.' He smiled down at her. 'So. Probably best we call it a night.' He let her hand go and took a step back. 'Can I call you?'

'Please,' she said. On a sudden impulse, she darted forward and stretched up to kiss him. His lips were dry and cool, and he made no attempt to pull her into an embrace. They stood, slightly awkward, smiling at each other. 'Goodnight,' she said softly. She'd been lucky tonight. Lucky to have found herself with a man who didn't dismiss her as damaged goods, leap to the desire to avenge her, or recoil with ill-disguised disgust. He hadn't drowned her in pity or outrage, hadn't asked how such a thing could happen to a woman like her. A clutch of negatives that added up to the first positive she'd encountered since the rape. It was, she imagined, how Tony would have reacted if he hadn't been so riven with guilt.

'Goodnight, Carol.' Jonathan reached for his helmet. 'I'll wait till you're inside,' he said, straddling the powerful machine.

She opened the gate and walked down the path, noticing for the first time that the light was on in the upstairs room that anyone else would have used as the master bedroom but which Tony had turned into a study. Her heart lurched and she hoped he hadn't seen the small drama they'd just played out.

Tony sat at his desk, eyes unfocused, turning over what he'd just witnessed. Ninety-nine times out of a hundred, he'd have missed it. Although his observational skills were the lynch-pin of what he did for a living, he didn't sit at his window spying on other people's worlds. And when he was working, engrossed in his reading, writing or analysis, it would take more than the unfamiliar note of a motorbike engine to rouse him from the focus of his concentration.

But when Jonathan France turned into his street, Tony was standing near the bay window, scanning rows of books for something he knew had to be there somewhere. That was the trouble with moving house; no matter how carefully you packed the books, they never ended up on the new shelves in quite the right place.

So when the motorbike stopped at his front gate, he was not in his customary state of oblivion towards the outside world. Curious, he glanced out of the window in time to see Carol shake her blonde hair free of the constraints of the helmet. His first instinct was to step away, to allow her privacy. But when she reached out her hand towards the tall man who had dismounted, he found he couldn't move. He told himself he was only watching to make sure she was safe. He knew that was a lie, but he didn't want to acknowledge the confused emotions tumbling beneath the surface. He watched as she avoided the first kiss, watched as the man stepped away, watched as they spoke and as Carol suddenly took the initiative.

Shamed, he made a harsh, dismissive noise and stepped back into the shadows as Carol turned towards the house. He dropped into his chair and slumped there, his face in his hands. Eventually he raised his head, blinking back tears.

Jealous. He was so jealous he could taste it like bile in his throat. He loved her; he'd known that for a long time now. But it looked as if the rift between them had grown too wide to cross. In spite of all his efforts, it appeared that Carol had chosen her own route to salvation. And it didn't include him.

The atmosphere in the incident room was heady with anticipation. A low buzz of speculation filled the air as the detectives wondered why DCI Jordan had called them together. 'I don't care what it is as long as it gets us out of talking to hookers in the rain,' Sam Evans confided in Kevin Matthews. 'It's like monkey city out there – see no evil, hear no evil, speak no evil.'

'You never know with Jordan,' Kevin said. 'If anybody's got off-the-wall tendencies, it's her.'

'But do they work?' Evans demanded. 'Her off-the-wall ideas?'

Kevin picked at a bit of dried food he'd just spotted on his trousers. 'She's got a spooky tendency to get it right,' he said. 'I've seen her float ideas that even Tony Hill thought were out of the box. And then she's turned out to be on the money.'

'Yeah, but after what happened to her . . . maybe she's lost her nerve for going out on a limb,' Evans pointed out. His late-night trawls through the desks of his fellow officers had yielded nothing from Carol Jordan. She seemed to commit very little to paper and even less to her computer. He needed to know what she was thinking if he was to achieve his goal, but it was taking a long time to get a handle on her. So far, he'd managed to avoid an opportunity to tell her about his surveillance on Hart. He was hoping Brandon would get to her first, make her feel vulnerable and put her on the back foot. But it didn't look as if that had happened yet.

'I wouldn't bank on it,' Kevin muttered as a hush fell over the room. He turned to see Carol making her way to the front through the serried ranks of officers. Don Merrick followed close on her heels. Kevin thought she was looking better than she had for weeks. Her skin had a glow to it and her eyes were bright.

Carol stopped by the murder board with its photographs of Sandie Foster and Jackie Mayall. She looked at their faces, made a silent promise to herself then turned to face the detectives. She'd been in the office since seven working on the undercover strategy, stifling her personal anxieties about the operation, and she still felt fresh and sharp. After leaving Jonathan, she'd gone straight to bed without even a nightcap. And she'd slept straight through till the alarm woke her at six. No nightmares, no restless tossing and turning. And almost no alcohol. Three glasses of wine with dinner scarcely counted, given her recent levels of consumption. She didn't think she'd climbed a mountain, but she thought she might have turned a corner, offering a new choice of direction.

'Good morning, everyone,' she said, her voice clear and brisk. 'First, I want to thank you for your hard work over the past few weeks. It's not the fault of anyone in this room that we have made so little progress. We're up against an organized and intelligent killer here, and we've had none of the breaks that open a case up. So it's time for an alternative strategy.'

There was a murmur of assent round the room. She saw nods of approval from her own team. She bit back her doubts and fears and carried on. 'It's a high-risk operation. It's going to mean a hundred per cent effort from every one of you. But I believe it can bring us results we're not going to get any other way.'

Carol opened the folder she carried and took out photographs of Derek Tyler's four victims. She pinned them up on the board behind her then swung back round to face the room. 'I know there's been a lot of speculation in the media about a connection between these two recent murders and the series of killings two years ago. At this point, there is no substantive doubt about Derek Tyler's guilt. However, one thing is clear: whoever is responsible for these murders is using Derek Tyler's crimes as a template. There's no point in wondering why. At this point, it's not going to take us any further forward. We simply have to accept that it's the case.

'What it does give us is a very clear idea of the physical type that our killer goes for. These women all have short blonde hair. They're all slim. They're all around the same height and build. These are his chosen victims.' Carol straightened her shoulders. 'With that in mind, we have decided to mount an undercover operation in an attempt to draw our killer to us.' A sudden hubbub of reaction threatened to drown out Carol's words and she raised her voice accordingly. 'The first part of that strategy came last night in the Chief Constable's press briefing. His comments were guided by advice from Dr Hill, and they were designed to goad our killer into action.'

She glanced across to Paula and nodded. Paula stood up. 'For those of you who don't know her, this is DC Paula McIntyre. She's going to act as our decoy on the streets.'

Paula grinned at the room. Carol's heart lurched. She remembered that gung-ho feeling, and where it had taken her. It was unbearable to think of someone else embarking on the same journey. But at least she could make sure Paula had blanket back-up, something she'd been forced to do without.

Sensing the excitement in the room, she immediately acted to subdue the natural thrill of anticipation provoked by the idea of something that would break the investigative logjam. 'I repeat, this is a high-risk strategy. We are going to saturate the area with undercover officers to make sure we keep Paula safe. That is our paramount consideration. If Paula is in any danger, then we abort. I want you all to be crystal clear about that.' She glanced at Paula. 'The first thing is to get Paula to look the part.'

'Hey, Paula, don't get too carried away now,' Kevin called.

'All right, Sergeant Matthews, save the adolescent humour for the little boys' room,' Carol said wearily. 'DS Shields, I want you to go with Paula over to one of the sex shops in Manchester, get her kitted out in the right sort of gear. We're not going to use anywhere local, on the off chance you might be spotted. Then we'll put Paula on the street tonight with full back-up. Don, can you run us through the technical stuff?'

Merrick stepped forward. 'Paula will be wearing a wire, naturally. We're also going to mount extra CCTV cameras at either end of the main drag in Temple Fields and at the bottom of Campion Boulevard, where they can't be easily seen. We'll have a team in the surveillance van, and there will be plainclothes units on the street. We'll stay in close radio contact. And we're trying to arrange it so that the wire feed will also be available in the cars so you will know what's going down.'

Carol spoke again. 'Like I said, the priority here is Paula's safety. I want you all to bear that in mind. She's taking all the risks. She deserves to know we're looking out for her. She deserves our best efforts. There'll be a full briefing here at six. Some of you – mostly the statement readers and the HOLMES team – will continue with what you've been doing. Others of you can take the rest of the day off. DI Merrick has your assignments.' Carol swept the room with a cool gaze. 'This could be our best chance to take this bastard off the streets before he kills again. I'm counting on you.'

She didn't wait for questions or comments. Anything she needed to hear would be relayed to her by Merrick, her eyes and ears among the thirty-odd detectives on the team. She concentrated on getting out of the room before her confident façade cracked wide open.

She'd barely made it back to the security of her own office, blinds drawn against the world, when there was a knock at her door. *If it's bloody Brandon, I'll scream.* 'Come in,' she said resignedly.

The door opened a few inches and Jonathan France's head appeared. 'Have you a minute?'

Flustered and surprised, Carol stammered, 'Yes, come in.' He slid round the door and closed it behind him. 'I didn't expect to see you so soon,' Carol gabbled. 'Have you got something for us already?'

'Not professionally,' he said. 'That'll take a little longer.' He pulled a plastic bag from his jacket pocket. Carol recognized the logo of a local independent bookshop. He held the bag out to her. 'I thought this might interest you,' he said.

Curious, Carol took it. She slipped the book from the bag. *Lucky* by Alice Sebold. She looked up, puzzled.

'It's a memoir of her own experience of rape,' Jonathan said. 'I don't mean to be presumptuous, but it struck me you might find it helpful.' He looked awkward, as if unsure of his ground. 'It's not schlocky or sensationalist or sentimental. And it's very well written.'

'You've read it?' Carol asked. It wasn't really the question she wanted to ask, but it filled the silence.

He looked faintly sheepish. 'Don't tell my rocky colleagues.' He stuck his hands in the pockets of his jeans. 'My sister is an arts bureaucrat. She's always punting stuff my way. I like things that make me think.'

Carol turned the book over and read the jacket blurb. She looked up. 'Thank you. I appreciate it.'

'You're welcome.' He backed towards the door. 'Look, I'll get off. We've both got work to do. Give me a call, yeah?'

More touched than she could express, Carol nodded. 'I'll do that.'

'I'll be in touch about the other thing – the photograph.' He gave her one last smile, then he was gone.

Carol stared at the door for a long time, trying to work out how she felt. His kindness was remarkable, not least because he delivered it with a grace that removed any sense of patronage. She'd enjoyed his company, found him attractive. But somehow, her heart remained untouched. Maybe she wasn't ready. Maybe it was still too soon.

Or maybe it was simply that he wasn't the one she wanted.

Before she could consider the matter further, another knock disturbed her. 'Come in,' she sighed.

Sam Evans stood in the doorway, his face giving nothing away. 'Can I have a word?' he said.

She gestured to the chair. 'Take a seat.'

He arranged himself in an attitude of confident relaxation. 'I thought I'd better come clean before Mr Brandon spoke to you,' he said without preamble.

Carol frowned. 'What are you talking about, Sam?'

'Aidan Hart.'

'Have I missed something? Only you're not making much sense.'

'I know you concluded that Aidan Hart was off the suspect list because of his alibi, but I wasn't convinced. So I've been following him.' Evans met her eyes, his mouth twisting in what might have been an apology. 'On my own time.'

'What?' Carol sounded incredulous.

'When I interviewed him, I got the feeling that there was something not quite on the square about Hart. And I was right,' he added. 'He's addicted to whores. Two or three times a week, he's buying sex from street girls.'

Carol stared at him in astonishment. She didn't know where to begin. She was furious that he'd taken matters into his own hands. But the gnawing bite of doubt had taken hold too. Had she been rash in discounting Hart? Was she losing her touch? Impatiently, she put such considerations to one side. 'And where does Mr Brandon come into this?'

Evans shrugged. 'He caught me entering the details on my computer. He wondered why I was following Dr Hart. So I had to explain.'

Carol felt a cold pit open inside her. 'You told the Chief Constable that you were pursuing a line of inquiry I had dismissed?' she said, her words clipped and tense.

He raised his eyebrows. 'I didn't put it like that. Not exactly.'

You bastard. She could barely trust herself to speak. The echo of betrayal rang in her head. 'I want a full report on your activities,' she said. 'I want it on my desk within the hour. And I don't ever want to hear anything like this from you again. This is not the OK Corral. We're a team or we're nothing. You expressed no hint of your doubts about Hart to me. If you had, I might have been more reluctant to let him off the hook. I won't have this sort of underhand behaviour on my team. It undermines all of us. Consider this a warning, DC Evans. Now get out of my sight.'

He stood up and walked out, back straight, head erect. Carol saw nothing of the smile that lifted the corners of his mouth.

A watery sun had broken through the grey haze, giving a pale gleam to the streets of Temple Fields. The rest of the city was bustling, but at ten on a weekday morning, there was an air of deserted sleepiness about the district. Those who lived there had already left for work; those who worked there were mostly still trying to recover from the night before. A man in a business suit, his raincoat flapping with the speed of his passage, briskly walked a bull terrier along the canal towpath. A couple of women in jeans and leather jackets swung along the street arm in arm, cocooned in a bubble of smug self-satisfaction. And Tony Hill stood on a street corner, fumbling with the index of a Bradfield A–Z and a sheet of paper.

Should have done this before I came out, he thought as he tried to work out a logical order in which to visit the six addresses he'd jotted down when the spectre of a copycat killer had first reared its head. He flicked through the pages of the gazetteer, trying to find the locations of the crime scenes and fix them on his own mental map of the area. That way, he could start to get a feel for the killer's own view of his world. He hadn't chosen his victims at random so the chances were good that the area he'd culled from was one he knew well, one he held in his mind as a shape. Everyone had their own topography of the patch they called their own, traced by their personal routes, limited by their own needs. They could be blissfully unaware of whole chunks of territory entirely bounded by their own activities. The killer's Temple Fields would be uniquely his, and discovering what that consisted of might help Tony to understand more of who he was. Or at least who he wasn't.

He'd needed activity that morning. Although he knew Carol would be briefing her officers about the proposed undercover operation, he wasn't ready to see her yet. All night, he'd kept drifting up from sleep, the images of her and the motorbike man morphing in his mind's eye into new shapes and patterns. He despised himself for the violence of his reaction, and he didn't want that to taint his next encounter with Carol.

Eventually, he had his route clear in his mind. He set off, heading into the warren of ginnels and lanes that threaded through the hinterland of Temple Fields. He turned into an alleyway and stopped outside a doorway. He looked up at the grimy redbrick building, wondering which window had opened on to the bed where Derek Tyler's first victim had bled to death. According to the notes, Lauren McCafferty had often taken punters back to the bedsit where she lived. She'd thought it was safer than their cars; she'd thought it meant she was in control, surrounded as she was by other bedsits whose occupants might hear if things got out of hand and she had to call for help.

She hadn't bargained on an encounter with a killer who had forgotten more about control than she had ever known.

Tony stood for a few moments, letting his mind freewheel, then set off for the next place on his list. Half an hour and another four locations later, he was outside the Woolpack Hotel. 'What do they have in common, these places of yours?' he said softly. 'They're part of a network that's invisible to most of the people who visit Temple Fields to drink or find a sexual partner. But you're comfortable with them. So maybe you live or work there? Maybe you make deliveries? A courier? A postman? All the sites are near the busy streets but not on them. You like to be private, but you want your victims to be discovered before too much time has gone by. You stay with them till they're dead and then you leave, knowing they won't be alone for long. Can you not bear them to be lonely?'

He walked slowly down the alley towards Bellwether Street, thronged at this time of day with shoppers and those members of the underclass for whom the prospect of covered shopping areas was an improvement on the alternative. 'No, that's not it,' he mumbled. 'You don't care enough about them. They're not women to you, they're disposables. You want us to see your kills when they're fresh so we can admire your art. It was just bad luck that Dee had a night off and it took us so long to find Sandie.' He looked up, a radiant smile on his face. 'You're showing off, that's what it is. You can't bear to hide your light under a bushel. You're rubbing our noses in your power. You want the credit, the gratification, and you don't want to wait for it.'

Tony made his way down Bellwether Street to the Woolmarket, where he sat down on one of the benches that looked across the busy square. Unpacking the underlying message of the killer's actions was only the first step, but it was a necessary one. He had to move backwards into the unravelling before he could extrapolate how those deep motivations might shape the public behaviour of the man who was perpetrating these vicious actions. Until he could do that, he wouldn't be much use to Carol. Or to the killer's future victims. 'You've always looked for praise.' He spoke quietly, his lips hardly moving. 'But they never gave you enough of it, did they? They never valued you for what you wanted to be valued for. You wanted the power that people's admiration would bring you, and it never happened. So what do you do for a living? You'll have chosen something that offered you the prospect of lording it over the rest of us. You'd have liked the armed forces or the police or the prison service, but I'd guess you're not disciplined enough to handle that. So maybe a security guard? A nightclub bouncer? Temple Fields has plenty of those. Something where you can throw your weight around anyway.' He raised his eyes and let his gaze drift over the assortment of humanity going about its business. On the far side of the square, a woman in a dark blue uniform was tapping a stylus against a handheld computer. 'Or a traffic warden,' Tony muttered. 'They know the streets.'

He got to his feet impatiently. He didn't feel as if he was getting anywhere. For some reason, this killer's mind felt as slippery as saturated autumn leaves that would fall apart in his hands before he could examine them. He couldn't grasp those central threads that would lead him through the labyrinth. He'd never had this experience before, and he couldn't understand why it was happening now, with this case. Was it that he was too focused on his own guilt and his need to keep Carol safe? Or was there something about this killer that set him apart from the other twisted minds Tony had encountered?

He'd spent too many years working with serial offenders – rapists, killers, arsonists and paedophiles – to see them as one homogeneous group. Some were highly intelligent. Others, like Derek Tyler, seemed scarcely bright enough to have pulled off their crimes. Some had superficial social skills. Others would trip any normal person's weirdo detector at a hundred paces. Some were almost grateful to be caught, to be relieved of the burden of their compulsion. Others gloried in the celebrity a perverse media culture persisted in granting them. One thing was certain: their actions carried the unique stamp of their particular mindset, and that had always been the route Tony had been able to travel with them.

But this time, it was different. This time, it felt impossible.

Peccadilloes was tucked away on a side street in Manchester's Northern Quarter, a revamped part of the city centre where the rag trade had slowly been squeezed out by the economics of labour and replaced by craft workshops, inner city housing and boutique shopping for the hip. An uneasy mixture of redbrick streets, remodelled Victorian monoliths and modern vernacular architecture struggling to look as if it fitted in hugged the narrow pavements. Jan Shields navigated the one-way system like a native, pointing out their destination as they drove past.

'You know your way around,' Paula commented as she negotiated a tricky junction in line with Jan's instructions.

'I've been doing my Christmas shopping in the Craft Village for years,' Jan said. 'It's nice to get people something a bit individual, something they won't have seen in Bradfield. And there are a couple of decent restaurants where you can relax afterwards.' She directed Paula into a small pay-and-display car park where they found a slot.

It had been a quiet drive over the Pennines. Jan had spent most of the journey engaged in a text message conversation that seemed to afford her considerable amusement. She hadn't shared the joke with Paula. Almost the only conversation they'd had centred round whether or not Carol Jordan was up to the job. Paula had defended her boss, in spite of her own doubts. It was one thing to question Carol's judgement with Don, but Jan Shields wasn't really one of their team, so loyalty demanded that Paula support Carol to the hilt. Seeing she was getting nowhere, Jan had given up and turned to her mobile.

As they approached Peccadilloes, Jan became more animated. 'This is going to be fun,' she announced. 'Nothing like a bit of game-playing to put a spring in the step.'

'That's easy for you to say,' Paula muttered. 'You're not the one who's going to have to stand on a street corner freezing her arse off and dealing with grubby little fucked-up punters.'

Jan chuckled. 'No, I get to appreciate the view.' She pushed open the door. The interior of Peccadilloes was less glossy than its counterpart in Bradfield. The lighting was dimmer, the wares less exuberantly displayed. Behind the counter, a woman glanced up at them. She looked to be in her late thirties, multi-coloured hair gelled and twisted into curlicues and spikes. Bizarrely, she was wearing a fawn cardigan that would have looked more at home on the proprietress of a wool shop. Paula suspected the outré hairdo was an attempt to draw attention from the strawberry birthmark that slid down one side of her face, looking as if someone had drawn a paintbrush loaded with blackberry sorbet down her cheek.

Jan glanced around, then led Paula to a rack of clothes at the rear of the shop. Jan flicked through the garments hanging on a rail and pulled out a skimpy black latex dress. 'Hey, girl, you'd knock them dead at Rainbow Flesh in this.'

'I wouldn't know,' Paula lied, trying to cling to her privacy in the teeth of Jan Shields' certainty. 'Anyway, it's not practical for tonight. I couldn't wear a wire under that.'

Jan grinned, her cherub's face looking incongruously wicked. 'Constable, you couldn't wear anything under that.'

She replaced the dress and raked along the rack. Her next pick was a scarlet PVC miniskirt. 'Now that is the business. Perfect for Temple Fields. You'll have Don Merrick slobbering into his tea in this.'

Paula giggled. 'That's meant to be a selling point?' But nevertheless, she took the skirt, setting it against her hips to gauge the fit.

Jan pointed to the skirt. 'You'll need to try it on,' she said. 'And you'll need a second opinion.'

Paula turned a frigid stare on the sergeant. 'I don't think that will be necessary,' she said, reacting to what felt like knee-jerk innuendo. She reached past Jan and pulled out a tight silver lurex top cut low in the neck. 'This should fit the bill.'

Jan raised her eyebrows. 'I swear you're starting to enjoy this altogether too much, DC McIntyre.'

This time, Jan's flirtatious tone made Paula feel flustered. There seemed to be a note of genuine appreciation in her voice that made Paula wonder fleetingly what it would be like to spend time with Jan outside work. 'I like to do my job properly,' she said, smacking down the idea. Relationships with colleagues were always a seriously bad idea. And besides, Jan Shields wasn't her type. Now, if Carol Jordan were to make a pass at her . . . Paula turned away, mentally rebuking herself for losing sight of why they were here.

'Of course you do. But maybe when all of this is over, you could give me a little fashion show all for myself?' Jan's voice was soft, her breath warm against Paula's neck.

'I swear, Jan, you're as bad as the guys,' she said wearily.

'Trust me, Paula, I'm better than any of them.' Jan put a hand on her shoulder, smiling when Paula flinched. 'The changing rooms are over there,' she said, pointing to a curtained-off cubicle behind the clothes rails. She stepped back, allowing Paula to pass without crowding her.

Five minutes later, Paula surveyed herself in the

changing cubicle mirror. Even without make-up and the right shoes, she knew her best friends would be hard pressed to recognize her. She barely knew herself. It was disconcerting how so superficial an alteration rendered her undeniably other. A shiver of apprehension gave her gooseflesh and she hastily stripped off and gratefully assumed her own personality along with her black jeans and white shirt. She yanked back the curtain, holding the clothes at arms' length. 'These'll do,' she said.

Jan held out a PVC bomber jacket that almost matched the skirt. 'What about this to finish it off?' she said. 'It'll be fucking freezing out there tonight.'

Paula shook her head. 'Jackie and Sandie weren't wearing jackets. I'm supposed to look as much like them as possible. But I do need some fuck-me shoes.'

'You need the jacket,' Jan insisted. 'You've got to have something to hide the wire going down your back and the bulge of the transmitter.'

'I hadn't thought of that. You're right.' Paula took her purchases to the counter and handed over her credit card. Thank goodness nobody she cared about would see the monthly statement.

'God, there's some weird stuff here,' Jan said, peering curiously into a cabinet containing bondage equipment.

'Takes all sorts,' the woman behind the counter said huffily.

Jan gave her a cool look. 'So it would seem.' She turned away. 'See you outside, Paula.'

When Paula joined her, Jan was leaning against the wall, rolling a cigarette. 'I didn't know you smoked,' Paula said.

'Only when I need to take the taste out of my mouth,' Jan said.

'I thought you were having a laugh in there.'

Jan licked the paper and efficiently finished the job. 'Did you? Whistling in the dark, Paula. That's what that was.' Her expression was unreadable, but her voice was softer than Paula had ever heard it. 'You're putting yourself on the line tonight. That's probably the scariest thing a cop can ever do.'

Paula sighed. 'Thanks, skip. And there was me trying to convince myself you lot would take care of me.'

Jan's smile looked forced. 'We will. Don't doubt it. But there are times, Paula, when it's sensible to be scared. And tonight is one of them.'

The day ticked relentlessly on. There was a ziggurat of paperwork in the incident room that Carol could have skimmed, but there were other officers to do that. Teams reading statements and reports, filling in slips for actions that needed to be pursued, detectives working their way through the actions in their in-trays, officers producing more paperwork for the statement readers to plough through. And Don Merrick to pull out the crucial stuff she needed to know about. The overwhelming volume of material in a case like this was terrifying, all the more so because it seemed to be taking them nowhere.

The undercover operation preyed on her like a fox on chickens. Every tiny intimation of what might go wrong multiplied in her mind, stirring up the silted memories of her own botched operation. Then there was Sam Evans. She couldn't figure out whether he was simply a glory-hunter or whether he was deliberately trying to undermine her. Either way, he must have planted doubts in Brandon's head at a time when she could least afford that. She didn't want him wondering if her own experience was going to affect Paula's undercover. Carol tried to force the poisonous thoughts away, but they wouldn't be ignored. Eventually, she gave in. If she couldn't evade the past, perhaps she should try confronting it. She took the book Jonathan had given her from the desk and gingerly opened it. She'd never been much of a reader outside her own very specific areas of interest, and since the rape she'd deliberately shied away from anything that smacked of self-help. But this seemed to be different. In spite of her reservations, Carol found herself drawn into a narrative that, while it had few parallels with her own experience, nevertheless seemed to speak to her at a level nothing and no one had touched before.

After forty pages, she had to put the book down. Her hands were trembling and she felt on the verge of tears. Her body craved a drink, but she was determined not to give in. For the first time in months, she understood that she had travelled so far down the route of survival that there was no longer any question but that she was going to make it. The Carol Jordan who emerged on the far side of what had happened to her would be very different, but she would be herself again. Damaged but not destroyed. Cracked but not broken. She wished Tony was there, not because she wanted to talk about it, but because she knew he would see the change in her and perhaps feel the beginnings of release.

As if in response to her wish, a knock sounded at her door. 'Come in,' she said, hastily shoving the book out of sight under some papers. But it wasn't Tony who appeared. Jonathan France was back again, clutching a folder under one arm. 'Twice in one day,' Carol said. 'People will talk.' She was idiotically pleased to see him, far more so than she expected to be.

He sat down, leaning back in the chair and stretching his long legs out. 'Much as I enjoy your company, this is a purely professional visit,' he said. 'I have some news for you.' He looked pleased with himself, a retriever carrying the soggy newspaper he knows will make somebody's day.

Carol's interest quickened. However much she might want to see Jonathan for personal reasons, that desire was always going to be trumped by her professional objectives. 'You've identified the location?'

He nodded. 'As soon as I saw the photograph, I thought I knew where it was. Not specifically, not down to pinpoint. But when I blew up the details on my computer, I realized I recognized it.' He opened the folder and drew out a couple of printed enlargements of sections of rock, passing them over to Carol.

She stared blankly at the photographs. To her, they looked like a couple of slabs of rock, grey with a faint reddish tinge, traced with what looked like dribbles and blobs of pale grey. 'What am I looking at?' she asked, almost immediately regretting the question. She knew only too well the perils of inviting experts to hold forth on their areas of specialism.

'It's called stromatactis,' Jonathan said eagerly. 'One of the persistent enigmas of the Devonian period. In lay terms, what you've got there is a flat-bottomed cavity with an irregular top filled with fibrous calcite. In geological terms, it's an autochthonous formation caused by the partial winnowing of unlithified sediment. Opinions differ as to how it was formed and what it represents. You see how it mimics the fabric of a coral reef? Some geologists say what you're looking at is the result of reef organisms, stromatoporoids, being piled up. Water filled the interstices and, under pressure, stromatactis was formed. Others believe they're essentially the fossils of soft-bodied organisms such as sponges. Yet others think they're the product of marine algae or cyanobacteria.' He grinned. 'And the creationists think they were thrown up from the deep ocean during Noah's flood.'

'All of which is fascinating, but . . .' Carol tried for an amused but quizzical expression.

'I know, I know – cut to the chase, that's what you want, right?' Jonathan said ruefully. 'OK. You get these formations in limestone. The Peak District has some remarkable examples. They tend to show up in clusters. And there are a few places in the White Peak that sad rockies like me positively salivate over. When I saw the blow-ups, I thought I could narrow it down to one place in particular. But I wanted to check it out first. So after I left here this morning, I went out there. And I was right. This is a piece of limestone reef in a spur off Chee Dale.'

Carol couldn't hide her excitement. 'You've identified it? Positively?'

Jonathan nodded. 'It's quite distinctive . . .'

Whatever he'd intended to say next was cut off by the opening of the door. Tony started speaking as he walked in, initially oblivious to the fact that Carol had company. 'Carol, I think he works in Temple Fields. Maybe a security guard or a bouncer in one of the bars or clubs.'

'Tony,' Carol said, her voice a warning, her head indicating Jonathan, half-hidden behind the open door.

Tony craned his head round. His voice was friendly enough but his face seemed to lose all animation. 'Oh, sorry. I didn't realize . . . I'll come back later.'

She knew from his reaction that he'd seen something the night before. And she knew him well enough to understand he wasn't going to make allusion to it. Not here, not now. Probably not ever, knowing Tony's capacity for avoidance of the life emotional. 'It's all right,' she said. 'Come on in. This is Dr Jonathan France. He's a geologist. Jonathan, this is Dr Tony Hill.' Jonathan eased out of his chair and shook hands, towering over Tony. 'Tony's a clinical psychologist. We do a lot of work together.'

'A geologist,' Tony said, moving quickly away from Jonathan. He perched on the corner of Carol's desk. She suspected his move was completely deliberate, putting himself alongside her, demonstrating their allegiance, making Jonathan the outsider. 'It must be relaxing to work with something that moves as slowly as a tectonic plate.'

Jonathan lowered himself back into his chair. 'It gets me out of the house.'

Tony smiled. 'That's what some of my patients say about their psychiatric conditions.'

Jonathan looked faintly puzzled, as if unsure whether he was being disparaged. 'Not the agoraphobics, though,' he said.

Tony conceded the point. Before he could throw down the next verbal challenge, Carol intervened. 'Jonathan has identified the site where Tim Golding was photographed.'

Tony's professional instincts leapt to life. 'Really?' he said. 'Tell me more.'

'As I was just explaining when you came in, the geological features in the background of the picture are quite distinctive. I've visited the site on field trips more than once. It's a particularly striking example of stromatactis.'

'What kind of a place is it?' Tony asked. 'Isolated? Somewhere walkers go?'

Jonathan pulled another sheet from his folder. 'I photocopied the relevant section of the map.' He laid it on the desk and leaned forward to illustrate his comments. 'This is Chee Dale. Carved out of the limestone by the River Wye.' He traced the winding ribbon on the map. 'As you can see, there's a public footpath goes down the dale. It's a popular walk. So much so that the National Park has built stepping stones where the river breaks its banks and covers the path.' He stabbed the map with a long finger. 'And this little spur up here is called Swindale. The entrance is very narrow – it's easy to miss it. But the dale opens out once you're through that narrow neck and climbs up for about quarter of a mile. There's no footpath as such, and I'd bet that ninety-nine people out of a hundred wouldn't even notice the way in.'

'And that's where this stroma-whatsit is?' Tony asked, gazing intently at the map.

'Yes. About halfway up on the left,' Jonathan said.

'So it's pretty secluded? Not somewhere people would go for a picnic?'

Jonathan shook his head. 'Not unless you like mud and brambles and no view. That's the thing about the Peak District, there's a lot of hidden space. You get a quarter of a million people there on a Bank Holiday and still you can lose yourself.'

'So who would go there?' Carol asked.

'Geologists, professional and amateur. I did once see three guys climbing there, but it's not a great pitch, and there are a lot better rock routes nearby. But that's about it. Like I said, it's not got much to commend it in terms of scenery.'

'So whoever took Tim Golding there could be pretty sure they weren't going to be disturbed,' Tony mused. 'Which means they knew the terrain.' He glanced up. 'How near can you get a car to here?'

'There's a car park about a mile away at the old Miller's Dale station.'

'That's a tall order with an unwilling victim,' Tony said softly. 'I don't suppose there's any way of telling what time of day this picture was taken?'

Jonathan took the original print from his folder. 'That depends on the time of year. When did the boy go missing?'

'The second week of August,' Carol said without having to check.

Jonathan studied the photograph. 'That part of the dale is east-facing. It takes a while for the sun to climb high enough to clear the opposite cliff. I'd guess around nine or ten in the morning.'

Tony stood up abruptly and turned away, pressing his hands to the sides of his head as if suffering a headache. 'Take a full team of SOCOs with you when you go, Carol. You're looking for a grave. Maybe even two.'

'You think Guy might be there too?'

Tony dropped his hands. 'Balance of probabilities? Yes. The overwhelming odds are that both Tim and Guy were taken by the same man. We both know that. If he's confident enough to put that picture out there, I'd say it's because he's already used that as his killing ground at least once.'

Carol caught Jonathan's dismayed expression. It was all too easy to forget how the horrors cops took in their stride could rip into the hearts of outsiders. Confronted with the uninflected reality that she and Tony had dealt with more times than they could count, the non-combatants in the war against chaos had no defences. 'It's too early to say,' she said, knowing in her heart Tony was right.

Tony whirled round, his face pale and drawn. Oblivious to Jonathan, he leaned his fists on Carol's desk and gazed into her eyes. 'He'll have got to the car park soon after first light. Tim was almost certainly lightly sedated. Enough to make him spaced out, docile, so he wouldn't put up a struggle. In that state, it will have taken a while to get him to Swindale. Then he'll have done his thing. Taken his time over it too. And taken his trophy pictures. So what does he do then? He's not going to risk walking back on a popular footpath with a messed-up kid on his hands. He's killed him, Carol. He's killed him there and disposed of the body in situ. A shallow grave under Jonathan's brambles.' He closed his eyes and muttered something she didn't catch.

'What?'

'I said, at least you can bring him home now.'

A long silence. Jonathan's face had sunk in on itself, his eyes slitted as if he was trying to block out the image Tony's words had conjured up. *Too much information for him,* Carol thought. She cleared her throat. 'We don't know that till we get there.' She pushed her chair back and stood up.

'Jonathan, there's nothing we can do today. The light is already going. But we need to get moving on your information as soon as we can. I know we're imposing a great deal on your time, but is there any possibility that you can take some of my officers to Swindale tomorrow and show them where this photograph was taken?'

His eyes widened, the implications of what he'd heard still reverberating in his head. 'I . . . I don't know,' he said.

'You wouldn't have to stick around,' Carol said gently. She moved to his side and put a hand on his shoulder. 'It would simply be a matter of leading us there, showing us the geological formation that corresponds to the picture. Then you'd be free to go. I promise you.'

'Will you be there?' His voice was neutral, but she sensed his need. It wasn't such a big thing to ask, not after what he had already done for her.

'I can't promise,' she said. 'I'm in the middle of another major inquiry. It depends on what happens tonight. If we make an arrest, I'll be needed here. But otherwise . . . yes, I'll be there. If you can be back here at eight tomorrow morning, we'll sort it out then.'

He nodded, reading the dismissal in her voice. 'Thanks, Carol.' He stood up.

'It's us who should be grateful, Jonathan. This is the first real break we've had since Tim went missing. If we do bring him home to his family, it'll be you they have to thank.' She patted his arm. 'See you tomorrow.'

Jonathan paused in the doorway and found a faint smile. 'Nice to meet you, Dr Hill.'

Tony nodded acknowledgement. As the door closed behind Jonathan, he said, 'I've lost count of the number of times I've heard that lie.'

Carol shook her head in affectionate exasperation. 'You really have to learn not to frighten the horses,' she said.

'I've always enjoyed a good stampede,' he said.

'If we find what you think we will, can you come out and take a look at the scene?' Carol asked.

'If you feel it will help.'

'Thanks.' She hesitated for a moment, wondering if and how she could raise the subject of Aidan Hart with him.

'So how are you doing?' he asked, returning to his perch on the end of Carol's desk. As he settled, he knocked into the pile of papers on her desk, revealing the Alice Sebold memoir. He frowned, picking it up. 'You reading this?' he said.

'No, I'm using it as a paperweight,' she snapped. 'What do you think?'

He raised his eyebrows. 'I think you might find it helpful.'

'You've read it?'

'Carol, I think I've read almost every serious work written about rape.' As she opened her mouth to speak he lifted a finger to stop her. 'And no, not because of you. Because of what I do.'

'So if you thought *Lucky* might be helpful, why didn't you suggest I read it?' Carol knew she sounded aggressive, but she didn't care.

'You would have listened?' Tony said mildly. 'You wouldn't have told me to butt out and let you deal with it in your own way?'

'Jonathan gave it to me,' she said baldly. 'He wasn't scared of being told to keep out.'

Tony's head moved back, as if avoiding a blow in slow motion. 'You told Jonathan.'

Straight to the wrong point, Carol thought bitterly. 'Yes, I told Jonathan.'

Tony nodded. 'Probably easier. Him being a stranger. No baggage. I'm sorry, Carol. If I'd thought you would have welcomed it, I would have suggested it. I read it wrong.' Suddenly he stood up. 'Right. Well, I'll be off.'

'You're not coming to the briefing?' He shook his head. 'And you're not going to run through the operation with Paula?'

'What would be the point?' he said. 'This isn't what I do. It's what you do.'

'You can give us insight,' Carol said.

'You've had my insight for the day. I think the killer works in Temple Fields. I think he's a security guard or a bouncer or maybe even a traffic warden. Other than that, I've got nothing to offer you right now.' He reached out and put the palm of his hand against the front of her shoulder.

She felt panic in her chest, a tight fist squeezing the air out of her lungs. 'You could help Paula.'

'I don't think so, Carol. You don't need me for this. This is cop business, not head business. There's nothing more convincing than experience. And nobody has more rigorous experience of undercover than you. You really don't need me.'

Paula found Don Merrick in the station canteen nursing a mug of tea. She slid into the seat opposite him, checking out his glum expression. 'You look like you could give Eeyore a run for his money,' she said.

'I got a letter delivered here from Lindy's solicitor. She wants a divorce.'

'Christ, she's not wasting any time, is she?'

Merrick sighed. 'She's right though, isn't she? We both know in our hearts that it's over. It's supposed to be blokes that are the tough ones, but when it comes to severing the ties and moving on, you women are bloody ruthless.'

'Not all of us,' Paula said, thinking back over her own calamitous past. Two relationships in the past six years, both of which she'd hung on to long past the sell-by date. They reminded her of a poem she'd once read about love being a kite you couldn't let go of till somebody gave you something better to do. Although she didn't like to see the effect Lindy's hard-headedness had on Merrick, she envied his wife her ability to cut herself free so readily.

But Merrick was too wrapped up in his own miseries to register Paula's regretful tone. 'At least if we get things formalized, I'll know where I am when it comes to seeing the lads,' he said. 'If I ever get any time off in this lifetime.'

'If we get lucky tonight, we'll be able to ease up a

bit,' Paula said, trying not to think what getting lucky would mean for her.

That got through. Merrick looked up, his mournful eyes showing a spark of interest. 'You all right about tonight?' he asked.

Paula twirled a short strand of hair round her finger. 'I'm a bit nervous,' she admitted.

'Nothing bad's going to happen to you,' Merrick reassured her.

'What? Like nothing bad happened to you when you were chasing the Queer Killer?' Paula said sarcastically. She'd only been a CID aide on the fringes of the investigation, but she vividly remembered the turban of bandages that had swathed Merrick's head after his own undercover operation had gone out of control.

Merrick looked embarrassed. 'That was my own fault,' he said. 'I put myself in harm's way. I thought I could handle the situation and I was wrong. So learn from my mistakes: don't take risks, don't leave anything to chance. If in doubt, abort. It's better we lose a chance at the killer than anything happens to you.'

Slightly uncomfortable in the face of his earnest concern, Paula said, 'I'm not really worried about something happening to me. I feel confident in the back-up. Face it, after what Jordan went through, she's not going to leave my back uncovered. If anything, she's going to go for overkill and scare him off.'

'So what is it that's eating you? Because I can see something's bothering you.'

'This is going to sound daft,' Paula said. 'But I don't

know if I can carry it off. I don't know if I can play the part. I don't think I've got the right kind of imagination.'

Merrick frowned. 'I'm not sure I understand you.'

'I'm a cop through and through, Don. I see the world in black and white. I don't get that empathy shit that Tony Hill's always banging on about. I don't catch villains by thinking the way they do. I catch them because they're stupid and I'm smart. Because I'm on the right side of the law and they're not. So how does somebody like me stand on a street corner and make some fucking psychopath believe I'm a hooker?' Paula said savagely.

Merrick struggled for an answer. 'Well, you've got the gear, right?'

'Yes, I've got the gear,' she said wearily. 'Shields knows all about picking the right trashy clothes. But I feel like a kid playing make-believe. You know how sometimes you dress up to go out, and you put something on that's a bit out of the usual run of what you wear and you think, "Yeah, wow, that's who I can be tonight"?'

Merrick looked at her as if she was talking Greek. 'I can't say I do.'

'Trust me, it goes that way. But when I put that stuff on, all I think is, "I so don't want to be this person." I'm not scared you guys are going to let me down. I'm scared I'm going to let you down.'

Carol tracked down John Brandon to the press briefing room, deep in discussion with one of the liaison staff. He looked up when she entered, and gave her a nod of acknowledgement. 'Carol, we're just talking about Tim Golding and Guy Lefevre. Shaheed's had one of the Sunday broadsheets on. They're apparently planning to revisit the cases this weekend.' He sighed. 'The way they go on, you'd think we'd been sitting on our hands for the past four months.'

Carol forced a smile. 'I might just have some news for you on that score, sir.' Briefly, she outlined the information Jonathan had given them.

Brandon's lugubrious face lit up. 'But that's excellent news, Carol. Whose idea was it to bring this geologist on board?'

'Mine, sir.' She was damned if she was going to refuse credit for the one good thing she'd achieved in a while.

'Good. Well done. Make sure you keep me posted on developments. And Shaheed too.' He stood up.

'If I might have a word, sir?' Carol said, drawing him to one side.

Brandon raised an eyebrow. 'Fire away.'

'I understand DC Evans told you he was following an unauthorized line of inquiry relating to Dr Aidan Hart?'

Brandon squared his shoulders. 'He did. And I'm bound to say I was most surprised that you had closed down that particular avenue. It's not as if you're awash with suspects on these prostitute murders. I know that Hart works with Tony, but . . .'

'That had nothing to do with my decision, sir,' Carol interrupted. 'I eliminated Dr Hart on the basis that he has an alibi for the time when the medical evidence says Sandie Foster was killed.'

Brandon shook his head. 'Not good enough, Carol.

We all know time of death is far from an accurate measurement.'

'Nevertheless, the timings don't stack up. He picked her up at half past eight. It would have taken a few minutes to get to her room. Then he's got to tie her up and brutalize her repeatedly. Then somehow he's got to drive across town, find a parking space and get to the restaurant by nine without a trace of blood on him. It's just not possible, sir, whatever bee Sam Evans has in his bonnet.'

Brandon scowled. 'In that case, DCI Jordan, you need to keep a tighter rein on your officers. Now, I'm sure you have work to do in preparation for this evening.' He walked past her and out the door, leaving Carol smarting at the injustice of his final remarks. Had she been wrong about Brandon? When the pressure for results was at its height, was he so very different from the others who had let her down before? One thing was certain: when all of this was over, there would be some adjustments in the Major Incident Team. But for now, she had to swallow her pride and get back to work.

Carol understood the disappointment she could read all over the faces of Kevin Matthews and Sam Evans. Tonight would be the first sniff of real frontline action they'd had since their supposedly elite squad had been inaugurated and she was pulling them off it for the sake of a good night's sleep. But if Tony was right about what lurked in Swindale, she wanted officers in charge who were alert to every possibility. She didn't want vital evidence slipping through their fingers either because the lead officers were dizzy and disorientated with tiredness or, conversely, high as kites because they'd got a result in another case.

She knew that when she'd called them in they'd been expecting some special assignment on the undercover duty. They'd both demonstrated all the eagerness and anticipation of lads let off the leash for a Saturday night on the town. She'd tried to let them down easy, but there was no way to sugar the pill. They wanted to be out there, standing shoulder to shoulder with their team mates, not tucked up in bed in preparation for the morrow's work, no matter how crucial that might turn out to be. No matter that they were all desperate to find out what had happened to Tim Golding and Guy Lefevre; when push came to shove, cops always wanted to be where the action was. And tonight, the action would be in Temple Fields.

'I thought we needed every body we could muster on the ground for this op,' Evans had protested even before she'd had the chance to brief them thoroughly.

'I'm not doubting your willingness, Sam,' she said, trying not to let her personal animus colour her response to what was close to insubordination. 'But I make the decisions about priorities round here. And as far as I'm concerned, finding out what happened to Tim Golding is every bit as high a priority as catching the person who killed Sandie Foster and Jackie Mayall before he can claim any more victims.'

'Even if it means putting an officer at greater risk?' Evans' betrayal of her to Brandon seemed to have given him a taste for undermining her. She had to end it here and now before it caused problems with the others.

'Believe me, Detective Constable, your absence will not be increasing the risk to DC McIntyre one jot. You are not so special that you can't be replaced. Tonight's team is at full strength. What I need is to have confidence that tomorrow morning's operation will be as thoroughly covered.' Carol's voice was sharp and cold as an icicle. Evans studied his shoes and mumbled something she was prepared to consider an apology.

'What's the drill tomorrow, guv?' Kevin asked, feeling sorry for his colleague and keen to divert Carol's annoyance.

'Dr France, the forensic geologist, thinks he's narrowed down where the photograph of Tim was taken. It's an isolated though not especially remote dale in Derbyshire. Dr Hill believes that there's a strong possibility Tim may have been murdered there and his body disposed of on site. So this isn't just a stroll in the country I'm sending you on. This could be the most significant development in these cases so far. You'll be going out with a full complement of SOCOs and you're going to treat the area as a crime scene. I need officers of your calibre because it's crucial that we don't miss anything that's down there that can take us nearer to what happened to Tim and who made it happen.'

'Do the local boys know we're going to be on their patch?' Kevin asked.

'I've spoken to them, yes. Stacey has the details of who you should liaise with if you come up with anything.' She stood up. 'I know you're both disappointed about tonight, but I've chosen you two because I have confidence in your ability to find whatever there is to be found out there in Swindale. So get a good night's sleep then go out tomorrow and prove me right.'

They filed out and Carol watched them glumly. *You're losing them,* she thought, trying not to panic. *You're losing them and they know why.*

The rules have changed. This time it's going to be different because the Voice says so. He doesn't make the rules, he just follows them. And if they change, there must be a reason. It doesn't worry him that he doesn't know what that reason is. He knows he probably wouldn't understand it even if he did. But the Voice understands. So even though things are going to be different this time, he'll still be OK.

Because it's going to be different, because there are new things for him to learn, the Voice is giving him longer to prepare. He has a new script to learn, a new set of instructions to be sure of. He's even got a new coat to make him look different.

He has a dim feeling that these changes mean danger. He's going to be taking more chances, which would be scary if it wasn't for the Voice giving him confidence. So tonight, he's staying home, making sure he knows without having to think about it what he'll have to do. He's sitting in his room, listening to the seductive voice on the minidisk running through the routine one more time. He's got a joint burning, good stuff he's been holding back for a special occasion.

As the words sink into his brain, spreading their warmth and comfort, he knows he was right to roll it. Occasions don't really come any more special than this.

Tony sat in the pool of light cast by the desk lamp in his office at Bradfield Moor. Like so many objects in the secure hospital, it had never been up to much in the first place, and now it was well past its best. The only two positions it would sustain for any length of time were either too high or too low for effective use. But at that particular moment, Tony was oblivious to his surroundings.

The killer was still eluding him. A disembodied voice he couldn't hear but which still seemed capable of pulling his strings. He had no more real sense of who this killer was now than he'd had on the morning after Sandie Foster's murder when he'd spoken to Carol about rape and murder and power.

He'd tried to speak to Derek Tyler again, but Tyler had refused to come out of his room. When Tony had attempted to see him there, Tyler had curled up in a ball on his bed and turned his face to the wall. There had been nothing equivocal in the gesture. So he'd gone back to his office and read through the case file that Carol had finally sent over. She'd been right. There was no wriggle room around Derek Tyler's conviction. Not unless he'd had a twin brother who shared his DNA. And there was no record of Tyler having any siblings, never mind a twin.

'What's in it for you?' he said, leaning back and staring at the ceiling. 'Where's the punchline in taking over someone else's crime?' He was at the point of beginning to doubt something he had always regarded as one of the few given truths in what he did: that no two people were subject to precisely the same reactions to stimulus in the area of sexual homicide. What if this case were to provide the exception that proved the rule?

He'd once been present at a forensic science conference where a prominent crime writer had been giving the after-dinner speech. He remembered the man leaning nonchalantly on the lectern, his soft Welsh accent making his words soothing and innocuous. Tony didn't have Carol's gift of total recall of speech, but he remembered the gist of it because it had chimed so perfectly with his own understanding. The writer was talking about a question that was frequently put to him by readers: did he worry about somebody stealing his imagined crimes and turning them into real ones? The writer said he didn't lose sleep over this for two reasons. Firstly, the chances of any individual having the identical motive springs for his action as the characters in the books was negligible. And even in the unlikely event of that happening, it still wasn't the writer's responsibility. The person committing the crime had to be predisposed in that direction; to blame the writer for the murderer's crime would be like blaming the breadknife for stabbing a spouse in the middle of a domestic.

But what if they'd both been wrong, the writer and Tony? What if a congruence of murderous fantasies wasn't as unlikely as he and his colleagues had always believed? What if someone out there had been so moved by Derek Tyler's crimes that he'd come to understand that the only way he could achieve his own dream of perfection was to act out what he'd realized was his fantasy too?

It was far-fetched. It would earn him ridicule from his colleagues. He could see the smirk on Aidan Hart's face at the conviction that Tony Hill had finally lost it completely.

More than that, it just didn't make sense. Because Tyler had confessed, because the forensic evidence had been believed to be impregnable, because he'd been deemed to be mad and not bad, the full story of Tyler's crimes had never been heard in open court. There were elements of the crimes that were not in the public domain, known only to Tyler himself, the police and the lawyers on both sides of the divide and those, like Tony himself, charged with his psychiatric care. And while it wasn't impossible that someone among that group could have gone to the bad, it wasn't a suggestion that was likely to inspire confidence from Carol or from Brandon.

Come to that, he didn't believe it himself. Trying it on for size only demonstrated what a bad fit it was.

He walked his chair back till he was out of the light and his head was touching the bookshelves behind him. Had he really lost his touch? Had he been out of the game for too long? Was he no better than those self-serving idiots who gave profiling a bad name?

It was a frightening thought. If he had lost the one thing he knew he was good at, what was left? He certainly couldn't console himself that he'd been able to use his professional acuity to help Carol. It had taken a man who spent his days looking at rocks to see at least something of what she needed and to act on it.

He wallowed for a few minutes longer, then abruptly sat upright. 'Mawkish self-pity,' he said loudly. 'Not a pretty sight.' Nor did it lead to behaviour he could be proud of. He'd walked away from tonight's undercover operation not because he genuinely believed there was nothing useful he could offer, but out of a combination of pique and a sense of acute failure. He'd let himself down. More importantly, he might have let Paula McIntyre down. And that was something Carol would find harder to forgive than his role in her own ruin.

'Oh, bugger,' Tony said, pushing himself out of the chair and grabbing his coat. It was time to stop the self-indulgence. It might not be too late to stop something very bad indeed happening to Paula McIntyre.

Carol watched the officers file out of the briefing room, their voices a low mutter of background noise. She'd pulled together just over thirty men and women to cover Paula's foray into the killer's world. Most would be on the streets in plain clothes, trying to blend in with the usual patrons of Temple Fields. Some would be parked up in cars just off the main drag, out of sight of Paula but in radio contact with the surveillance van. Others would be strategically placed in the warren of back alleys, ready to cut off any escape attempt. Carol herself would be in the surveillance van with Don Merrick, Stacey Chen, Jan Shields and a couple of technicians, sweating it out, staring into the CCTV screens, straining to hear what came in over the wire Paula would be wearing.

Carol tried to convince herself she was confident of a good outcome. She thought they'd achieved saturation coverage; any more officers and they'd have started to have a significant impact on the ambience. She knew that murderers like this were often finely tuned to their killing ground, and it was important not to alter the environment so much that their target would sense a disturbance in the atmosphere. That much she'd learned from Tony over the years. She could have used his input this afternoon. It wasn't that she didn't believe in her own ability to organize a major operation; it was more that she wanted another angle on what she had planned. She wanted Tony because he could look at it with the eyes of the hunted rather than the hunter. Paula would be offered up as prey; Carol didn't want her to end up as a sacrificial lamb, but equally she didn't want the wolf to sniff the air and take fright.

Tony was, she thought, behaving oddly. Given the level of concern he'd been showing for her since she'd come back to Bradfield, she'd expected him to be glued to her side tonight. It was hard not to see his absence as a reproach.

The last of the team left the room and Carol took a final look at the whiteboards where the strategy was outlined. Time to go and reassure Paula.

She found the young DC sitting in her office with Jan Shields. Paula was kitted up and ready to roll. She looked curiously pathetic in her trashy outfit, her bare legs already goosepimpled above the strappy stilettos Jan had found on a cheap market stall. Paula's face was masked with the exaggerated make-up of a street girl, eyes outlined in kohl and lips a scarlet slash. She looked as comfortable as a white mouse in a pit of vipers.

Carol looked her up and down. 'I know it feels horrible, but you look the business. Well, from a distance anyway. Up close, you look far too sussed and healthy.'

'Thanks, chief,' Paula said ironically.

Carol put a hand on her shoulder, feeling the stiff PVC cold against her fingers. 'We'll be close, all the time. We'll be watching you. We've got officers on the street as well as in vehicles. Have they wired you up yet?'

Paula nodded, swivelling in her chair and lifting the back of her jacket. Although the sparkly silver top revealed her midriff, the jacket reached the top of her hips, hiding the wire that ran from the mike between her breasts, round the line of her bra and down her back into the transmitter that was fixed just below the waistline of her skirt. The wire wasn't taped to her skin; there was enough slack to make sure it wouldn't be ripped out by accident if she had to bend over or crouch to speak to the driver of a car.

'You can't see anything when she's standing or walking,' Jan said. 'We've checked.'

'Good,' Carol said. 'What about an earpiece?'

Paula shook her head. 'The techies said it was too visible with my hair being so short.'

'And you're OK about that? About us not being able to talk to you?'

Paula shrugged. 'I'll be fine.'

'If we need to abort, one of us will do a walk-past. You're clear on the rest of the drill?' Carol asked.

She nodded unhappily. 'If I get a punter, I walk round the corner with him and find out what he wants. If he's just a regular punter, I flash my warrant card and tell him to disappear before he gets arrested.'

'That's right. We're not interested in saddo sales reps tonight. Save them for Jan's colleagues another time.'

'Thanks,' Jan said sarcastically.

'And when I get someone who wants a bit of bondage, I go along with him?'

Carol could see Paula was trying hard to maintain

bravado. But she knew the worm of anxious fear that was eating her. She knew because she'd lived with it for longer than she ever wanted to again. 'That's right,' she said. 'Then you ask him exactly what he's got in mind. If he's got somewhere to go or if he wants to use your place. Whether we think he's the killer or not, that's when we move in. Either to warn him off in no uncertain terms or to lift him. We'll be right behind you. We need to give him a bit of rope, but we'll be keeping close tabs to make sure nothing goes wrong.'

Paula braced herself visibly. 'But nothing's going to go wrong. Right?'

'Right.' The male voice came from behind them. The three women turned to see the Chief Constable in the doorway. 'I have every confidence in you and your team, DCI Jordan. You're in the best possible hands, DC McIntyre. I'm sure we're going to get a result. If not tonight, then very soon.'

Carol felt Paula stiffen under her hand. She realized that the DC hadn't understood that this might not simply be a one-off. 'Thank you, sir,' she said.

'I'd like a word, DCI Jordan?' Brandon said.

Jan and Paula left them to it. 'We'll wait in the briefing room,' Jan said, closing the door behind her.

'How are you doing, Carol?' Brandon asked, his brow furrowed in concern.

'I'm fine, sir,' she said, her voice clipped, inviting neither sympathy nor indulgence. After their earlier encounter, she found it hard to accept his concern was sincere. 'It's not me who's taking the risks tonight.'

'No, but it can't be easy for you, sending an officer out on an operation like this. After what you –'

'I do my job, sir,' Carol interrupted. 'If I thought my own feelings were compromising the operation, I would have asked you to relieve me of command.'

Brandon looked embarrassed. 'I wasn't suggesting that for a moment, Carol. And it wasn't what I was implying when we spoke before. All I meant was that I do understand that this must bring back uncomfortable memories.'

Carol fought to stay in command of herself against the rising tide of frustration and anger. 'With respect, sir, that's my business.'

Rebuked, Brandon turned away. 'As you say. Is Tony in the building?'

'No, sir. Dr Hill felt he had contributed all he could to this evening's undercover. He indicated that he thought the arrangements I had put in place were sufficient.' *Unlike you,* she thought with some bitterness. Suddenly, it dawned on her that Tony's absence might not be an admonishment. It could be his way of showing her that he thought she was back in command of herself again, back on top of her game.

If that's what it is, he couldn't be more wrong. She was more anxious than she'd been for a long time. But she was damned if she was going to let Brandon see that. She nailed a smile to her face and said, 'If you'll excuse me, sir, I need to show my support for DC McIntyre. It's time we got to work.'

Brandon stood aside to let her pass. 'Good luck, Carol,' he said.

She swung round. 'If we catch him, it won't be about luck, sir. It'll be about good police work.'

* * *

Temple Fields on a weekday evening. Sharp night air with an acrid edge of city pollution that caught the throat. Two generations back, the base note would have been the smoke from thousands of coal fires. Now it was the greenhouse gases from car exhausts and the stale exhalations of the city's hundreds of food outlets, from burger bars to Bollinger bistros. The garish neon lighting looked blurred through the lenses of the CCTV system. The four cameras that fed into the surveillance van were all targeted on Paula from a variety of angles and distances, showing her against the backdrop of a bustling street where all appetites could be met. People shopped in the mini-market on the corner, moved in and out of pubs, cafés and restaurants. Sex workers of all genders and sexes dawdled, their impatience for custom mostly numbed by alcohol or drugs. Cars cruised and drifted, some looking for parking spaces, others looking for sex. What their drivers didn't know was that every number plate was being logged by another set of cameras strategically placed at the main access routes into the area. If the killer didn't show his hand, each of those registered owners would have to be visited in a tedious, time-consuming ritual where everyone was assumed to have something to hide until they demonstrated otherwise. Marriages might founder in the wake of tonight's operation.

Carol Jordan didn't care. She knew the price that taking chances sometimes demanded and she had little sympathy for those who took their risks for such venal rewards. She stared into the screens, watching Paula intently. The young DC had staked out a corner by a mini-roundabout. She'd learned quickly, clocking the attitude and style of the other women on the street and now she was strutting her stuff like the rest of them. A few steps in one direction; a cocking of the hip, an insolent stare at the traffic. Then back to where she started.

When she'd taken up position, she'd been challenged by another woman whose pitch she'd inadvertently invaded. A quick flash of her warrant card would have seen off the opposition but might have threatened the whole strategy. So Paula had done a deal. The other woman backed off in exchange for a twenty-pound note. It wasn't much of a bribe, but Paula had invested her words with enough of a threat for the other woman to move a few yards down a side street without further complaint. Carol had been impressed. Given how nervous Paula had been earlier, it was a bravura performance.

'She did good,' Jan had said. 'That's one of the advantages of us clearing out the pimps. Not that long ago, if she'd have tried that stunt, she'd have had a knife at her throat in five minutes. But the women don't go in for that kind of response.'

'Don't they look out for each other?' Stacey asked, looking up from the computer screen where she was running the car numbers from the other cameras against the Police National Computer.

'Up to a point. But they're not exactly what you'd call a trade union,' Jan said sardonically.

It wasn't a busy night on the street as far as the hookers were concerned. But it was early yet. According to Jan, there would be more action after ten o'clock, reaching a peak between midnight and one. Carol, however, had already decided to close down the operation at midnight. All of the killer's victims, whether you counted it as two or six, had been taken off the streets between six and ten. This killer clearly didn't like working the night shift.

By half past eight, Paula hadn't had a serious nibble. The team in the van had been aware of a dozen or so transactions on the street, but none of the women involved had looked remotely like the killer's type, so they'd let them run their course without interference.

Suddenly, Jan pointed to one of the screens. 'Well, well, well,' she said. 'Look who it is.'

Walking down the street towards Paula, head down and jacket collar turned up, was the unmistakable figure of Tony Hill. Carol leaned into the screen, watching intently as he walked past Paula without a second glance. Then he turned into the first pub he came to. What the hell was he up to? Part of Carol wanted to jump out of the van and chase after him. But the better part of her knew she must sit tight. If anything went down, her place was here, right on top of the game, not running round the streets demanding to know what Tony was playing at. Besides, it went against all the rules of surveillance to have foot traffic in and out of the vehicle, drawing attention to its presence.

Her decision was made for her when a car glided to a halt next to Paula. 'Punter alert,' Merrick shouted. The tension in the van ratcheted up palpably.

Paula bent down to speak into the lowered window. The car obscured her face, but the camera behind her showed she was free and clear, and the wire gave a crackly but comprehensible rendering of the conversation.

'You working?' the driver asked.

'What are you after?' Paula said, the harshness in her tone evident even through the attrition of transmission.

'You take it up the arse?' the man said.

'You want me to take it up the arse, it'll cost you more than you could ever afford. Fuck off, pervert,' Paula snarled.

'Fucking cunt,' the driver spat back, shifting the car into gear and moving further down the street.

Paula stepped back from the kerb. 'I guess the price wasn't right.'

'Attagirl, Paula. Keep whistling in the dark,' Carol said softly. They all sat back in their seats and allowed themselves a degree of relaxation.

'He's sitting in the window,' Jan said.

'What?' Carol was still replaying Paula's encounter in her head.

'Dr Hill.' Jan pointed at one of the screens. It was just possible to make out a face that might possibly belong to Tony. 'He's just sat down. He's got a drink – look. He's found a seat where he can watch the street.'

'Just so long as he stays put,' Carol muttered.

Another fifteen minutes passed without incident. Then Merrick said, 'That bloke. He's walked past three times.' He pointed with his pen at a middle-aged, balding man, stocky but with a slight stoop. 'He's eyeing up Paula. Look.'

He was right. The man slowed as he approached Paula, his head moving up and down as he scrutinized her from the side and from behind. He passed her, then crossed the street. At the corner, he turned back. He sauntered in Paula's direction, then, when he was almost level with her, he crossed the street, quickening his pace.

'Uh, oh,' Jan said as he hit the pavement, crowding Paula so she had to take a backward step.

'Let's do some business, you and me.' The man's voice was a loud growl in their earpieces.

'What are you after?' Paula said, trying to stand her ground but having to back up as he moved in on her.

'I want you to suck me off,' he demanded, keeping up the pressure, angling Paula towards a break in the buildings where a narrow alley led to back yards.

'Team A, move into position,' Carol yelled. At once, four of the apparently aimless strollers on the street began to converge on Paula's position.

Now they were in the alley. It was hard to see what was going on, but they heard a thud then a cry of protest from Paula. 'Hey, shithead, cut the rough stuff,' she shouted.

'Shut your fucking hole,' the man grunted.

'Team A, stand by,' Carol said. The four bodies flanked the alley mouth. Carol heard sounds of movement in her ear. Then a yelp of pain. Then Paula's voice. 'This is a warrant card, asshole.'

'What the fu—'

'Yeah, I'm a cop.' Carol could hear Paula's breath coming fast and hard. 'Now fuck off fast before I'm tempted to do you for assault, shithead.'

Carol laughed out loud. 'Team A, stand down.'

The man shot out of the alley, breaking into a shambling trot, nearly stumbling as he looked over his shoulder, panic written all over his face. Behind him, Paula emerged from the alley, brushing down her skirt.

'She's good,' Jan said.

Carol wiped the sheen of sweat from her upper lip. 'She's very good. Let's just hope the killer thinks so too.'

Tony had his glass halfway to his lips when the hand descended on his shoulder. He started, slopping lager down his shirt. 'Shit!' he said, jerking backwards and batting pointlessly at the spreading stain. He looked up. 'Where did you come from?' he demanded.

Carol jerked her head towards the rear of the bar. 'Through the back door.' She put two bottles of Stella on the table.

'You scared the hell out of me,' Tony complained, reaching for one of the bottles and topping up his almost-empty glass.

'I'm supposed to scare the hell out of people. I'm a cop.' Carol sat down and took a swig of her beer. 'As you will have noticed, we just wound up for the night. I got the van to drop me off round the corner.'

'I noticed. I was just finishing up my drink then I was off to get the night bus.'

Carol grinned. 'Your sophistication never ceases to amaze me. What's wrong with a taxi?'

'You get a better class of nutter on the night bus. I blend in perfectly.'

She couldn't argue with that. 'So why are you here? I thought you were washing your hands of the undercover.'

He shook his head. 'I never said that. Just that I didn't think I had anything useful to offer.' He gave her a shrewd look. 'But I do now.'

She raised her eyebrows in a question.

'It's not going to work, Carol,' Tony said flatly.

From anyone else, it would have been grounds for offence. But she knew him better than that. 'What's the problem? You don't think Brandon's line will force his hand?'

Tony pulled a face. 'The challenge was fine. It's the bait that's the problem.'

'You don't think Paula looks like a hooker? I thought Jan had done a good job getting her kitted out. Or is it that you think she's not close enough to his type?'

He shook his head. 'She looks like a hooker. And she's his type. That's not it. Paula's right on the money. It's what you're doing with her that's the issue. Carol, this man knows Temple Fields. It's his stamping ground. Like I said earlier, I think the chances are high that he works here. Which means he knows these streets, he knows the women who work them. So if he saw Paula out there tonight, he knows she's new meat. And what did she do tonight?'

Carol thought for a moment. 'She acted like a street hooker.'

Tony put his glass down heavily. 'No. She didn't. Carol, she didn't go with a single punter. As a whore, she was a total failure. Now, if our man was watching her, he'll have thought one of two things. Either that she's a decoy, in which case you're blown. Or that she's so new to the game she's being too picky. In which case he's not going to chance an approach.'

Carol closed her eyes momentarily. With all she'd learned from Tony about putting herself in the shoes of the enemy, why hadn't she thought of that?

Because she'd been too wrapped up in her own reactions. Her priority had been taking care of Paula, not making sure the honeytrap was tempting enough. 'So what do I do now?' she asked wearily.

'You go back out on the street with Paula tomorrow night. And you set up some fake punters. A couple of guys in cars, a couple on foot. Make it look like she's learned not to be so fussy. Make it look like she's working and not standing around like cheese in a mousetrap.' He smiled. 'That's all I wanted to say. Now, are you going to give me a lift home or should I go and get the night bus?'

Rain drizzled depressingly from a battleship-grey sky, leaching all colour from the Derbyshire landscape. Their small cavalcade had swept out of Bradfield against the incoming tide of the morning rush hour, arriving at the car park by the remains of the old railway station in Miller's Dale just after nine. The brown gritstone of the walls seemed to weep moisture. Carol turned to Jonathan France, white-faced beside her in the back seat. 'Are you OK?' she asked.

They had spoken little in the car on the way over from Bradfield. Carol was lost in her plans for the next stage of the undercover. But even if she hadn't been, the presence of Sam Evans driving the unmarked CID car would have kept the conversation within narrow limits. As it was, Jonathan hadn't shown much inclination for talk. He'd mostly stared straight ahead, as if mesmerized by the sweep of the windscreen wipers.

'I'm ready, if that's what you mean,' he said, a deep breath lifting his shoulders. He grabbed the waxed jacket that he'd placed on the seat between them, opened the door and got out.

Carol joined him. 'I do appreciate you helping us with this,' she said. 'As soon as you've identified the site, I'll have someone take you back to Bradfield.'

He nodded. 'I don't know how you deal with this stuff day in, day out,' he confessed. 'Just thinking about it makes me shiver.'

'Keeping faith with the dead. That's what Tony calls it.' Carol looked around her. The team was gathering, scenes of crime officers in their familiar white suits, designed to avoid any contamination of evidence. Kevin and Sam were struggling into their suits, both muttering complaints about the general level of discomfort. 'We should suit up too,' Carol said. She retrieved a couple of suits from the SOCO van and took the opportunity to have a word with Kevin and Sam. 'I didn't plan on being here,' she said. 'But Dr France had cold feet. It's your operation, I'm only here to observe. I won't stay long.'

Kevin gave her a tight smile. 'Thanks, guv.'

When everyone was ready, they set off along what had been the railway track. Now it was a public footpath, the rough stone chippings making for awkward going. It must have been a breathtaking journey back when the steam trains plied this route, Carol thought. Even on a miserable winter's morning, the light poor and the visibility worse, the drama of the landscape was obvious. Striated limestone cliffs and reefs loomed above them, occasional hardy patches of vegetation sprouting from the cracks. Mottled with more shades of grey than she could count, the huge bluffs stretched skywards, seeming to move towards closure above her head. She tried not to think how threatening it must have seemed to Tim Golding.

After a short distance, they left the track and cut down a steep slope towards a meadow. A handful of sodden sheep munched miserably at the pale grass while others huddled beneath the bare branches of a clump of trees. The ground was heavy underfoot and Carol could feel her walking boots add weight as the mud began to stick to them. It was a long and tiring forty minutes to the mouth of Swindale. They gathered at what looked like a cleft in the rock, no more than four feet across. Carol was sweating inside her protective suit, but her feet were freezing. Not even good quality boots could keep the water out when you had to walk through the river overflow. She turned to Jonathan. 'The scenes of crime officers will go in first. They'll tape off a narrow route as they go. That will be the route that we use in and out from now on. So if you go just behind them and direct them to the place you think we're looking for . . .?'

He nodded. He unzipped his suit and took out the blown-up photo of the rock formation. He'd laminated it, a sensible precaution against the weather. Carol stayed close on his heels as he followed the SOCOs through the narrow neck of the dale. To her astonishment, a few yards in, the walls of rock spread open dramatically, becoming a valley about fifty feet across. The rough vegetation on the valley floor thinned out in places, offering a faint path forwards. They carried on in, Jonathan occasionally steering them with a few words. 'Just there on the right,' he said eventually. Carol looked at her watch. Eight minutes from the mouth of the dale. She stepped up beside Jonathan and compared the picture in his hand to the rock in front of her. Even to her untutored eye, there seemed little room for doubt. But Jonathan took her through the common features, indicating the points of identity. 'I can't imagine there are two sets of stromatactis formations with those identical configurations,' he concluded.

Carol asked the photographer to start on a set of pictures, then she collared one of the uniformed officers she'd requisitioned for the search. 'Bryant? I want you to drive Dr France back to Bradfield. And then I want you to come back for me. I'll meet you in the station car park at one.' She turned to Jonathan. 'I'll keep you informed,' she said, putting a hand on his arm. 'Don't brood on it.'

He gave a rueful smile. 'I'll try not to.'

She turned back and watched Kevin go to his task. 'Right,' he said to the waiting team. 'Let's fan out from here. Three metres apart. Any sign of disturbed ground, uprooted plants . . . You know what we're looking for. Let's do it.'

Carol hung back, trying to find some shelter in the lee of the bluff a few yards from the site of the photograph. The officers were making slow progress, hampered by the brambles that twined through the dense undergrowth. While she waited, she took out her phone and started making the calls to reshape the undercover operation for that night. She'd just finished talking to Paula when a shout went up from one of the officers towards the right-hand end of the line. 'Over here,' he called.

At once, everyone froze. Two of the SOCOs who had remained behind headed for the man who had called out, spooling crime-scene tape behind them to make another narrow corridor of access. It took them a few minutes to reach the man, then another couple of nail-biting minutes while they looked at what had stopped him in his tracks. Then one of them turned back towards Carol and gave her the thumbs-up sign.

She reached the spot at almost the same moment as Kevin. They crouched down, the better to see what was being pointed out. Below the brambles, dead bracken had been piled in a vain bid to disguise the unmistakable hump of a shallow grave. To one side, the earth had been disturbed, presumably by a fox or badger. At first glance, it looked as if someone had strewn a handful of short grey-white sticks on the soil. But Carol knew different, knew what a scatter of finger bones looked like.

She stood up, head bowed, rain streaking her face. It looked as if they'd finally found Tim Golding. Or Guy Lefevre.

Or both.

Midnight. Carol rubbed eyes made tired by hours of peering at CCTV screens and sighed. They'd done everything Tony had suggested. But they were no further forward than they had been when Brandon had first insisted that they try the undercover. Carol wondered how long he would continue to sanction this level of expenditure and staff on such a labour-intensive operation. Following the discovery in the dale, they had two major murder inquiries on their hands. If the press got a whiff of how many officers were involved in the prostitute killings, there would be an outcry. Hysterical demands that more officers be allocated to the paedophile murders, that saving children was more important than saving hookers. It was logical to devote more attention to the Temple Fields murders at this point, because the killer was clearly active now, whereas the paedophile murderer seemed to be dormant for the time being. But logic was always the first victim when the press got their teeth into a campaign. They needed a quick result, both for morale and so that they could be seen to be throwing every resource at finding Tim Golding's killer. If they couldn't manage that, it would be Carol who would carry the stigma of failure in the eyes of her colleagues and junior officers. It wasn't the sort of start a supposedly elite unit needed, though she suspected there would be plenty who would savour her lack of success.

She pressed the transmission button on her radio and said, 'All units, stand down. Tango Charlie two three, pick up DC McIntyre. Full briefing tomorrow afternoon at four.' A man emerged from the café bar behind the van and climbed in, driving them back to base. Nobody spoke. They were all too tired and disheartened. When they arrived at the police station, the others filed out, leaving Carol and Merrick slumped in their seats.

Merrick glanced across at her. 'We're not going anywhere with this, are we?'

Carol shrugged. 'At least it stopped raining. What else is there to try?'

'We should be concentrating on finding Tim's killer. We both know he's going to kill again if we don't find him. And I don't want another kid's blood on my hands.'

'The man who killed Sandie Foster and Jackie Mayall is also going to kill again, Don. And he's got a much shorter killing cycle. The women on the streets deserve our protection as much as the kids do. We don't have the right to create a hierarchy of deserving victims. We leave that to the press. We treat them all the same, and we devote our resources where they're most likely to get a result.'

From the look on his face, Carol could tell Merrick didn't agree with her assessment. 'We can't keep this up indefinitely,' he said.

'And if Tony's right, we won't have to. Once our man accepts Paula as a fixture, he'll bite.' Carol sounded more confident than she felt.

Merrick pursed his lips. 'And until then, we keep putting Paula on the line?'

Carol reached for her jacket and stood up. 'It's her call. If she wants out, she only has to say.'

'But she's not going to say, is she?' Merrick challenged her. 'She's ambitious, she wants to do well. She wants you to think well of her. She sees backing down as bottling it.'

'You seem to be very clued up on Paula's thoughts,' Carol said. 'Has she told you she wants out?'

Merrick seemed embarrassed. 'Not in so many words, no. But I can see it for myself.'

Carol sighed. Sometimes she couldn't resist the feeling that Merrick had been shoved one rung up the ladder too far. He'd been a terrific sergeant, but he wasn't cutting it as a DI. 'Don, you're probably not wrong. But we haven't got the right to pull this rug out from under Paula. She's been asked to do something – asked, not ordered – and until she says she's reached her limit, she deserves not to have her courage undermined by us second-guessing her. So unless you think she's either a danger to herself or to anyone else, she keeps on keeping on.'

Merrick's dark eyes took on a sulky look. 'If you say so, ma'am.'

'I do, Don. And now I'm going home to bed. It's been a bitch of a day, and I've got to brief the Tim Golding team first thing in the morning.' As soon as the words were out of her mouth, Carol cursed herself.

'I was going to ask you about that,' Merrick said. 'I want you to put me on that inquiry.'

Carol shook her head. 'No, Don. I need you working this case. There has to be an inspector in charge of the statement readers and the action assignments. Somebody has to have an overview.'

'So get someone else,' he said impatiently. 'Tim Golding was my case. I worked on Guy Lefevre's disappearance too. Nobody's put more into finding those lads than me. I lost sleep over them, I worked my arse off for them. I know those cases inside out. I know the families. And they know me. Anybody else would be starting from scratch. And it would be just another case to them.'

Carol considered diplomacy and rejected it. She was too tired to go round the houses. And besides, it would probably be wasted on Merrick. 'That's a large part of the reason why I'm not transferring you. We've got a fresh scenario and I want someone running the shop who isn't bringing any preconceptions to it.' Merrick recoiled as if she'd slapped him. But Carol ploughed on. 'The other reason is that the Foster and Mayall cases are live and ongoing. Bringing someone else in to replace you would mean they'd have the impossible task of reviewing all that's already been done while still trying to keep on top of fresh statements and actions.' Belatedly, she tried to soften her response. 'Don, I know you took these disappearances very personally. And that's not a bad thing. It means you went the extra mile for Tim and Guy. But now it's time to step back. Sandie and Jackie had families too. They deserve answers as much as the Goldings and the Lefevres. And I need you by my side on this one.'

Merrick looked momentarily as if he wanted to argue. Instead his shoulders slumped and he stood up, bending over so he wouldn't crack his head on the roof of the van. 'I'll see you in the morning, ma'am,' he said bitterly. Then he was gone, leaving her to contemplate another piece of botched staff management.

'What a fucking day,' she said under her breath as she climbed out of the van and made for her car. She'd stood over a child's grave, then driven to the Goldings' home to tell them that in all probability it belonged to their son. Next she'd had to break the news to Jonathan before he heard it on the radio or the TV. Then four hours stuck in a van in an atmosphere pregnant with expectation. And now she'd pissed off her number two. Her nerves were shot. She needed a large drink, and she needed it soon.

The last thing she expected when she pulled up outside the house was to see Jonathan huddled over his motorbike. She glanced up at Tony's windows and was reassured to see they were all dark. She stifled a groan and got out. As she approached, he dismounted stiffly, stretching his long limbs and straightening his spine. She couldn't help admiring the sight. 'This is a surprise,' she said.

'I'm sorry,' he said. 'I didn't realize you'd be working this late. But once I'd waited an hour . . .' He shrugged and spread his hands.

'There's nothing more I can tell you, Jonathan. We don't have a positive ID yet, never mind a cause of death . . .'

'I didn't come because I wanted more information,' he said. 'I came because . . . well, I just couldn't settle. The whole thing kept going round in my head, and I thought how much worse it must be for you, and I thought it might help both of us . . .' He saw the look on her face and began to turn away. 'Obviously I was wrong.'

'No, no,' she said hastily. 'I was just taken aback, that's all. I'm not used to . . .' Her voice tailed off.

'People regarding you as human?'

She sighed. 'Something like that. Now you're here, would you like to come in for a drink?'

He looked uncertain. 'It's late, you probably want to get some sleep.'

'Both of those statements are true, but the first thing I was planning to do was to pour myself a very large glass of wine. You're welcome to join me.'

'If you're sure?'

Carol shook her head in mock exasperation. 'Can we not waste good drinking time standing here talking about it?'

She'd thought the ceilings in her flat were relatively

high, but Jonathan had barely a few inches of clearance. He sat down hastily, looked around her living room and smiled. 'You've not been here long, have you?'

Carol pulled a face. 'Does it feel so unlived in?'

'It's not that, it's just that there's no clutter. Me, I can make a place look like the wreck of the *Hesperus* in three days.'

'I'm not greatly given to clutter,' Carol said. 'But what there is of it is in my London flat.' She spoke over her shoulder as she headed for the fridge. 'White wine or beer?'

'Wine, please. So are you planning on selling your London flat?' he called after her.

Carol came back with the bottle and two glasses. 'Not sure yet. Right now it feels like too much of a commitment.' She handed Jonathan a glass and poured the wine. She turned on the CD player and slotted in Arvo Pärt's *Alina*, then sat down next to him. There was enough distance between them for the decision not to seem weighty. The lambent notes of the piano and violin eased the way into conversation.

'How do you get through this stuff?' he asked.

'I just open my mouth and swallow,' Carol joked. 'It's not that bad, is it?'

'You know that's not what I meant. OK, we'll talk about something else.'

'I'm sorry. I get so used to flippancy and graveyard humour I sometimes find it hard to shake off. You waited for hours in the cold, you deserve an answer. Except that I don't really have one. Some cops drink too much. Some focus so hard on catching the person who did it that they deliberately lose sight of the victim. Some go home and hug their kids. Some go home and beat their wives. And some crack up.'

'And you? What do you do?'

Carol stared into her glass. 'I try to turn the anger into positive energy. I try to feed off it, use it to drive myself to the edge of exhaustion and beyond.'

'Does that work?'

Carol could feel tears pricking at the back of her eyes. 'I don't know any more. I don't know a lot of things any more. Things I thought were bred in the bone. Now they sometimes feel like fairy tales I used to tell myself to stop me being afraid of the dark.'

He reached out and curled his arm round her shoulders. Without hesitation, she moved against his side. 'You haven't lost it, you know. You're still a good person. And a good cop.'

'How would you know?'

'I saw you out there today. I saw how you managed the scene without anybody realizing you were doing it. And with all that going on, you still found the time to be kind to me. And here you are, being kind to me again.'

Carol sighed, an exhalation that seemed to come from the very core of herself. 'Doesn't it occur to you that the person I'm being kind to is myself? Jonathan, I don't want to be alone tonight.'

She felt his muscles tense. 'You mean . . .?'

Another deep, heartfelt sigh. 'Yes, that's what I mean. But, Jonathan . . .' She pulled away so that she could see his face. 'Only if you're absolutely sure you're not in love with me.'

* * *

Just after five, Tony abandoned the unequal fight against wakefulness. He'd been drifting in and out of sleep for a while, troubled by thoughts of Tim Golding. And Guy Lefevre, the child almost forgotten in all the excitement. The message Carol had left telling him about the discovery in Swindale hadn't specifically asked him for help, but he had promised her he would look at the scene and he felt Bradfield police were still in credit on that case. He'd been asked for a profile in the early stages by Don Merrick, and he was painfully aware that he'd only been able to provide a very limited outline. That hadn't been his fault; he'd said right from the start that he needed more data before he could be of much use. But now he had more information, and a visit to Derbyshire would offer even more. It should be possible to come up with something a little more detailed.

He lay on his back, arms folded behind his head. The room was dark, but that was fine. He didn't have to see to think. He ran through what he thought he knew about the man who had taken Tim Golding and killed him. And probably done the same previously to Guy Lefevre. It would have been a man. There was an infinitesimal degree of doubt on that point. It was always about probabilities. But you had to keep an open mind at the same time, because the nature of sexual homicide was also very particular; it was about appetites that didn't occur often enough to form a proper statistical base.

So, a man. In age, anywhere between his late twenties and his early forties. It took time to mature into this kind of killer. Teenagers and men in their early twenties were often sexual predators but seldom took it to the point of no return. Sometimes they became murderers almost by accident, when restraining their victims went too far and ended in death. If they liked the way it made them feel, then the next time it wouldn't be an accident and another serial killer would be walking the streets. But mostly that first time was deliberate. And it took time for a man's fantasies to develop the commanding power that would drive him to take a life. So it was mostly safe to assume a higher starting age than for rape or sexual assault. The upper limit wasn't arbitrary either. By their mid-forties, the urgent rage of youth had faded or been dulled by alcohol. If they hadn't started killing by then, the chances were they were never going to take that step.

The fucked-up childhood was more or less a given too. Of course, it was possible to have all the markers without growing up to embrace the darkness. Tony knew that only too well; anyone examining his own past would have found a series of indicators that, in another man, would have been the first steps on the tortuous route to psychopathy. For him, they had provided the foundation of his empathy with those who had ended up on a different path. He was never entirely sure where the crucial fork in the road had been, but he had ended up a different kind of hunter. And just as the serial killer had a sure instinct for his victims, so Tony had an apparent sixth sense for tracking his prey. In spite of his public insistence that his was a scientific approach, he was well aware that his most crucial insights were drawn directly from the well of intuition. He was practised in hiding this aspect of his work; Carol was probably the only person who understood and forgave it.

So what could he safely say now about the abductor of Guy Lefevre and Tim Golding? Gender, age. Probably a loner, probably with superficial social skills but an inability to make deeper personal connections. He was at home in the countryside; he'd known a location isolated enough for a killing ground, and he'd known the area well enough to feel safe about parking in a public car park and transporting the boy a mile through the landscape to the final destination. He must have known there would be few people around at that time of the morning. But he was also comfortable in the environs of the city, since it was assumed he'd lifted Tim from a street in broad daylight.

At that point, Tony's thoughts stumbled. Assumption wasn't fact. There had been no witnesses. The cops had struggled to believe it could have happened without someone seeing something, even though there were precedents in this sort of case. The notorious child abductor and murderer Robert Black had snatched at least two of his victims from the street without anyone noticing. But what if it hadn't happened like that?

Tony reviewed the evidence. Guy had gone off into woodland to search for birds' nests. He'd never been seen again, though his map of the nests had been found near the canal. Tim had told his friends he was going down to the railway embankment to watch the freight trains. The women at the bus stop said they thought they'd glimpsed his yellow football shirt between the trees. What if their killer hadn't been in a vehicle on the streets? What if he'd been on the embankment or in the woods, waiting, ready with some tale that would enrapture a young boy and make him come willingly? Maybe a particularly exotic nest, or some piece of railway machinery? Interestingly, both locations were connected by transport links to the Derbyshire peaks, only a dozen or so miles from Swindale, though not links that the killer could have used. The canal led to a railhead with a direct line down into the dales. And that particular spur of the railway line led to a quarry on the fringes of the Peak District.

Galvanized by the thought, Tony jumped out of bed, grabbed his dressing gown and hurried through to his study. He wanted to get something down on screen, to make his ideas concrete so he could present them to Carol before the morning briefing he knew she'd be leading. They could discuss them over a coffee before she left for work.

While he waited for the computer to boot up, he ran downstairs and brewed some coffee. Mug in hand, he went back upstairs and crossed to the window to stare out at the sky while he marshalled the words he wanted to express his insight.

But it wasn't the sky that drew his eyes like a magnet. It was Jonathan France's motorbike, the one incongruity in a streetscape Tony had already grown familiar with. The bike squatted between Carol's car and the next-door neighbour's people carrier, imposing its presence with all the malevolence of a tank on the streets of Baghdad. Tony felt as if the breath had been sucked out of him, leaving him hollow.

Then emotion surged in, raw and relentless. It was more than jealousy; it was ragged pain, tearing at him like lacerating claws. *It's your own fault. Because you couldn't give her what she needed. Because you're a pathetic excuse for a man. Because you led her into the lion's den but you couldn't rescue her. Because love is only worth something if the actions match the words.*

Tony hurled his mug at the door, splattering the fresh paintwork and the nearby books with coffee. 'Fuck it,' he shouted. Then he threw himself into his chair and pulled his keyboard towards him.

Don Merrick was on his second cigarette of the morning when Paula pushed open the kitchen door. Her hair stuck up in an angled wedge on one side of her head, her eyes were puffy with sleep and her navy dressing gown had a streak of toothpaste on the lapel. 'How the fuck do you get to look so sorted first thing?' she grumbled on her way to the kettle.

'It's something to do with shaving,' he said. 'Even when you feel like shit, when you've had a shave you look better.'

'I'll have to give it a try some time,' Paula muttered.

'You not sleeping?' Merrick asked.

Paula coughed and poured boiling water on instant coffee. 'I'm OK once I get off. But that seems to be taking a while.' She sniffed, added milk to her drink and plonked herself down at the table opposite him. She reached for his cigarettes but he adroitly swiped them out of her reach.

'Slippery slope, Paula. You start cadging fags this early in the day, you'll be back on two packs before you know it.' He wagged a finger at her.

'Grrr.' She snarled, showing her teeth. 'I didn't realize I was inviting my mother to stay.'

'Your mother wouldn't have fags for you to nick. So, what are you planning to do today?'

She shrugged. 'Dunno. Might go down to the Spa, have a swim, see if I can get a massage. I need to do something to make me feel good about my body after two nights on the meat rack.'

'You don't have to do this, you know.'

Paula gave him a sidelong look. 'What do you mean?'

'I mean you could say you've had enough. That it's freaking you out.'

Paula snorted. 'Yeah, right. What a good career move that would be.'

Merrick's expression mingled concern and sympathy. 'Jordan would understand. She knows what it's like, she was on the sharp end when it all went pear-shaped. She's not going to hold it against you.'

'Even if you're right – which I'm not convinced of, by the way – that'd barely be fine if Jordan was the only senior cop in the world. I walk away from this, I'll always be the girl whose bottle went.'

'Better that than you end up as fucked up as Jordan.' Merrick studied the table. 'I'd never live with myself if anything happened to you on this one, Paula.'

Paula squared her shoulders. 'Get over it, Don. This is about you, not me. I'm holding together. I can do this.' She pushed the chair back, its legs grating on the tiled floor. 'You've got to stop trying to be the knight in shining armour. You can't save the world, Don. Concentrate on saving yourself.' She looked at the clock as she stood up. 'Isn't it about time you were getting a move on? Isn't there a briefing on Tim Golding at nine?'

Merrick grunted. 'I'm not invited to the party.

Jordan wants me to stick with the hooker murders. She wants a fresh pair of eyes on Tim Golding.'

Paula felt for him. She knew how much of himself he'd poured into the hunt for the boy. 'I'm sorry, Don. But maybe it's for the best. That case really ripped into you.'

He looked up at her, eyes wounded. 'So you think I blew it too?'

'Of course not. If they do crack it now, it'll be on the shoulders of your groundwork. Maybe Jordan's right, maybe she's wrong. But I'm your friend, and I'm glad you're not going there again.' She leaned over and hugged him, her breasts swinging against his chest. Hastily, she pulled back, embarrassed by the sudden flare of surprised interest in his face. 'I'll see you in the afternoon briefing, then.'

Merrick watched her go, conscious of her backside moving under her robe. He'd been disciplining himself, not allowing himself to appreciate her body, her air of contained sexuality. But now, finally, he was beginning to wonder whether he was in with a chance after all, whether her offer of the spare bed was really the disinterested kindness of a friend or something more. It was a cheering thought to take with him to the grimness of the murder room.

Carol waltzed into the station, conscious that her mood was not appropriate to what her day held. For the moment, she didn't care. She'd moved mountains in the night, shifted her world on its axis and she was going to savour the feeling for as long as she could. It wasn't that Jonathan had been the greatest lover she'd ever had; he'd been too cautious, too solicitous, too damn anxious about his steps in the ritual dance. The cynical cop's reaction occurred to her: perhaps he had culled his textbook responses from the very book he'd given her. Even if that were true, it didn't really matter. What was important was that she'd crossed the invisible, intangible line that had separated her from a crucial part of herself. She hadn't exorcized the rape. But she'd moved beyond it. Her body was hers again.

Jonathan had left shortly after six, and she hadn't been sorry to see him go. He'd tried to pin her down to another date, but she'd sidestepped neatly, calling on work to shelter her from an encounter she didn't want. She liked him well enough, but she didn't want to slip heedlessly into some sort of relationship with him. He wasn't the one she wanted to be with; but she'd always known that she couldn't expect Tony to be the one to bring her back to sex. That was a journey she would have to make without him. But having made it opened possibilities for them that had been closed down since Berlin.

She took the stairs two at a time and walked into the squadroom radiating confidence and good humour. Stacey glanced up casually from her computer at her entrance then did so obvious a double-take that it was almost comic. 'Good morning, Stacey,' Carol said cheerfully.

'Morning, ma'am,' Stacey said automatically.

'I've got a good feeling about today,' Carol said. 'You know how sometimes it feels like this is going to be the day when something breaks, when finally we get what we need to move forward?' Stacey nodded. 'Well, that's exactly how I feel this morning.'

'Dr Hill sent a document file for you,' Stacey said, not sure how else to respond to what seemed like unfounded optimism. Machines she could do; but people left her bemused, constantly searching for a way to exert the same mastery she applied so effortlessly to the cyber world.

Carol's mood sobered suddenly. 'What is it?' she asked.

'He's done a profile on the Tim Golding case. I printed it out. It's on your desk.'

'Thanks.' Carol was already moving, making for her office. She snatched up the printout as she shrugged out of her coat and started reading. At once, she recognized the familiar opening disclaimer:

Re: Tim Golding

The following offender profile is for guidance only and should not be regarded as an identikit portrait. The offender is unlikely to match the profile in every detail, though I would expect there to be a high degree of congruence between the characteristics outlined below and the reality. All of the statements in the profile express probabilities and possibilities, not hard facts.

A perpetrator of sexual homicide produces signals and indicators in the commission of his crimes. Everything he does is intended, consciously or not, as part of a pattern. Uncovering the underlying pattern reveals the killer's logic. It may not appear logical to us, but to him it is crucial. Because his logic is so idiosyncratic, straightforward traps will not capture him. As he is unique, so must be the means of catching him, interviewing him and reconstructing his acts.

This is a supplement to the draft profile I prepared earlier at the request of DI Merrick. As I stated previously, the perpetrator is likely to be male, between the ages of 27 and 42. He will probably live alone. It is likely that he has superficial social skills but he is unlikely to be capable of forming close friendships with either sex. In this case, given the age of the victim, I believe it to be unlikely that he has ever had a sexually functional relationship with any adult. He will have obsessive personal traits and may have an interest in the sort of hobby that provides an outlet for obsessional list-making such as trainspotting, birdwatching or philately. He is probably intelligent and functional enough to hold down a job, but it will not involve teamwork. He will prefer a role that allows at least the illusion of autonomy and will ideally spend much of his working day alone.

I believe that the same perpetrator is responsible for the abduction and probable murder of Guy Lefevre. However, given that only the body of Tim Golding has been discovered to date, I will confine myself initially to the specifics of his case.

It is clear that the killer is very familiar with the crime scene. He knew that the car park would be deserted at the time of day he chose to arrive. He knew he would be able to transport Tim Golding to Swindale without interference. He knew he would be able to use Swindale for his purposes without interruption. Therefore he must have a high degree of familiarity with the area. By taking Tim Golding to this particular spot, the killer is signalling that this is his place, somewhere special to him. When looking at suspects, a search of their home/workplace/computer will almost certainly uncover photographs or even paintings of the dale. I would suggest canvassing universities to see whether their field trips include Swindale; local amateur geological societies; climbing organizations; old railway enthusiasts; and of course, the Peak National Park ranger service, who, as well as being familiar with the area, are likely to know which other groups frequent Chee Dale and Swindale. I would also recommend a trawl of the literature; guide books, rambling publications. If this trawl proves negative, it strengthens the case against any putative suspect who can be shown to be familiar with the terrain.

It is likely that the killer may previously have attempted to lure other victims to Swindale. I would recommend checking with local police for any reports of stranger approaches to children in this area. The killer may have used the children's natural curiosity about their environment to draw them in (see below).

I have been giving further consideration to the means of Tim Golding s abduction. Given the absence of witnesses to support the theory that he was snatched from the street, and given we now know we have a perpetrator who is comfortable in a more rural environment, I would suggest that the killer made his contact with the victim AFTER he had left the street and made his way down the railway embankment. Given his familiarity with the countryside, the perpetrator could have found a credible approach to the boy along the lines of having something to show him: a fox's earth, a badger's sett, a bird's nest. (This is even more probable in the case of Guy Lefevre, who was looking for birds' nests at the time of his disappearance.) Alternatively, playing on the boy's interest in trains, he could have posed as a railway enthusiast or employee promising him access to some special treat. There are several points further down the line where it would have been easy to take a child from the trackside to a parked vehicle with a low risk of being seen. In support of this contention, I offer the fact that this freight line runs away from Bradfield in the direction of the Peak District. Its terminus is a mere dozen miles as the crow flies from Swindale. The line moves from what we know now is our perpetrator's territory into Tim Golding's home territory. This is a connection that should not be ignored. We should also therefore consider the possibility that the perpetrator may be a railway worker or a railway enthusiast, particularly since part of the route he must have walked Tim Golding down is a former railway track.

He is more likely to live near the body dump than to the place where he originally picked up Tim Golding. He is more comfortable in the country than in an urban environment.

The perpetrator will also have private access to a computer. Given that the image of Tim Golding ended up on the computer of a known paedophile, it would be worth liaising with colleagues involved in the investigations into internet child pornography. It may well be that they have cases pending against others who have seen images of Tim Golding. These offenders may be willing to reveal their sources in exchange for some sort of deal. It may also be that in the vast volume of information held by Operation Ore but not yet acted upon is the name of our perpetrator. It may be worth running any names that crop up in the Tim Golding investigation against those in Operation Ore's databanks.

Finally, I would like to return to the disappearance of Guy Lefevre. As previously outlined, I believe there is a strong likelihood that whoever was responsible for the abduction of Tim Golding was the same person who took Guy Lefevre. That being the case, I think it is extremely likely that Guy's body will also be found in Swindale. The killer is clearly comfortable with his choice of body dump and his ability to get his victims there. It's likely he had already tested it out on Guy. When Tim's remains are clear of the grave, I suggest exploring the area immediately beneath him. If that produces no result, I would recommend widening the search to the rest of the dale.

Carol reread the profile. 'Thank you, Tony,' she said softly. As always, his concision and his insight had moved her inquiry further forward. She could go into the briefing this morning with a series of positive suggestions. Hitting the team with definite lines of inquiry always provoked their best work.

The only thing niggling at the back of her mind was why he had chosen to email the profile to her rather than bringing it in himself and going through it with her. They had always found it productive to test his hypotheses in argument and discussion. And there was no mention of a proposed visit to the crime scene. It cut into her good mood and made her feel uneasy.

Carol shrugged the thought aside and picked up

her phone. 'Stacey, can you find out who's in charge of the SOCOs we've been working with in Derbyshire? I need them to go back to Swindale and look for another body.'

Evans was looking pleased with himself. 'It's a start, at least,' he said. They were sitting in a tearoom in Tideswell, a pile of hot buttered teacakes on a plate in front of them next to a couple of slices of lemon meringue pie. Kevin had arrived first after supervising the further excavation of Tim Golding's grave. A mere fifteen inches below the first set of bones, more human remains had been unearthed. Carol Jordan had been right on the money, Kevin thought, pleased that his boss was so evidently back on form.

Now a full fingertip search of Swindale was under way. Two dozen cops were still on their hands and knees in protective white suits inching through the vegetation. Kevin felt he deserved self-indulgence after two hours standing in the rain feeling the waves of hatred from the officers Derbyshire had loaned them for the search, but Evans seemed oblivious to the treats on the table.

'Run it past me,' Kevin said.

'OK. I tracked down one of the three rangers who covers this patch. Nick Sanders, his name is. He told me that he had a report from some hikers earlier this summer of a flasher down that end of Chee Dale, near the entrance to Swindale. They'd spotted him exposing himself to a bunch of kids, and they chased him. But they lost him. Said he just seemed to disappear into thin air. Which of course fits with the entrance to Swindale. Later that afternoon, Sanders ran into them when he was doing a routine patrol and they gave him a description.' Evans flipped open his notebook and read it out. 'Early thirties. About five foot eight or nine, slim build, dark hair, bald on top. Wearing a Leeds Rhinos shirt, blue jeans and trainers.'

'It is a start, I suppose,' Kevin said, reaching for a teacake. 'But it's not like we're going to pull him based on that description.'

'We could release it, though. Somebody might recognize it.'

Kevin looked sceptical. 'Did Sanders report it to the local lads?'

Evans' lip curled in contempt. 'No. He says he meant to but it slipped his mind.'

'Great. Fucking woodentops out here.'

'But he logged it in his daily report. He's going to email me a copy of it when he gets back to base. He's also going to email me a set of photos the rangers took of Swindale and Chee Dale back in July.'

'What were they doing taking pictures down there?'

'It wasn't just there specifically. They did a photographic record of the whole of that part of the Wye Valley. Him and the other two guys who cover this patch were proposing a series of footpath improvements and they wanted to back it up with photographic evidence of the effectiveness of work that had been done in the past. Plus where it needed to be done now. He also told me that there was a team of conservation volunteers working in that part of the dale back in May. He didn't have names, but he says the Peak Park HQ should be able to provide those.'

'Helpful bloke, your Nick Sanders,' Kevin said. 'I wish the turnips Derbyshire sent us were as keen to do the business. Talk about "send in the clowns . . ."'

'He seemed genuinely upset about Tim and Guy,' Evans said. 'Nearly as upset as he was about the idea of somebody fucking with his precious park.'

'Nice work, Sam. So, have you got the other two rangers lined up for a chat?'

Evans glanced at his watch. 'Sorted. Gotta meet one in half an hour. Some place called Wormhill. Sounds tasty. The other one's on his day off today; I'll catch him first thing in the morning.'

'Better tuck in, then. Can't be expected to work on an empty stomach.'

Evans reached for a teacake. 'It'd be nice to nail this one. Make up for missing out on the action in Temple Fields.'

Kevin snorted. 'What action? That's turning into the biggest waste of time and money this side of the Yorkshire Ripper inquiry. A career graveyard, that's what that one's going to be, mark my words. A career graveyard.'

'It's brass monkeys out here.' Paula's words crackled in Carol's ears. She felt for the young DC. It was hard to imagine a worse night to be out on the streets. Freezing fog hung over the canal, sending tendrils of chill mist into the streets of Temple Fields. Moisture almost too fine to merit the name rain soaked through clothes, plastering Paula's hair to her head. There were few pedestrians, and those there were hustled down the street, heads down, umbrellas up. In all conscience, Carol knew she couldn't keep Paula out there for four hours. She made a mental promise to herself to knock it on the head at ten.

'Rather her than me,' Jan Shields muttered.

'She looks better in a miniskirt than you would,' Merrick commented.

'And light years better than you would, Don,' Carol pointed out. She chuckled suddenly. 'Hey, remember when you guys had to stake out the gay club on the Thorpe case? You made such a sweet leather queen, Don.'

'All right, all right, point taken,' he grumbled.

'Hang about, looks like we've got some action,' Jan said urgently.

The man had been walking down the street, snorkel parka hood pulled over his head, hiding his face. There was nothing suspicious about that in itself on such a night. But as he approached Paula, he slowed down. He came up to her from the side, obviously moving so quietly she hadn't heard his approach. He stretched out a gloved hand and touched her, one finger on her arm.

'Jesus Christ, are you trying to give me a fucking heart attack?' Paula's voice, loud and clear. She turned to face him.

'You working?' The man's voice was barely audible. It sounded muffled, as if he was speaking through a scarf.

'What does it look like?'

'I'm looking for something a bit unusual. You up for that?'

'Depends what you have in mind.'

'I'm willing to pay. Up front.' His hand emerged from his pocket. It was impossible to tell from the cameras what he was holding.

'That'll buy you a lot of unusual. But you still haven't said what you want. You gotta use a condom, you know that?'

'That's not a problem. Listen, I've got a place. You let me tie you up, I'll pay you two hundred. Straight up.'

Carol's mouth dried up. She pressed the button on her mike and croaked, 'All units, stand by. The eagle is hovering. Repeat, all units, stand by.'

Paula was still talking. 'Two hundred? Up front? Now?'

Even through the intermediary of the camera, the action was unmistakable. He peeled off notes and offered them to her.

Carol's nose was practically up against the screen but she still couldn't distinguish any of the man's details. 'Shit. We can't see his face.'

'Sounds like the real thing,' Jan said excitedly.

'All units, move to takedown positions. Move to takedown positions. Close off the area. Repeat, close off the area.' Carol's pulse was racing, the beat of her blood loud in her ears. On the screen, Paula was rounding the corner, the man's hand on her elbow. On the street, other bodies were closing in on them. It was going to work. Thank Christ, it was going to work.

Adrenaline had Paula in its electric grasp. Her breathing was shallow, her heart pumping like a drum. As they rounded the corner, she felt herself being shunted into a narrow ginnel between buildings. 'Where are we going?' she said.

In reply, he pulled her into an embrace, one hand

roughly groping her breast, the other circling her back. Paula was so focused on the pain in her tweaked nipple that she never felt the sharpened electrician's snips slicing cleanly through the wire that ran from her mike to the power pack.

She pushed him away, saying, 'Oy! I thought you said you had a place to go to?'

He swung her round by the arm. 'It's just here.' He leaned past her and opened a gate in the wall, so grubby it was almost invisible against the blackened brick. He steered her inside then slipped the snib on the lock, closing it fast behind them. He ushered Paula towards the back door of a building.

Nervous, but secure in the mistaken belief that she was still transmitting, Paula said sarcastically, 'Mmm, very glamorous back yard. Who'd have thought such a nondescript gate in the wall would hide so lovely a place? We going into this building here then? This your place?'

'Yeah,' the man said. 'Come on, get a move on. We haven't got all night.'

Carol was on her feet. 'Paula's gone dead. There's nothing coming through.' She turned to the two technical support staff. 'Is it our end or hers?'

Thirty seconds of unbearable suspense. Breath held. Prayers offered. Fingers crossed. Then one of the technicians shook his head. 'It's not our end. She's not transmitting.'

At once, chaos broke out. Carol shouted, 'Take down. Repeat, take down. The eagle has landed. All units, pursuit, pursuit.'

'Fuck, shit, fuck, shit,' Merrick kept repeating like

a mantra as he wrenched open the side door of the van. He leapt out into the street as Carol ripped off her headset and tore after him, Jan in their wake. Stacey stared after them, open-mouthed, uncertain whether to stay put and hold the fort or follow. She settled for closing the van door and picking up Carol's discarded comms equipment. Somebody had to keep track of what was happening. She didn't mind. She who controls the technology controls the world, she told herself. It was a far more interesting option than running around on the street. Nothing would happen without her knowledge here.

Carol pounded down the pavement, nightmare visions flooding her head. 'No, no, no,' she gasped on her out breaths as she covered the twenty yards to the corner where she'd last seen Paula. As she rounded the corner, she ran into the back of another officer, winding both of them. Carol staggered, then found her footing. She pushed past and found more officers milling around in the narrow ginnel where Paula had disappeared with the man. She shoved her way through, following the ginnel to its end. It led into another street intersected with lanes, alleys and back entries. It was a labyrinth.

'Fan out,' Carol shouted. 'Cover the area. They can't have gone far. Shit!'

'It's a rabbit warren round here, they could be anywhere,' Merrick said, his face haggard, his voice cracking.

'So don't stand here talking, start looking. And somebody get this gate open,' she added, pounding her fist against the door in the wall of the ginnel. 'See where it takes us and go through it with a fine-tooth comb.' Carol ran her hand through her hair. A sharp pain was rising from the base of her skull. How could this be happening?

Merrick was talking urgently into his radio. 'All units. Begin search of immediate area. Officer missing. Repeat, officer missing.' He glanced across at Carol. 'You want us to start door-to-door?'

She nodded. 'Jan, you take charge of that. And start with whatever's behind this gate.' Carol turned away, choking on her anger. As the officers around her dispersed, Carol wondered what she could have done differently. The worst of it was, she couldn't think of a single thing.

This one's a keeper. He doesn't know why, he just knows that's the way it has to be. The Voice makes the decisions, the Voice knows best, the Voice doesn't ever let him down.

She looks like all the others, like a whore, but this one's a cop. Knowing that makes him scared, but he still manages to do what he's supposed to. He can't get over how simple it's been to capture her. Just like the Voice said it would be. The Voice said she would come along with him, meek as a lamb, good as gold, and she has.

He plucks her off the street, easy as could be. Easier than the others, in a way, because he doesn't know this one from before. It isn't hard to think of her as a dirty piece of meat because she's never done anything to make him think otherwise. He gets her into the ginnel, then he cuts her wire just like he'd been practising all afternoon. Snip, snap, just like that. She doesn't notice a thing.

Into the yard, through the door, up the stairs. She never pauses for a moment, just keeps wittering on, thinking there's somebody listening to her giving directions to the room that's been prepared for her. She doesn't even hesitate at the double door that looks just like a cupboard when you open the outer door on the landing. She comments on it, though, thinking she's passing the message on. When he tells her to lie down on the bed and spread her legs and arms, she does as she's told. He can smell the anxiety coming off her, but she isn't scared, not really scared, not nearly scared enough. The cuffs go on and still he can tell she's waiting for the cavalry to burst through the door and save her. She doesn't even kick when he fastens the ankle restraints.

But when the gag goes on, that's a different story. He can tell she doesn't like that, not one bit. Her eyes widen and a tide of colour sweeps up from her juicy round tits to her hairline. All at once it's dawning on her that maybe it isn't going to play out the way it's supposed to. That he is in control, not her and the pathetic plods on her side. He smiles at her then, the relaxed, triumphant smile of the winner.

'They're not coming,' he says. 'You're on your own.' He leans over and reaches under her body. He pulls the transmitter out from under her skirt. Then he reaches into her cleavage and yanks out the mike and its cable. He waves the cut ends in front of her eyes. 'You've been talking to yourself,' he taunts her. 'They don't have a fucking clue where you are. You could be anywhere in Temple Fields by now. You thought you could beat us, but you were wrong. You're fucked, plod.'

He turns away, ignoring the mewling noises coming through the gag. He takes out the dildo he prepared earlier. The bright light gleams on the sharp edges of the razor blades. It's fucking wicked, this death machine. He swivels on the balls of his feet, spinning round to face her. When she sees the dildo, the colour drains from her face, leaving her chest blotchy and ugly. He steps forward, pushes up her skirt and rips her pants away. He waves the dildo in her face and grins.

That's when she pisses herself. Which annoys him, because it's going to make the room smell, and that's not very nice. Because this one's a keeper.

PART FOUR

It's a well-known fact that there exist books that change people's lives. If anyone were to ask me if such a book had ever swept through my life, I imagine they'd be profoundly surprised by the answer. But I can still remember the impact I felt when I first read John Buchan's The Three Hostages.

We were on a family holiday on the Norfolk Broads. It was as if my parents were aware of the concept of holidays but didn't really understand how they should be done. Other people got to spend the week messing about on boats, exploring the waterways and experiencing a way of life utterly different from their normal routines – locks, fens, waterfowl, the strange sensation of unreality when their feet hit solid ground after days on the water. But not us. My parents had rented a static caravan on a site where hundreds of the metal boxes sat in serried rows along a low bluff that looked out over the blue-grey waters of the North Sea. The van we'd ended up in didn't even have that view to commend it. All we could see from the windows was other caravans. It wasn't an improvement on home; even in a two-bedroomed council house, there was more space and privacy than in this thirty-two-foot tin can. I hated it, resented the other kids whose parents had taken them on a proper holiday, counted the hours till we'd be on the road home.

The weather didn't help either. A typically English summer week, grey drizzle alternating with days of watery sunlight when everybody from the caravan site trooped off to the shingle beach, stripped down to their bathing suits, hopping from one foot to the other over the painful stones to the water's edge. Then they screamed at the temperature, turned round and hopped shivering back up the beach again to flasks of hot weak coffee and egg sandwiches.

One afternoon when the rain was particularly undeniable my parents decided to go and play bingo in the community-hall-cum-snack-bar that squatted in a low concrete block in the middle of the vans. I had to go too, because at twelve I wasn't legally old enough to be left on my own. And my parents were always nauseatingly law-abiding. Smarting at the indignity, I trailed behind them, grudging and resentful. I wanted to hang out with Amanda, the beautiful blonde girl from the van two rows down, not watch a bunch of old fogeys playing bingo.

Dad bought me a Coke and a bag of crisps, pointed me in the direction of the ping-pong table and told me to amuse myself for a couple of hours and not to wander off. Like I was a little kid. Fuming, I stomped off. The ping-pong room was noisy with kids who looked at me like I'd dropped in from another planet. I slouched off towards the furthest corner and that's when I spotted the shelf of tattered hardbacks. I took a couple down from the shelves, but they didn't grab me. Then I picked The Three Hostages *and from the first page, with its images of a social milieu whose lives were utterly alien to mine, I was hooked.*

Until that moment I'd never imagined it was possible to achieve total domination over another's conscious will. The Three Hostages *spoke to me of two things I wanted above everything else: absolute superiority, and access to a world of power and success. I'd been deprived of the latter by birth, but if I seized the former for myself, I could grasp at something almost as fine.*

The Three Hostages *was the first step on a long journey to the heart of other people's minds. That control was possible, I never doubted. That I could achieve it, I never doubted. That I could use it to change the world around me remained to be seen. But on balance, I thought I could probably manage it.*

At first, my path was less than clear. I chose information as my highway, tracking down everything I could about hypnosis, altered states, brainwashing and mind control. And the more I learned, the more I tried to demonstrate my abilities to myself. I practised on school friends, I sneaked under the guard of lovers, I even tried it at work. I soon learned that my skills weren't all I had hoped for. Sometimes I achieved remarkable results. But, more often, I failed. Most minds remained resolutely beyond my grasp. And no matter how hard I tried, I just couldn't break through.

Then I discovered that there was a category of weaker minds that had few defences against my techniques. People the rest of the world dismissed as slow and stupid could be bent to my will. Not perhaps the world-shattering effect I had dreamed of, but something that offered distinct possibilities.

The question then became what I would do with the

power I had prepared myself to wield. How could I magnify what was in my grasp?

The answer came out of nowhere. The power of two.

If knowledge was power, then the choice of how to disseminate it was power in action. So Sam Evans was always willing to trade a little to get a lot. It was surprising how much people would spill if they thought you were being candid with them. So it was with Kevin. In exchange for a couple of snippets he'd picked up about Stacey Chen's background, Evans had garnered a wealth of information about Don, Paula and Kevin himself. Just the sort of things that could come in useful as subtle little pressure points if he ever needed to push them off balance.

They were sitting in a country pub a few miles from Swindale, recharging their batteries with a well-earned pint after a long and frustrating day fighting petty turf wars and conducting painstaking interviews. They were supposed to be formulating a plan of action for the morning, but they'd tacitly acknowledged that they'd had enough of the grinding depression of dealing with the deaths of children. Station gossip was far more appealing.

Kevin broke off from the story he was telling when his mobile beeped, indicating the arrival of a text message. He looked incredulously at the screen. 'Is she at the wind-up, or what?' he exclaimed, turning the phone so Evans could read the screen.

Under the heading STACEY MOBY, it read 'Killr hs capturd Paula. She's missng.'

Evans shook his head. 'Not Stacey. Not her style.'

Kevin was already dialling. As soon as the line opened, he said, 'What do you mean, the killer has captured Paula? Is this some kind of sick joke?'

'I wouldn't joke about something like that,' Stacey said, clearly offended at the suggestion. 'I meant just what I said. He's got Paula. He took her into an alley and she went off the air. By the time we got there, they'd vanished. That was about half an hour ago and we've not seen hide nor hair of either of them since.'

'Shit,' Kevin swore. 'We're coming over. We'll be there inside the hour.' He ended the call and turned to Evans. 'She meant it. While we were sitting here enjoying a pint, our fucking colleagues sat on their hands and let the killer snatch Paula from under their noses.' He jumped to his feet. 'Come on, we're going back to Bradfield.'

Evans abandoned his half-drunk pint and led the way to the door. 'How the hell did that happen?' he said.

'I don't know,' Kevin said. 'Carol Jordan was so sure she had all the bases covered.'

Evans raised his eyebrows as he followed Kevin to the car. If anything happened to Paula, it would be goodnight, Vienna for Carol Jordan. He was glad he was well clear of the night's debacle, working a case that had a better prospect of resolution. It was every man for himself out there. Anyone who thought otherwise was prey. And prey got eaten.

He had no intention of being anyone's next meal.

It was just after three in the morning when Carol made it home. Paula McIntyre had been missing for a little over six hours. Every door in Temple Fields that would respond to a thunderous tattoo of knocking had opened, every respondent had been questioned. They'd shaken down massage parlours and brothels, accosted whores and rent boys, disrupted bars and clubs. Short of taking a battering ram to all the remaining doors of Temple Fields – shops, offices, flats, bedsits and who knew what else – they had done everything they could to find Paula. But it was as if she and her assailant had vanished into thin air. The maze of alleys, back yards and lanes had yielded nothing in the way of clues. Jan Shields had led a team through the gate in the wall and into the building behind it, which seemed mostly to serve as storage for a local printshop. Their search had turned up nothing to indicate that anyone had passed that way for days.

Finally, Carol had called it a night. Several officers had protested, expressing their willingness to continue searching, but Carol had vetoed their requests. Nothing of use could be done before daybreak, she said firmly. The best service they could offer Paula now was to get some sleep. What none of them was prepared to voice was their conviction that they were already too late.

Carol had walked back to the surveillance van with Jan Shields and Don Merrick in a despondent silence.

When they got there, Jan had shaken her head. 'I'm not coming back yet. I've still got contacts out there. There are people I need to talk to. You'll be amazed who ends up on our side once they realize it's a cop on the missing list. They'll want this sorted nearly as badly as we do.'

'Bad for business, is it?' Merrick said sourly.

'Yeah, you could say that.' Jan pulled her soft leather jacket closer to her face. 'I'll see you at the briefing.'

Carol made no attempt to stop her. They watched till she was swallowed up by the mist. 'I told her this morning she didn't need to go through with this,' Merrick said.

Carol could feel the heat of his hostility but was too weary to get into it with him. 'She knew that already, Don. It was her choice,' she said heavily. She yanked open the door of the van and climbed inside. 'I'm going home to get some sleep. I suggest you do the same rather than chase your tail round Temple Fields for the rest of the night.' She didn't wait for his response. When he hadn't followed her after twenty seconds, she slammed the door shut and ordered the driver to take them back to the station.

She thanked Stacey for holding the fort, then asked one of the technicians to run the CCTV footage of Paula's last encounter again. They watched it half a dozen times on the journey, but none of them saw anything new. When they arrived back at base, she ordered the technicians to do everything they could to enhance both sound and vision. Then she walked to her car, feeling so old and tired she could hardly put one foot in front of the other.

By the time she got to her door, she was trembling with a mixture of despair and exhaustion. She was pathetically grateful to see a light burning in Tony's study. She leaned on his doorbell. He opened the door dressed in jogging pants and a T-shirt, a puzzled look on his face.

'He's got Paula,' Carol said. Each word felt as if it had been dragged out of her. She closed her eyes tightly, tilting her head back. Tony stepped on to the freezing doorstep and put his arms round her. For a few seconds, her body remained rigid. Then her head was on his shoulder, tears coursing down her face. Tony said nothing. He supported her weight, letting her lean into him, feeling her body shudder as she let go her grief.

Eventually, the storm abated. Carol withdrew slightly, meeting his concerned look. 'I'm OK,' she said shakily.

'No, you're not.' Tony led her indoors and helped her sit. 'You want a drink?'

Carol nodded, wiping the tracks of her tears from her cheeks. 'Please.'

He nodded, heading for the kitchen. He reappeared a minute later with two glasses of white wine, handing one to Carol before sitting down next to her. 'You want to talk about it?'

Carol took a mouthful of wine. It tasted alien, as if something had chemically altered her tastebuds. 'Call it displacement activity if you want, but I can't talk about Paula until I know where we stand with each other.'

'Then you need to tell me what I need to know.'

Carol drank more wine. This time, it tasted closer

to what she expected. 'Since the rape, I've felt like I didn't own my body any more. It took me a while to realize that I needed a sexual experience that would show me I was still in control of my responses. I needed it to be about me and I needed it to be uncomplicated.' She put the palm of her hand on his back, feeling the warmth of his skin through his shirt.

He snorted. 'Which ruled me out on both counts.'

Her half-smile signalled agreement. 'And suddenly there was Jonathan. Understanding, generous, attractive and absolutely not somebody I could fall in love with. So I used him. I'm not particularly proud of that, but there's no reason for you to feel jealous. You get more of me every day than I let him have.'

'But I am jealous. I'm jealous that it's so easy for him and so hard for me.'

'I was trying to make it easier for both of us.'

'I know. But that's not going to happen any time soon, is it? For you and me to be at ease with each other?'

His voice was sadder than she'd ever heard it. 'I don't know,' she said bleakly. 'I just know that I . . .'

'Don't say it.' He cut across her harshly. 'I feel the same. But the timing's never right, is it? There's always something with a greater claim on us, something that pushes us apart. And right now, it's Paula. So tell me what happened tonight.'

Carol outlined the evening's events. 'She's dead. And I let it happen. Knowing what I know about how these things can go wrong, I still let it happen.'

Tony jumped to his feet and started pacing. 'I don't think she is dead. This killer wants his victims found, and found while they're still fresh. He sets it up so they will be found. Paula hasn't been found, so logic dictates she's probably still alive.'

Carol shook her head. 'But why would he change his MO?'

'That's a good question. Maybe because he realized Paula's a cop. If you remember, I said to you after the first night that he might have spotted that she was a decoy.'

'Even so, why would that make a difference?'

'He likes power. It may be that he's keeping her alive because it gives him even more power to savour, having a cop under control. It gives him power over us as well as over her. He's the stage manager, the conductor of the orchestra. We have to dance to his tune if we want Paula back alive.'

Carol frowned. 'What do you mean, "dance to his tune"?'

Tony waved a hand impatiently. 'I don't know yet. Either he'll make that clear to us or we'll have to figure it out for ourselves.' He paced again then stopped abruptly and whirled round to face her. 'Carol, how did he know she was wearing a wire?'

'You answered that yourself. He must have figured out she was a decoy and realized she would be wired. That's probably why he started pawing her as soon as he got her in the alley.'

'This is way too sophisticated for Derek Tyler,' he muttered.

'But it wasn't Derek Tyler last night. Derek Tyler's banged up in Bradfield Moor.'

'I know, I know. But these are the same crimes, the same brain behind them. And it's not Derek Tyler's brain. He's not smart enough, not controlled enough.' He fixed Carol with a freshly energized stare. 'The person behind this isn't just pulling our strings. He's pulling the killer's strings too.'

Carol shook her head stubbornly. 'I don't buy it. People don't kill because somebody asks them to. Only contract killers do that. And if this is a contract killer, then he's doing it at the behest of someone who wants to send Derek Tyler a "Get out of jail free" card. We need to go back through his life again, find out who might want him out and why.'

'You're wrong, Carol,' Tony sighed. 'But if you're determined to go down that path, then maybe you should be looking into the lives of his victims, not Tyler himself.'

Carol drained her glass and stood up. 'His victims?'

'If I loved someone who was murdered, and their killer didn't even get life, if he just got sent to a mental hospital that theoretically he could be released from at any time, I probably wouldn't feel that justice had been done. I'd want that killer in my grasp. Given the kind of circles his victims moved in, it's not beyond the bounds of possibility that there's someone who loved one of his victims and who is now in a position to hire a contract killer to replicate those crimes, in the expectation that you'll have to let Tyler go as a result.' He shrugged. 'It has a kind of logic to it.'

Carol stared at him, her mouth open. 'Logic?' she stammered.

'No, Carol. It's bollocks. If there was anything in what I've just suggested, the person hiring the contract killer would also have sent a lawyer in to

Tyler, pushing him towards an appeal. And that hasn't happened.'

'There's time,' she said. 'Maybe he'll try to use Paula as a bargaining chip.'

'Carol, if you get a demand from the killer offering you Paula in exchange for an admission that Derek Tyler was wrongly convicted, I will buy you dinner every night for a year.'

'Deal,' she said.

He swallowed the last of his wine. 'And now I think it's time for sleep. We've both got important work to do . . .' He glanced at his watch and groaned. 'Starting in a few hours.'

'I didn't thank you for the profile in the Tim Golding case,' Carol said, following him to the front door 'It was very helpful.'

'You're welcome. I didn't think you got your money's worth before.'

'Will you go out and take a look at the scene?'

He spread his hands in a gesture of helplessness. 'I was thinking about going out there tomorrow. But with Paula missing . . .'

'It can probably wait.'

'Who have you got on it?' he asked.

'Kevin and Sam. And Stacey will do the liaison with the paedophile unit. Don wanted it back, but frankly I'm not convinced he's up to it. When all this shit is over, I think I'm going to ask Brandon to move him back to mainstream CID. Maybe by then Chris Devine will be able to move north. She'd make a good DI.' Her face clouded over. 'God, when I think how much I was looking forward to this assignment. I thought it was going to be my salvation. But right now, it feels like the last nail in the coffin.'

Stacey Chen loved her job. Her parents had embraced computer technology with eagerness when it first became generally available in the late eighties. They owned a chain of Chinese supermarkets and the capacity of the machines to keep track of stock and transactions enchanted them. Stacey could hardly remember a time when there hadn't been computers in her life. An only child, she'd taken to silicon the way other children took to Barbie dolls or books. Frustrated by the limitations of those early home computers, she'd learned programming code so she could write her own games for machines that had only ever been meant to do word processing and simple accounts. By the time she started studying computer science at UMIST, she'd already earned enough to buy a city-centre loft, thanks to a neat little piece of code she'd sold to a US software giant which secured their operating system against potential software conflicts. Her lecturers predicted a meteoric career for her in the dotcom world. None of them could quite believe it when she'd announced that she planned to join the police.

It made absolute sense to Stacey, however. She loved the unpicking of problems. Rooting around in other people's systems was meat and drink to her, and here was a way she could satisfy her urges without breaking any laws. And she had enough time off to pursue her own commercial interests without any of the potential clashes that might have arisen if she'd been working for a software company. So what if her police salary was peanuts compared to what she made in her own time? Her job gave her legitimate sanction to invade other people's secrets, and that was satisfaction enough.

She didn't even need to be in the office to creep through everyone else's data. She'd set up her own home computing systems to allow her network access to all the machines used by the Major Incident Team. And because she'd designated herself as a systems operator she didn't even have to go through the tiresome process of capturing their passwords. She could simply wander at will through their machines. And so she knew Kevin's taste for soft-porn sites where he could browse for free without handing over any personal details. She knew Don Merrick's penchant for American baseball, Paula's addiction to news websites and Jan's habit of ordering books from an online women's bookstore in York. She'd been intrigued by Carol Jordan's wariness to commit to the machine until she'd uncovered the information that her brother worked in software development. Carol was clearly only too aware of the footprints that any activity left on a computer.

She also knew about Sam Evans' late-night trawls. She'd sat in her flat noting his keystrokes, watching him trying to break into his colleagues' files and failing every time at the password hurdle. She should have felt that Sam was a kindred spirit, but instead she despised him for his incompetence. He should stick to hanging out on those gross post-mortem sites he liked so much. That was about his speed. God, but cops were weird.

Tonight she was alone on the system, however.

Wherever Sam was, he wasn't skulking round the office, trying to steal a march on the rest of them. And there was nothing new on the hard drive to interest her. She wondered what was happening over in Temple Fields. A few keyboard commands and a couple of mouse clicks and she could see what the cameras were feeding back to the computer.

Stacey poured herself another cup of coffee from the Thermos on her desk and settled down for a long hard look.

Paula had no idea how long she had been lying in the stark, oppressive room with its bare bulb making everything brutally vivid. At first, all she'd felt was overwhelming relief and gratitude that she was still alive. She had no idea why that should be; she knew his previous victims must have been attacked almost as soon as he'd snatched them from the street. And when he had produced that vile, horrifying implement, she'd been sure she was going the same way. But no. He'd simply exposed her genitals to the camera, brandished the lethal dildo in front of her and giggled. Then he'd checked her bindings and stepped back, fingering his cock through the faded denim of his baggy trousers. She'd thought then he was going to rape her, but that fear wasn't realized either. He'd gazed hungrily at her for a few minutes, stroking his erection as if it were a pet rat. Then he'd checked the video camera and the webcam and left.

Since then, she'd been alone. She'd struggled to free herself, but soon gave up, understanding that the only thing she was achieving was the fruitless expenditure of energy she might need later. She'd tried shouting for help, but the gag pressing against her mouth was far too effective to allow anything other than a moan to escape. There was nothing to do but lie there, shivering with cold and fear. The puddle of piss beneath her had soaked into the thin mattress and spread out, making her even colder.

Paula tried to convince herself they'd be coming to get her soon. Carol Jordan would never abandon her. That he'd left her alive made her think he believed they were close on his heels. He'd gone because he didn't expect to have the time to sit and watch her die once he'd cut her. But as the time trickled by, she began to lose faith. At one point she'd thought she heard faint footfalls and muffled conversation. But even as she strained to hear, the sounds faded and she was left wondering if it had all been her imagination.

This was all her own fault. How could she have missed him cutting the wire? If she'd been paying attention to her mission instead of freaking out because he'd pinched her nipple so painfully, she'd have known she was on her own. Then, as soon as they reached the room and she'd seen confirmation in the tools of his trade arranged on the table, she could have taken him by surprise and nailed him. But she'd dropped the ball. She'd focused on her reactions rather than on the job and now she was paying the price.

But she was still alive. As long as she was still alive, she could believe in rescue. Carol Jordan would break down every door in Temple Fields if she had to. She knew what it was like to be hung out to dry by her bosses, and there was no way she would allow that to happen to Paula. Whatever it took, Carol would find her.

The minutes ground by inexorably. Exhausted, Paula was drifting in and out of an altered state that bordered sleep but never quite crossed over. When the door opened, she couldn't be sure initially whether she was dreaming it. Her heart leapt in her chest. They'd found her!

Hope perished in seconds when the cruelly familiar shape of her kidnapper came into view. He'd swapped the parka for a hooded top, presumably to avoid being recognized. But she knew who he was only too well. 'Only me,' he said. 'Come to change the tape. The webcam's not very good, that's why we need the video too. So we can enjoy watching you suffer.'

If she strained her neck, she could see him move behind the video camera and remove the tape. He put it in his pocket, then leaned over and did something to the webcam. He leered at her. 'I'm not supposed to touch you. The Voice says I've to wait till the time is right. But the Voice doesn't see everything.'

He came towards her, one hand rubbing himself. He climbed awkwardly on to the bed. Paula smelled stale cannabis smoke and the acid tang of half-digested beer as he moved on top of her. He was heavy and clumsy, the zip on his jacket scratching the soft skin of her belly. Suddenly, she felt the smoothness of latex between her labia, fumbling towards her vagina. She tensed herself against him and he grunted. 'Don't make it harder on yourself, you silly cunt,' he growled in her ear. She tried to twist away, but her bonds were too tight and he was too heavy.

Then he was inside her, fingers pounding and thrusting while he rode her thigh. She could feel his cock rigid through his clothes. Paula bit down on the gag, fighting tears. She didn't want him to see how much he'd got to her. She tried to dissociate herself from what was happening to her body, but it didn't work.

Mercifully, it was over quickly. He hammered his hand into her, his hips forcing her thigh deep into the mattress as he speeded up. His head arched back and he yelped like a kicked puppy. Then he collapsed on top of her, his fingers slithering out of her bruised vagina. He rolled over and grinned. 'Tight bitch. I like that. It'll be more fun when I do you.'

He clambered off the bed, adjusting his jacket to cover the damp patch on his trousers. He slotted a new tape into the video camera, set the webcam running again and headed for the door. 'See you later, alligator,' he said, waving as he went.

The door slammed shut. Only then did Paula begin to weep.

Carol was in her office making notes for the briefing when Kevin and Sam arrived. 'Guv, can we have a word?' Kevin asked.

She waved them to take a seat with a resigned nod. She'd been half-expecting this. Just another messy conversation that would end up making her feel about as much use as a blind man in an archery contest. 'Let me guess. You want to help find Paula?'

'She's one of us, guv. You said at the start we had to be a team. It doesn't feel right that you've pulled me and DC Evans off on something else when one of the team is on the line,' Kevin said.

'I do understand how you feel,' Carol said. 'But I need to know I have the best possible officers running the Golding and Lefevre inquiry. You must have seen the papers this morning – they know two bodies have been found. They're speculating. The anti-paedophile hysterics are building up a head of steam, and we're directly in their paths. We have to be seen to be devoting our resources to finding their killer.'

'But they're dead, and Paula might still be alive,' Evans protested.

'They may be dead, but they're still important. And whoever killed them is still out there, possibly planning his next crime.'

'We're not saying they're not important, guv,' Kevin argued. 'What Sam means is that there's less urgency.'

'Yeah, it wouldn't hurt if we put it on hold for a day or two, just while the hunt for Paula's going on,' Evans interjected.

'We can't put it on hold, however much you might like to.' Carol tapped her finger on a file on her desk. 'Two positive IDs: Tim Golding and Guy Lefevre. Cause of death in both cases is most probably manual strangulation. We can't keep that from the press. You've already started stirring the pot with the park service and with other groups who may have visited Swindale. Unless our man is deaf and blind, he's going to know we're looking for him. I don't want to give him space to wriggle out from under. We need to keep up the pressure. I'm sorry, guys. You stay with Tim and Guy.'

Both men still looked mutinous. 'But, guv . . .' Kevin began.

'Kevin, the best thing you can do for Paula is to get an early result on this case. You know that'll boost morale, help everyone believe we can bring Paula home safe and catch whoever has taken her. There's no great skill in knocking on doors and chasing up official records, which is more or less all we have to go at this morning. Please, use your talents to give us something positive.' Carol felt faintly surprised at herself. It was the kind of persuasion she would have used without a thought in previous times. That it came so easily to her now restored some of the confidence she'd lost overnight.

Kevin at least fell for the bait. He visibly puffed up, basking in the glow of Carol's flattery. 'We'll do our best,' he said, getting to his feet.

Evans looked at him, then back at Carol. He shook his head in disbelief then followed Kevin out of the door. As they went, she heard him say, 'I can't believe you fell for that bollocks . . .'

Carol was on her feet and at the door. 'Evans,' she shouted. 'Back here. Now.' Startled, he turned back. 'Kevin, I'm taking Evans off you. Don't let me down.' She glared at Evans. 'My office. Now.'

Carol shut the door behind them. 'We're all under strain here, but that's no excuse for insubordination. I do not want my officers working with anything less than a whole heart, and it's clear to me that you are not prepared to give a hundred per cent to easing the pain of two sets of parents whose sons have been murdered.'

'That's not fair.' Evans' expression was mutinous.

'Don't talk back to me, Constable,' Carol said, each word enunciated with chill clarity. 'If you want to stay on this squad, you had better understand that I do not care about your personal preferences when it comes to assignments. I thought I'd already made that clear to you? I choose people for particular tasks because I think they are fitted to them. You're a talented detective, Evans, but that doesn't mean you have the right to question my decisions, especially not in my hearing. I'm reassigning you to the Temple Fields inquiry. But don't think you've won. As of now, you are number one on my shit list and it's going to take something very special indeed to get you out of that slot.'

A flicker of arrogance crossed Evans' face. 'You won't be waiting long,' he said. 'Ma'am.'

Carol shook her head in exasperation. 'It's time to grow up, Evans. Now get out of my sight before I have you reassigned to Traffic.' She watched him leave and sighed. One step forward and two steps back. Time to change the dance, she thought bitterly. Time to pick up momentum and crack the case.

On the giant TV screen, Paula once more stood on a misty street corner. The man in the parka approached and touched her arm. The dialogue boomed out, still crackly but more clear than it had been in Carol's earpiece the night before. Paula and the man rounded the corner and the screen faded to static. The soundtrack continued to the point where it ended as abruptly as a slap to the face. There was absolute silence in the room as the lights went back on. Most of the team looked about as shit as Carol felt. *Showtime,* she thought, squaring her shoulders and stretching her fingers like a pianist. 'OK,' she said. 'That's the last we saw of Paula. She is still missing. Our job is to find her. Dr Hill believes the chances are good that Paula is alive. This killer wants his victims found while they're fresh. The fact that we haven't found Paula suggests she's not a victim yet. So let's get to her before that changes. Does anyone recognize that voice? Does that man look familiar? These are the questions we need to be asking.

'We have photographs of Paula at the back of the room. There are also stills from the video available to you. And we've got a limited number of microcassette recorders with tapes of the man's voice that you can play to people in Temple Fields, see if we can get an ID that way. There should be more tape machines available later in the day.

'I'm splitting you into three teams. DI Merrick will remain here, collating information as it comes in via statement readers and HOLMES operators. Sergeant MacLeod from uniform will be in charge of the team extracting details from the council tax registers of every property in Temple Fields. DS Shields will be in charge of the team who will interview every tenant and resident in the area, assisted by information from Sergeant MacLeod's team. No stone unturned, people. We've got an officer out there depending on us. And we're not going to let her down.' Carol's voice rang out with a confidence she didn't entirely feel. But it was her job to make them feel gung-ho, and she was determined to succeed. As they filed out, she called, 'DI Merrick, DS Shields and DC Chen, a word, please.'

The remnants of her squad gathered around her.

'You've all worked closely with Paula. Is there anyone we should inform about what's happened? Parents? Partner?'

'Her mum and dad live in Manchester,' Merrick volunteered. 'I can get an address. Do you want me to go and talk to them?'

'No, it's fine, Don. Get me the address and I'll deal with it myself.' *If anyone's going to get a kicking, it should be me.* 'So, that's it? Parents, no partner?'

'She hasn't got a girlfriend at the moment,' Jan said absently.

Merrick rounded on her angrily. 'What do you mean, a girlfriend?'

Jan gave Merrick a pitying look. 'A lover, a significant other, whatever. Who happens to be female, in Paula's case.'

'Bullshit,' Merrick exploded. 'Paula's not a dyke.'

Jan snorted with laughter. 'You're living under her roof and you hadn't noticed she's gay? Call yourself a detective?'

Carol did a double-take. Her DI was living with one of her DCs? Who happened to be gay? And she'd known nothing of it? There was something seriously amiss with the bush telegraph on this squad, which she'd have to rectify once they had recovered Paula and things had returned to something approaching normal. It wasn't that Carol wanted prurient gossip; simply that, if the squad was to work properly, she had to understand the personal dynamics.

'In your dreams, Shields. You're talking shite,' Merrick said contemptuously.

Jan shook her head, her cherub's face registering

amusement. 'If you say so, Inspector.' Merrick glared at her, frustrated.

Stacey, who had been watching the exchange like a Wimbledon spectator, suddenly spoke up. 'What does it matter who she likes to sleep with? She's not been abducted because she's gay or straight, she's been abducted because she's a cop and we put her out there to do our dirty work. And I'm going back to my computer to do what I can to put things right. Ma'am?' She looked to Carol.

'I couldn't have put it better myself, Stacey. For Christ's sake, you two, get with the programme. We've got a job to do. Shall we get on with it?'

Tony stared at the man curled up on the bed with his back to the room. Again, Tyler had refused to come either to Tony's office or to an interview room. But this time, Tony was not to be denied. He was going to prise something from the man. If Paula McIntyre didn't come out of this alive, he knew Carol would never work as a police officer again, and much as he found that idea personally attractive, he knew he couldn't sit idly by while she lost the one thing that had shaped her sense of herself as an adult.

He pulled up a chair close to the bed and leaned forward, elbows on knees. He gathered his thoughts, focused his energies and spoke conversationally. 'It's not nice, is it? Knowing you've been dumped in favour of somebody else?' Tyler didn't move a muscle.

'I mean, when you hear voices, the least you expect is that they'll be faithful to you. Not abandon you like a pair of worn-out shoes just because you can't deliver the goods any more.' Tyler's leg twitched.

'I can see that's a notion that upsets you. And no wonder. I'd be upset in your shoes. You've been cast adrift, Derek. I bet you thought your voice was going to get you out of here, didn't you? I bet that's why you played the "mad not bad" game, because the voice told you to keep your mouth shut. So one day you could start talking again and we'd think you were cured.' A definite movement, Tony thought. The shoulders tightened, the legs drew further up.

'It's a funny thing, but I've noticed over the years that with most people who hear voices, at some level they're using the voice as their excuse. Now me, if I thought the Virgin Mary was telling me to kill prostitutes, I wouldn't do it, because I've got no deep-seated desire to kill prostitutes. But a man who secretly believed prostitutes were evil would use the voice as an excuse to do what he thought was the right thing. Like Peter Sutcliffe claimed when he was trying to play the "mad not bad" game.'

Tony deepened his voice, aiming for warmth and sympathy. 'But I don't think that's how it was with you, Derek. I don't think you used the voice. I think the voice used you. And now it's using somebody else. Face it, Derek, you're not as special as you thought you were.'

Suddenly Tyler uncoiled and rolled over. He jerked into a sitting position on the edge of the bed, his face inches from Tony. Tony maintained his expression of compassion and concern. Time to play his ace. 'You've been loyal to the voice, but it's let you down. It's left you here to rot. It's found somebody else to do its bidding. It's betrayed you, Derek. So you might as well return the favour.'

The silence dragged out between them for a long minute. Then Tyler leaned even closer. Tony could feel the heat of the other man's breath against his skin. 'I've been waiting for you,' he croaked.

Tony nodded gently. 'I know, Derek.'

His eyes opened so wide Tony could see the iris as a perfect circle against the white. 'I'm supposed to be slow. All these doctors, they're supposed to be clever. But they never got it.'

'I know.'

'They all thought it was the voice of God or something. But I'm not daft, you know. I might be slow, but I'm not daft.'

'I know that too. So whose voice was it?'

Tyler's lips curled back in a triumphant sneer. 'The Creeper.'

'The Creeper?' Tony tried not to show disappointment. 'Who's the Creeper?'

Tyler withdrew a few inches and tapped the side of his nose. 'You're so bloody smart, you figure it out.' Then, in one single fluid movement, he rolled back into his foetal crouch, facing the wall.

If they'd only sussed it out soon enough, it could have been a field day for Bradfield's opportunist criminals. Every available officer was out on the streets in a kaleidoscope of encounters.

On a corner near the sex shop, putting potential customers off, PC Danny Wells: 'Have you seen this woman in the past twenty-four hours?' The photograph of Paula, grinning at the camera on a girls' night out with her colleagues. 'Do you recognize this man?' The video still. *It could be anybody, really,* Danny thought. 'Listen to this voice. Do you recognize it?' Play, stop, rewind.

In the newsagent's down the street from Paula's pitch, DS Jan Shields. The Asian behind the counter had the air of a man puffed up with righteous indignation. 'Have you seen this woman?' Paula's photo placed on a pile of morning papers. A shake of the head. 'Do you know this man?' The video still placed next to Paula. A shrug.

'How do I know? It could be anybody. It could be you,' he said insolently.

'Do you own this property?'

'No, I just rent the shop.'

'Only the shop? What about the upper floors?'

'Flats. Nothing to do with me.'

'OK. I'm going to need the name and contact details of your landlord.'

The shopkeeper scowled. 'Why is this your business? Is there a problem?'

'Yeah, there's a problem, but it's probably not yours. Can I see your back room?'

Suddenly his bluster was replaced with apprehension. 'Why do you want to do that? It's just a storeroom.'

Jan, not in any mood to argue, leaned on the counter. 'Listen, I don't give a toss if you've got wall-to-wall smuggled fags back there; that's not what I'm looking for. Just let me take a look, OK? Then I'll be out of here. Otherwise, I'll be on the phone to Customs and Excise right now, pal.'

He glared at her, then lifted the counter flap to let her through. 'I can explain . . .'

And in the offices of Bradfield Metropolitan

Council, Sergeant Phil MacLeod. He stood at the head of a group of five officers at the reception desk of the local taxation office. The woman behind the desk looked dubious. 'We shut at twelve today. It's Saturday,' she said.

'Not today you don't. This is a murder inquiry.'

She looked perplexed and frightened. 'I don't know what the procedure is,' she said.

'It's a matter of public record. All you need to do is show me the council tax register for these streets.' Sergeant MacLeod produced a list of the streets of Temple Fields.

'I'm going to have to get my boss.'

'Whatever. Just do it,' MacLeod snapped.

And in a house converted from former Victorian glory to an aggregate of bedsits, DC Laura Blythe. She knocked on a door. No reply. She walked down a hallway smelling of curry and cabbage and knocked on the next door. A bleary-eyed young man in boxers and a T-shirt opened up. Blythe produced her warrant card. 'DC Blythe, Bradfield Police. We're looking for a woman who has been abducted. I wonder if I might take a look inside your flat?'

'Do what?' He looked flabbergasted.

'I just need to satisfy myself that she's not here.'

'You think I've kidnapped somebody?' Incredulity and confusion.

'No, but she went missing very near here and it's my job to eliminate people from our inquiry. So, can I take a quick look?'

'You got a warrant?'

Blythe lowered her voice and went for menacing. 'Don't make me get one. I'm having a very bad day.'

She produced Paula's photo. 'I'm not interested in anything else. Just her.'

He gave a bemused shake of the head and pushed the door open to reveal the scuzzy chaos within. 'She's not my type, love,' he said ironically.

Carol stood in the doorway of Tony's office at Bradfield Moor. It looked like everywhere he'd ever worked – so crowded with books and paper it was impossible to discern any fundamental architecture. He was like a squirrel, building the same nest around himself year after year. 'You left a message on my phone? Sounded urgent.'

He looked up from his computer and smiled. 'Thanks for coming. I thought you'd just phone.'

'I was already heading out of town. I'm on my way to see Paula's parents.' She came in and sat down.

'Ah.'

'Quite. So, what have you got for me?'

'Tyler talked,' Tony said.

'You're kidding,' she exclaimed.

'Don't get too excited.' He ran through the conversation then looked expectantly at Carol.

She ran her hands through her hair. 'The Creeper? That's it?'

He nodded eagerly. 'I told you Derek Tyler hadn't got the wit to commit organized offences like this off his own bat. These murders weren't Tyler's idea. It was never his set-up.'

'So we're back to your theory of some puppet-master pulling Derek Tyler's strings? And now he's back at his old tricks?'

'That's one possibility. It would mean he's found

someone as suggestible as Tyler, which can't have been that easy. But maybe he's spent the last two years plucking up the courage to do it himself.'

'Oh God,' she groaned. 'You know how crazy this sounds?'

'I know. But it's the one thing that makes sense of all the information we have. Either the ringmaster has someone new to control or he's doing it himself.'

An anxious thought crept into Carol's mind. 'What sort of person would be able to control another person to this degree?' she asked, almost reluctant.

Tony frowned. 'You'd be looking at a strong personality. Someone with the ability to charm people, to get under their skin. They'd know a lot about brainwashing techniques. They would probably have developed skills in hypnosis.'

'Someone like you, in fact?' Carol tried to make it sound like a tease but failed.

Tony gave her an odd look. 'They'd have to have better social skills than me,' he said ironically. 'But yes, a practising clinical psychologist could probably do it.' He tilted his head to one side. 'Carol, what are you not telling me?'

'Nothing,' she said with a nervous laugh. This wasn't the time to mention Evans' obsession with Aidan Hart. First she wanted to figure out what she thought herself. 'I need to find the connection to Tyler. Whoever the Creeper is, he was in Tyler's life back then. And I need to get the teams on the streets asking if anyone's heard of the Creeper.'

Tony studied her for a long moment, puzzling over her words. Then he stood up and reached for his coat. 'And I need to think. I'm going back to where Paula went missing.' He paused on his way out the door. 'She's still alive, Carol. I'm sure of it.'

And the kaleidoscope shifted. Inside a chichi pub with bed-and-breakfast rooms on the upper floors, DC Sam Evans. The publican was thirty-something, shaved head, leather waistcoat over a bare torso and leather trousers, polishing glasses with a bar towel. The questions, the photos and the tape. The publican shrugged. 'Doesn't ring any bells, mate.'

'So how many rooms do you have?'

'Eight doubles and two singles.'

'I'd like to take a look at them.'

'Four of them are occupied.' The publican put down his towel.

'I'd especially like to take a look at those ones.'

The publican leered at Evans. 'Into voyeurism, are you, pet?'

Evans leaned on the bar. He fixed the publican with a menacing stare. 'When does your licence come up for renewal? Sir?'

And in a room not fifty yards from the pub, Paula lay glassy-eyed on the bed, the fly captured by the spider. Her mouth was so dry her lips were gummed to the gag. Her captor had been back again to change the tape, but this time he'd left her alone, contenting himself with brandishing the dildo in her face. She had never been so afraid in her life. Her mind was beginning to slip its cogs, strange ideas tumbling over each other in her head. What if this was her punishment for doubting Carol Jordan? What if this was her punishment for being gay? Nothing made sense any more. All she lived for was the opening of the door and for it not to be him on the other side of it.

And on the streets that formed the web around the spider's prey, life went on in patterns too deep-set to be altered by the heavy weight of the police presence. People were more cautious than usual, but still the regular transactions continued. Dee had already found another fuckpad to entertain her customers in; that afternoon, she was bouncing mechanically on top of an office furniture sales rep whose wife was walking their two children home from school while he grunted under Dee. Honey was scoring a wrap of heroin from Carl Mackenzie, both of them well aware that the cops swarming the streets wouldn't have cared if it had been a kilo of pure Chinese white.

And a killer was swaggering on the streets of Temple Fields, wrapped in a sense of contemptuous invulnerability.

Alone in the elite squad's room, Stacey Chen noted the arrival of new email. Seeing there was an attachment, she ran it through her personal virus checker, then, satisfied it was safe to do so, she opened it. It came from Nick Sanders, a ranger in the Peak National Park, and included his log from July as well as a couple of dozen photographs of Chee Dale and Swindale. As she flicked through them, another program activated itself. Stacey had set up a capture program to analyse every JPEG file that her machine encountered, classifying them according to camera serial number when it could be found. She planned to offer the software to the paedophile investigation unit to help them sort files from a variety of sources into associated batches so they could see possible connections between different individuals, but she needed to be sure she'd ironed out any bugs first.

As she turned back to the files she'd been working on previously, one of the SOCOs came in. 'DCI Jordan around?' he asked.

'She's gone to Manchester. Can I help?'

He dropped a file on her desk. 'We managed to extract DNA from the contaminated sample on Jackie Mayall. It's a bit degraded – not good enough to run against the national database for a positive match, but certainly enough for elimination purposes. It won't nail your guy absolutely, but it'll give you a decent pointer if you get the right man.'

'Cheers. I'll make sure she sees it as soon as she gets back,' Stacey said absently, her mind already turning back to the task in hand.

She was surprised when she looked back at the screen to see a flashing window in the centre. <Camera match> it said. She sighed. Probably the same old glitch she'd been trying to solve for a week or two now. Instead of reading a group of images from the same source as a single batch, it was picking each of them up individually and telling her they were in fact matches against something already on the system. She'd thought she'd finally ironed it out, but clearly she'd been mistaken. All it would be telling her was that some of the photos in Sanders' attachment had been taken by the same camera as each other. Hardly earth-shattering stuff, and something she was going to have to work harder to sort out before she could let anybody else loose with the program. With no great hopes, she clicked on the window. And sat there staring, hardly able to believe the evidence of her eyes.

'Holy shit,' she muttered, reaching for the phone.

It had taken Tony longer than he would have liked to make it to Temple Fields. As he'd been leaving Bradfield Moor, he'd been collared by Aidan Hart demanding a case conference on one of Tony's patients. 'Not now, Aidan,' he'd said impatiently.

'Yes, Tony, now. This is one of the mornings you're contracted to work here, after all,' Hart had said implacably.

'You know that's just a formality. I put my hours in – hell, I put more than my hours in – at times that suit me and my patients.'

Hart had tried a conciliatory smile. 'What's so important that it can't wait a couple of hours?'

Tony ran a hand through his hair. 'It's the prostitute killer. He's kidnapped a police officer. I think she's still alive.'

'Surely that's a matter for the police? They don't expect you to search for her, do they?' Hart said, aiming for impish irony.

'No. But I've got something from Tyler and I need to figure out how it moves us forward.'

Hart looked startled. 'Tyler talked to you?'

'A bit. We've got a nickname for the killer. Or at least, the person behind the killer.'

Hart's eyes widened. 'A nickname?'

'I can't tell you, Aidan. It's still confidential.'

Hart's tongue flicked at the corners of his mouth. 'I think I understand confidentiality, Tony.'

'Even so . . .'

'OK, OK. But what do you mean by "the person behind the killer"?'

Tony frowned. 'I haven't got time for this now, Aidan. I need to get into town.'

Hart clamped a hand on his shoulder. 'I'm sorry, Tony. I need you at this case conference.' He steered him back down the corridor. 'So, what's this about a person behind the killer?'

'It's just an idea. I'm not really ready to talk about it,' Tony hedged, uncomfortable at what was starting to feel like an intrusion into the other part of his professional life. He'd clammed up then and sat through the case conference, his spirit chafing but his sense of duty requiring him to support his patient as best he could.

Eventually, however, he'd escaped. Now he was back on the streets of Temple Fields, retracing the steps of Paula's abductor, trying to figure out where he might have come from. As he walked, his lips moved, but he didn't notice the stares he earned from other pedestrians. Twice, he was stopped by police officers, brandishing photos of Paula, officers who were mildly embarrassed when he explained who he was and what he was doing.

'So where is she? Why haven't you given her back to us? You gave us all the others. Why not Paula? We know you've got the power. What are you trying to prove?' he said under his breath as he walked, the questions taking him round in circles that were far smaller than the ones his feet were tracing on the pavements and alleys.

He rounded another corner and walked straight into Jan Shields and Sam Evans, deep in conversation in the lee of a betting-shop awning. Not bothering with preliminaries, he said, 'The Creeper – what does that mean to you?'

Evans shrugged. 'Virginia creeper? Brothel creepers?'

Jan shook her head. 'Not a clue. Sounds like a nickname, but it's not one I've ever heard.'

Tony nodded. 'Pimps have nicknames, don't they?'

'Some of them, yeah. But, like I keep saying, we don't have many pimps left around here,' Jan said.

'Can you ask around, see if anyone's ever heard it?' Tony asked.

'Sure. But what's the relevance?' Evans asked.

Tony looked about him as if the answer might be lurking in one of the adjacent buildings.

'Tony?' Jan prompted.

'I think it's someone Derek Tyler knew,' Tony said, collecting himself. 'Someone who might be able to shed some light on these killings.'

'I don't remember seeing that in his file,' Evans said.

'It's not in his file. He told me himself.' Tony was still looking around, his mind already somewhere else.

'You got Tyler to talk?' Evans asked, incredulous.

Distracted, Tony took half a step beyond them. 'Not nearly enough,' he mumbled. 'And I don't think he's going to give me any more till I can prove I deserve it.'

He walked away, unaware of their looks of astonishment. He carried on to the end of the street, then traced a path through the lanes and alleys till he was in the place where Paula was last heard. 'I thought so,' he said. 'There had to be a circle.'

He leaned against the gate, entirely oblivious of its significance. 'You like to send us messages. So why have you gone off the air? You're the Creeper. You love the sound of your own voice. So why aren't you talking to us any more? Is it something we've done? Something we've said? Or is it the opposite?' He groaned and put his head in his hands. 'I wish I could work out what the hell is going on here.'

Kevin was already waiting for Carol when she returned to the office. She'd driven back from Manchester in the grip of conflicting emotions. Her encounter with Paula's parents had been harrowing. Paula's father, a self-employed electrician, had already been in a state of panic at her request that they both meet her. He was convinced she was coming with news of his daughter's death. Mrs McIntyre had seemed frozen, as if trying to hold back time so she wouldn't have to absorb what Carol told her.

Once Carol had explained the situation, her father's fear had turned predictably to anger. He wanted answers that Carol couldn't provide and he wanted to blame someone. Carol weathered the storm of his anger, did what she could to reassure them and eased out of the drab three-bedroomed semi with promises to keep them informed of any developments.

But the encounter had left her drained and guilty. The excitement she'd felt at Stacey's news had made her feel even more guilty; how could she take pleasure in anything when Paula was in the hands of a ruthless killer who savoured death too much to allow her to live indefinitely?

As if that wasn't enough, she had the troubling

problem of what to do about Aidan Hart. If Tony's bizarre hypothesis was right and a master manipulator had induced someone else to commit his crimes for him, she couldn't ignore what Sam Evans had uncovered about the clinical director of Bradfield Moor. No one was better placed to know every detail of Derek Tyler's crimes. He'd indisputably been in Temple Fields just before Sandie Foster's murder. And he had precisely the sort of skills Tony had outlined as necessary for that sort of mind control over another.

She knew she should discuss it with Brandon, but until she had something stronger to lay before him, she was reluctant to put herself so firmly in the wrong. She wanted to talk it over with Tony, but she was concerned about the possible conflict of interest. She'd never met Hart herself and knew little about Tony's relationship with his boss. She knew they weren't close, if only because nobody was close to Tony. Except possibly her. But she didn't want to put him in a difficult position if Hart was someone he liked and respected.

So she was glad of Kevin's presence because it meant she had something concrete to do, something that left no brooding space. 'Good news, isn't it?' she said, throwing her coat on top of the filing cabinet.

'That Stacey's bloody amazing,' Kevin agreed. 'It would never have occurred to me to do what she did.'

'Me neither. Where is she, by the way?'

'Gone to get a vase. Apparently we don't have one.'

Carol did a double-take. 'A vase?'

'You know, tall thing, you put flowers in it.' The grin was cheeky.

'Thank you, Kevin. And why do we need a tall thing for putting flowers in?'

'Because you got a bouquet,' he said, clearly delighted to be scoring a point off the boss.

'I got a bouquet?' she echoed, feeling stupid. 'Where?'

He gestured with his thumb in the direction of the main office. 'Stacey sat them in her wastepaper basket while she went to get a vase.'

Carol was already on her way back into the squad-room. She rounded Stacey's desk and stopped short at the huge bunch of roses and lilies propped up against the desk. 'Oh, fuck,' she muttered, reaching for the card pinned to the cellophane.

She ripped it open and her heart sank as she read: *Welcome back to the world. You're a very special woman. Love, J.* 'Fuck, fuck, fuck,' she said, screwing it into a ball and remembering at the last minute to stuff it in her pocket rather than toss it in the bin. She strode back into her office and gave Kevin a tight smile. 'So, what have we got?'

'Well, you've got flowers,' he said, not noticing her mood had slipped to the wrong side of geniality.

'Enough about the flowers. Show me what you've got,' Carol snapped.

Kevin covered the desk with the printouts Stacey had given him, arranging them in four groups. 'These are the photos Nick Sanders emailed to us. They've been taken by four separate cameras. The ones that we're interested in are these three –' He pointed to a trio of shots that Carol immediately recognized as being of Swindale. 'According to Stacey's program, they were shot on the same camera that took the picture of Tim Golding that turned up on Ron Alexander's computer.'

A slow, satisfied smile crept across Carol's face. 'So it's fair to assume that one of these three Park Rangers took that photo of Tim?' she said.

'Looks that way.'

'How do you want to proceed?' Carol asked.

'Well, given that we know the camera in question was bought for cash in Birmingham, it's not likely to be one of the ones that belongs to the National Park. So I thought I'd ask Derbyshire to do a simultaneous search of their homes and offices, bring in any cameras they find and see if we get a match.'

Carol considered the idea. 'Too much wriggle room,' she said. 'We start searching, we alert the killer that we're on to him. It gives him time to concoct an alibi, or even to disappear. No. Get their home addresses from the National Park. Take three teams down to Derbyshire, get on their tails and, when you're all in place, bring them in simultaneously. Arrest them on suspicion of murder. Then we'll ask Derbyshire to do the searches while we're questioning them back here. I want this guy scared, I want him off his patch, I want him sweating.'

'Where am I going to get three teams from?' Kevin asked.

'Go and see DI Merrick. Tell him I said you could have five bodies.' She raised a warning finger. 'But not Sam Evans.'

Kevin frowned. 'But it was him that got Sanders to send us the pix in the first place.'

'Exactly,' Carol said. 'But he didn't care enough to want to follow it through. Keep him away from the endgame, Kevin. Maybe it'll teach him something.' She knew she was being harsh, but she wanted to rein in Sam Evans' maverick instincts, to make them work for him and not against him. It was a lesson Carol understood; it was the one she'd had most difficulty with herself in the early stages of her career. Going out on a limb was all very well, but you had to learn how to tell the solid wood from the rotten. And she suspected Evans was still a long way from that knowledge.

I'm savouring every minute of this, I admit it: the cops running around in circles because I've spirited away one of their own; front-page headline in the evening paper and an editorial slagging off the force hierarchy for putting an officer in harm's way without adequate back-up. Of course, it wasn't incompetence that cost them Paula McIntyre, it was my superiority. But I forgive the media that lack of insight, because it serves to make the police even more powerless. And power is like energy: finite. If one group loses it, somebody else benefits. And in this instance, it's me. I have the power to manipulate them, to frustrate them and to make fools of them.

My power is evident all around me. Even when I'm alone in my home, the wonders of modern technology allow me instant access to Paula's terror and pain. And my trained monkey brings me the digital videos at regular intervals. I can watch her, debased and helpless, on my TV screen or computer monitor while I lie on the sofa, naked and glorious. Whatever I want done to her, I can make it happen. I stroke my body, imagining her mouth on me, doing my bidding, her eyes fixed on mine, anxious to please. Imagination can be so much better than the reality, which so often disap-

points. Not that I'm averse to taking my pleasure when it presents itself. I've always had a taste and a talent for making women do what I want. But compared to this exercise of total domination, that's just an appetizer. Soon the blades will slice into her cunt, the blood will start to flow and pool between her legs, and her body will arch and twist in a frenzy of pain . . .

Sometimes I play one of the other videos, one of the ones that takes it all the way. But those make me come too quickly, and then I have to start all over again enjoying Paula.

The only thing that worries me is how I'm going to improve on this one.

After Kevin left, Carol had found it impossible to settle. She'd tried to call Tony, but only reached voicemail and answering machine. She'd had a cup of coffee with Stacey, congratulating her on her inspired work and insisting she accept Jonathan's flowers. She'd spent half an hour in the murder room with Don Merrick, growing depressed at the dozens of names their street trawl had attached to the unidentified man who had snatched Paula. Finally, she'd decided to do what she'd previously criticized Merrick for; she needed to get out on the streets, to feel she was doing something more constructive than reviewing everyone else's work.

At first, she'd just walked around Temple Fields, speaking to the officers who were still knocking on doors and canvassing passers-by. It never hurt to offer the troops a word of encouragement, to let them see you were putting in the hours, just like them. As she chatted to one of the young uniformed officers, she noticed Dee Smart slipping into a well-lit doorway opposite. Carol ended the conversation with a metaphorical pat on the back and headed across the street and into Stan's Café.

Dee was already seated alone at a table with a mug of tea and a cigarette. Carol took the chair opposite and smiled. 'Hi, Dee.'

Dee rolled her eyes. 'Look, I've told you lot everything – you know more about me than my ex-husband. You're very bad for business, you know that?'

'And I appreciate your help, Dee. But something new's come up that I wanted to run past you. Did Sandie ever mention someone called the Creeper?'

Dee stared at her, open mouth revealing an unappetizing array of ugly fillings and stained teeth. 'The Creeper?'

Carol gave an apologetic shrug. 'I know, it sounds ridiculous. But did Sandie ever talk about anyone by that name?'

Dee shook her head, incredulity in her expression. '*You're* asking *me* about the Creeper?'

Carol's attention quickened. This wasn't the reaction she'd expected. Dee's incredulity was not sparked by the nickname but by the very fact that Carol was asking the question. 'You know who I'm talking about,' Carol said, knowing she was right.

Dee snorted. 'You think I'm going to tell you, of all people?'

This wasn't making any sense. 'What do you mean, me of all people?'

Dee said nothing. She shifted in her chair, as if she wanted to put visible distance between herself and Carol.

Carol persisted. It would have been impossible for her to do otherwise. 'Dee, if you know anything, anything at all, you'd better tell me. There's a woman's life at stake, and I'm not playing games. If I have to arrest you for police obstruction, I will.'

Dee crushed out her cigarette and stood up. 'You think you frighten me with your threats? Listen, cop, there are people out there I'm a lot more scared of than I am of anything you can do to me. I don't know what the fuck you're on about, OK?'

Carol jumped to her feet, trying to get between Dee and the door. But Dee pushed her to one side and picked up speed. 'Dee!' Carol shouted. A hush fell on the café as every pair of eyes turned towards them.

'Fuck off! I got nothing to say to you,' Dee shouted desperately over her shoulder as she barged out of the door.

Carol flushed scarlet, aware she was the remaining centre of attention. She felt a touch on her arm and swung round, ready to rip into anyone who was willing to have a go. 'Tony?' she said, taken aback. 'I didn't see you. Are you stalking me?' She wondered for one mad moment if he was on some mission to protect her.

'No, Carol. I've been walking and thinking.' He steered her towards the corner table in the rear where he'd been nursing a coffee and absorbing the atmosphere when Carol had arrived. 'You only had eyes for the woman you were talking to,' he said.

'That was Dee Smart.'

'The one who shared the room with Sandie?'

Carol folded her arms across her chest. 'I fucked

that up so badly.' She pursed her lips, furious with herself. 'She knows something about the Creeper. As soon as I mentioned him, she freaked out. She knows something and she sure as hell isn't going to tell me now.'

'What exactly did she say?'

Carol closed her eyes and summoned to her service her gift of perfect recall. 'She said, "You think I'm going to tell you, of all people?" And then she said, "You think you frighten me with your threats? Listen, cop, there are people out there I'm a lot more scared of than I am of anything you can do to me."'

'Interesting,' Tony said.

'Meaning what?'

'Not sure yet. There's something I'm close to, but I'm not quite there,' he said slowly. Carol knew there was no point in pushing him. Even though his hypotheses sometimes sounded like the product of a mind deranged, he never put them forward till he was sure they had assumed the shape of validity. She'd just have to wait till he was ready, frustrating though that might be when a life was at stake.

'It'd be nice if you could make it soon,' she grumbled.

'Do you want me to have a chat with Dee?'

Carol considered. It probably wasn't such a bad idea. 'You think you might get somewhere?'

He spread his hands in a self-deprecating gesture. 'Well, I'm not a cop. And I'm not a woman.'

She couldn't resist. 'I had noticed.'

He pulled a face. 'Maybe Dee will too.' He pushed his chair back.

'Tony . . .' Carol began.

He gave her a quizzical look. 'Yes?'

She sighed. 'Nothing. It'll keep. This isn't the place.'

He glanced around. 'I see what you mean. Later, then.'

She watched him leave, wondering when exactly would be the right moment to tell Tony she thought his boss might be a serial killer.

Sam Evans didn't believe in luck. Suckers believed in luck. He believed in hard work, preparing the ground and seizing the moment. That was the difference between making it big and never getting off the slow track to nowhere. So you had to go looking for whatever it was that would give you the edge. And that was what Evans had been doing all day. He was desperate to get off Carol Jordan's shit list. He didn't mind undermining her, but he didn't want her trying that on him. Besides, although he craved the attention of his bosses, this was definitely the wrong kind of attention and he needed to make it history, and fast. So in spite of the repetitiveness of his task, he'd had his antennae tuned for that little something a bit out of the ordinary. Tony Hill's account of Tyler and the Creeper seemed to offer the breakthrough he'd been looking for. It would be good to find someone who fitted the bill.

It had grown dark and chill on the streets of Temple Fields yet still he hadn't found a crack he could pry open. But just when he had almost given up hope, he felt that prickle along his hairline that told him he was on to something. He'd stopped a bleary-eyed young hooker and thrust Paula's picture under her nose. She'd looked away too hastily and shivered.

Evans was prepared to bet that it wasn't because of the cold night air.

'Let's go for a drink, you and me,' he said, taking her elbow and steering her into the nearest pub. Luckily for him it was low-life enough not to be bothered by his choice of company. He found a table near the back of the room and asked her what she wanted to drink.

When he came back with the Bacardi Breezer and his own pint of Guinness, she was still there. 'So, how come you know Paula?' he asked.

She swigged from the bottle and wiped her mouth with the back of her hand. It made her look about twelve. 'She was nice to me after Jackie died. She reminded me of Jackie, you know? Like, kind. But still a no-shit.'

'That's Paula all right. So, what's your name?' He placed a hand flat on his chest. 'I'm Sam.'

'Hi, Sammy. I'm Honey. So, has he got Paula, then? The geezer that did Jackie?' She dug a pack of cigarettes out and offered him one.

'Looks that way.'

'So you're really out to get him now, then?'

'We were always out to get him. I expect Paula told you that.'

Honey shrugged one shoulder. 'So she said. But, like, I knew you wasn't going to get your knickers in too much of a twist about a pair of dead prossies.'

'You knew Jackie?'

Honey sighed out a thin stream of smoke. 'That's why Paula wanted to talk to me. To see if I knew anything about who'd topped her. She even got me to look at some photos of geezers. But there wasn't anybody I knew.'

Evans wasn't about to let it go. 'You've had time to think since then, though. Have you remembered Jackie being scared of anybody?'

Honey gave him a derisive look. 'In this game, you'd be daft if you weren't scared out your mind half the time.'

'But was there anyone in particular that bothered Jackie?' Evans swirled his glass nonchalantly, making the creamy head stick to the inside.

'After I spoke to Paula, I remembered Jackie once warned me off a punter. I was going to get in his car and she practically dragged me out. Said he'd smacked her about one time and dumped her without paying.'

The door to the bar opened and Jan Shields walked in. Evans caught her out of the corner of his peripheral vision and gently shook his head. Either she didn't see the gesture or she had something that wouldn't wait. She headed towards them. 'What kind of car?' Evans asked quickly.

'One of them big four-wheel-drive jeep things. A black one.'

The connection sparked in Evans' mind: *Aidan fucking Hart.* He'd been right and Jordan had been wrong. If he fitted the frame as this Creeper that Tony Hill reckoned was involved in the murders, that alibi didn't necessarily clear him. 'You don't know what make?' he asked urgently. 'What model?'

Honey cast her eyes upwards. 'Do I look like somebody who knows about cars, Sammy?'

Jan arrived at the table and sat down. Honey jumped as if she'd been stroked with a cattle prod. She grabbed for her fags and began to slide off the banquette. Jan put up a hand to stop her. 'It's all right,

Honey, I'm not wearing my Vice hat. Nothing so trivial.'

Honey ducked under the hand. 'Yeah, well, I've got my rent to earn. See ya, Sammy.'

'Shit,' he said as Honey disappeared back to the streets. 'I thought I was getting somewhere with that one.'

Jan looked apologetic. 'Sorry, mate. My past working Vice has its downsides as well as its advantages. How're you doing?'

Evans pushed the remains of his drink away from him. He wasn't about to share his ideas with anybody else. 'Getting nowhere slowly. You?'

'Likewise. Nobody's ever heard of Tony Hill's Creeper. Not a hooker, not a pimp, not a punter. Waste of time, if you ask me.'

Evans got to his feet. 'So, nothing new there, then. Let's go make some more people miserable.'

Jan fell into step beside him. 'I keep seeing Paula's face. It's as if she's haunting me. Like I've failed her.'

'What do you think the chances are of us getting her back alive?'

Jan closed her eyes momentarily, as if a stab of pain had hit her. 'My honest opinion?'

'Yeah.'

'I think Tony Hill's full of shit. I think she's dead already.'

Kevin closed the door of the interview room behind him. He'd just spent forty minutes with the last of the three Park Rangers they'd arrested on suspicion of murder. He'd been determined to interview all three himself, in spite of the complaints of the duty solicitors about being kept waiting. But he hadn't found a single discrepancy in their stories to offer any leverage. Nick Sanders, Callum Donaldson and Pete Siveright all denied having taken the photographs of Swindale.

They'd been happy enough to identify the other shots they had taken, but they were all adamant that they hadn't photographed the secret dale. They'd all denied ever having seen Tim Golding or Guy Lefevre other than via the media. They all claimed their worksheets would show they'd been nowhere near Bradfield on the day of his abduction. That in itself was pretty worthless, however, since they all finished work at six and neither boy had been taken till after seven. Plenty of time to get from the Peak Park to Bradfield.

Bronwen Scott followed him out of the room. The solicitor looked depressingly fresh and alert. 'You've got nothing on my client,' she said. 'I'm going to make representations to the custody sergeant that Callum Donaldson should be released.'

Kevin leaned against the wall. As always when he was tired, his skin had paled to the colour of milk, his freckles standing out like miniature stigmata. 'Nobody's going anywhere till we get the results of the searches that Derbyshire Police are carrying out on our behalf.'

'That could take hours,' she protested.

'So go home. We'll call you when we're ready with the outcome of those searches and to reinterview,' he said, not bothering to hide his hostility. 'One of those three men abducted and killed two young boys. So your convenience isn't very high on my list of priorities, Ms Scott.'

She raised her eyebrows. 'I had hoped that DCI Jordan might introduce the concept of civility round here. Clearly I was wrong.' She swept past him towards the custody suite. As she reached the door, the custody sergeant yanked it open.

'Kevin,' he shouted, 'I've got some DC from Buxton on the line for you.'

Bronwen Scott turned as he hurried down the corridor. Her mouth looked as if she'd just bitten a pickle. Kevin enjoyed beaming broadly at her as he brushed past. 'Looks like you might not have so long to wait after all.' He snatched up the phone and introduced himself. For a couple of minutes he listened, saying nothing more than, 'Yeah . . . yeah . . .' Finally, he said, 'Give me that make and model and serial number again.' He reached for a pen and paper and scribbled down the details. Then: 'Thanks, mate. I owe you one. Let me have the paperwork soon as.'

He replaced the receiver and turned to give Bronwen Scott the full benefit of his smile. 'Derbyshire Police have just informed me that they have found a camera whose serial number corresponds to the camera that took the photographs of Swindale and the photograph of Tim Golding. Guess where they found it?'

Scott's lip curled in disdain. 'Get on with it, Sergeant.'

'They found it in the bedroom of your client.' He leaned against the custody counter and folded his arms. 'I guess you won't be going anywhere in a hurry, will you, Ms Scott?'

* * *

Driving round Temple Fields at night was a different experience from being a pedestrian, Tony thought. The perspective on the terrain was quite different. Walking around, the prostitution impinged, but it wasn't hard to ignore. Behind the wheel, the sex for sale was totally in his face; the vendors set out their stalls for the carriage trade, not the foot traffic.

On his first pass through, Tony was so absorbed in the distinctive feel of the night streets that he missed Dee. Second time round, he saw her on a corner, kerbside, legs apart, leaning towards the road. He slowed and pulled up beside her. As his window went down, she stepped forward and dipped, offering a view of her cleavage. 'What's it to be, then?'

'You're Dee?'

'That's right. Somebody recommend me, did they, sweetheart? Well, you came to the right place. What are you after?'

Tony felt faintly flustered. It was all so much more complicated in reality. 'I'm not a punter, Dee. I just want to talk to you.'

She backed up a step, but kept the cleavage on show. 'You a cop?' she said suspiciously.

He gestured at the car then at himself. 'Does this look like "cop" to you? No, I'm not a cop.'

'In that case, you want to talk, it'll cost.'

Tony nodded. It seemed reasonable. People paid to talk to him, after all. 'Fine. I'll pay. Do you want to get in?'

Ten minutes later, he pulled up outside a smart café bar on the edge of the financial district. Dee had tried to talk in the car, but he had asked her to wait.

'I'm not good at navigating and talking,' he said. 'We'll only end up in the middle of nowhere.'

They walked together to the entrance, where, to Dee's obvious astonishment, Tony held the door open for her. As they walked in, the unmistakable cube of a bouncer approached them. 'Hang on a minute, where do you think you're going?' he demanded, all belligerence and brashness.

'What's it to you, meathead?' Dee snapped.

'We don't want your type in here,' the bouncer said.

Tony intervened with a suaveness he could only achieve when it was nothing personal. 'And what type would that be?'

'Keep out of it, pal,' the bouncer advised him.

'This lady is with me. We came here for a quiet drink,' Tony said politely.

'Not in here, you don't.'

Dee put a hand on his arm. 'Leave it, Tony. We'll go somewhere else.'

He patted her hand. 'No, Dee. We won't.' He turned to the bouncer, ice and steel on full display. 'You have no basis for refusing my friend entry. She is dressed no less discreetly than at least three other women in here. She's not touting for trade, unlike the financial services jerks at the bar, and also unlike many of your other customers, she's not going to be using your toilet to take drugs. So unless you can come up with a compelling reason why we shouldn't, we are going to sit at one of your tables while we have a drink and a chat.' He nodded politely to the bouncer and steered Dee past him.

The bouncer, baffled, stared after them like a bull

who'd just missed the matador. Tony chose a table, pulled out a chair for Dee then sat down opposite her. She grinned at him. 'How did you get away with that?'

Tony looked pained. 'Natural charisma?'

Dee laughed, a deep, throaty sound that spoke of Embassy Regal and too many late nights. 'Balls of steel, more like.'

'Ah, that's what the problem's been all these years . . .' Tony looked up as the cocktail waitress approached and dumped a bowl of Japanese rice crackers on the table. He suspected the swiftness of her arrival came from curiosity to see the man who had bested the bouncer. Tony smiled sunnily at her. 'Good evening. My friend would like . . . ?' He gave Dee a questioning look.

'Rum and black,' Dee said.

'And I'll have a glass of your Shiraz Cabernet. Thanks.' The waitress departed, giving them a final curious glance.

Dee scrunched down in the leather armchair, savouring its comfort. 'So, what is it you want to talk to me about?'

'I think you know.'

Dee tipped her head back and sighed, as if to say she'd known it was too good to be true. 'Is this to do with what that woman cop was asking me about?'

Tony said nothing, simply fixing her with an expectant look.

Dee jackknifed forward, leaning across the table towards him. 'What's she to you, then? Why are you doing her dirty work for her if you're not a cop?' she asked savagely.

'I'm a psychologist.'

'A shrink? You going to make me lie down on a couch and tell you about my childhood?' she said scornfully.

'I don't have a couch.'

Dee gave a louche smile. 'Pity. I wouldn't mind lying on a couch for you.'

'Life is full of disappointments, Dee. Why are you so scared of the Creeper?'

'Who said I was scared?' The defiance was so fake it was almost laughable.

'Why else would you refuse to tell us what you know when there's a woman's life at stake? I don't think you're keeping schtum out of loyalty.'

Dee looked away. 'Why should I stick my neck out for some copper?' She shifted impatiently in her seat. 'You've no idea what you're dealing with here, do you?'

'Whatever it is, we can protect you. Who's the Creeper, Dee?'

Now she was angry, covering up her fear with spitting rage. 'You don't get it, do you? You might not be a cop, but you're still on the team. The only ones you look after are your own. Yeah, I'm scared. And I'm right to be scared. Nothing you can promise me can make any difference.' Suddenly she was on her feet, grabbing her bag.

'Wait, Dee!' Tony said urgently. But she walked away without a backward glance. 'You haven't even had your . . .' The waitress approached with her tray balanced at shoulder level. '. . . rum and black,' he sighed.

He sat alone for a long time, staring into his red

wine and occasionally over at the glass of rum and blackcurrant opposite him. Thoughts flashed in and out of his mind as he struggled to make a logical sequence from what he knew and what he surmised. The early-evening crowd dispersed, and the bar entered a hiatus before it would come alive again after nine. When he was almost the only person left in the place, he took out his phone and dialled the familiar number.

'Carol Jordan,' he heard.

'It's me. Can we talk?'

'I'm in the office. Do you want to come round?'

The last place he wanted to have this particular conversation. 'I don't think so,' he said. 'Can you come to mine?'

'I'm in the middle of something,' she said. 'It looks like we're close to cracking Tim Golding and Guy Lefevre.'

'That's great news. But I do need to talk to you, and not in the office.'

He heard her sigh. 'Give me an hour. I'll meet you at your place. And, Tony . . .?'

'Yes?'

'This better be good.'

Under pressure from the solicitors representing Nick Sanders and Pete Siveright, Kevin had released both men. He'd had no real choice once he'd given them the disclosure that was their right: namely, that the results of the searches had produced no evidence against their clients. Once Bronwen Scott had indicated she'd had enough time to consult with Callum Donaldson, he gave himself a few more minutes to prepare. He anticipated that Scott would advise Donaldson to go 'no comment', but he didn't want to take any chances.

Kevin felt the low thrum of excitement in his veins that always came when he was so close to a result he could touch it. These days, every good arrest, every conviction felt like another step towards rehabilitation. It was as if his previous disastrous mistake was a stain, like a street vandal's spraypainted tag. And everything that went well was another brushful of paint towards covering up the blemish. One day, there would only be a freshly painted wall, and he'd finally be back on track again.

Callum Donaldson felt right. He fitted the profile. He lived alone in a remote cottage between Chapel-en-le-Frith and Castleton. He was an avid birdwatcher who often led school trips into the Peak Park to show them the bird life. He was technologically adept – he had a state-of-the-art computer and a pager that automatically alerted him to the arrival of any rare species in the UK. Kevin had found him awkward and uncomfortable in their preliminary interview, and if he'd had to pick a killer from the three, Donaldson would have been his chosen one.

He gathered his papers together and walked into the interview room. He'd barely started the twin tape-decks and made the formal introduction when Bronwen Scott said, 'My client wishes to make a statement.'

Kevin couldn't hide his surprise. He smiled, wondering if it was really going to be that easy after all. 'Fine. Let's hear it.'

Scott perched a pair of rimless glasses on the end

of her nose and cleared her throat. 'My name is Callum Donaldson and I am employed as a ranger with the Peak National Park Service. I wish to make a statement regarding a Canon Elph digital camera which is presently in my possession. I purchased this camera on approximately 15th September of this year from my colleague Nick Sanders.'

Scott paused and looked up. Kevin understood she was enjoying the sight of the rug being pulled out from under his feet and he struggled to remain impassive. She allowed herself a tight little smile and continued. 'I paid him one hundred and fifty pounds for the camera. I paid this sum by cheque. The transaction took place in the Red Lion pub in Litton. Among those present were David Adams of Litton Mill and Maria Tomlinson, also of Litton Mill. I am willing to allow access to my bank records to verify this transaction and I am confident that David Adams and Maria Tomlinson will remember the occasion since we all took photographs with the camera in the pub that night.'

Scott handed him the statement, written out in her neat italic hand. 'Duly signed and witnessed,' she said. 'How soon will you be releasing my client?'

Kevin stared dully at the piece of paper, seeing his good night crumble before his eyes. He knew he should still ask his prepared questions, but suddenly time was of the essence. 'I'll need to speak to DCI Jordan,' he stalled. 'Interview terminated at seven forty-three p.m.,' he added, getting to his feet and hurrying out.

He ran down to the custody suite. 'When did you let Sanders go?' he asked the sergeant.

'When you said. About forty minutes ago,' the sergeant said.

'Who's driving him back?'

'They both declined the offer of transport. Said they'd seen enough of us for one day, they'd rather get back under their own steam.'

'Fuck,' Kevin exploded.

'We got a problem?'

'Too fucking right. We've let the wrong one go,' Kevin growled. He reached across and grabbed the phone. 'I need to speak to Buxton CID,' he told the switchboard. When the phone was finally answered, he identified himself then said, 'I need to speak to DC Thom . . . What do you mean, he's gone home?' After a prolonged conversation that led Kevin through three different officers, he finally secured a reluctant promise to go to Nick Sanders' cottage in Chelmorton and rearrest him when he arrived back home. Provided Kevin could have the request ratified by a senior officer.

He took the stairs two at a time and found Carol in her office, signing off on a stack of paperwork. She looked up expectantly, knowing how confident Kevin had been of a result. Quickly, he outlined what had happened. 'Oh, Christ,' Carol said, making no attempt to hide her dismay. 'Not your fault, Kevin, but . . . oh, Christ. Leave it with me, I'll speak to Derbyshire. And you'd better release Donaldson on police bail before Bronwen Scott starts waving the bloody Human Rights Act at us.'

As she watched Kevin go, she thought, *Actually, it was my fault.* They should have waited until they had the search results in from Derbyshire before interviewing the three men. But Kevin had been eager to get going and he was concerned that Derbyshire would drag their heels over the searches out of sheer bloody-mindedness. And because of the terms of the Police and Criminal Evidence Act, they could only hold the men for thirty-six hours before they'd have to go before the magistrates who would probably not understand the complex evidence relating to the camera and so would throw out the request for extended custody. Kevin had told her Derbyshire were becoming increasingly restive at what they perceived to be the big city boys expecting them to do the shit work. So, against her better judgement, she had sanctioned a series of preliminary interviews.

Carol squeezed the bridge of her nose between her fingers. She was making too many mistakes. It wasn't like her. It frightened her, with Paula's life at stake. Screwing up was bad enough on its own, but concern over screwing up could make her hesitate fatally; failure to reach a decision could be as damaging as making the wrong one in a case of this sensitivity. She sighed and made the call to Derbyshire. Then she reached for her coat. Time to go and see what Tony was being so mysterious about. And maybe she could get at least one of her worries off her chest at the same time.

She stopped in at the murder room, where Merrick was still ploughing through statements, his eyes heavy, his shoulders bowed. He looked up as she entered and slowly shook his head. Carol moved round the room, a supportive word for everyone. She ended up at his side, a hand on his shoulder. 'We'll find her, Don,' she said. 'Why don't you go home and get some rest?'

His face twisted in pain. 'Home? Ma'am, I'm living in her house. Going home just makes it worse. It feels like a reproach.'

Carol cursed herself for her insensitivity. 'Can't you go back to Lindy and the kids? Just for a few nights?'

'Too late for that. She's not even speaking to me.'

Carol squeezed his shoulder. 'Check yourself into a hotel, Don. Charge it to the inquiry. But get some rest, please.'

He gave her a crooked smile. 'I will if you will, ma'am.'

'Touché. But I am at least leaving the building now, Don. You should do the same.'

She was halfway down the corridor, lost in thought, when the familiar sight of Jonathan France swaggering towards her in his bike leathers jolted her back to earth. He grinned and quickened his step, not taking in the frozen expression on Carol's face.

'What are you doing here? How did you get in?' she demanded.

His step and his smile faltered. 'I wanted to see you. The guy on the front counter remembered me being here before, so he let me come up.' He looked hurt. 'I thought you'd be pleased to see me,' he added plaintively.

In reply, Carol threw open the nearest door, which led into an empty meeting room. 'In here,' she indicated with a jerk of the head. He followed her, perking up at the prospect of privacy, in spite of the contra-indications. Carol shut the door behind them and glared at him. 'What did you think you were doing, sending those flowers here?'

Shock flattened his features. 'I thought you'd like them.'

'So why not send them to my house?'

He shrugged. 'You're never there.'

'The florist would have left them with a neighbour. But no, you sent them here. Didn't it occur to you that a police station is a gossip factory? That my private life is now the subject of speculation from the canteen to the Chief Constable's office?'

'I didn't think . . .'

'No, you didn't. I'm running two major murder inquiries here, and the last thing I want is this kind of distraction.'

Stung, he rounded on her. 'Distraction? That's how you see me? A distraction?' Carol shrugged. Two patches of colour burned on his cheekbones. 'You used me,' he said, light dawning. 'You used me to prove to yourself you could get past the rape.'

She raised her eyebrows. 'You got what you wanted too – an image of yourself as the strong, sensitive saviour. But that wasn't enough for you, was it? You wanted it to matter to me, you wanted to be the man who would heal my heart. Well, Jonathan, I've got news for you. You never came near my heart, because somebody else has first claim to that.'

As so often happens in the throes of emotional argument, he seized on the least relevant point. 'You told me you weren't seeing anybody else. That night we had dinner, you told me.'

Carol clenched her fists. 'I'm not seeing anybody

else. Not in the sense you mean. But you can't reduce relationships to the simplicity of playground games.'

'You were dishonest,' he said bitterly. 'You were never emotionally available.'

She shook her head vehemently. 'I never said I was. You presumed. You saw what you wanted to see and you presumed the rest.'

'I don't deserve this,' he said, his voice shaky.

Carol's anger suddenly fizzled out, leaving her hollow and weary. 'No,' she said. 'You probably don't.' She opened the door. 'I'm not ungrateful, Jonathan. And I would have liked it if we could have been friends. But that's not going to happen now.'

He stepped through the open door. 'I don't envy him, this man you love,' he said bitterly.

'That's the first sensible thing you've said tonight,' Carol said sadly. 'Goodbye, Jonathan.'

She watched him go, feeling the last traces of adrenaline leave her. Christ, how much worse could it get tonight?

Tony sat at his desk, staring out at the cityscape that flowed down the hill towards the centre of Bradfield. In the distance, the office towers in the financial district showed irregular squares of light like half-completed seaside bingo games. 'You're out there somewhere,' he said softly. 'Making your plans, figuring out how to get us to play your game, deciding what to do with Paula.' A picture was starting to form in his mind of the person behind these crimes. It had been a struggle to grasp the shadowy mind of the puppetmaster, but at last he was piecing it together, gradually making sense out of the jumble of information in his head. Convincing Carol was going to be a lot harder, he thought.

He saw her car draw up and ran downstairs to let her in. He was shocked by how drained she looked. Her eyes were hollow, her skin slack and pale. 'You look shattered,' he said, stepping aside to let her in.

'I fucked up on the Tim Golding interviews. It looks like we ended up cutting the right man loose and holding on to the wrong one. Kevin seems to think the suspect is confident enough to go home so we can rearrest him. I'm not so sure. We're getting nowhere on the search for Paula. Don and Jan are at each other's throats because Jan says Paula's gay and Don says she's not. And Sam Evans thinks somebody died and made him God. The only one who's not doing my head in is Stacey, and that's because she only talks to machines.' She took off her coat and threw it over the newel post at the foot of the stairs. 'Where are we?'

'You want a drink? Or are you still working?'

'Yes, and yes. I'm waiting to hear from Kevin, but I'm out of the office now for the night unless something breaks on Paula.'

'Kitchen, then. I'll open a bottle.'

While Tony got the drinks, Carol settled herself at the kitchen table. 'I just gave Jonathan his marching orders,' she said.

Tony had his back to her, which he was grateful for. It meant she missed the leap of joy in his eyes, the smile that lit up his face. 'And how do you feel about that?'

Carol snorted with laughter. 'Oh, Tony, you're such a fucking shrink.'

He glanced over his shoulder at her. 'Sorry. But it wasn't a shrink question. It was a friendly enquiry.'

'I feel pissed off with him for pushing me into a corner. He sent the most ridiculous bouquet of flowers to the office, then he turned up there this evening. If he'd have just let it lie, we could have been friends. But it was that presumption, you know?'

Tony brought the glasses to the table. 'I know. "You slept with me, so how can you resist loving me?"'

'Exactly. And you know how I get when I'm cornered.'

He winced. 'Not a pretty sight.'

'I was horrible to him,' she admitted. 'But I didn't want there to be any room for doubt. I haven't got the time or the energy for that right now.' She sipped her drink gratefully. 'I just hope I haven't blown him as an expert witness.'

'I shouldn't think so. Given his behaviour so far, I suspect he'll want to impress you with his magnanimity. And of course, he'll want to believe that once a bit of time has passed, you'll realize what a good thing you let go by you. Don't worry, Carol, he'll be back.' Tony raised his glass to her.

She groaned. 'I hate you sometimes,' she said.

'You're going to hate me even more when you hear what I have to say.'

'Oh yes,' she said. 'There was a reason why I'm here, wasn't there? OK, spill.'

He'd never been good at the politics of information. Direct, uncomfortable, unvarnished, that was how his delivery always went. Even for Carol, he couldn't do diplomacy. 'Somewhere at the heart of this case, you're going to find either a cop or someone who's tight with the cops. A SOCO, that sort of thing.'

Carol's hand stopped halfway to her mouth. Carefully, she replaced her glass on the table. 'That's a hell of an allegation.'

'It's what makes sense. I believe Derek Tyler could not have constructed these crimes. Tyler's of low intelligence. He's stubborn, but he's also suggestible. If he was going to kill a prostitute off his own bat, he wouldn't have planned it like this. It would have happened on the street, with a knife or a half-brick. There would have been forensics all over the place. You'd have had him in custody the same night. He's not a sophisticated game player like our killer. But nobody fitted up Derek Tyler. So we come to the Creeper. Because there's one irresistible psychological fact here: Derek Tyler could not have imagined those crimes. This is somebody else's fantasy. Somebody else pulled the strings.'

'What if it's Tyler who's pulling the strings now? Getting someone else to do the crimes so he won't have to do the time?' She knew she should tell him about Hart. But she wanted to see where he was going with this, untainted by her suspicions.

Tony shook his head. 'Believe me, Carol. I've spent time with him. He just isn't smart enough.'

'So if it's the Creeper who's behind it all, why wait two years to start again?'

Tony closed his eyes and laid his hands, palms down, on the table. 'Because I'm careful. Because I want the dust to settle. Because it takes time to find another Derek Tyler. Because I don't have the desire to get my own hands dirty. Because the joy comes from exercising power twice over. Not just the power over the victim but also the power over the killer. And this time around, the power over the police.' He opened his eyes. 'But mostly because I don't want to be caught, and it takes time to arrange things in such a way that I can protect myself.'

'OK. That all makes some sort of sense,' Carol said grudgingly. 'What I don't see is how it points to a cop.'

'I spoke to Dee tonight.'

'And?'

'She won't tell us what we want to know about the Creeper. And she won't tell us because she doesn't trust us to protect her. That suggests either a cop or someone who is owed a duty of care by the cops. Someone on the team. Or even an informant . . .?'

Carol shook her head. 'No, I'm sorry, I don't buy it. It's just as likely that the Creeper is somebody out there who she sees as powerful enough to breach whatever protection we put round her. That doesn't spell cop to me. It could just as well be a pimp, a dealer.'

'She doesn't have a pimp. Jan says they've cleared out most of the hard nuts. And why would she imagine a dealer could breach witness protection?'

Carol gave him a cynical, knowing look. 'Because there is a perpetual assumption that drugs squad cops are bent, that you don't get to be a high-level dealer without having some cop in your pocket.'

Tony slumped in his chair. He'd given it his best shot, but he hadn't really expected her to go for it. 'Do me a favour: keep it in mind.'

She drained her glass and reached for the bottle.

'I appreciate your input on this, I really do. But I think you're way off beam.'

'Fair enough,' he said.

'Not the theory, Tony. I think that's nothing short of brilliant. But where you're pointing the finger, that's where you're off the mark,' she said.

Puzzled, he paused with his glass halfway to his mouth. 'What have I missed?'

'Someone with the skills to brainwash another person. Someone who has access to Derek Tyler, who can make sure he never tells what he knows. Someone who was in Temple Fields the night Sandie Foster was killed.'

Tony's eyes widened. 'What are you saying, Carol?'

'I'm saying that Aidan Hart fits your profile better than any cop.'

Tony snorted with laughter. 'Aidan Hart? You're kidding me.'

'Aidan Hart had sex with Sandie Foster the night she died. We traced his car and he admitted it. He had an alibi for the time of the murder so I didn't pursue it. But Sam Evans did. And he discovered that Hart uses prostitutes two or three times a week. I didn't think that was grounds for suspicion either. But if you're right, and the same person has orchestrated both series of murders, the alibi is worthless and everything else becomes more significant.'

Tony shook his head, struggling to take in what Carol was saying. 'No, that can't be right. The man's a buffoon. A careerist buffoon.'

'Or maybe he's just very good at presenting a fake front?' Carol said.

Tony swallowed a mouthful of wine, his brow

furrowed in thought. 'It doesn't work, Carol. It doesn't fit with what Dee said. There's no reason why she should know who Hart is, never mind be shit scared of him.'

'No? What do we know about her mental-health history? A man with Hart's power could write her up as delusional, have her sectioned, surely? Locked away forever?'

Tony looked doubtful. 'I don't know . . .' He jumped to his feet and paced. 'Wait a minute,' he said triumphantly. 'Two years ago. When Derek Tyler was active. Hart wasn't here then. He was still at Rampton. He's been in post here less than a year. He can't have been the man behind Derek Tyler's crimes. And if you concede that Derek couldn't have conceived those murders on his own, you have to concede that the same person is behind both series. Which rules out Aidan Hart.'

Carol stared at him. 'You're sure about that? He couldn't have been seconded here?'

'I'm sure as I can be. But it won't be hard for you to check out.' Tony pulled a rueful face. 'I'm sorry to rob you of a suspect. But, leaving aside the practicalities, I just don't figure Hart for this. I just don't think he's got what it takes.'

She sighed, not entirely convinced but unable to find a counter-argument. 'Fuck. Oh well, at least I don't have to make a fool of myself with Brandon.' She finished her drink. 'I need to get some sleep. It's been a shit of a day.'

'Keep me posted, yeah?' He walked her to the front door.

On the threshold, she turned and put a hand on

his shoulder, leaning into him and kissing his cheek. 'Thank you,' she said.

'What for?' He was surprised.

She grinned. 'You're the psychologist, you work it out.'

Then she was gone, leaving him alone to continue his journey into the dark spaces of someone else's mind.

Morning dawns sunny for a change, and I imagine those dull-witted coppers seeing it as a good omen. That's the thing about superstitions. The morons who believe in them never seem to consider that, by their very nature, omens must be indiscriminate. They look out their bedroom window and see the perfect rainbow arcing across the landscape and decide it means good fortune for them without realizing that it means precisely the same for their next-door neighbour who is their sworn enemy. So if the sunny morning is a good omen for my enemies, it must be one for me too.

I check out the webcam again. The refresh rate isn't brilliant, even with broadband, but at least it lets me keep an eye on Paula in real time. Except when that fuckwit leaned on the pause button by mistake the first time he changed the videotape. At least he noticed what he'd done and put it right before he left. He won't do that again in a hurry; I made my displeasure known and it reduced him to a pathetic jelly, desperate to win back my good graces.

So there she is, spread out the way I like her. I start to feel aroused by the sight, but I haven't got time to enjoy it, so I force myself to think of more practical things. I've never kept one this long before, and it does present certain problems. I know she can go without food for a long time, but I'm not sure how long she can manage without water. I don't mind her getting delirious, but I don't want her to die. Not until I decide the time is right. And when it is, she'll die the way I dictate, not according to her physiology. I decide to check it out on the net when I get a minute.

Letting her drink will be a problem. If he takes the gag off, she'll try to scream. It should be possible to drip water into her mouth through her teeth, but I'm not convinced the trained monkey can manage something so delicate. I might have to do it myself. Far from ideal. Not because there's any danger she'll live to tell the tale, but because if she saw me it would destroy the mystique.

The tip of my tongue slides between my teeth as I watch her. She's good enough to eat.

Another fantasy to keep for later. But for now, there's work to be done.

Paula was oblivious to the dawn. Inside her brightly lit prison there was no day or night, just endless mute brilliance. When she closed her eyes, the light burned red through her eyelids, reminding her of the sea of blood that had made islands of Sandie Foster and Jackie Mayall. Her head hurt, a dull ache that had started at the base of her skull and crept forward like the vanguard of an enemy army till her brain felt as if it would burst.

She could no longer keep her thoughts under control. Something would pop into her mind, but before she could examine it, it would slither away or morph into something different. Memories segued and elided into each other, people turned up in places she knew they'd never been, their mouths uttering things she knew they'd never said. Lovers shape-shifted into colleagues, old school friends shimmered and reformed as relative strangers. It was unnerving.

Sometimes she could barely remember who she was and how she'd got here. Her limbs felt heavy, as if they belonged to someone much bigger and softer. But that was more bearable than the agonizing cramps that shot through her arms and legs at unpredictable intervals.

The only clear knowledge Paula still managed to hold on to was that someone would come for her. She no longer knew who it would be; but she knew that, sooner or later, one way or another, it would end.

Tony closed the front door behind him and stood for a moment, savouring the sun on his face. He'd slept better than he'd expected but didn't want to think about why that might be. The sudden image of Paula McIntyre's face flashed into his mind and all at once, his pleasure in the morning evaporated. He hoped desperately that he was right, that she was still alive.

He got into the car and turned the key in the ignition. It coughed, wheezed like an emphysemic octogenarian and died. He frowned and tried again. A click, then nothing. He looked around as if there might be an answer inside the car. There was, of course. After Carol had returned to the office, he'd gone out for a Chinese takeaway. And he'd left the lights on. 'Bugger,' he sighed. Even if he could have laid hands on his roadside assistance membership card, he didn't have time to wait for the patrolman to turn up and jump-start him. And Carol had already left. He'd have bet serious money on her having a set of jump leads tucked away in her boot.

Grumpy now, he got out of the car and set off for the bus stop. He knew there was a bus that went near Bradfield Moor, but knew too from the complaints of visitors that the bus stop was a mile from the hospital gates.

Forty minutes later, a bus pulled up in the middle of nowhere and Tony got out. He stood for a moment, trying to figure out exactly where he was, then set off up a nearby lane. Freed from the clammy fug of the bus and its uneasy assortment of passengers, he let his mind run free over its problem.

'Two kinds of people are drawn to power: those who have it and those who don't,' he mused as he trudged on. 'That's where we have to start from.

'Those who don't have it usually don't have it for a good reason. Maybe they're not very bright or not very motivated or not very organized. Doesn't sound like you, does it?'

He was silent for a while, mulling it over. 'So we should probably assume that you have access to some degree of power. Which would work, if you're a cop – only Carol thinks I'm completely off the page on that one. The thing about having power is that those who have it always want more. Absolute power corrupts absolutely. And you like corruption, don't you? You like the taste and the smell of it. If you're a cop, you're a bent cop.' He stopped for a moment, digesting the implications of that thought.

'And that's why Dee's so scared of you. Because she already knows you don't play by the rules.' He was startled out of his reverie by a vast black all-terrain vehicle pulling up alongside him. The tinted window on the passenger side slid down and Tony found himself looking into the smug face of Aidan Hart. Given what he had learned from Carol about Hart's sexual proclivities, it was hard to resist the knowing remark that would wipe the smile from his mouth forever.

'Are you walking for pleasure or would you like a lift?' his boss asked.

Tony grinned. 'All things considered,' he said, 'I think I'd rather walk.'

'This is getting to be a bit of a habit,' Carol said, walking into her office with Kevin at her heels. 'People will talk.'

Kevin gave a tired smile. 'I don't think so. They all know I'm too cheap to send expensive bunches of flowers.'

'Kevin,' she said, her voice a dark warning.

'Sorry, guv,' he said ruefully.

'So, where are we up to?'

'Sanders never went home last night. After he left here, he disappeared into thin air. Siveright says Sanders told him he was going to visit friends in Bradfield and then he set off on foot. We've got Sanders withdrawing cash from the ATM in the Woolmarket about ten minutes after he left here. We've spoken to his colleagues at the park and I've alerted ports and airports but nothing's come up.'

'Shit,' Carol said. 'We need to put out an urgent press release with a photo. I want him caught, Kevin. I don't want him disappearing into some underground paedophile support network. He'll have contacts. People who will hide him. People who will give him transport, money, shelter.'

Before Kevin could speak, there was a knock at the door. 'Come in,' Carol said impatiently.

Stacey hovered on the threshold. 'Sorry to interrupt, but I just came up with something on Nick Sanders I thought you might both want to hear.'

Carol waved her in. 'Please tell me you know where he is,' she said with a half-smile.

Stacey frowned, as if uncertain whether Carol was serious. 'No. But I do have something that strengthens our case against him. You know he sent us his log from July with that report of the alleged flasher?'

'When he was being so "helpful",' Kevin said, his hands making speech marks in the air.

'Well, I dug a bit deeper. Guess what? That log was altered within an hour of the first news reports of a body being found in Swindale. He made up that log entry to divert attention away from himself.' Stacey looked pleased with herself.

'Thanks, Stacey, that's really useful. Well done,' Carol said. As she spoke, Don Merrick stuck his head round the door.

'Can I come in?' he asked. Carol nodded. 'I was looking for Kevin, actually,' he said. He consulted a sheet of paper. 'We've had an anonymous call from a punter claiming to be a former friend of Nick Sanders. The friendship ended because he caught Sanders taking pictures of his young son in the bath. He kept quiet at the time because he didn't want his kid being put through the ordeal of an investigation, but when a mate who works for the Peak Park told him Sanders was a suspect and that he'd legged it, he decided to come forward. Anyway, he reckoned Sanders would head for open country. He's got the skills to live off the land. Apparently there's a place in Sutherland, in the north-west of Scotland – Achmelvich Bay,' he said, stumbling over the unfamiliar name. 'Sanders was the warden at the Youth Hostel there years ago. We checked that out, by the way. It's on the CV he submitted to the Ranger Service. Anyway, according to our caller, Sanders spoke about something called the Hermit's Castle. He couldn't remember much about it except that some guy from London built it right out on the headland. Like a concrete pillbox, only smaller. Lived in it for a year, wouldn't speak to a soul. The caller said Sanders might head for there. I think we should check it out,' Merrick concluded eagerly.

'It's a pretty long shot,' Carol said.

Kevin made a noncommittal gesture. 'We could ask the local boys to keep an eye out.'

'If he worked up there, he probably knows the local boys,' Merrick pointed out. 'I think Kevin should go. There's a flight to Inverness at noon.'

Carol considered for a moment, then shook her head. 'It's too insubstantial. Kevin, speak to the local lads, ask them to check it out. But discreetly, yes? If there's any trace of Sanders, we'll follow it up. In the meantime, we concentrate on getting an appeal out nationally. Now, if you'll excuse me, I've got a briefing to prepare.'

There was pitifully little to impart at the morning briefing. And they all knew it. The determination of the morning before was tinged with desperation. They all knew that with every passing hour the chances of finding Paula alive diminished dramatically.

'We'll continue to follow up on the council-tax

data,' Carol said, trying to keep the energy in her voice high. 'I want us to speak to every landlord and tenant within the search area on the map here. I know it's a scattergun approach, but until we have something to narrow it down, we will do whatever it takes to find Paula. Inspector Merrick has the full list of assignments for today. In addition, I want you to ask in every interview whether the subject has ever heard anyone referred to as the Creeper.' She was conscious of a dubious stirring in the room.

'I'm aware it sounds bizarre. But this is good information. Derek Tyler has said nothing for two years. While it's possible he may have mischief in mind, Dr Hill is inclined to think he hasn't the wit to mislead us on this. So bear it in mind.

'The good news from forensics is that we do have DNA. Unfortunately, the sample is not of sufficiently high quality to run it for comparison against the national database.' Groans all round. 'However,' she said, raising her voice, 'it's good enough for elimination purposes. And I'm told that if we do get the right person, there will be enough common ground for it to have evidential value.'

She turned and pointed to the large-scale map of Temple Fields. 'She's there somewhere. So let's find Paula.'

As the briefing ended, officers moved in clusters towards Don Merrick, who looked as if he hadn't slept in this lifetime. 'Sam,' Carol called over the hubbub. He turned and gave her an enquiring look. 'A moment, please.'

He wove his way against the tide to her side. 'Yes, ma'am?' he said smartly.

'I want you to pull the files on the cases from two years back.'

'The Derek Tyler murders?'

'That's right. Once we'd arrested Tyler, everything else came to a halt. You and I are going to have a very boring morning going over those files and identifying any actions that were slated but never followed up.'

Evans tried to look enthusiastic. It wasn't convincing. Before Carol could say anything, she saw John Brandon's familiar figure moving through the press of bodies. He was plotting a course straight for her. 'Off you go, Sam,' she said firmly.

Brandon reached her and steered her to one side. 'Carol, is Tony fully abreast of the investigation?'

'Yes, sir.'

'I think we need a formal profile from him. I've got a press conference at noon and I'd like to give them something that makes it look as if we're making a degree of forward movement. Especially since we've lost Nick Sanders,' he added acerbically.

She tried not to smart under the implied criticism. 'Can we give them some of the video footage? To see if anyone recognizes the man?'

'I don't see why not. Whether they'll use it is another matter. The media care a lot less about a police officer at risk than we do. They're more excited about having a serial killer in their midst than they are about saving DC McIntyre.' Brandon moved away, taking the time to dole out some words of encouragement as he headed back to the relative peace of his office.

Carol looked around to see which of her officers was nearest. 'Jan?' she called.

Jan looked up from the sheaf of papers she was reading, caught Carol's eye and came over. 'Something for me?'

'Can you track down Dr Hill and get him to come over?'

'Sure. Have you got his mobile number?'

Carol reached for a piece of paper and scribbled it down. As she wrote, she said, 'He'll either have it turned off or he'll ignore it, though. I'm giving you his home address as well. I think he said he'd be there this morning.'

'And if he's not there?'

Carol shrugged. 'Try Bradfield Moor.'

Jan smiled. 'Like calling to like, eh?'

Carol bridled. It was precisely the sort of thing she would have said to Tony herself. But that was the prerogative of a friend, not the kind of sly remark she wanted to hear from her junior officers. 'We need him more than he needs us, Sergeant. Let's not forget that, eh?'

Jan shrugged an apology and left. Merrick approached Carol and ran a hand over hair greasy from lack of washing. Hollow-eyed, he stared at her bleakly over the rim of his mug, one leg jittering with nervous energy. 'I keep feeling there must be something else we should be doing,' he said, his voice gravelly with exhaustion.

'I know. But it's hard to imagine what that could be. And it's not going to help anyone if you drive yourself into the ground over this, Don,' she said gently.

She saw anger spurt into his eyes. 'Paula's not just one of my officers,' he said tightly. 'She's my friend. I know that might seem odd. I know most people can't get their heads round the idea of a woman and a man being mates. But that's how it is with us.'

And yet you didn't know she was gay, Carol thought. That probably said as much about Paula's instinctive caution as it did about Merrick's lack of insight. 'I believe you, Don,' she said. 'And I do understand how that makes it harder on you.'

'Do you?' He shook his head. 'She was like a dog with two tails when she got the posting to the squad, you know? She was excited about working with you. Ever since the Thorpe case, you've been her hero. That's why she agreed to the undercover even though it freaked her out. She wanted you to think well of her. She was determined that anything you could do, she could do too.'

His words cut Carol to the quick, even though she understood he was lashing out to ease his own guilty sense of failure. 'I think she was doing it for herself, Don. Not to impress me, but to keep faith with her own idea of what a cop should be,' she said. 'But whatever Paula's motives, there's no point in chucking blame around. We've got to concentrate on finding her.'

'You think I don't know that? But what's to concentrate on? There's hundreds of bits of paper there, and they all say the same shit. It's like she vanished into thin air.'

'We're getting there. We're narrowing down the possibilities all the time. We've covered a huge amount of ground in Temple Fields. According to your own figures, we've physically been inside more than seventy-five per cent of all the properties in the area. It comes down to time and method.'

He sighed. 'I know. I'm not thinking straight. Look, ma'am, if you don't mind, I'm going to take off and get some sleep. I'll check into a motel, get my head down for a few hours.'

'Good idea, Don. It won't look so bleak once you've slept.'

He turned away without a word and shambled off. It was only half past nine, but Carol felt she'd already done a day's work. When she'd taken on the challenge of a specialist squad, she hadn't considered quite how tiring it would be to spend her days trying to corral a bunch of cops whose natural abilities made them as difficult and bolshie as she'd been herself in her younger days. Sometimes, she found herself almost longing for Traffic.

The grounds at Bradfield Moor had not been designed for anything other than easy maintenance. But on a wintry morning, with the leaves off the trees, they offered a long vista across the moors to the north through the tall chainlink fence. It was possible to lose sight of the city below, to cut one's connections to the life of the streets. To walk there with a patient wasn't generally an option that staff were encouraged to take, but Tony had decided Tom Storey would only benefit from a short respite away from the oppressive surroundings of the hospital. They'd been out in the open for the best part of an hour, taking stock of Tom's most pressing current concerns.

They had come to a halt among a stand of birch trees, close to the fence, looking across the valley at the sparkle of a reservoir on the moors. Tony checked his watch. 'We should probably head back. I've got another appointment in a quarter of an hour.'

With one last look at the landscape, they turned back towards the ugly Victorian Gothic pile. 'I'm glad you came today,' Storey said.

'We had an appointment. Where else would I be?'

'I thought your police business might keep you away.'

'My patients come first with me. I work with the police, but that doesn't give them the power to dictate my movements.'

Storey gave him an odd look. 'That's a funny way to put it.'

'It is, isn't it? I suppose it's because I've been thinking a lot about power this morning.'

They walked in silence for a couple of minutes, then Tony said, 'What's your line on power, Tom?'

Twin lines formed between Storey's eyebrows as he tried to find a way to express what he felt. He was finding it less easy to communicate his thoughts now. 'You take it where you find it,' he said. 'It's always circumstantial. One man's power means another man's pathos.'

Tony stopped in his tracks. He wasn't quite sure how, but something in Tom Storey's words had triggered an idea in his head. He spoke so softly his patient had to strain to hear him. 'You look at the overpowered, there's a direct line back to the oppressor . . .' Tony raised his face to the sky. 'Find the thread, you find the killer.' He turned to Storey and smiled beatifically. 'Thank you, Tom. Thank you for that beautiful thought. I do believe I'm starting to see the light.'

But the light had to wait. As he'd said, Tony had another patient to see, a patient whose psychosis required the full focus of his attention. An hour later, he finally emerged from his office, head down, paying no attention to his surroundings. He was vaguely aware of shapes passing him, but he was almost at the end of the corridor when something penetrated his consciousness. He stopped and frowned, looking round impatiently as a voice repeated its Bugs Bunny impersonation.

Jan Shields was leaning against the wall outside his office, grinning. 'I said, "Nya . . . What's up, Doc?"'

He felt a quick surge of apprehension then dismissed it. If something bad had happened, she wouldn't be clowning with him. 'Don't give up the day job,' he said, walking back towards her.

'I wouldn't dream of it. I like it far too much.'

He drew abreast. 'Something happened?'

She pushed off from the wall. 'No. That's the trouble. Mr Brandon wants a profile. That way he'll have something to feed the reptiles. I'm here to drive you back. Shall we?' She gestured towards the main corridor and fell into step beside him.

'How did you know where I was? And that I didn't have my own car?'

She winked at him. 'I'm a detective.'

'What I do with my life isn't exactly a secret. You asked Carol.'

Jan smiled. 'When your car was at the house and you weren't, I called Carol. She said you'd probably have left the lights on. Or run out of petrol. So I called here.'

When they emerged in the car park, Tony was

surprised to see they were heading not for a nondescript saloon car but a low-slung Japanese sports two-seater. 'Nice to see Bradfield CID taking care of their officers,' he said, bending to fold himself into the passenger seat.

'You really do have a weird sense of humour, Dr Hill,' Jan said.

'Tony, please.' He gasped as she floored the accelerator and sped out into the narrow lane.

'So, what's in it for you?' Jan asked as she rattled through the gears.

'In what?' he said, confused.

'The nutters in Bradfield Moor. Why bother? You could spend your life profiling and teaching. Why earn a pittance dealing with the dregs?'

He thought for a moment. 'Hope,' he said finally.

'That's it? Hope?'

'Don't underestimate the power of hope. And besides,' he added, 'I'm good at it. There's a satisfaction in doing something you know you do better than most people in the field. Don't you find?'

She drove fast into a tight bend, throwing him against the door. 'Thanks for the implied compliment,' she said. 'And do they help you with your current profiling cases, your nutters?'

He grinned. 'Oddly enough, I place more trust in my own judgement. Which is not to say they don't occasionally offer an accidental insight.'

'Any insights today, then?'

Tony shook his head. 'Just a timely reminder that I really should have been looking more closely at victims. And what links them.'

'That's easy. They were all whores.'

'Apart from Paula.'

Jan pulled up at the junction with the main road and took the opportunity to give him a puzzled stare. 'But she looked like a whore.'

'If looks could kill, they probably will.' He smiled at her bafflement. 'There's something else they have in common.'

'What's that?'

'If your mission as a killer was cleaning up the streets, you might think getting rid of cops was as socially useful as getting rid of prostitutes. But of course that would only make sense if Paula was a bent cop . . .'

'There's more than one way of being bent.'

'Ah, yes, I'd heard you produced that revelation. Don Merrick seemed a bit put out at the notion.'

This time, there was no warmth in Jan's smile. 'It's so predictable, isn't it? Pretty girl like that, how could she be a dyke?'

'Still, you picked up on it,' Tony said. 'But then, I suppose you would.'

'Meaning what?' she said.

'Takes one to know one. Isn't that what they say?'

She flashed a quick glance at him. 'What makes you think I'm gay?'

'Is it supposed to be a secret?'

Jan blew a raspberry. 'Shrink's trick. Answer the question: what makes you think I'm gay?'

Because of the way you are with Carol, he thought, but was not prepared to say it because of what it would reveal about himself. He paused for a moment, finding another way of saying the same thing. 'Because of the way you are with men.'

'You think I hate men? What a cliché.'

'That's not what I said. You treat all of us with exactly the same mixture of amusement and charm and disdain. It doesn't matter if we're attractive or ugly, bright or dim, you don't differentiate. You're not interested in us beyond our professional interactions. It could be that you're one of those people who's just not interested in sex with either gender, but I don't think so. I sense a certain sexual charisma there. Does that answer your question?'

She slowed down and looked across at him. 'Thank you for taking it seriously. You're right, as it happens. And I'm right about Paula.'

'And you thought it was fair to out her?' Tony asked, curious rather than combative.

'Hey, you're the one saying we should be looking at every aspect of the victims. You think it matters? That she's gay?'

'I never gave it a moment's thought. It never seemed relevant,' he said indifferently.

'It can make you vulnerable on the street. Unless you take steps to turn it to your advantage. You can't rely on anybody else to do it for you. Of course, it's not the only thing that makes you vulnerable. Any sort of difference can have the same effect: race, being disabled . . . They're all things people have to compensate for.'

In every exploration he had made into the criminal mind, Tony had arrived at a moment where something crucial fell into place and made sense of everything. It wouldn't have registered if he hadn't been thinking so hard about power and vulnerability that morning, but because his mind was already running on those lines, it assumed the correct significance. At last he thought he understood. And he also knew he hadn't a hope in hell of convincing Carol or anyone else. Not wanting Jan to see his reaction, he looked out of the passenger window. 'I suppose. Must be just as hard for Evans and Chen,' he said nonchalantly.

'I wouldn't know, I've never asked them.'

'What? No solidarity among minorities?' Tony asked.

'I've got nothing against them. But I've got nothing in common with them either. Why should I expect them to fight my battles?'

'Fair enough. So I suppose Brandon wants this profile yesterday? That would be why they took the trouble to send someone to fetch me?'

'I guess so. Nothing else is going anywhere. Carol's even going over the old Derek Tyler cases with Sam to see if there were any loose ends they can chase up now.' She reached out and turned on the CD player. Bonnie Raitt sang that love had no pride.

'You think you're going to bring Paula home alive?' Tony asked.

'Honest answer?'

'Honest answer.'

'I think she's already dead. I think he's playing with us.'

More than anything else he'd heard that day, the words thrust a chill spear of fear into Tony's heart.

Evans marked his place with a finger and looked up. 'DCI Jordan? I can't seem to find any mention of Paula on the original inquiry list.'

Carol thought for a moment. 'She probably wasn't on it, Sam. She was a CID aide on the Thorpe case, but that was only a six-month posting. She'd probably have gone back to uniform by then. You think there's any significance in that?'

'If there is, I don't know what it could be,' he said. 'Just clutching at straws.' They went back to work, heads bent, minds on full alert, mining the mountain of paper.

Half an hour of silence later, they were disturbed by a SOCO. 'Are you DCI Jordan?' he said.

'Yes.' Carol tried to squash the quickening of interest. She couldn't bear any more false hope.

'We've been going through the bins in the search area and we've found the radio mike and transmitter that DC McIntyre was wearing,' he said, sounding pleased with himself.

Carol snapped to full attention. 'And?' She was half-aware of the arrival of Jan and Tony, but all her focus was on the SOCO.

'The wire from the mike to the transmitter had been snipped. There are two partial prints on the transmitter. We're working on them right now. We should know soon if they match anything on AFIS.'

Tony stayed discreetly in the background, but Jan dumped her coat and bag by her desk and moved closer to the action.

'Why has it taken this long to find?' Carol demanded. 'What have you people been doing for the past two days?'

He looked wounded. 'It turned up a couple of hundred yards away from where she was last seen. That's a lot of rubbish to get through.'

'It is when you work nine to five. Jan, see who you can rustle up to get back on the streets with you. Then widen the search area out from where they found the mike. Sam, you go too.'

Jan didn't pause to discuss the order, heading straight out the door towards the murder room. Evans capped his Cross fountain pen, slipped it into his inside pocket and followed her. Meanwhile, Tony casually sat down at Jan's desk, apparently waiting for Carol's attention.

'How long will it be before you get a result from AFIS?' she asked.

Unnoticed by anyone, Tony leaned down and flipped open Jan's handbag. He slid his fingers inside, probing till her found her bunch of keys. He closed his hand round them then silently lifted them clear and slipped them in his pocket.

'Hard to say,' the SOCO replied. 'It depends how much traffic there is on the system.'

Tony stood up. 'I'm just going for a coffee.'

Carol barely registered his words. 'Can't we put a priority status on it?'

'I already did,' Tony heard the SOCO say as he walked out of the office. He hurried downstairs and out into the front reception of the police station. He paused at the counter.

'Do you know where the nearest heel bar is?' he asked.

The civilian behind the counter thought for a moment. 'If you go into the mini-mall round the corner, there's one up the back in the basement.'

Tony left at a trot. He was breathing hard by the time he reached the heel bar. The smell of solvents and glue caught his throat and made his eyes water. Luckily there was no one waiting to be served ahead of him. He deposited the bunch of keys on the counter. As well as the car keys, there was a Chubb mortice, a couple of Yales and two small keys. 'I need copies of all of these, except for the car keys,' he said. 'And I'm in a hurry, I'm afraid.'

The youth behind the counter gave the keys a swift appraisal. 'No problem. Ten minutes do you?'

'Brilliant. I'll be right back.' He hurried out of the shop and ran through the arcade of stalls to the coffee shop by the escalators. Again, he was spared the tension of waiting in a queue. 'Large macchiato to go, please.' He drummed his fingers on the counter while he waited for the pitifully slow barista to get to grips with his technology and assemble the drink. He grabbed the carton then walked briskly back to the heel bar.

Five minutes later, he walked nonchalantly up to Jan's sports car. He put his coffee on the ground, unlocked the car and put the keys in the ignition. Then, trying to look like a man with nothing more demanding on his mind than coffee and a serial killer profile, he made his way back up to the squadroom.

He walked in just as Jan was upending the contents of her bag on to her desk. She looked up, frustration on her face. 'You didn't see what I did with my keys, did you?'

Tony scratched his head, frowning in recollection. 'You know, I don't remember you actually locking the car,' he said.

'Fuck.' Jan shovelled everything back into her bag, grabbed her jacket and ran from the room. Evans raised his eyebrows at Tony as he followed her at a more leisurely pace.

Tony shrugged. 'What can I say? I have that effect on women.'

Honey – whose real name was Emma Thwaite – had started to think of herself as streetwise. It had only been a matter of months since she'd left the shitty council flat in Blackburn to escape the responsibilities of raising three younger brothers while her mother spent her time in the pub, cadging drinks from men she would bring back and fuck on the living-room settee. But it felt like a lifetime. She could hardly remember who she'd been back then.

She knew she'd been lucky to end up under Jackie's wing, and she'd been naïve enough to believe she'd learned enough from that position of relative safety to manage on her own. But the past few days had thrust upon her the realization that she was a lot less capable of dealing with the world than she had thought. She wanted someone to take Jackie's place, someone to help take the edge off the fear and the loneliness.

So when she walked into Stan's Café that afternoon, she gravitated straight to the table where Dee Smart sat alone, smoking and staring out of the window. 'Hiya, Dee,' she said. 'Fancy another cuppa?'

Dee looked her up and down, as if calculating what the price might be. 'Yeah, go on,' she said with a shallow sigh.

Honey clattered off on her high heels, returning with two mugs and two chocolate biscuits. 'There you go,' she said, settling in opposite Dee and stripping the wrapper off her biscuit.

Dee carried on staring into the street. 'Bastard cops everywhere. They're scaring the punters away.'

'Sooner they catch whoever's doing this, the better for us,' Honey said.

Dee gave her a contemptuous look. 'That's not going to happen any time soon.'

'You think?' Honey tried not to let her apprehension show.

'I know. You think the Creeper isn't pulling the strings?'

The name took Honey by surprise. It had never occurred to her to connect it with the crimes that had turned her world difficult and sour. 'This has got something to do with the Creeper?' she asked.

'Of course it has,' Dee said impatiently. 'I've had them all over me, asking their questions. Do I know the Creeper? Do I know anybody who had it in for Sandie? Blah blah blah.'

'And you haven't told them?' Honey couldn't figure out why Dee would have kept silent about something so important.

Dee's eyes narrowed. 'You crazy? You think I want to be next on the hit list?'

Honey frowned. She knew she wasn't exactly Brain of Britain, but she didn't think what Dee was saying made sense. 'There won't be no hit list if the Creeper's locked up,' she pointed out.

Dee flicked the ash from her cigarette in a gesture of exasperation. 'Grow up, Honey. They're never going to lay a finger on the Creeper.'

'All the same . . .'

Dee shook her head vigorously. 'Don't even think about it. It'd be your funeral, girl.' She pushed her tea away from her, as if deciding that drinking it would place her under too much of an obligation. 'I'd have thought you'd have learned your lesson from what happened to Jackie. If you don't want to end up like her, keep your nose out of the Creeper's business.'

Honey watched Dee walk out. It hurt that her overture had been rejected, but she was more disconcerted by the reason than the fact itself. Maybe Dee was right, the best thing was to keep her head down and make sure she didn't rock the boat. But what if Dee was wrong?

Don Merrick decided he didn't like the Scottish Highlands. He'd never been anywhere so empty in his whole life. He remembered a trip he and Lindy had taken before the kids came along, a four-wheel-drive safari into the Sahara. Compared to this louring emptiness, the desert had felt positively thronged. It hadn't been so bad for a few miles after he'd left Inverness airport in the hire car, but when he'd turned off the main arterial road to strike out west, he had rapidly found himself in the middle of absolutely bloody nowhere. According to the map, this was supposed to be an A-road, but it was more like one of the narrow back roads of the Peak District.

You could go mad out here, he thought. Nothing but grey rock and greeny-brown vegetation. Correction. Nothing but grey rock and greeny-brown vegetation and the occasional grey-brown pond. Sometimes the grey rock manifested itself as the crumbling gable end of what might once have been a house or a barn. But signs of human life were few and far between. The only living things he could see were sheep. In an hour's driving he'd passed two vehicles, both travelling in the opposite direction: a Land Rover and a red minibus with PostBus emblazoned along the side. Don supposed some people might like the grandeur and the isolation, but he found himself longing for the bustle and scrum of the city.

When he'd looked at the map, he'd thought he could check out Nick Sanders' putative foxhole in a matter of hours. Before anyone would even notice he'd been gone. He'd capture the fugitive and restore his self-respect in one. Then the glory of success would bring forgiveness for his insubordination. Carol would be forced to respect his abilities if he brought Nick Sanders in before nightfall.

But the light faded faster up here too. It was only mid-afternoon, and already he felt twilight closing in. He'd be lucky if he made it to Achmelvich by nightfall, never mind back to Bradfield. He wished he'd brought a torch with him. He had a feeling that Achmelvich wasn't going to be well endowed with streetlights. If he ever found anything approximating civilization again, he'd stop and stock up on some essentials.

He wondered if they had chocolate up here.

Tony had chosen to sit at the desk Kevin Matthews normally occupied for the good reason that, from her office, Carol couldn't see what he was doing. She was still busy on the phone, which gave him the freedom to flick through the pages of the phone book. With one ear cocked, he ran his finger down a column of names. God, it was getting harder to read the small print, he thought. Time to have his eyes tested.

It sounded as if Carol was winding up her call. 'Yes, I do know that everybody thinks their request is a priority. But I've got an officer who's been abducted by a killer . . .' A pause. 'OK. I appreciate it.'

Just in time, he found what he was looking for. He jotted it on a piece of scrap paper and shoved it into his pocket as Carol emerged from her office and headed towards him. 'Did Jan fill you in?' she asked.

'Jan? Fill me in?' he echoed.

'Brandon wants a profile. He already told the noon press conference he was calling on the services of a psychological profiler. Which of course the local media will assume is you.'

'Oh, that. Right. Yes, she did say something,' he said, aware he was sounding flustered and hoping Carol would put it down to his customary vagueness. 'I take it you don't want me to refer to what we discussed last night?' he asked, hoping that might divert her from noticing anything unusual in his behaviour.

Carol raised her eyebrows. 'Not if you want Brandon to take anything else you say seriously.'

'And you? Have you thought about it?'

Carol pushed a hand through her hair. She looked frazzled and unhappy. 'Yeah, but it doesn't seem to take me any further forward. I'm sorry, Tony, but unless you've got something concrete, I haven't got time for this now.'

He stood up. 'That's OK. I understand. I'm going home. I'll work better there.'

'Fine, we'll talk later,' she said absently. Her mind was already on the next thing, the phone to her ear, her fingers on the buttons.

Out on the street, Tony hailed a taxi. He pulled the paper from his pocket and gave the driver the address. He sagged back into the seat and stared into the middle distance. So deep in his thoughts was he that he wasn't even aware of it when he started to speak out loud. Nor was he conscious of the apprehensive eyes of the driver in the rear-view mirror. All that interested him was the process of a killer's mind.

'You didn't get what you wanted,' he muttered. 'The bad fairy at the christening gave you a shit deal, and the brains to see how shit it was. So you learn how to take the power, hide the vulnerability. Get your retaliation in first. Hide your weakness behind a show of force. But sooner or later, the cracks start to show. You stop believing in your own publicity. You have to find a way to reassure yourself. A way to take more power to yourself. You become the voice.' He nodded in satisfaction. It made sense. It had the structure of a logical argument. Pretzel logic, but logic all the same.

'At first, you take your power from the weak. You find your listener in Derek. You make him do your bidding. You make him take your prey and you control every move of the puppet show. But Derek fucks up and you're back where you started. And it takes time to carve another will into the shape of your own.

'But, eventually, you get there. You find another mind you can dominate, another head you can perch inside. And it begins again. And then you get the chance to take on someone your own size. And you can't resist, can you?'

His reverie was broken by the anxious voice of the taxi driver. 'You all right, mate?' he asked.

Tony leaned forward. 'Not really,' he said. 'But I will be soon, I hope.'

One of the reasons for my success is my ability to think on my feet, to adapt my plans to accommodate changing circumstances. After the time it took to train him, I'd hoped to get more use out of this monkey, but it's become clear that sooner rather than later he's going to be fingered – and that presents a risk I'm not prepared to take. I was sure of Tyler, sure he would keep the faith because he had such a personal stake in the work I set him. But this one is weaker. He'll give me up without even knowing he's doing it.

I pull up round the corner from the shithole where he lives. It's getting dark now, and everyone's in too much of a hurry to get somewhere warm to pay attention to anybody else. I check the mirrors, just in case anybody's watching, then remove the gun from the glove compartment, enjoying the heft of it in my hand.

When the coast is clear, I get out, head down, and walk briskly to my destination. I have a key to the street door and I run up the stairs to the first landing. Two grubby green doors open off it. I reach up with a gloved hand and knock on the door with the number four painted on it.

I can feel my heart rate speeding up. I've never done this face to face before, and I'm curious to see how it will feel. Seconds pass, then the door inches open. Carl is peering out through the gap, dressed only in grey sagging jockey shorts and a crumpled T-shirt. He looks as if he's just woken up. His expression is suspicious, but when he sees it's me, his face clears.

'Hiya,' he says, a goofy grin on his greasy face. 'I wasn't expecting you.'

He steps back to allow me to enter. It's a dank, untidy room. Unmade bed, clothes in piles, Britney poster on the wall. It smells of masturbation and sweat. Every time I've been here, it's depressed me to think this was the best I could do.

Carl is gibbering something, but this afternoon I've no time for small talk. I'm supposed to be somewhere else. I pull out the gun and take pleasure in the panic that spreads across his face. He's not very bright, but even he knows what a gun means when it's at his head. I back him towards the bed.

'I did what you said. I never told anybody,' he whimpers. His legs hit the edge of the bed and he tumbles backwards. He scrambles towards the head of the bed. He's crying now. 'I promise, I won't give you up.'

I find the voice within myself. The one I know he is conditioned to obey. 'Lie down, Carl. Lie down and everything will be all right. I am the Voice. I am your Voice. Whatever I tell you to do is for the best. I am the Voice, Carl. Lie down.' And it works. His subconscious mind overrides his panic enough for him to do as he is told. He's shivering and sweating, but he's doing what he's told.

I reach for the pillow and put it to the side of his head. I press the gun barrel into the pillow. His eyes are wide with trust. 'I am the Voice,' I remind him. 'I am your Voice.' And I pull the trigger.

Carol looked up from the file she was reading and recognized the man who'd just entered the squad-room as one of the fingerprint technicians. 'We've got a result from AFIS,' he said.

'Who is it?' she demanded, getting to her feet and reaching for the sheet of paper in the technician's hand.

'Carl Mackenzie. Twenty-six. Possession of cannabis, possession of ecstasy, indecent exposure . . .'

'I know him, he's a small-time street dealer,' Kevin said. 'He hangs out in Stan's Café.'

'Last known address, Flat 4, 7 Grove Terrace, Bradfield,' Carol said. 'Come on, Kevin, let's hit it.' She pushed past the fingerprint officer, shouting for Merrick.

'He went off to get some sleep,' Kevin reminded her. 'I could call his mobile.'

Carol shook her head. 'Never mind. Stacey, get your coat,' she called across the room.

The technician stood in the doorway of Carol's office watching them go. 'Thanks for all your hard work, lads,' he mimicked sarcastically.

Carol, Kevin and Stacey pounded pell-mell down the corridor. 'We'll take my car,' Kevin shouted. 'I've got a noddy light.'

Carol nodded agreement as they hurtled down the stairs and into the car park. They piled into Kevin's car, Carol yanking open the glove box and pulling out the blue flashing light. Fumbling with the connector, she finally managed to plug it into the cigarette lighter slot, then opened the window and slammed it on the roof.

They were already out in the traffic, the rush hour jamming the streets with cars. Kevin leaned on the horn, the light flashed and it gradually dawned on other drivers that they needed to pull over. But it still felt like painfully slow progress.

Carol chewed on the skin by her thumbnail. *Please, God, let us find Carl Mackenzie. And please, God, let him lead us to Paula.*

* * *

Tony paid off the taxi and stood for a long moment, taking in the house in front of him. It was a modern detached brick building, part of a depressingly uninspired development on the outskirts of the city centre. It occupied the central plot at the head of a cul-de-sac with an unimpeded view of any car coming up the street. He wasn't in the least surprised. The Creeper would need to be in control of every possible aspect of her environment.

Jan Shields' house was even more lacking in personality than its neighbours, if that were possible. White paintwork, white front door, white garage door. Boring block paving on the drive and pathway. A tidy lawn with evenly spaced shrubs and conifers round the edge, all trimmed with obsessive neatness. Nothing that surprised Tony one whit.

He walked up the path and tried the mortice key in the lock. It was reluctant to turn at first, but Tony jiggled it a little and the tongue slipped back into its bed. The first Yale wouldn't fit, but the second slipped home easily. As the door opened, he heard the insistent beep of a burglar alarm's warning tone. He looked around for the control box, eventually spotting it behind him. His luck was still running; it was a key-operated system rather than one controlled by an electronic combination. He fumbled with the two small keys, his hands sweating as he jammed the first of them into the lock and turned.

Silence fell. Tony wiped the sweat from his face with both hands and turned to examine the house he believed to be the Creeper's lair. His evidence for that conviction was not the sort that would cut any ice with a cop. He could imagine Carol's face. 'It was the way she spoke about power and vulnerability. Her contempt for the weak,' he'd say. And then he'd see the struggle on Carol's face between her desire to believe him and her copper's dependence on tangible evidence. Actually, there was something else too, but that was equally intangible. From the very beginning the cutting of the wire had troubled him. If Paula had noticed it happening, she'd have kicked off there and then. For her not to have noticed, it must have been done without fumbling. And for it to have been done without fumbling, whoever abducted her couldn't have relied on a lucky guess. He had to have known. And that narrowed it down to Carol and her team.

At first, he'd been more interested in Chen and Evans. They were the most obvious outsiders because of their racial backgrounds. It wasn't hard to imagine the resentments building up over the years as they perceived themselves powerless in the face of an organization that was implacably geared towards handing control to others. Chen had seemed particularly appealing because of her obsession with machines. Interacting with people was something that didn't come easily to her, which, if she was the killer, might tempt her to use the agency of another. There was a coldness in Evans too, a distance that suggested he might enjoy exploiting others for his own ends.

And then he'd realized Jan was not only another outsider but one with a unique connection to Paula. So he'd driven that morning's conversation in a direction that he hoped would tell him more about her. Which it had done. And then he'd remembered Carol mentioning that Jan had been with Paula when she'd chosen her outfit. Nobody was better placed to make sure the wire was where it was supposed to be. And so he was here, staking everything on his gut instinct.

He flicked on the light switches in the hall. It was a risk, but there wasn't any point in being here in the dark. The floor was covered in thick cream carpet as far as the eye could see. It extended into the living room and up the stairs and it was spotless. No children or animals here. He looked down at his feet and saw a pair of slippers by the front door. Nothing from the outside world was going to be allowed to soil this place.

He moved through to the living room, standing on the threshold and drinking it all in, moving from first impression to a fuller scrutiny. The room was big, an archway leading from the seating area to a dining space. Two big cream sofas dominated the first part of the room, each replete with four precisely placed burgundy velvet cushions. In front of one there was a glass-and-wood coffee table. On it sat a *Radio Times* and that morning's paper, each perfectly aligned. The walls were painted a deeper shade of cream than the carpet. Above the fake coal fire hung a reproduction of a geometric Mondrian painting. A flat-screen TV dominated one corner of the room, DVD and video players underneath it.

On the other side of the chimney breast bookshelves had been built into the wall. Tony crossed to look at them, but he was distracted by the sight of a laptop on the dining table. He ducked through the arch, opened it and pressed the button to turn it on. While he waited for it to boot up, he went back to the bookshelves. 'There's got to be a record,' he murmured.

The lower shelves contained videos, the upper ones books. Most of the books were lesbian fiction, from pulp romance to more serious literature by writers such as Sarah Waters, Ali Smith and Jeanette Winterson. Incongruously, half a dozen tattered hardbacks of John Buchan thrillers. On the top shelf, legal textbooks, police manuals. He bent over to study the videos. American cop shows like *CSI, NYPD Blue, Law & Order* dominated, though there were also a few lesbian classics such as *Bound* and *Show Me Love*. He took out a couple of cases at random, but the contents matched the covers.

'Gotta be a record,' he repeated. He went back to the computer and gazed at it. The trouble was, he wasn't much of a techie. He knew enough to run the programs he wanted to run and that was about it. He needed Stacey Chen. But that was about as likely as a moonwalk right now. 'It's not going to be here. You're too clever for that. You know what people like Stacey can do. No, you're going to want something tangible, something you can access without leaving footprints.' He looked around the room. There was nowhere to hide anything down here. Wherever the puppetmaster kept the records of her exercises in power, they weren't here.

Purposefully, Tony headed for the stairs. He wasn't worried about being disturbed; all Carol's officers were working flat out round the clock. Jan wouldn't be back for hours yet. Plenty of time to have a good look round.

The three cops thundered up the dimly lit stairs of 7 Grove Terrace, ignoring the open-mouthed student who had let them in and who was now shouting, 'Hey, what the fuck . . .'

They stumbled into one another on the landing outside the door of flat 4. Carol banged the door with the side of her fist. 'Police, open up,' she shouted, venting all the anger, fear and frustration of the past few days.

No reply. Kevin pushed his way to the door and hammered so hard the wooden panel cracked. 'Open up, Carl. The party's over.'

'Kick it in,' Carol said.

Kevin stepped back and threw himself at the door. It vibrated, but didn't break open. As he backed up for another attempt, Stacey intervened. 'Gimme a chance,' she said.

Kevin almost burst out laughing. 'You what?'

But Stacey was already somewhere else. She stood side-on to the door, breathing deeply. She seemed to coil into herself then she erupted in a blur of movement, one leg shooting out and hitting the door right next to the lock. There was a splintering of wood and the door sagged open.

'Fucking hell,' Kevin said.

Carol gave Stacey a perplexed glance. 'You're full of surprises,' she said, pushing the door open. What faced them stripped away any sense of wonder or levity. Carl Mackenzie lay sprawled on the bed, blood and brains on the covers and the wall behind him. The air was thick with the salt metallic taste of blood. In his right hand, a gun lay, his fingers curled loosely around the grip.

'Gunshot wound to the right temple. Gun in his hand,' Carol said automatically.

'Oh Jesus, no,' Kevin shouted. 'Fucking bastard, why couldn't you give us Paula first? Fucking selfish bastard.'

'Looks like suicide to me,' Stacey said.

Carol bent forward to peer closely at the body on the bed. 'Except I can't see any powder burns round the wound.' She reached out and laid the back of her hand against his arm. 'Still warm. Very fucking convenient.'

Stacey frowned. 'Convenient for who?'

'For whoever wants us to believe that Carl Mackenzie was smart enough to plan a series of murders and to kidnap a cop.'

'I don't understand. His prints were on Paula's powerpack. Do you mean he was working with someone?'

Carol sighed. 'Not with someone, Stacey. For someone.'

It wasn't so bad after all. Nothing like as exciting as making the others do the work, but still a thrill. Having the power to take a life and having the nerve to exercise it; how could that not be close to as good as it gets?

I wonder how long the suicide scenario will hold water. It depends on whether they find him because they know they're looking for him for the murders or whether they just find him. If it's the ice blonde and her team of nodding dogs, it won't take them long to realize Carl wasn't alone when he died. It's a pity I had to use the pillow, but I didn't have a silencer and it was more important that I got away than that I made the scene watertight and some nosy neighbour clocked me leaving after the gunshot.

Maybe I should have tried the line that I was interviewing him when suddenly he reached for the gun and shot himself. I could have been the hero of the hour. But that would have been a high-risk strategy, and I haven't got this far by taking unnecessary risks. I've always stacked the odds in my favour. Like with the trained monkeys: I always made sure they were well in my debt before I started pushing the buttons to make them perform. With Derek, there was the evidence of the rape that I conveniently made disappear. With Carl, there were the drugs.

Now it's time to finish clearing up. I'm keeping an eye open for what I need, doubling down the side streets a couple of miles from Carl's place. And there it is, tucked down an alley. A builder's skip, full of wood and broken furniture and rubble. I pull up at the mouth of the alley and grab the ruined pillow. I stuff it under a broken sheet of chipboard and I'm back in the car inside a minute.

I need to get back on to the visible plane, but I want to see her first. I'm aching for her; it's been a long time since this morning, and Carl won't be bringing any more videos. I'm going to have to go there myself later to change the video cassette and to check on her. Shoving a dildo garnished with razor blades into a woman's vagina myself will be less satisfying. Making someone else do it, now that's worth the candle. But getting my own hands dirty was never part of the game plan.

But there's no other way out. Left to her own devices, she'll take too long to die. They'll have found where I'm keeping her long before that happens. And even though there's nothing there to point the finger at me, I'd prefer her to be dead when they get to her.

Of course, there might be more pleasure to be had in her staying alive . . . Watching her struggle with the damage my power has inflicted might just offer something rather special to savour. It's possible that would amuse me while I look for another monkey to train.

Yes. Perhaps for once the exercise of mercy might be a more entertaining route to take.

But first I want to see her suffer some more.

The immaculate cream carpet continued throughout the upper floor of the house. The room straight ahead was clearly the main bedroom. Although it was as perfectly ordered as the living room – no clothes thrown over chairs, bed neatly made, dressing table as organized as Dr Vernon's instrument tray in the pathology lab – it wasn't what he'd expected. Somehow, though the overall effect managed to be sterile, this was undoubtedly intended to be a boudoir. Decorated in peaches and cream, the curtains matching the bed linen, the room contained more flounces and frills than Tony had ever seen outside the bedding department of John Lewis.

'Who are you trying to be here?' he asked out loud. 'Who do you bring here? Are you trying to lull them into a false sense of security? Are you trying to kid them that you're not really a shark?' He walked over to the chest of drawers and, feeling uncomfortably like the sort of sexual pervert that ended up as his patient, he slid open the top drawer. It was crammed with excessively feminine lingerie of the kind Tony had only ever seen in expensive shops and then only in occasional glimpses. But even here, order prevailed. Bras on one side of the drawer, briefs that deserved their name on the other. He gingerly moved his hand among the lace and silk. Nothing untoward met his fingers.

The next drawer contained carefully folded T-shirts, many of them silk, and an assortment of hosiery. The bottom drawer was packed with sweaters. He closed it, having found nothing except clothes.

He looked over at the bed. Kingsize, traditional iron bedstead painted cream. It was, Tony thought, a measure of his intellectual investment in perversion that he could never contemplate such a bed without automatically thinking of bondage. On either side there was a bedside table complete with lamp. It was impossible to tell which side Jan slept on.

He checked the drawer of the bedside table nearest the door. Empty. The other offered a couple of books of lesbian erotica, one with an S&M theme, a dildo and a small anal probe. Nothing very remarkable, he thought. 'Of course, I could be wrong about you. It does run counter to the probabilities,' he muttered. 'And if I am, that could be very embarrassing.' He shut the drawer and looked around purposefully.

One wall of the room appeared to consist solely of doors. Tony tried the first and found himself inside a small en suite shower room. Not a hiding place in sight. The next door opened into a walk-in wardrobe stretching the rest of the length of the room. He moved slowly along, flicking through the clothes. Suits, trousers, jackets, blouses, a couple of formal evening dresses. Everything clean and ironed, some items still in their dry-cleaning bags. He got down on his knees to look behind the shoes. She had what he thought Carol would find a depressing penchant for cowboy boots.

Probing among the boots, his fingers brushed against the coolness of metal. Scrabbling under the footwear, he discovered a metal file case pushed back into a recess in the wall. 'Bingo,' he breathed. He pulled it out into the light and tried the remaining key he'd had cut.

The lock turned with the smoothness of frequent use. Hoping for more than a stash of porn, Tony opened the lid.

Carol stood on the landing in Grove Terrace, watching the SOCOs work their tedious magic. She could hear Stacey's voice floating down from the floor above.

'How well did you know Carl Mackenzie?'

Then a woman replying, 'I wouldn't say I knew him. We'd speak on the stairs, that sort of thing. But that's as far as it went. He wasn't the full shilling, poor lad.'

'Did you ever see other people coming and going from his flat?'

'Can't say I noticed anybody. A proper Billy No-Mates, that was Carl. Eager to please, but not the sort you'd want following you round.'

'And did you hear anything this afternoon?'

'Not me, love. I was watching the telly.'

Kevin walked up from the floor below. He shook his head. 'Nobody heard a thing.'

Carol sighed. 'They really didn't, or they conveniently didn't?'

'I think they were telling the truth,' he said despairingly. 'There's a little old lady downstairs, she'd love to have heard or seen something. She hasn't had this much excitement since the Boer War.'

'You know, Kevin, if Carl Mackenzie killed himself,

I'll apply for a transfer to Traffic. Get the uniforms to search the bins.'

'The bins? What are we looking for?'

'Look at the bed. What's wrong with this picture?'

Kevin looked but he couldn't see past the body steadily cooling on the soiled sheets. He shrugged.

'There's no pillow. Can you sleep without a pillow, Kevin?'

The penny dropped. 'A pillow with a hole in the middle.'

Sam Evans was fed up. He wasn't even sure what he was supposed to be doing. Jan Shields had marshalled half a dozen of them back down to Temple Fields to go over what was, as far as he was concerned, old ground. They were ordered to carry out another canvass of the area immediately surrounding the bin where the transmitter pack had been found. They'd dispersed on their rounds and he hadn't seen Shields since. He'd knocked on the doors assigned to him, asked the same questions, logged the same negative responses.

He decided to have a quick pit stop in Stan's Café. The coffee was terrible, but the atmosphere was marginally less depressing than that inside the police station. As he walked down the street towards the greasy spoon, he saw Honey on the kerb, touting for trade. 'Hey, girl, how're you doing?' he said easily.

'Hi, Sammy,' she said. 'Crap, actually. You lot are killing the trade.'

'Fancy a coffee?' He'd thought she had something for him in the pub, but Jan Shields' arrival had closed her down tight as a drum. Maybe he could loosen her up again.

'You buying?'

'I'm buying.'

'In that case, you can treat me to an all-day breakfast.'

He grinned. He'd always admired bottle. 'Come on, then.'

A few minutes later, Honey was attacking a monstrous fry-up with all the gusto of a starving dog. Mouth full of sausage and egg, she mumbled, 'Brilliant, Sammy.'

'It'll kill you, that shit,' he said censoriously. 'Clog up your arteries, make you fat.'

She shook her head. 'I never put a pound on, me.'

Evans gave her a cynical look. 'Can't imagine why that would be.'

She winked. 'All that exercise.'

'Not to mention the recreational drugs . . .'

She looked disappointed. 'Aw, Sammy, don't spoil it.'

'I'm a cop, Honey, I can't help it.' She acknowledged his reply with a sad little twist of her mouth. 'You know the other day when we were having a chat?' he continued. She nodded. 'I had the feeling you were going to tell me something. And then DS Shields turned up and you did one.'

Honey swallowed, buying herself some time, considering. Then she said, 'She disgusts me, that one.'

He shrugged. 'She's only doing her job. Just like me.'

Honey gave him a disbelieving look. 'Is that what it's called?'

This wasn't going quite where he'd expected but Evans was nothing if not a good listener, especially when it meant adding to his store of knowledge. 'Meaning what?' he prompted.

Honey cast her eyes upwards. 'Come on, Sammy. Don't tell me you don't know about the Vice and their freebies?'

At first, he didn't get it. 'Are you saying Jan Shields is on the take?'

She picked a piece of bacon rind from between her small, feral teeth. 'Not like you mean it. Not in money.' She understood his stillness. She knew he wanted her to spell it out, as if that would somehow make it easier to believe. 'She takes it in sex. She makes some of the girls have sex with her.'

Evans didn't much like Jan, but he thought she was a good cop. She'd been the one who'd spotted the Tim Golding photo. And she'd worked her arse off trying to find Paula. He didn't want to think of her in the light Holly was shining. 'Come off it, Honey,' he protested. 'That's just people taking a pop at a cop because she's an easy target.'

Honey put down her fork and knife. She looked both serious and miserable. 'She's had me. Face down on a table, rough and ready. She fisted me. I couldn't walk straight for days. Another time, she fucked me in the arse with a Coke bottle. Do you have any idea how fucking scary that is, someone ramming a glass bottle into you? That's what your precious detective sergeant likes.'

He recognized truth when he heard it, but he still didn't want to accept it. 'I'm finding this hard to believe, Honey.'

Her mouth twisted in a bitter line. 'Which is why she's been getting away with it for so long. You lot don't want to hear this kind of shit about one of your own.'

'You should have made a complaint.'

'Yeah, right. Like anyone would believe that a nice lady cop would hit on a slag like me.' She picked up her cutlery and attacked a slice of fried bread, dipping it in her egg yolk and crunching angrily.

'Has this happened with other women?'

'Only a few, as far as I can make out. She's choosy. And we know to keep our mouths shut unless we want to be banged up on a charge. We all hate her. She drools all over us, makes us kiss her. And, like, that's the thing we don't do with punters, you know? It's sick. And you never know when she's going to be back for more. Out of the blue, suddenly she's there.' She gave him a sidelong glance, knowing she was about to deliver the killer punch. 'That's why we call her the Creeper.'

He stared at her, open-mouthed and horrified.

'See, I knew you wouldn't believe me,' she said with a kind of sad triumph.

'What did you call her?' Evans strained to get the words out.

'The Creeper. It's what the girls she screws call her.'

He gave her the standard-issue policeman's hard stare. 'This better be the truth, Honey,' he said, pushing his chair back.

'I got no reason to lie about it, Sammy,' she said huffily.

Evans jumped to his feet and threw some money on the table. 'Right, Honey. On your feet. You're coming with me.' He marched her protesting to the door, pulling out his mobile as he went.

* * *

The first thing out of the file case was a thin stack of photographs. Tony recognized the top one immediately. Jackie Mayall lay spreadeagled on the bed where she'd died. But there wasn't as much blood as he remembered. In the following two pictures, more blood appeared. The final two shots showed crime-scene tape at the edges; in one a SOCO stood by the bed with a ruler in his hand. Tony's stomach turned over as he realized what he was looking at. 'Official crime-scene photos . . . and very unofficial ones.'

With a gesture of disgust, he put them aside and carried on looking. There were more photos, this time of Sandie Foster. They fell into the same two categories: official and unofficial. Under the photos he found a handful of DVD-ROMs. He leaned back on his heels and stared at them. 'Memories,' he said softly.

He'd been right. It had taken him far too long to get there, but he'd been right. He thought about phoning Carol, but the need to know, to be certain, was stronger. He gathered everything together and retraced his steps down to the dining-room table.

He sat down in front of the laptop and pressed the button to open the CD/DVD drive. Empty. He was about to insert one of the disks when it occurred to him that it might be worth checking out which websites Jan had bookmarked. He clicked on her comms program, then on the icon for favourite places. Her bank. The BBC website. Amazon. Something called lesbiout.co.uk. And one called simply 'webcam'. 'Oh shit,' he said.

Hurriedly, he checked there was a cable connecting the laptop to a phone line, then he clicked the icon to get online. Against the background sound of modems warbling to each other, he spread out the photographs on the table around him. A bright voice said, 'Welcome. You have mail.'

Ignoring the prompt to access the incoming mail box, Tony clicked on the webcam link. The screen went black. Then it filled with a blurred image. Seconds later, the pixels shunted into place and with pinprick clarity Paula McIntyre appeared on the screen. 'Holy fuck,' Tony said.

At first, he couldn't tell if she was dead or alive. There was no blood, which was a mercy. He frowned at the screen, trying to work out how to control the image, whether he could zoom in or not, whether there was any way to find where the image was coming from. He was so intent on what he was doing, he completely missed the drift of headlights up the cul-de-sac and the sound of a car engine cutting out only yards from the house.

She knew as soon as she turned into her street that something was seriously wrong. Her house was a blaze of light, upstairs and down. But there were no cars in sight, other than the ones she knew belonged to her neighbours. For a moment, she considered making a run for it. She'd have a head start and she had plans in place for precisely this contingency. However, she reasoned, if it was her colleagues who were on to her, she would have picked up something unusual in the radio traffic. But all afternoon, the police radio in her car had spat out the usual crap. Nothing out of the ordinary at all. She'd heard the call for support when Carl's body had been found and was glad she'd had the foresight to get rid of him before the fingerprint evidence came back. Besides, if it was her lot, Jordan the ice maiden would have made damn sure that she was well out of the way during the search, performing some pointless task on the other side of town.

So if it wasn't the cops inside the house, it had to be Tony Hill. She'd sensed something this morning in the car with him, but she'd thought she was being paranoid. Now, it seemed her instinctual nervousness might have been justified. Sudden realization dawned. He must have lifted her keys and had them copied. She swore under her breath. That's what had happened earlier. She hadn't been losing it at all. He'd tricked her. Outrage swelled inside her and she knew she wasn't about to run. Nobody got one over on her. Nobody.

If it was Hill and he was there alone, she could finesse the whole problem out of existence. Get rid of him, move her souvenirs where they couldn't be found, show terrible remorse at killing the psychologist she'd mistaken in the dark for a burglar. At the most, she'd do a couple of years.

If that was going to play, however, she'd need to make it look like she'd come home as normal. About thirty yards from her house, she cut the lights and switched off the engine, coasting into her drive on momentum and habit. She got out of the car, closing the door with the gentlest of clicks. From the darkness of the drive, she could see the length of her living room.

There he was, the cheeky bastard. Sitting at her dining table, using her laptop like he was Goldilocks and she was the three bears. Well, there was no doubt about it now. She was going all the way.

She crept round to the back of the house, ducking beneath the dining-room window as she passed. She leaned against the wall by the back door, raking through her bag to find the back door key, which she always kept loose, just in case she lost the rest of her keys. A cautious planner, that's what she was. And why she should have realized earlier that Carl wasn't her only problem.

She slipped the key into the lock and turned it with infinitesimal care. The click as the tumblers released was barely audible. She kicked off her shoes, pushed down on the handle and inched the door open. Gingerly she stepped through the gap and stood listening. She felt wonderfully alive, buzzing with the knowledge that she was in control, and he had no fucking idea. Through the half-open door between kitchen and dining area, she could hear the tap of keys and the click of the track-pad buttons.

So taut was she that she physically jerked when the sound of his voice cut through the silence. 'Where are you? Come on, tell me. Where are you, Paula?' Her heart rate dropped back as soon as she realized he was talking to the image on the screen, not to her.

She took a deep, silent breath. In the dim city glow bleeding in through the kitchen window, she could see the outline of her neat, sterile, modern kitchen. One of the few women she'd brought back to the house to fuck had commented that it looked like somewhere serious microwaving went on. She hadn't been invited back a second time. By the cooker, the knife block sat, its contents seldom used and still factory sharp. She reached out and gently removed a long-bladed boning knife, then walked soundlessly towards the dining-room door.

Carol reached out her free hand to the wall, unconsciously supporting herself against the weight of the information coming down the phone at her. 'Are you sure, Sam?' she said, knowing in her gut that he was right, that Tony had been right, that this was the worst of all possible scenarios for Paula McIntyre. The knowledge wormed its way into her brain, making sense of the loose connections that had been troubling her for days.

'I'm as sure as I can be,' Evans said solemnly.

'Where is she right now?' Carol asked. Kevin stopped on his way down the stairs, alarmed by the stricken look on her face, the dull inevitability in her voice.

'I don't know. I haven't seen her for hours.'

'We need to find her. Get out on the streets and see if you can track her down. Ask who's seen her. But keep it off the radio, you understand?'

'I understand.'

'Good work, Sam,' Carol said, knowing nobody else would ever thank him for what he'd achieved. She ended the call. She wanted to curl up in a ball and weep, but that would have to wait for later.

'Guv?' Kevin said, his tone concerned. Carol knew his anxiety wasn't really for her, but she forgave him anyway.

'The Creeper,' she said. 'Sam's got an ID from one of the street girls.'

Kevin's face lit up. 'But that's great news.'

'No, it's not,' Carol said flatly. It was as if she

couldn't bring herself to tell him. She turned away and began to run down the stairs. 'Stacey,' she shouted. 'And you too, Kevin. With me, now.'

Kevin caught up with her at the car, Stacey at his heels. 'Who is it?' he demanded. 'Who is it?'

Carol's face clenched momentarily in pain. 'Jan Shields,' she said.

Kevin recoiled as if he'd been struck in the face. He gave an incredulous little laugh. 'It's a wind-up,' he said. 'Somebody with a score to settle.'

'Sam says not,' she said heavily. 'I should have listened to Tony,' she added, running a hand through her hair. 'Can we get a move on, please, Kevin?'

Dazed, he unlocked the car and they piled in. 'Stacey, call the station and get a home address for Jan Shields,' Carol said over her shoulder. 'Fuck, I should have listened to Tony.'

'What? He said it was Jan Shields?' Kevin sounded incredulous.

'He said there was a cop behind this. I wouldn't believe him.'

'Where am I going?' Kevin said as Carol slammed the noddy light back on the roof.

From the back seat, Stacey shouted the address. 'It's on the Micklefield estate,' she said.

'We've still only got one hooker's word for it,' Kevin said as he carved a line through the traffic. 'And it makes no sense.'

Carol sighed as if she had the weight of the world on her shoulders. 'Oh, it makes sense all right. It's the first thing that's made sense since this whole fucking business began.'

* * *

Tony clicked another button, hoping it might provide some indication of where the webcam feed was coming from. He'd left the screen itself, unable to bear the sight of Paula's vulnerability. At least she was still alive. It was, he knew, time to call Carol. Stacey Chen was far better equipped for this task than he was.

He reached for his mobile. He'd barely got his hand out of his pocket when he heard a low voice behind him that chilled him to the bone.

'You're a burglar. I'm quite within my rights.'

He froze and slowly turned. Jan Shields was inches from him, her weight balanced perfectly, a glittering blade held almost carelessly in her hand. Her eyes were cold and steady, her whole attitude one of carefully contained violence. 'Drop the phone on the floor,' she added.

He did as he was told. He didn't doubt for a moment that she would have had no hesitation in cutting him if he hadn't complied. 'Might be a bit hard to argue reasonable force. I mean, everybody knows I'm a weed.'

Her lip curled in contempt. 'I don't think I'll ever have to make the argument. Because nobody knows you're here, do they?'

'Carol knows.' He said it casually, trying to make it convincing.

She shook her head. 'I don't think so. She does things by the book, does the lovely Carol. She would never let you come out to play by yourself. I rather think you're all mine, Dr Hill.'

She was so accustomed to dominating, he thought. The only way under her guard was to take the power from her. Which was fine in theory. His problem was that he was woefully short on leverage. 'This isn't your style, Jan,' he tried for starters.

For some reason, his words had amused her. 'You think not?'

'It's way too hands-on. You like somebody else to do the dirty work.'

She raised one eyebrow. 'Are you suggesting I've got something to do with these murders?' she said, her cherub's face assuming a look of injured innocence.

'They're your murders, Jan. You should be proud of them. They're interesting pieces of work.'

'That's as maybe. But they're nothing to do with me, Dr Hill. Derek Tyler killed four women. And a retard called Carl Mackenzie did three more copycat murders before he topped himself in remorse only this afternoon. That's what the evidence shows.'

Oh Christ, she's killed with her own hands. The knowledge hit Tony with the force of a lightning strike. He felt his own chances shrivel to ash. But still, he had to try. 'Come on, Jan. There's no point in lying now. Carl Mackenzie hasn't done three murders. Paula McIntyre is still very much alive.'

'You obviously know more about it than I do. Maybe you're the person behind it all. Maybe you've set me up. Maybe you're the person who's been sending me all this sick stuff.'

He shook his head, aiming for an air of disappointment. 'That dog won't hunt. Carol Jordan knows me too well to fall for that.'

'I can make it look that way. With you dead and the ends all tied up, who's going to listen to your favourite blonde? Everybody knows she's lost it. Face it, Dr Hill, you're a busted flush.'

Kevin turned into the Micklefield estate and slowed to a halt at the end of the street where Jan Shields lived. 'What now?' he said. 'It's a cul-de-sac. If she's looking out for us, she's going to see us the minute we turn into it.'

'Your car's pretty nondescript. We could drive up and just turn into somebody's drive near her house. There's not much light, and it's not like we'd be doing anything suspicious.'

Kevin drove slowly up the cul-de-sac. Almost at once, he spotted Jan's distinctive car. 'Looks like she's at home,' he said.

'Stick to the plan,' Carol replied. 'There, that one on the right a couple of doors down from hers. The house will shield us from her line of sight if we pull right up the drive.'

'What now?' Kevin asked. 'We could just front her up. Arrest her on suspicion and do a search.'

Something was niggling at the corner of Carol's mind. 'Does anyone know where Tony is?'

'He said he was going home to write his profile,' Stacey reminded her.

Carol took out her phone and speed-dialled Tony's home number. It rang a few times then the machine kicked in. She waited for the beep, then said, 'Tony, it's Carol. If you're there, pick up. It's urgent.' She waited for half a minute, then cut off the call. She tried his mobile, but it rang out interminably without an answer. 'Oh shit,' she said, a terrible apprehension hitting her.

'There's no reason to suppose he's in there,' Kevin said anxiously.

'Apart from that little pantomime with Jan's lost keys earlier.' Carol felt the pieces sliding into place, the picture forming in her mind's eye.

'What little pantomime?'

'Jan mislaid her keys. And Tony stepped out of absent-minded professor role long enough to remind her she hadn't locked her car. How likely is that, on both counts? But I just didn't see it at the time.' She swallowed hard. 'He's in there, Kevin. In there with her.'

'We don't know that,' he said.

'We need to find out. Stay there,' Carol ordered, opening the car door, ignoring the looks of dismay on her colleagues' faces. She walked to the corner of the building and sneaked a look round it. She was at a tangent to Jan's house. She could see part of the living room, which was empty. The front window upstairs was also brightly lit. Anyone watching from in there would be visible from where Carol was standing. Time to take a chance.

She sprinted along the front of the house, jumping a low hedge and crossing the garden of the house next door. That brought her to the edge of Jan's drive, alongside her car. A big window towards the rear of the gable end spilled light on to the paved blocks of the drive and splashed it up the side of the garage. She calculated that if she could make it to the far end of the window undetected, she could use the shelter of the garage to look into the window from far enough away not to be obvious to anyone inside.

She crouched down and circled behind the car, making it to the gable end and flattening herself against the wall. She edged up until she was almost level with the window, then crouched down and crept along below the sill for a few feet before straightening up. She was just outside the oblong of light. Taking a deep breath, she covered the distance to the rear of the garage in seconds.

Relying on the pool of shadow to obscure her, Carol turned and stood up. She had a clear line of angled vision into the dining room. She could see Jan from the waist up. And, slightly to one side of her, she could see the back of Tony's head. Her chest tightened. *Why the fuck didn't you call me?* As she watched, Jan's right hand came up into view in what looked from that distance to be a casual gesture.

But there was nothing casual about the knife that refracted light in a gleaming line that seemed to cut to Carol's very heart.

The insistent chirrup of Tony's mobile stopped as suddenly as it had begun. Jan nodded. 'Good boy. You didn't even try to answer it.'

'This is what you like, isn't it? The moment of power. Control. The world bent to your will.'

She cocked her head. 'If you say so.'

'I know so. It was a beautiful idea. Working on mentally susceptible men, making them your tools. A double dose of power. You control them and they control the victim according to your script. I take my hat off to you. It can't have been easy, getting them word perfect.'

She smiled. 'I know what you're trying to do. And

it isn't going to work. There's no point in playing for time when the cavalry don't know where you are.'

He stood up. 'I'm not playing for time.'

'Sit down,' she ordered him.

'I don't think so,' he said. 'You know there's no way out for you.'

Her eyes narrowed. 'I told you. I can make it look like you tried to set me up. I caught you in the act, we struggled, you died.'

'Underestimating the opposition. It's the one mistake that brings people down more than any other.'

She gave a derisory snort. 'What's to underestimate? We both know where the power resides. I'm a cop. You? You're just a very strange little man who weirds people out.'

'No, no, you misunderstand me. I'm not your problem. I don't actually mind dying, you see. No, your problem is Carol Jordan. I told her what I suspected. OK, she laughed at me. But if anything happens to me, she'll come after you.'

She looked scornful. 'Carol Jordan doesn't scare me.'

'That's what I mean about underestimating the opposition. She should scare you. Because, contrary to what you think about her, she's not afraid of getting her hands dirty. She won't be hiding behind some poor inadequate sod like Derek Tyler or Carl Mackenzie. She'll take you down, and she'll do it in the worst way.'

'I'll take my chances.'

He turned away. 'I don't think so. You're too accustomed to making other people take them for you.'

'Where do you think you're going?' she yelled, her control suddenly slipping.

He glanced back at her. 'I'm tired of talking. You're history and I'm going home.'

Galvanized into action, she lunged forward and grabbed his arm, spinning him towards her. Then the knife was in the air, gleaming between them, searching for flesh.

As soon as she saw the knife, Carol knew there was no time for anything other than action. She raced to the back door of the house, making a lunge for the door handle. To her surprise, it gave under her hand and she half-tumbled, half-ran into the kitchen. She saw a freeze-frame of Jan bearing down on Tony, the weapon hidden from her by their bodies. His mouth opened in a scream of pain. 'Drop the knife,' Carol yelled desperately at the top of her voice as she crossed the kitchen in a handful of strides.

At the sound of her cry, Jan hesitated long enough for Tony to stagger out of the arc of her knife. She glanced back at Carol, turned to flash a look of hatred at him before Carol launched herself across the last few feet between them.

Carol's momentum drove them both crashing to the floor in a struggling tangle of limbs. At first, Carol had no idea where the knife was and she scrabbled for purchase so she could pin down Jan's wrist.

'Let me go,' Jan shouted. 'You're hurting me.'

'Drop the knife,' Carol yelled back, her face inches from the other woman's.

'I dropped it already.' The words came out almost as a scream. 'Get off me.' Her body bucked under

Carol. Then suddenly Tony was on the floor beside them, pinning Jan's shoulders to the floor with his knees. Blood was streaming from one of his hands, and he clutched it to his chest.

'The knife's on the floor, Carol,' he said.

Carol eased back, panting, her weight keeping Jan's lower body immobilized. 'You're making a big mistake,' Jan gasped.

'I don't think so,' Carol said. 'Jan Shields, I am arresting you on suspicion of conspiracy to commit murder . . .'

'You don't get it, do you?' Jan howled.

'Save it for the interview room. You do not have to say anything . . .'

'Carol, listen to me,' Jan said, dragging all her resources together to give her voice the note of assured command. 'I'm the victim here. You need to listen to me.'

Don Merrick couldn't remember ever having been so cold in his life. He'd gone beyond shivering and into a kind of physical trance, his body numb and heavy. And still no sign of Nick Sanders.

He'd reached Achmelvich in the early evening, at the end of a single-track road that cut high above the slender finger of a sea loch. The occasional tree he'd passed had been bent double, a marker to indicate the force and direction of the prevailing wind.

It was hardly worth giving a name to, he thought. There was the youth hostel, closed for the winter, and a handful of low cottages hunched along a spine of rock that stretched out into the sea. Only one of the cottages was showing a light. He wondered if he should ask for directions, but figured it couldn't be that hard to find this Hermit's Castle.

He'd been wrong, of course. He'd spent the best part of an hour clambering over rocks in the wrong shoes, stumbling on loose stones, nearly tumbling headlong into the sea at one point. When he'd finally found it, he'd almost walked straight past it.

Exhausted, cold and bruised, he shone his torch over the tiny concrete structure. It was nestled in a gap in the rocks, a grey box scarcely seven feet high with a small chimney curved over the roof like a tail. There was a doorway but no door. It led to a narrow passage that curved round, apparently designed to keep out the wind and the rain. It gave on to a tiny cell, barely six feet across. Along one side was a concrete shelf the size and shape of a single bed. Opposite was an open hearth. And that was it. Nowhere to hide, nowhere to do anything much. He couldn't imagine spending a day there, never mind a year.

Merrick went back outside and shone his torch around. Nothing to do but wait. He'd give it till ten, he decided, then leave. If Nick Sanders arrived after that, he wouldn't be going anywhere before morning. If, of course, he was coming there at all.

A short distance beyond the hideaway, Merrick found a sheltered space in the rocks and hunkered down. He'd come across a petrol station earlier where he'd managed to buy a heavy rubber torch, some cans of Coke, a couple of packets of biscuits and some crisps. He'd also bought a hideous handknitted jumper which he'd hoped might protect him against the cold. It didn't seem to be helping much.

The sound of the sea crashing against the rocks was hypnotic. There were moments when he felt himself drifting into a doze, starting awake only because his body shifted and some part of him hit a different bit of rock. Thoughts of Lindy and his sons drifted in confusion around his head. They were why he was here. Somewhere in the deep recesses of his mind, he knew that a large part of the reason he was so determined to bring Tim and Guy's murderer to justice personally was that he felt it would be a kind of talisman, an act that would protect him from the prospect of losing his own boys. It almost assuaged the guilt he felt at abandoning Paula. But there were dozens of people out there working to bring Paula back, and nobody but him who cared enough about Tim and Guy to take a chance on this most slender of leads.

It was just after seven when he realized that there was another sound in the distance, a different note from the surge and crash of the sea. There was no doubt about it. It was a car. He shifted his position, trying to rub some life back into his frozen limbs. Either it was one of the cottage residents returning after a day doing who knew what in the back of this godforsaken beyond. Or it was Nick Sanders, going to ground where he thought he'd be safe.

The minutes passed, slow as hours. Then a glimmer of light rose behind the rocks. It grew brighter and clearer then, as it rounded an outcropping, became clearly identifiable as the steady beam of a big torch. Merrick ducked lower, though he knew there was little chance of anyone seeing him against the mass of black rock.

The beam swung round and illuminated the Hermit's Castle. Merrick could see nothing of the person behind the torch at first. But as the light disappeared inside the narrow passage, he could make out the shape of someone with a tall rucksack on his back. The height and bulk of the figure was, as far as he could make out, much the same as the description he'd read of Nick Sanders.

Merrick counted to sixty, then he stood up. It took a couple of minutes for his legs to feel capable of carrying him. He used the time to make sure his handcuffs were open and ready, his grip firm on his torch. Then he picked his way across the rocks in the darkness and stepped into the mouth of the passage. He walked as lightly as he could, picking up the sounds of someone moving around. The clank of tins. The rustle of plastic bags. Then he was in the chamber, looking down at the man crouched by the concrete shelf, illuminated by the light of a lantern-style torch. There was no doubt about it. This was the man whose photograph was pinned to the whiteboard in the squadroom.

A slow smile of satisfaction spread across Merrick's face. 'Nick Sanders, I am arresting you on suspicion of murder,' he said, enjoying every word.

He relaxed too soon. Sanders sprang up from his crouch, his momentum carrying him into Merrick and knocking him off his feet. Sanders tried to scramble over him and into the tunnel, but the space was too confined. Merrick lunged at his leg and caught him off balance. Sanders crashed into the wall and tripped up, falling backwards and cracking his head on the bed shelf.

He grunted once, then went slack. Merrick dragged himself upright and staggered across to Sanders. He was, to Merrick's regret, still breathing. He rolled Sanders over on to his side, not caring about the first rule of head injuries, seeing with satisfaction a swelling welt across the man's forehead. He glanced away as he went for his handcuffs. Suddenly Sanders uncoiled and sprang upwards, grabbing the heavy torch and swinging it savagely at Merrick's head. It caught him on the temple and at once, everything went red then black.

Carol stared at Jan Shields, incredulity on her face. 'You're the victim here? Bullshit. Where's Paula?'

Jan's voice dropped into a warm, lower register. 'I have no idea, Carol. Why don't you ask Dr Hill? Like I said, I'm the victim here. I came home to find he'd made an illegal entry into my home. I found him typing something into my laptop. I grabbed a kitchen knife to defend myself against an intruder. I have no idea how long he has been here or what he might have planted.'

'Nice try, Jan,' Tony said, his voice strained. 'Carol, there's a webcam feed. She's got it saved in her favourites. It's Paula. She's still alive.'

'Does it say where she is?'

He shook his head. 'Maybe Stacey can find something?'

Jan continued as if neither of them had spoken. 'Like I said, Carol, I found him in my home. I have no idea what he's talking about.'

'Shut up,' Carol said savagely. She shifted her position so she could reach her phone. She dialled Kevin's number. 'Kevin, get up here now. Back door. Bring

Stacey with you. Call for an ambulance, a SOCO team and uniformed back-up, please.'

'You're going to look very foolish, Carol,' Jan said, a pitying smile on her lips. 'A well-respected police officer with commendations for bravery and experience of working with the FBI defends herself against an intruder in her home, an intruder intent on framing her for murder purely to protect the failing reputation of the woman he loves . . . That'll play beautifully in court, don't you think?'

Carol wished she could cover her ears and shut out the insidious poison coming from Jan Shields' mouth. 'Like I said, save it for the interview room. I hope you've got something put aside for a rainy day. Bronwen Scott doesn't come cheap.'

Jan chuckled. 'Oh, I think I can afford a few hours of her time. That's all it'll take before Mr Brandon realizes what a trumped-up mess of lies there is against me. And who's behind it.'

Carol was spared listening to any more by the hasty arrival of Kevin and Stacey. She summoned them with a jerk of her head. 'Cuff her and caution her, Kevin. I only got as far as "suspicion of conspiracy to commit murder". You might want to throw assault in for good measure. Tony, you can move away now,' she said. She waited till he was clear and Jan was flanked by the other two before she rolled off Jan's legs and got to her feet.

'I'm sorry you're being forced to take part in this charade, guys,' Jan said apologetically. 'I keep telling Carol I'm the victim here, but she's got her own reasons for preferring to believe Tony, hasn't she?' She smirked at Carol as she spoke.

'Get her out of my sight,' Carol said, crossing to Tony. 'As soon as we get some uniforms here, I want her taken back to HQ and banged up till I'm ready to talk to her.' She took in his pallor and pulled a dining chair across for him. He slumped on the chair, holding his hand against his blood-soaked sweater. 'How bad is it?' she asked.

'It hurts like hell. Won't stop bleeding.' Beads of sweat formed on his forehead. Carol hurried through to the kitchen and grabbed a couple of dishtowels from their hooks. She folded them into pads and made him press them against the long slash that transversed his hand.

After a couple of minutes that felt much longer, flashing blue lights washed across the front window. 'That's the ambulance,' Carol said. 'Come on, let's get you on your feet.'

By the time the paramedics had loaded Tony into the ambulance, Kevin was escorting Jan into the back seat of a police car. Stacey was about to climb in with them when Carol called her name. 'I need you back here,' she said. Stacey followed her into the house. 'There's a laptop picking up a webcam feed with live pictures of Paula. I need you to find out whatever you can, Stacey.'

The younger woman nodded. 'I'd be better off taking it back to the station,' she said. 'That way I have access to all my diagnostics.'

'Fine. Just do it as fast as you can. Paula's still alive. It's obvious Jan's not going to give her up, so we need to do whatever it takes to find her before that changes,' Carol said bleakly. She watched Stacey packing up the laptop, thoughts tumbling over each other in her head. She couldn't remember the last time she'd ever faced so complicated an endgame. It should have scared her, but instead it exhilarated her. She was definitely herself again. 'Oh, and Stacey – when you get back, can you call Don Merrick on his mobile and tell him I need him here. I'm going to the hospital to take a statement from Tony. I want Don to run the search here.'

Fifteen minutes later, she was addressing a mixed team of SOCOs and detectives. 'We need to find where Paula is. There must be something – a rent book, a utility bill, something. You have to be fast, but you also have to be unimpeachable. I don't have to tell you how vital this search is. Do what you need to do. Take up the carpets, shred the cushions if you have to. I don't care if you leave the place looking like a war zone, find Paula for me.'

She turned away and spoke to the senior officer at the scene. 'I'm going to the hospital to take a statement from Dr Hill before I interview Shields. As soon as you get anything, call me. I'll have my phone switched on. To hell with their bloody heart monitors.' She stopped on the threshold and gave the team a last level stare. 'I know I can rely on all of you. And so does Paula.'

Tony sat on the edge of the examination couch, a polystyrene cup of some indeterminate brownish liquid in his left hand. He'd waited less than ten minutes to be seen by the medical staff at Bradfield Cross A&E. Something to do with the amount of blood on his sweater, he suspected. Since then he'd been given a local anaesthetic, eight stitches and a cautious opinion that he probably hadn't done any permanent damage to his hand.

The curtains surrounding his cubicle moved and Carol's familiar face appeared in the gap. 'Hi,' she said. She slipped inside, closing the curtains behind her. 'How are you doing?'

'I'll live,' he said.

Carol hitched herself up on the bed beside him. 'I need to take a statement from you.'

He gave a tired, sad smile. 'What do you need to know?'

'I need to know what happened between you and Jan. The earlier stuff – how you got there, what the hell you thought you were playing at – that can wait for later. But I want to know how it went down.'

'I couldn't think of a way to make you believe me other than hard evidence,' he said. 'My failure.' He sipped from the cup. Tea, he thought, though he wouldn't have been willing to wager anything he cared about on it. 'Inside a file case that was hidden in her wardrobe, I found a bunch of photos and some DVD-ROMs. Photos of the victims before they were discovered. Photos presumably taken by Carl Mackenzie.'

'You know about Carl?'

He nodded. 'Jan told me the bare bones.' He continued with the story, up to the point where he had turned to walk away.

'She came after me,' he said. 'I thought she would. I wanted to make her feel powerless, to lose control. That was my only chance of finding a chink in her armour that might have got me out of there alive.' He smiled. 'And that's when you arrived.'

'She didn't actually confess?'

He shook his head. 'No. Sorry. She was already practising the line she used on you.'

'Never mind,' Carol said. 'We'll nail her.'

'Paula?' Tony asked.

'We're locking. We'll find her.' He could see the restored confidence in her face and hear it in her voice.

In spite of his concerns for Paula, part of Tony rejoiced.

Nick Sanders kicked the lifeless body at his feet. Bastard plod had screwed everything. He'd got it all planned. He was going to lie low for a week or two, until the hue and cry had died down and he'd had time to grow a beard. Then he was going to take the ferry across to Larne, drive down into Eire and disappear. It had all gone up in smoke now, thanks to this interfering copper. He'd have to hole up in some mountain bothy near the snow line, unable to risk venturing into populated areas. A child murderer would be off the front pages in a week by Sanders's reckoning, but a cop killer would be Public Enemy No.1 until he was caught. Sanders had no intention of allowing that to happen.

He repacked his rucksack, wiped the blood from the torch on Don Merrick's sweater, then set off back across the rocky outcropping to the place where he'd left the car. It was near the end of the narrow tarmacked track that led down into the hamlet of Achmelvich, tucked away between the last cottage and the rocky headland. The low cloud robbed the landscape of light, and Sanders had to use his torch to prevent himself breaking a leg on the jagged rocks that lay between him and safety.

Eventually he emerged on the narrow path between the boulders, his breath white in the chill air, a thin film of sweat on his back. He broke into a shambling trot. He was only feet away from his car when a set of headlights on full beam snapped on and blinded him, silhouetting his tall frame against the uneven skyline.

A strong Highland voice rang out across the short distance between them. 'Police. We'd like a word, sir.'

Sanders didn't pause. He took to his heels, running back down the path towards the sea. He heard the sound of heavy feet behind him and panicked. He veered from the path and started scrambling over the boulders. He'd barely gone a dozen yards when a pair of powerful torch beams started playing over the rocks around him, pinning him down after a few seconds. He carried on gamely, but his pursuers had the advantage of being fresh and being able to see where they were going.

It was over in minutes. Two burly officers hauled Sanders to his feet, handcuffed him and half-dragged, half-carried him back to the path and to their waiting car. 'What's this all about?' Sanders blustered as they went.

'You tell us, sir. Innocent people don't normally run away from the police,' the older of the two officers said.

'I was scared,' he said. 'I couldn't see if you really were the police. For all I knew you could have been going to rob me.'

'Aye, right.' At the car, they shoved him in the

back seat and turned on the interior light. 'Nasty bump you've got there,' the officer observed. 'It's not much of a disguise, though, Mr Sanders. We were expecting you. But we thought you'd be heading towards the Hermit's Castle, not running away from it.'

Sanders said nothing, mostly because he couldn't think of anything to say. A single tear slithered from the corner of his eye and trickled slowly down his cheek.

The older officer nodded. 'Fine. Constable Mackie is going to stay here with you while I go and take a wee look down by the sea. I'll not be long.'

The hospital had discharged Tony under the mistaken belief that he was going straight home to bed. Instead, he asked the taxi driver to take him to the police station. He was tired and in pain, but there was still work to be done. He knew the only practical thing he could do to help Paula was to advise Carol on the interview techniques that might penetrate Jan Shields' defences. So going home wasn't an option.

He arrived to find Carol deep in frustrated discussion with John Brandon. Jan Shields was refusing legal representation. She was also refusing to say anything whatsoever in a formal interview. Brandon looked surprisingly relieved to see Tony. 'How are you?' he asked, his expression one of concern and bonhomie.

'Sir,' Carol said, her voice a warning.

'I know, Carol, I know. But let me at least run it past him.'

'Sir, Dr Hill has suffered a traumatic experience tonight. He's been attacked and injured, he's exhausted and probably stuffed full of painkillers,' she said plaintively.

'Only local anaesthetic,' Tony said. 'I refused the painkillers. I thought I might need to have my wits about me if I was going to be questioned about planting evidence and illegal entry.'

Carol rolled her eyes at the ceiling. 'This is not the time or the place,' she muttered.

'Tony, we have a very unusual situation,' Brandon said. 'As you know, we have Jan Shields in custody. She is refusing to speak to anyone other than you. She says she will consent to a taped interview, but only if it's conducted by you. Anybody else and she will go no comment.'

'Would it be admissible evidence in court?' Tony asked.

Brandon shrugged. 'I don't know. I'll let the lawyers worry about that. What I'm concerned about is recovering Paula McIntyre alive. If Carol's right, then Shields knows where she is. I'm willing to take a chance on losing the product of your interview with her if it means getting to Paula. What do you say?'

'I think she just wants to play games with you, Tony,' Carol interjected.

'You're probably right,' he acknowledged. 'But so's John. If there's any chance of saving Paula, I have to take it.'

Tony took a last look over the notes Sam Evans had given him from his interview with Honey then took a deep breath and walked into the interview room. Jan Shields sat at the table, looking as relaxed as if she were conducting the interview. As he crossed the room, her eyes never left him. 'Nice of you to come by, Dr Hill,' she said. 'I imagine our positions will soon be reversed, just as soon as we can persuade a detective who isn't DCI Jordan to look at the evidence. Not that I'm saying you two are in cahoots. No, I think you acted entirely off your own bat. But you did it for her, and I'm sure she feels obliged to stand by you now.'

'You might as well save it for the tape,' he said genially, pressing the twin buttons as he'd been instructed. He intoned the date, time and names of those present. 'Just for the benefit of the tape,' he said, 'can you make clear the circumstances of this interview?'

'Certainly. I have waived the right to legal representation at this point. I have refused to communicate with any police officer and I have asked to speak to you, Dr Hill. The reason for this is that I wanted to confront personally the man who broke into my home and planted evidence there that would tend to incriminate me.'

'I don't think I've ever encountered anyone with a stronger taste for power,' Tony said conversationally. 'When did it start? What was the point where you understood that life had dealt you a crap hand? How did you come to realize that nobody gives power, that it has to be taken? What made you realize you could strip other people to the core and steal their power from them? How did you learn the hypnotic techniques you used on Carl and Derek? I tell you, it's going to be tough for you from now on, Jan. Because it's like a drug to you, isn't it? You can't give it up, can you? Even now, when you must know in your heart that it's over, you still need to play the power games.'

'You're the one whose career is over, Dr Hill. You broke into my house.'

Tony shook his head. 'I had the set of keys you lent me.'

'Why would I lend you my keys?'

'I wanted to borrow your set of *NYPD Blue* videos and you didn't know what time you were going to get off work.' He pushed back in his chair. 'Any fiction you produce, I can counter it. But the weapon I've got that you can't trump is truth.'

'I don't think so.' She smiled.

'We'll see, shall we? Let's start with your sexual abuse of prostitutes.'

He thought he spotted a momentary flash of unease, but it was gone before he could be sure. 'You must be confusing me with someone else. I don't pay for sex.'

'I didn't say you paid for it. We've got a statement from a young woman saying you coerced her into violent sex by threatening her with arrest if she wouldn't co-operate.'

Jan laughed, a delighted gurgling chuckle. 'They're coming out of the woodwork tonight, aren't they? Dr Hill, one of the perennial risks of working Vice is malicious accusation. I can produce plenty of women with whom I have had consensual, non-violent sex. I don't need to threaten street hookers to get laid. I think, on balance, any court will take the word of a career cop with commendations over that of some junkie whore.'

'It's not a chance I'd be willing to take,' Tony said,

his manner mild and relaxed. 'Let's move on to the hard physical evidence I found in your house. Not just the computer, Jan. I found your stash. The photographs, the CD-ROMs. They'll have your prints on them.'

She sighed and looked down at the table. 'You've caught me out there, Dr Hill. Maybe I'll make it easier on myself if I just come clean now. Yes, I do possess the material you're talking about. But all I'm guilty of is withholding evidence. That material arrived anonymously in the post at my home. Maybe you have some idea where it came from? I know I should have turned the evidence in, but . . .' She spread her hands in a disarming gesture. 'What can I say? I'm not proud of this. I wanted to make a name for myself. I wanted to solve these crimes myself. Yes, I should have handed it over to DCI Jordan. But I wanted the glory for myself.' She lifted her gaze and met his eye. She gave him the twinkling cherub smile. 'I can only say how sorry I am.'

Tony couldn't help a sneaking admiration for her. He'd never seen anyone hold it together so well on the surface. He'd interviewed more than his share of stone-cold psychopaths, but he'd never encountered such supreme control. 'I've got to say, I don't know how you did it. It must have been a hell of a challenge, to get Derek and Carl to carry out your bidding so precisely. I've seen some skilled hypnotherapists in my time, but I doubt any of them could have exerted this level of mind and impulse control.'

She shook her head pityingly. 'I have no idea what you're talking about,' she said.

'No? I'd have thought you'd have wanted to share

the secrets of your success. You could make a lot of money teaching people like me how to achieve complete control over another human. Even if they are only pretty pathetic specimens like Carl and Derek.' Nothing. Not a twitch. He tried another tack. 'It's a shame Carl Mackenzie's dead. I'm sure he had an interesting tale to tell.'

'I think so too. And I suspect I'm more sorry than you that he's dead, because he could certainly have exonerated me. If someone was directing these murders – which I'm not convinced is true, by the way – Carl would have been able to reassure you that person was not me.'

'An interesting thought, Jan. But there is one person who can still set our minds to rest on this point. Once he realizes his voice isn't the omnipotent creature it pretends to be, once he knows we've got you in custody, Derek Tyler's going to talk. Derek is alive and well, and he will talk, I promise you.'

This time, her smile was cruel, her eyes dark with a savage humour. 'I wouldn't be too sure about that. About any of it, in fact.'

A sudden chill crept into Tony's heart. His mind flashed up the image of Jan leaning against the wall inside Bradfield Moor. How long had she been there waiting for him? Had she been anywhere near Derek Tyler? Had she had the chance to activate some long-buried suggestion?

'What's up, Doc?' Jan asked, clearly enjoying the confusion she could read on his face. 'Remembered something?'

Tony leapt to his feet and ran for the door. Carol emerged from the observation room at the same moment. They met in the corridor. 'She came to Bradfield Moor to fetch me,' he said urgently. He went for his phone, keying in the number of the hospital one-handed. 'This is Dr Hill, I need to speak to the duty charge nurse.' He looked at Carol as he waited to be connected. 'You need to get over there. Bring Derek Tyler here, keep someone with him twenty-four seven until I can persuade him to make a statement. He mustn't be left alone. She'll have programmed him to self-destruct.' He turned his attention to the phone. 'Vincent? It's Tony Hill. This is really important. How was Derek Tyler today?'

'Funny you should ask, Doc. He seemed quite bright, almost cheerful. Silent as usual, but a bit more animated somehow.'

'When did you last check on him?'

'Lights out, I suppose. There's no reason why he would have been checked again.'

Fuck. 'Vincent, can you do me a favour? Can you go and check on him yourself? Right now?'

The nurse sounded bemused. 'Sure, but . . .'

'And Vincent? Call me back as soon as you've done that.' He ended the call. 'Why are you still here, Carol? We need to get Tyler before it's too late. I need to talk to him.'

'Wouldn't it be better if you went and interviewed him there?'

He shook his head. 'Suicide watch there means observations every fifteen minutes. But you can put somebody in with him round the clock. That's what we need if we're going to keep him alive. Carol, you have to trust me on this.'

She hesitated for a second, then said, 'OK, you've

got it.' She took off down the corridor at a fast clip and Tony walked into the observation room. He stared through the one-way mirror at an apparently untroubled Jan Shields. Her arrogance was monumental. Even when she knew her nickname was being bandied around in the investigation, she hadn't cut and run. She'd just carried on blithely, clearing up every potential problem before it caused her any difficulty. The scary thing was that she'd almost got him believing in her invincibility. She seemed to have an almost plausible answer for everything. She could, he feared, make a jury love her just enough to believe her. Or at least forgive her.

The minutes ticked by and Tony grew more and more restless. The longer the wait, the more he feared the worst. Four, five minutes at most from the nurses' station to Tyler's room. A minute to check, then the walk back. Ten minutes, no more. That's how long it should take Vincent to get back to him if all was well.

Ten minutes stretched to fifteen, fifteen to twenty. When his phone finally rang, Tony almost dropped it in his haste to answer it left-handed. 'Hello? Vincent?'

'It's me,' Carol said. Those two words told Tony all he needed to know.

'Shit,' he said.

'I got here five minutes ago,' she said. 'The place is in an uproar. They just found Derek Tyler dead in his room. Apparently he swallowed his tongue.'

'I don't believe it,' Tony groaned.

'Believe it,' Carol said grimly. 'This case is going belly-up and we're no nearer to finding Paula. I could weep.'

'You and me both.'

'I'll see you back at the station. Tony – don't go back in to Jan until I get back, OK?'

'Yeah. We need to figure out where we're going with this.' If indeed there was anywhere left to go.

The police station Stacey had returned to a few hours earlier bore little resemblance to the one she had left. Nothing travels faster than bad news within an organization as driven by information as the police. For days, Paula McIntyre's abduction had fuelled conversation and ambience alike with a mixture of outrage, hindsight and criticism. Everybody had an opinion. But the news of Jan Shields' apparent betrayal had delivered a shockwave to Bradfield police that had created something like the moment after an explosion when air and sound have been sucked from the epicentre. Corridors were hushed, movements subdued, faces angry and baffled. When she'd walked into the murder room, Stacey had felt hostile eyes on her, as if by having been present at the event she was somehow responsible for so brutal a blow to the force's self-esteem. Already, she knew, people would be rewriting history; some searching for ways to exculpate Shields; others who had been close colleagues distancing themselves from her; still others claiming always to have known she was dodgy. The fallout was going to be grim and painful.

Back at her own desk, Stacey dry-swallowed two paracetamol caplets and scrunched her face into an expression of concentration. It didn't take her long to determine that there was no easy route to the location of the webcam from the image on the screen. It made her stomach churn to see her colleague staked out like that, and she made a mental promise to Paula that she would make sure the images disappeared for good from every computer they'd ever contaminated once Paula was rescued. There was no way the sleaze-bags were going to get their hands on this. Paula wasn't going to end up as late-night entertainment for scummy vice cops. Or anybody else.

One of the officers from the HOLMES computer team had taken on the task of wading through all the easily accessible files on the laptop's hard disk. So far, he'd found nothing except a depressing amount of hardcore porn.

Stacey wasn't interested in what was visible. She knew that a criminal as organized as Jan Shields was not going to have left crucial information in plain view. She would have deleted anything incriminating and, because of her involvement with the paedophile investigations, she'd probably have learned to take basic steps to clean up her hard disk regularly.

That didn't mean there wasn't anything to find, and Stacey was determined to find it. After an hour's intensive investigation, she'd managed to isolate only three stray file fragments. At first glance, they'd looked like gibberish. But Stacey had tools at her disposal and it didn't take her long to translate the jumbled symbols into splintered words and phrases.

The first fragment yielded nothing of interest. It looked like the remains of an email attachment, probably one of the thousands of jokes that circled the globe, given text such as 'wim in the pool' and 'so god sai' and 'out of the fish'.

The second fragment hit Stacey like a shot of vodka. '. . . rent in advan. . .osit in cash. . .edsit at !%. . .tron

Lane, Temp . . .rl Macke. . .' While the printer wheezed into life, she ran down the hall to the murder room, where a large-scale map of Temple Fields hung on the wall. She traced the street names with her finger. There it was. Citron Lane. The alley behind the street where Paula had disappeared.

Excitement welling up, she hurried back to her desk. The symbols ! and % were the shifted versions of 1 and 5. She'd got it.

Carol leaned her head on the steering wheel and felt the pain from her stressed muscles spread across her shoulders in a tight series of cramps. She couldn't get her head round Jan Shields. How much evidence could the woman wriggle out from? She'd clearly used all her experience in the job to figure out the perfect set of excuses and explanations for every aspect of her criminal activity. Carol was used to bluster from captured criminals, but she knew this went far beyond bluster into the realms of a kind of perverted credibility.

All of which she could possibly learn to live with if only she could bring Paula home. But that prospect looked no more likely now than at any point since her abduction.

Wearily she straightened up and started the engine just as her phone rang. 'Carol Jordan,' she said dully.

'It's Stacey,' the voice said. 'I've got it, I think.'

'Got what?' Carol couldn't let herself believe.

'Where Paula is – a bedsit at 15 Citron Lane, Temple Fields. Rented in Carl Mackenzie's name. We searched it on the night, but it was Sergeant Shields who led the search team and gave it the all clear.'

Carol felt her throat suddenly closing with emotion. 'Thank you, Stacey,' she managed to say before she choked up completely. 'I'll take it from here.' She ended the call and dialled Merrick's number. No reply. Where the hell was he? She didn't have time to chase him now, but she'd kick his arse when he finally reappeared. Cursing Merrick under her breath, she tried Kevin's number. He answered on the second ring. 'Kevin – 15 Citron Lane, Temple Fields. Meet me there. Bring a team. Do not, I repeat, do not go in till I get there. Is that clear?' She ended the call, shoved the car in gear and reached for her radio mike with one hand.

'DCI Jordan to control. Paramedic unit required at 15 Citron Lane, Temple Fields. Repeat, paramedic unit required at 15 Citron Lane, Temple Fields. Over.'

The radio crackled acknowledgement of her message. 'And I need someone to get over there with a set of boltcutters,' she added as an afterthought.

'Did you say boltcutters?' the radio operator asked.

'Yeah. The kind that cut through handcuffs.'

The room was on the third floor. As Stacey had said, Jan Shields had been responsible for giving the all clear to the building beyond the gate in the wall. Even if she hadn't managed to annex that search for herself, it would have been easy for officers in a hurry to miss its existence. At some time in the past, someone had created a double door. When the landing door was opened, it revealed a shallow cupboard with dusty shelves. But on closer examination, hidden under one of the shelves was a keyhole and a countersunk handle. The building was on the list of properties whose tenants were still to be queried with landlords. Another day and they'd have tied Carl Mackenzie's name to it.

Kevin Matthews and Sam Evans threw themselves at the inner door. It collapsed in a shatter of splinters and dust. Carol pushed her way through and entered ahead of them, heart in her mouth. At first sight, she thought they were too late. Paula lay motionless on the bed, eyes closed, unmoving. The room stank of sweat and piss. 'Get those cuffs off her,' Carol ordered, grabbing the corner of the sheet and yanking it free so she could cover Paula's nakedness. Evans rushed past her, boltcutters in his hand.

'Oh Jesus, Paula,' he moaned as he worked the boltcutters on the handcuff chain.

The paramedics crowded in, demanding room to do their job. Carol leaned over Paula and stroked her head. Her skin was warm and feverish, and Carol's heart sang. She stepped back to let the paramedics work, just as the metal on the second set of cuffs snapped under Evans' strength.

'How is she?' she asked anxiously as the paramedics started their tests.

'She's alive. But she's very weak,' one said without taking his eyes off her.

'Don't you dare lose her,' Carol said, backing towards the landing. She reached for her phone and called Tony. He answered on the first ring. 'Tony, we found her. We found Paula.'

'Alive?'

'Yes. Alive.'

'Thank God,' he sighed.

When she came off the phone, Carol was surrounded

by delighted detectives congratulating themselves and each other. The jubilation was so overwhelming that nobody, not even Carol, noticed the face that was missing. They were making so much noise she almost didn't hear her mobile ringing. She moved back into the room where Paula was being moved on to a stretcher so she could hear the call more clearly.

The voice at the other end was unfamiliar. 'Is that DCI Jordan?'

'Yes, speaking. Who is this?'

'This is Inspector Macgregor. I'm up here in Achmelvich,' he said, his voice gruff and solemn.

'Have you got Nick Sanders?' Carol hardly dared hope. But she could think of no other reason why someone of Macgregor's rank would be in a hamlet at this time of night unless a major arrest had happened. It was almost too good to be true. They'd found Paula, they had Jan Shields under arrest, and now they'd captured the man who had abused and murdered Tim Golding and Guy Lefevre.

There was a pause. Then Macgregor spoke, his voice packed with reservations. 'Aye. We do have Sanders in custody.'

'Is there a problem?' she asked, sidestepping to let the paramedics past with their burden. She reached out to brush her fingers along Paula's arm as she passed.

'DCI Jordan,' he said, 'do you have an Inspector Merrick on your team?'

A horrible suspicion formed in Carol's mind. 'What's happened?' she demanded.

'Look, I'm awful sorry. There's no easy way to say this: Inspector Merrick is dead, ma'am.'

Carol felt her legs collapse under her as she slid down the wall in a heap. It was too much to take in, on top of everything else that had happened in the past few hours. 'No,' she whispered. 'That can't be right. He's supposed to be here. Sleeping. In a motel. That can't be right.'

'I don't think there's any room for doubt, ma'am. He matches up with the photo ID he was carrying. It looks like he was staking the place out, waiting for Sanders. They had a fight and he took a bad blow to the head. We should have more information in the morning. I'm really, really sorry, ma'am.'

Carol ended the call and let the phone fall back into her pocket. She buried her face in her hands. Then she forced herself to her feet. There would be time for her grief later. For now, she had responsibilities.

She walked slowly to the door, planting one foot carefully in front of the other like a drunk. She took a long, shuddering breath and spoke as clearly and loudly as she could. 'I've got some bad news,' she began.

Tony was still standing by the one-way mirror. He knew he should be elated at the news of Paula's release, but all he could taste was the bitterness of failure. He'd finally met his match: a criminal who could withstand his probing, apparently effortlessly. The techniques she had developed to control the minds of others had given her the gift of control over her own responses to a remarkable degree. Perhaps with time he could break down her barriers. But he suspected he wasn't going to be granted time with her. If this ever went to trial, she would be charming, plausible – and would probably be declared not guilty.

If she did lose, she might well end up in a secure mental hospital, but he could guarantee it would be a long way away from anywhere he was practising.

Paula's survival was a huge consolation, of course. On a human level, it was the best possible outcome. But it didn't balance the despair he felt as he stared down at Jan Shields' complacency.

He had no idea how much time had passed when he heard a knock. Tony crossed the room and opened the door. A uniformed constable stood uncertainly on the threshold. 'I'm sorry to disturb you, Dr Hill. But this just came for you.' He thrust a small brown envelope at Tony. 'One of the nurses from Bradfield Moor brought it in.'

'Thanks,' Tony said. He closed the door and studied the envelope. His name was written in straggling capitals across the front. He didn't recognize the handwriting. He ripped open the flap and pulled out a single flimsy sheet of cheap writing paper. The same straggling capitals filled half the page. Beneath them was an awkward signature which read, DEREK TYLER.

Tony could hardly believe the evidence of his eyes.

DEAR DOCTOR HILL. DETECTIVE SARGENT
JAN SHIELDS IS THE CREEPER. JAN
SHIELDS MADE ME DO IT. SHE MADE
TAPES FOR ME. THEY ARE BEHIND THE
WATER TANK IN THE ROOFSPACE IN 7
ROMNEY WALK WERE I USED TO HAVE A
BEDSIT. I AM NOT SORY FOR WHAT WE
DID BUT I DONT WANT TO TAKE ALL
THE BLAME.

There are few things more moving than the full pomp of a police funeral. Dozens of officers in dress uniforms, family and friends stunned with grief and carried along on the formal wave of an organizational farewell, the full solemnity that the Church of England can muster. Carol stood surrounded by her team, eyes front, chin tucked in, cap under her arm. John Brandon read the encomium she'd written to honour Don Merrick's memory while his boys clung to their mother, the only familiar element in this extraordinary scene.

Tony stood off to one side, his eyes never straying far from Carol and, next to her, a hollow-eyed and twitchy Paula. When he'd shown Tyler's note to Carol, she'd descended on the building where he'd had a ground-floor bedsit like one of the Furies. All her grief and rage at Merrick's death had manifested itself in the absolute determination to nail Jan Shields.

The tapes had still been there, three floors up, rammed down between the water cistern and the angle of the roof. And their chilling message was irrefutable and inescapable. The only person who didn't recognize the fact was Jan herself. But that didn't matter. No jury would free her now. Tony felt a shudder of pity for whichever establishment was unlucky enough to acquire her as an inmate.

The past few weeks had been a baptism of fire for Carol, he thought. There had been several points where he'd feared she wasn't going to make it. But she'd proved him wrong, and for once he was glad to be wrong.

Brandon reached the end of his eulogy and bowed his head. The twenty-one-gun salute crackled out across the graveyard. Carol turned her head to meet Tony's eyes. A small, almost imperceptible nod passed between them. It was, he thought, amazing how little we needed to survive.

ISBN-13: 978-0-00-714285-9
ISBN-10: 0-00-714285-4